A NOVEL

KEEP THE JEWS OUT!

MIKE EVANS

KEEP THE JEWS OUT!

A NOVEL

TimeWorthy BOOKS

P.O. BOX 30000, PHOENIX, AZ 85046

Keep the Jews Out!
(a novel)

Copyright 2019 by Time Worthy Books
P. O. Box 30000
Phoenix, AZ 85046

Design: Peter Gloege | LOOK Design Studio

Hardcover: 978-1-62961-199-0
Paperback: 978-1-62961-201-0
Canada: 978-1-62961-202-7

This book is lovingly dedicated to my dear friend,
Rabbi Yisroel Goldstein

In April 2019, a 19-year old man with an AR-15 rifle entered a synagogue in Poway, California, on the last day of Passover, which also fell on Shabbat. He fired shots, killing Lori Gilbert-Kaye, and injuring three others, including Rabbi Goldstein. Another congregant was struck in the leg, and his eight-year-old niece was wounded by flying shrapnel.

When I met Rabbi Goldstein at the White House later that May, I asked him what the greatest need of his synagogue was. With tears in his eyes, he told me that the children were afraid to come to the school for fear of another anti-Semitic attack. I was able to raise the funds for Rabbi Goldstein and his synagogue to help pay for 24-hour security at their facility for an entire year. We did that to combat anti-Semitism and show God's love for the Jewish people.

In May 2019, I was invited to the United Nations in New York City where Rabbi Goldstein spoke at a symposium on battling anti-Semitism in the online world. At the end of the symposium, Rabbi Goldstein called, asking if he could come to my room and pray with me. He placed the Telfillin, a pair of black leather boxes containing Hebrew parchment scrolls, on my forehead and arm.

Shortly after the meeting at the UN, I flew to Israel to host the initial anniversary of the moving of the U.S. Embassy to Jerusalem. Sitting next to me was the Chief Rabbi of Jerusalem who had flown to New York City to comfort Rabbi Goldstein. The Chief Rabbi informed him that a Jewish man had just hosted an amazing event. Rabbi Goldstein exclaimed, "He's my friend, Mike Evans." The Chief Rabbi prayed a blessing over our friendship and informed Rabbi Goldstein that I had never experienced a Bar Mitzvah.

When I went to greet Rabbi Goldstein, he asked, "Would you allow me to conduct a Bar Mitzvah for you?" I laughed and replied, "That ceremony is for a 13-year old boy, not a 71-year old man." I quickly agreed, and Rabbi Goldstein then performed the ritual with his hand still bandaged from the California attack.

Rabbi Goldstein looked into the face of death with a holy boldness. The fire inside him was greater than the fire outside him.

CHAPTER ONE

Snow crunched beneath Schleman Lewin's feet as he trudged through the village. In the distance, beyond the rooftops and outbuildings, the tree-lined hills were covered with snow, creating a magnificent landscape. Overhead, the sun peeked through a layer of clouds, but to him even the clouds were a thing of beauty. For all of his life, Lewin had marveled at the natural wonder and splendor that surrounded him every day, but right there, in that moment, the air was thick with smoke and heavy with the stench of burning bodies.

Around the world, leaders argued and railed against the supposed causes of the Great War, a calamity just ended barely a month earlier. Already news of their narrow-minded and angry rant had reached the village and, indeed, all of Belarus. When he read the first accounts of it in a newspaper from Odessa, Lewin shook his head. "It's almost 1919," he muttered to himself. "Can't they do better than this?" But it seemed the leaders of the world were destined never to escape the prejudices they had brought to the conflict and now appeared to lead them toward yet another conflict—one, no doubt, that would be far worse than all of those that Europe had so far endured.

In Naroulia, a Jewish village, Lewin and his fellow residents in the Pale of Settlement were likewise locked in a struggle against a culture ruled by the prejudices and apprehensions of the past. They were the victims, not the aggressors. Created by

Catherine the Great, the Pale had been a place for Russian Jews to live following the monarchy's ineffective attempts to remove them from the country. Later, the region with its Jewish population was greatly expanded with the annexation of Poland, a consequence of Russia having won the Polish-Russian War. For Jews of the Russian Empire, it was the only location in which they could enjoy Russian citizenship and a measure of peace. Right then, for Lewin and his fellow Jews of Naroulia, that citizenship afforded them little joy and only intermittent peace.

Beginning in the nineteenth century and continuing well into the twentieth, Belarus, and the entire Pale, was subject to deadly attacks known to historians as the Pogroms. In waves of violence that sometimes lasted for decades, angry mobs, organized by czarist officials and operating with czarist approval, descended on hapless Jewish villages and raped, beat, burned, and killed all they found. Now, even after the Russian Revolution had ended the empire, those attacks continued.

As Lewin made his way through Naroulia that morning, he saw the aftermath of the attack that had occurred the night before. His house had been spared but many others were not. After checking on his nearest neighbors, he set out to learn the condition of his relatives, some of whom were quite old.

Lewin's first stop was at the home of his uncle Isaac, his father's brother. Approaching eighty, Isaac spent most days sitting alone in his kitchen, huddled by the wood-burning stove, reading and drinking coffee. He was able to get about on his own but lacked the agility necessary to escape an angry mob. Lewin had worried about his uncle all night and when he'd first left the house to see about him, he had been anxious. But as Isaac's house came into view, he felt the muscles in his neck relax. Tension left his body and a sense of relief swept over him. Even from the street Lewin could see that the structure had sustained only minor damage—a broken window, probably from a rock, was all.

Lewin quickened his pace, made his way onto the porch, and rapped on the door. Isaac greeted him with coffee cup in hand. He invited Lewin inside and ushered him into the kitchen, where they sat together and talked.

Isaac said in response to Lewin's concern. "It was nothing. I have seen worse." He gestured with his cup. "You have, too."

Lewin nodded in reply. "I have seen worse."

"Perhaps they are tiring of their torture against us."

Lewin sighed. "I do not think so."

Isaac paused to take a sip of coffee. "I do not suppose so, either."

They talked awhile longer, then Lewin left to check on his aunts who lived three houses from Isaac—they were Isaac's sisters—and found that they, too, had endured the night without injury. Lewin was relieved by what he'd learned so far, but his cousin Naum lived on the opposite side of town. Reports and rumors circulating through the night and even after sunup indicated that area of the village was hardest hit. So, after finding his uncle and aunts were well, Lewin started toward Naum's house.

Lewin and Naum had grown up together in a neighborhood not far from where Isaac and his sisters resided. Their parents were cousins, and got along well together, but the interests of the two families diverged greatly. Naum's father was a writer, scholar, and teacher. Lewin's was a businessman and entrepreneur.

At first, the difference meant very little to Lewin and Naum. They spent their childhood running through the forests and playing between the houses on their street. As they grew older, however, their lives began to move apart. Naum attended school, first in Naroulia and then in towns that were farther and farther away. He grew in stature as a respected scholar but, until the last five years, he was rarely in town, only returning after his parents died and he inherited their house.

Lewin followed his father into business as a merchant, which he operated from a warehouse in Naroulia. And, like his father, he leased a field outside of town that he sublet to a farmer. Rent from the sublease provided a source of steady income that protected him and his family from the vagaries of the mercantile business—a fact that his wife, Michla, and their two children very much appreciated. Lately, however, business had not been so good.

Past the center of town and around a bend in the road, Lewin caught sight of Naum standing in the street. Before him lay the smoldering ruins of his house. Lewin hurried forward and halted by Naum's side. He opened his mouth to speak but when Naum did not respond to his presence, words escaped him and he simply stood there with an arm around his cousin's shoulder.

The house had been large with many rooms. It had a sink with running water piped from a spring on the hill that rose behind the house. Now ashes and a few charred boards were all that remained. Staring at the rubble brought back memories of the fun they'd had as boys chasing through it, laughing and shouting as they went. Their laughter would echo through the house above the rumble of their footsteps. Naum's mother never seemed to mind, though, and always had a plate of cookies ready for them when they tired of play. Those were good years. Happy years that were intertwined with the house in a nostalgic emotion that made Lewin long for those days again.

After a while of standing in the snow, the acrid smell of smoke filling his nostrils, Lewin grew tired of the silence. His feet grew cold, too, and finally he removed his arm from Naum's shoulder, then glanced over at him. "What shall we do about this?" He gestured to the ruins that lay before them.

"We should kill them all." Naum's voice was flat, as if the words came from a cold, dark resolve that lay deep within his soul.

Lewin was unsettled by the response and gestured again toward the rubble. "I mean about your house." He used both hands to emphasize his point. "We must rebuild your house.

Better and bigger than before. A house worthy of the laughter of your children, as the one we knew was worthy of ours." He was deliberately grandiose in the hope that he might at least raise a smile on Naum's sullen face.

Naum was unmoved and shook his head. "I am not rebuilding." His words came in that same flat tone. "Not today. Not tomorrow. Not ever." He glanced at Lewin. "My children will grace the floor of some other dwelling."

Lewin frowned. "What do you mean you aren't rebuilding? We always rebuild. This is what we do. We don't give in. We don't give up. We persevere." Lewin felt nervous from Naum's odd mood and spoke in rapid fire, as if a torrent of words could somehow overwhelm the moment and bring Naum back to himself.

Again Naum shook his head. "You can have it. Take the whole place. The ashes. The charred lumber. The pipe from the spring. And the land, too. I'm leaving this place." He looked over at Lewin with a cold, hard glare. "You should leave, too." With that, Naum turned and walked away.

Lewin watched for a moment, startled by the abruptness of his cousin's departure, then called after him, "Where will you go?"

"Anywhere but here," Naum replied. "Maybe America." He turned to one side and looked back in Lewin's direction. "Do you think Esther will help me?"

Esther was Lewin's sister. She and her husband had left Naroulia following a pogrom several years earlier. Unlike many others, they got out—out of the village and out of Russia—and moved to America. By all accounts, they had a good life there and they were spoken of on numerous occasions. Many in the village referred to them as an example they wished to follow.

"I am sure Esther will be glad to help you," Lewin answered. "If you ask."

"Then I will write to her today." Naum turned away for a final time and waved as he moved up the street at a deliberate pace.

Soon he turned the corner by the cobbler's shop and was out of sight.

Lewin remained at the site of Naum's former residence awhile longer, thinking of what it meant that Naum and his family were leaving. Many others had departed also, but most of Lewin's extended family remained in the village and the surrounding countryside where they and their forebears had lived for centuries.

Leaving was not an easy decision to make, and although many of his relatives chose to remain, most of them thought that going was the wisest choice. It was a quandary for them—a Lewin family trait, it seemed. Thinking to do a thing but never following through with purpose.

Staying isn't such a bad idea, Lewin thought to himself.

In fact, there were advantages to remaining. His business was established and, though activity was slow right then, it afforded him a good living and enabled him to provide for his family. Moving to America meant uprooting his family from their familiar surroundings, closing the businesses, disposing of his assets, winding things up in Naroulia, then starting over in a strange and foreign land. True, his sister was there with her family. And he knew others that had made the trek across the Atlantic. But though he read and spoke English, he knew not the first thing about how business was conducted there. It would be like starting from scratch, he thought. *Only without Papa or Mama to show me how. And without the reputation of our family.*

After a few minutes alone to consider the matter, Lewin turned away and started up the street toward home. When he arrived, he found Michla preparing lunch in the kitchen. Their two sons were playing near the fireplace in the front room.

She asked as he entered, "How was it?" She remained at the counter with her eyes focused on her work. When Lewin did not answer immediately, she turned toward him. "How much damage did they do this time?"

Lewin slid a chair from the kitchen table and dropped wearily onto it. He slouched to one side and propped an elbow against the tabletop to brace himself. "The area around Isaac and the others was not hard hit. Just a few broken windows. But from the center of the village eastward toward Naum's house, they were devastated."

Michla wiped her hands on a towel and turned her attention fully to him. "Devastated?"

"Houses burned. Buildings looted. Many people dead or injured." Lewin spoke with a sense of sorrow in his voice. "It was awful."

"Who?" she insisted. "Who is dead? Who is injured?"

"Itzhak, Sarah—"

"Itzhak and Sarah are dead?" Michla asked, interrupting him. Her eyes were wide with a look of terror as she rubbed her hands on the towel.

Lewin nodded. "They and many more."

"But what about their children? Are they alright? Did you find the children?"

"They are with a neighbor."

Michla removed the apron from her waist. "I must go and help them."

Lewin gestured for her to wait. "There is one more thing."

"What? What more can there be?"

Lewin looked over at her. "Naum's house burned to the ground."

"Burned to the ground! Why didn't you tell me that first? You come in here and sit and chatter on about everyone else and you don't tell me about family? What about his wife and children? How can you sit there and tell me these things when his wife and children have nowhere to go? You should have brought them here with you. Why didn't you bring them here?"

Lewin gestured for calm. "They knew that trouble was coming. He had sent them to stay with Gesya and Zerach two days ago."

Michla's shoulders slumped with relief and her body relaxed visibly. "Even so, we must help them rebuild."

Lewin shook his head. "He doesn't want to rebuild."

Michla was startled. "Then, what is he going to do?"

"He says that he is leaving the village."

"To go where?"

"He mentioned he might go to America. I think he was serious."

"That's a fine idea, except for one thing."

"And what is that?"

"He has a wife and children. He can't just leave."

"Perhaps he will not go to America, but I think he is serious about leaving Naroulia. Maybe even Belarus."

"But what will he do about his house? He can't just leave it, too."

"There is nothing left of the house now," Lewin sighed. "And besides, he gave what is left of it to me."

Michla's mouth dropped open. "Really?"

Lewin nodded. "Really."

Michla seemed pleased to have the property but did her best not to show it because of the circumstances. Then she noticed the troubled look on Lewin's face. "What is it? What is wrong?" He did not respond immediately, and she continued talking. "We can rebuild the house. We can make it better than it was before." She took a seat beside him and held his hand in hers. "We could move there ourselves. They have a beautiful garden in back. And running water in the kitchen. Or we could sell it. Many people would want to live there."

"It's not that," he said quietly.

"Then, what is it?"

He looked her in the eyes. "I wonder if we should leave."

Michla drew back from him and let go of his hand. "Leave the village? Where would we go?"

"To America. This is not a good place for us now. There will only be more attacks. It will only get worse."

"That's what Esther said when she let Isador convince her to leave. You want to be like Isador? Just run off and live somewhere else? Among people we have never known?"

"I think we must consider it." Lewin glanced toward the children. "At least for their sakes."

Michla was astounded by the suggestion that they should leave the village. Three times she opened her mouth to speak, but each time she was caught up short by the sense that she should keep silent, which was uncharacteristic for her. She yielded to it nonetheless, choosing to sit in silence and watch while Lewin processed the events of the night before, the reality of the scene that morning, and the sadness at the news that Naum was leaving.

After a while, however, the duties of the day caught up with Michla and she rose from the chair at the table, wiped her hands on the towel, and returned to her work at the kitchen counter. Lewin seemed hardly to notice but remained in his seat, remembering again the day Esther and Isador left with their children to travel to America.

Leaving was a difficult decision for them. In spite of all that had been said about Isador, Lewin had seen him agonizing over the choice—whether to leave home, travel by ship across the ocean, and settle in a new country, or remain in Naroulia hoping to endure the pogroms without serious consequences, an outcome that seemed increasingly unlikely.

After their arrival in New York, Lewin received letters from Esther telling about their many adventures. It seemed they had found none of the obstacles insurmountable. Even finding a job had not been difficult. And although they had encountered some resistance to their presence in the new country, it had not deterred them from making their way. They had a cousin who was there already and that helped, at least until they could find an apartment of their own.

Lewin was certain Esther and Isador would do the same for him and Michla and the boys. Give them a chance to make a new start. It would not be easy, but as he sat at the table that day, with the stench of the attack still in his nostrils, Lewin felt certain he and Michla should follow suit. That they should leave the village and move their family to America. And the sooner the better.

CHAPTER 2

Afew days after the attack on Naroulia, Lewin took the train to Mazyr, a town located about forty kilometers northwest of the village. There were stops in between, though—one for water and coal to keep the locomotive operating running; one for passengers and freight at a flag stop.

The trip, though not very far, took more than two hours. When he arrived in Mazyr, Lewin made his way to a building in town where Yakov Chernigov, a friend he knew through trading finished lumber and raw timber, conducted business. Chernigov was several years older and known in the region as an expert on the world beyond the Pale of Settlement. They talked in his cluttered and dusty office.

"What brings you up here?" Chernigov began when they were seated.

Lewin leaned close and spoke in a low voice. "What does it take to travel to America? How it's done?"

"You remember. . .I helped your sister, Esther."

"That is why I came to see you. Can you help me?"

Chernigov nodded slowly. "I can help you. But it is not an easy trip."

"I know."

"And it is expensive."

"I understand." Lewin was growing impatient. "Tell me how it is done."

Chernigov glanced around, as if checking to make certain no one was listening. "First," he began, "you would travel by train from Naroulia into Lithuania and spend the night in Vilnius."

Lewin thought that much did not seem so bad. "I have a friend who lives there."

"Good. From there you will go to Klaipėda."

"The port."

"Yes," Chernigov acknowledged. "In Klaipėda, you would book passage on a ship of the Russian American Line."

Mention of the Russians troubled Lewin. "*Russian* American?"

"It is only a name," Chernigov reassured. "It is a Danish company. Not Russian."

"Oh."

"They have the best reputation for protecting our people."

Lewin thought for a moment. "And I must wait until I am there, in Klaipėda, to buy the ticket?"

"Yes."

Lewin looked perplexed. "I cannot buy it now? Here?"

"You will buy it when you get there."

"But what if the ship is full?"

Chernigov looked away. "This is how everyone has done it."

"You have been there? To Klaipėda? It is safe for us there?"

Chernigov looked away once more. "I have assisted many who have gone in this manner. The details are always the same."

Lewin pressed the issue. "And this is how my sister did it?"

Chernigov glanced down. "This is how she did it."

Something about the expression on Chernigov's face made Lewin suspicious. Not that his friend would lie but that his information might be old and outdated. Chernigov was a proud man and would never admit to not knowing. There had been rumors about him recently, too. Despite his reputation in foreign matters, some questioned whether Chernigov had ever ventured beyond the borders of Belarus at all. Still, he had helped Esther; that much was certain. And he was the only person Lewin knew who was conversant on the topic. So he decided to raise the question that troubled him most—one that touched Lewin's own pride.

"There is one more issue I wanted to ask about. I have enough money to pay for my own passage but not enough for my entire family."

"You are—"

Lewin held up his hand to cut him off. "I am not asking for a loan," but surely others must have faced this problem."

"It is not a problem," Chernigov replied. "That is what I was going to say when you stopped me."

"How is this done?"

"You go first." Chernigov smiled. "When you arrive in America, you get a job. Earn some money. Send for the others later."

"How long does that take?"

Chernigov shrugged. "That depends on your diligence. My brother did it in a year."

Lewin's eyes opened wider. He had not heard of Chernigov's brother. "Your brother went to America?"

"Yes. Five years ago."

"And he worked for a year and sent for his family?"

Chernigov nodded confidently. "Yes. They live in Newark now. Newark, New Jersey. I have never been there, but I have seen it on a map."

Lewin leaned back in his chair. A year without Michla and the boys. That was a long time to be apart. And he wasn't even sure he could do it. What if he failed? What if he couldn't find a job?

Chernigov noticed the look on his face. "This troubles you?"

"A year." Lewin sighed. "I don't know if I can do it."

Chernigov reached over and patted Lewin on the back of the hand. "You can do what must be done."

✦ ✦ ✦

After talking to Chernigov, Lewin caught the southbound afternoon train for the return to Naroulia. It was almost dark when he arrived but instead of going straight home, he stopped in the village to see Michla's father, Rabbi Michael Katznelson.

As with many of the area's residents, Katznelson had grown up in the region. He left to study but returned with his wife to oversee the congregation at the village's main synagogue, a massive wooden structure located near the center of town, not far from the train station. Under his guidance and tutelage, the congregation had become known throughout the Pale as a group that valued learning, wisdom, insight, and discipline—principles that Lewin felt he could use in making a final decision about the move to America.

Lewin found Katznelson alone at his house. They sat by the fireplace in the front room and talked. "You look troubled," Katznelson observed.

"I have many things on my mind."

"And one of them is moving your family to America."

"Michla told you?"

"She is my daughter. We talk all the time." Lewin nodded in response. Katznelson peered intently at him. "You are serious about this?"

"I went to see Chernigov. To ask about the details of the journey."

Katznelson smiled. "Michla told me that also."

"Michla knows everything."

"She is a good woman." Katznelson spoke with a sense of pride. "And she is diligent. She notices everything that touches her family."

"You would be sad to see her go."

Katznelson nodded. "And sad for the arduous times that would lie ahead for her."

"My sister is already there with her husband and their family."

"I was at the station when they boarded the train to leave."

"I believe they will help us."

"We all must help each other." Katznelson rose from his chair. "Would you like some coffee?"

Katznelson always brewed a large pot of coffee early in the morning and allowed it to sit on the hot stove all day. By late afternoon, it was usually strong, bitter, and, for Lewin, quite undrinkable. But he didn't want to turn down his father-in-law's hospitality, so he smiled, "Sure. A cup of coffee would be great."

When the coffee was poured and both had a sip, Katznelson returned to the topic at hand. "You spoke to Chernigov about your desire to move to America?"

"Yes," Lewin replied. He still thought of it as a decision in progress but there was no point in quibbling over the details. Besides, he wasn't sure if Katznelson was asking about his own decision, or about Chernigov. "Why? Is there a problem with Chernigov?"

"He is a good man." There was a tentative note in Katznelson's voice.

"But . . .?"

Katznelson glanced down at his coffee cup. "I have heard reports that his information is. . .no longer reliable."

Lewin frowned. "Intentionally unreliable?"

"No." Katznelson shook his head. "I don't think he is being intentional about it."

"Then, what?"

"In the past," Katznelson began, "when Esther and Isador departed for America, Chernigov had recently returned from a trip to Lithuania. From that trip, he knew much about the region beyond the Pale and had experience in navigating a portion of it. He was able to help your sister and others of that time make the trip. Everyone who knew him stood in awe of his abilities. On the basis of your sister's success and the success of others from that time, Chernigov became known as an expert on matters related to the American passage. But that was then. This is now. In the intervening time, he has not kept up with the latest developments."

"You think I should not have consulted him?"

"I think you must not rely on him being correct in every matter."

They both sat quietly and sipped their coffee. Finally Lewin asked, "You are opposed to this move?"

"I am not opposed," Katznelson responded. "I understand your reasoning. But I am saddened by it."

"You think we should stay?"

Katznelson smiled kindly. "You are the head of your own family. It is given to you to make decisions for others. You must do as seems right to you." Katznelson opened his palm and traced a circle in the center of it with his index finger. "You are in the center. An array of choices surrounds you." He traced around the base of his fingers in a circle. "Each of the choices is good. You must choose the one most right for you and your family."

"There will be more trouble here. The situation will not improve, and the current government is no more interested in solving our problems than the czar."

Katznelson nodded. "You are correct."

"Then, will you come with us?"

Katznelson shook his head. "You remember the *Proverbs*?"

"I read them every day."

"Then you know it is written, 'A wise man sees trouble coming and prepares for it.'"

"Yes."

"We see the same trouble, but we do not all prepare for it in the same way. We each must prepare in our *own* way. My preparation is here. I cannot leave." He made a sweeping gesture. "These are my people. This is my place. I do not want to be anywhere else. You, however, must work things out as they apply to you and your family. Perhaps America is best." He had a tight smile. "Perhaps it would afford a better life for my daughter and my grandsons."

"A move like this is complicated." Lewin sighed.

"Complication is not a thing to avoid."

"It would take some time to complete," Lewin said.

Katznelson nodded again. "I expect it would."

"I would go first, alone," Lewin explained. "Then find a job over there and send for them later."

"I have heard of others who have done that, as well."

"It could take a year to do that. Maybe longer." Lewin looked over at him. "Michla and the boys would be here without me."

Katznelson smiled. "If that is what you must do, we will care for them until you make arrangements for them to join you." He took another sip of coffee. "We will not allow them to lack for anything."

+ + +

When Lewin finally arrived at home, Michla was waiting for him in the front room. "You missed supper."

"I know."

"Where have you been?"

"You know where I have been."

She scowled. "I do not know why you put so much faith in Chernigov."

"He is the only one I know who is familiar with the world."

"And did he tell you what you wanted to know?"

"He told me the basics."

Michla placed her hands on her hips. "And you believed him?"

"Your father does not think I should."

"My father thinks you should be careful," she replied. "That is all. He is concerned."

"About what?"

"He hears many things about Chernigov."

"He told you that?"

She moved her hands from her hips and folded her arms across her midriff. "He and I talk all the time."

"That's what he said."

"Why should you complain?" she argued. "You stopped to see him just now. Before you came to me."

"He knows Chernigov. I wanted his assessment."

"And what did he tell you?"

"That time has passed since Chernigov actually traveled. He questions how accurate his information might be."

Michla gestured with a wave of her hand. "As I told you. Chernigov can no longer be trusted."

Lewin smiled at her. "You are worried about me?"

A puzzled frown wrinkled Michla's forehead. "You?"

"Yes," Lewin replied. "Are you worried that I will get halfway to America and not be able to complete the journey?"

Michla's eyes opened wide. "You would go alone?"

Lewin sighed. He had not meant to tell her in that manner, but there was no point in avoiding the issue. "Business is not so good right now. There is only money enough for one."

She became angry. "So, you are abandoning us?"

"No." Lewin held out his arms to embrace her, but she drew back. "In order for us to make this move, I must go first, find a job in America, and send money for you and the boys."

"Maybe you should work here," she suggested. "And we will save enough for all of us to go together."

Lewin shook his head. "We have not been able to do that so far."

Michla's shoulders sagged and her countenance softened with a look of resignation. "How long would this take?"

"Chernigov says—"

Her eyes darkened at the mention of him. "This is what I

mean. We are betting our lives and the lives of our children on what Chernigov says."

"No," Lewin responded. "We are not betting on him. We are betting on me. That I am making the right decision. That I will be able to complete the trip and find a job."

"And you think this is the way?"

"Others did it in this manner."

"Esther and Isador did not do it this way. They went together with their entire family."

"But, they were younger when they went."

"This is the only place I have ever known," Michla countered. "The only place *we* have ever known. The only place our children have ever lived. And now we have your cousin's property, too. We have made something here. We can make more of it and live just fine."

"This place has given us many things," Lewin replied. "But this place lacks the most important thing."

"What is that?"

"The future. This place has no future."

They talked awhile longer but gradually, reluctantly, Michla agreed with Lewin's assessment of their situation and his conclusion that America offered their only hope of escaping the prejudice and persecution that had come to characterize life in Naroulia.

The following day, Lewin sent a letter to Esther in America asking if she would help them make the move by giving him a place to live until he could get established.

While they waited for Esther's response, Lewin began arranging their affairs. He would make the trip before summer's end. Michla would remain with the boys until he was established in a job and had found a place for them to live. In the meantime, they needed a means to survive. For that to happen Lewin needed someone to operate his business in the village and tend to his farming lease. They also needed someone to take over their house when Michla and the boys departed to join him. Resolving those issues kept them up late at night, discussing options and arguing over the possibilities.

After much thought and not a little argument, Lewin looked over at Michla and smiled. "What about Yisroel?"

Yisroel Katznelson was Michla's younger brother. He had recently returned to Naroulia from Odessa where he had been apprenticed to a grain merchant. The life of a businessman came easily for him, but there were few opportunities for new trade in the village and he had been forced to take a job at the tannery. His work placed him in contact with dead animals every day and, according to orthodox practice, made him ceremonially unclean, which prevented him from attending worship at the synagogue. Many from the village shunned him as well and left him with a solitary life, a situation he found unsatisfactory. When he wasn't working, Yisroel spent his time in the small cabin where he lived near the tannery, or in the woods that surrounded it.

The work was an adventure at first, a chance to get hands-on experience in a craft he'd never tried before, but more recently the limitations it imposed were weighing heavily upon him and he was thinking of moving on. Perhaps going as far away as Paris where a friend from Odessa lived. Michla's father did not want him to leave, so bringing him into the business would help him and them.

At the mention of Yisroel's name, a broad grin burst across Michla's face. "He would be perfect." She leaned forward and kissed Lewin on the lips. "You are smart for thinking of him."

CHAPTER 3

The next day, Lewin took the horse and wagon out to the tannery. He found Yisroel stirring hides in a vat with a wooden paddle. "You should not be here," Yisroel advised. "If anyone finds out, they will not let you enter the synagogue on the Sabbath."

Lewin made a dismissive gesture. "I am not worried about that. Not attending would give me a true Sabbath."

Yisroel laughed. "What brings you out here? Has something happened?"

"I wanted to talk to you about business."

"What sort of business?"

"My business."

Yisroel glanced in Lewin's direction. "What about it?"

"I was wondering if you would like for it to become *our* business?"

Yisroel stopped stirring the vat. "Our business? You want to take me into your business?"

"I want to make you my partner."

Yisroel put down the paddle and turned to face Lewin. "Why? Why would you do that?"

"You're good at business," Lewin explained. "Working in a tannery is not your calling in life. And I need your help."

Yisroel picked up the paddle and stirred the vat once more. "What sort of help?"

"Put down your paddle and we can talk."

"I can't stop the process right now. It will ruin the hides."

"Very well," Lewin decided. "I will return this evening. We can talk at your cabin."

That evening, Lewin and Yisroel discussed the matter fully. Yisroel recounted. "Let me get this straight. You will bring me into your business as your partner. We will operate the business in that manner until Michla and the boys are safely with you in America. Once all of you are over there, the business will be fully mine, along with your house and the place where Naum used to live."

Lewin nodded. "That is correct."

"Do we need a paper to that effect?"

"I trust you," Lewin answered. "Will you trust me?"

"Yes. Of course."

"Then all we need is a handshake."

"Very well."

And with that, the two men clasped hands.

"Promise me one more thing," Lewin added.

"What is that?"

"When things begin to fall apart here, you will leave Naroulia at once."

Yisroel frowned. "You think things will fall apart?"

"That is why we are going to America."

"And if that day comes, where should I go?"

Lewin looked him in the eye. "Come to us in America."

✦ ✦ ✦

Three days later, Yisroel left his job at the tannery and moved back home with his parents. Early the next morning, he met Lewin at the warehouse. "You smell like boiling cowhide," Lewin sniffed when he arrived.

"I am afraid the scent of their skin has permeated mine."

Lewin grinned. "Then we shall have to sweat it out of you."

All that day, and for every day after that, Lewin and Yisroel worked together as Lewin taught him the business and introduced him to existing customers. It was slow at first; Yisroel had many questions and he challenged some of Lewin's practices, but as the days went by he came to understand how Lewin had made it work and how he might improve upon it once the business became fully his own.

Meanwhile, Lewin began selling off some of his belongings—hand tools he no longer needed, books he could not transport with him, and items of jewelry he had acquired along the way. The proceeds, he hoped, would speed the time when he would have enough to cover the expense of the trip to America, a matter that was very much at the forefront of his thoughts.

In spite of the information he had obtained from Chernigov, calculating an exact cost for the trip had proved elusive. In addition to the cost of passage on a ship, he needed train fare to get to the port and money for food to eat along the way. And he needed to arrive in New York with enough money to sustain himself until he found a job.

As sales of his belongings continued, Lewin deposited the money in a metal box that was hidden in a safe spot beneath the floorboards under his bed, where he and Michla kept their important papers. Each day that he sold something, he added the money to the box. On Fridays, just before the Sabbath began, he counted to see how much cash he had. From late winter and into spring, progress came slowly.

Though business was slow at first, Yisroel proved to be a quick study and very astute at handling transactions. Others seemed to notice his enthusiasm, and as winter began to wane, business increased. Soon the money in the metal box beneath the bed totaled more than enough to supply Lewin's needs for the trip. Only one thing remained—a response from Esther telling him that she would make a place for him in their apartment. When weeks passed without a response, Lewin began to wonder if something had happened to her.

Every evening when he came home and sat at the kitchen table before supper, he asked the same questions: Is she sick? Has she died? Is she no longer in New York?

And each time, Michla reassured him, "America is a long way away. And Esther has a life besides writing to you."

"But it has been weeks."

"She will write. And if something has happened, someone would know it by now. And if not, Esther will write to you."

Weeks turned into months and gradually the snow melted, turning the ground to mud. Then the trees began to bud as spring drew near and the planting season approached. Lewin showed Yisroel how to manage the farmer who worked the lease on the field at the edge of town and instructed him on where and how he sold his share of the grain that the land produced. Once or twice each week they watched as the land was tilled, and when the time came to plant the seeds, they spent an entire day sitting in the shade of a tree, watching as the farmer and his laborers worked.

"We should consider switching from wheat to rye," Yisroel suggested.

"Wheat has done well each year," Lewin replied.

"But alternating the years with rye would help the land," Yisroel noted. "And it would avoid the threat of disease."

"You learned this in Odessa?" Lewin's voice had a hint of disdain, as if he did not appreciate Yisroel's suggestion. "They have rye fields in the city?"

Yisroel ignored the tone of his voice. "I heard the grain merchants talking about it. It is a technique used in other places." Yisroel glanced in Lewin's direction. "It is how they do it in America."

"These grain merchants have been to America?"

"No," Yisroel replied. "But they read."

"I read," Lewin responded.

"I know. But you do not read about farming."

"This is true," Lewin conceded with a chuckle. They continued to discuss the farm, and by the end of the day Lewin was impressed with Yisroel's ideas. Perhaps he would make a go of it after all, a thought that left him feeling more comfortable about traveling to America. If he ever got to make the trip. As of yet, there had been no response from Esther.

At the house one evening later in the week, Lewin took a seat at the table in the kitchen and slipped off his work boots, as was his routine. Just then, Michla entered the room with a troubled look he could recognize even in the flickering light of the kerosene lamp that sat near the center of the table. "What is the matter?"

"This came for you." Michla reached into the pocket of her apron and brought out an envelope. She laid it on the table in front of Lewin and took a seat beside him.

The envelope was postmarked from New York and at the sight of it Lewin smiled. "This is from Esther."

With a flick of his finger, Lewin opened the letter and began to read. "Of course, you can stay with us," Esther wrote. "And Isador will help you get a job." She went on to talk about the latest news from family members living in New York, but offered no explanation for the delay in responding to his earlier inquiry. When Lewin finished reading, he handed the letter to Michla.

She scanned it quickly, then handed it back. "I guess that settles it."

"I know you don't like the idea of moving," Lewin responded. "But it is best for all of us that we go."

Michla scooted back her chair from the table and stood. "Then you get to explain it to our sons."

Lewin glanced through the doorway into the front room where his sons sat reading by the light of an oil lamp. The thought of not seeing them for a year was overwhelming. Still, he was resolved to make the change and, after a moment longer to reflect, rose from the table and went to the front room to explain it to them.

✦ ✦ ✦

Arranging final details for Lewin's trip—putting the business's books in order, confirming with Yisroel the distributions of profit to be given to Michla, arranging for train tickets to take him all the way to Klaipėda, and contacting friends in Vilnius where he could overnight along the way—took several letters and several more weeks.

Finally—on a bright, clear morning near the middle of summer—the time came for Lewin to begin his journey to America. On the morning of his departure he packed his clothes into a single satchel made of leather and cloth, cinched it closed with the straps, and gripped the handle tightly. "It is time," he announced.

At the sound of his voice, both boys grabbed his legs, locking their arms around him tightly as if to hold him in place. They seemed determined to prevent him from going, but after a moment of coaxing, Michla pulled them away. "Let your father go," she instructed. "This is something he must do for us."

Lewin bent down and gave each of them a hug, then sent the boys from the room. When they were gone, Lewin put his arms around Michla and pulled her close. "You will not forget me?"

Tears filled her eyes. "It is not of me you should ask such things. But yourself."

"I will not forget you."

A tear slid down her cheek. "I am scared."

"So am I," he whispered.

"We will join you. I promise we will make the trip as soon as we can. But as for Yisroel and the other members of our family, I think you will never see them again."

"As your father told me, we each must make our own way,

with our own decisions, choosing what is right and best for our families," Lewin explained. "This is best for us. Maybe not in the short term but in the years to come you will see. This is a good thing."

"You have seen or heard something that lets you know this?"

"I have not seen a vision." Lewin placed his hand on his chest. "But I know it in my heart."

As Lewin and Michla walked from the room, the boys joined them and they all said their final good-byes at the front door. Then Lewin stepped from the porch and started alone up the street toward the train station. Three times he paused and glanced over his shoulder, considering whether to abandon the trip and return to the house, and each time he resolved anew to see it through to the end, whatever that end might be.

When he arrived at the train station, Lewin found his father-in-law waiting for him. "I came to see you off," Katznelson explained. "I knew Michla would not be here."

"She doesn't like good-byes."

"More to the point," Katznelson added, "she doesn't like others to see her cry."

Lewin smiled. "You know her well."

"She is my daughter."

"You will check on them?"

"I have always checked on them."

"Now I have mostly questions. Except for this move to America." Lewin looked Katznelson in the eye. "This is the thing for us to do."

Katznelson nodded. "I can see you have made up your mind."

"I have set my face toward New York."

"Well put."

They stood in silence for a while, with the birds singing in the distance followed by the sounds of the village as it came to life for the day, and then the train came into sight. A few minutes later, the locomotive brought the cars to a stop beside the station. Lewin waited while the conductor opened the doors and passengers stepped down from the nearest one. When all was set for boarding, he turned to Katznelson and offered his hand. "This is good-bye, Michael."

"This is only *farewell*." Katznelson grasped Lewin's hand firmly and smiled energetically, but the look in his eyes said he knew they would never meet again. "May everything you touch turn to gold." He spoke it as a blessing and followed with a hug.

Lewin savored his father-in-law's embrace, and his eyes were full. "Thank you. May we meet again, in Jerusalem." And with that, Lewin pulled away and stepped into the train car. He gave one final wave at the door, and then started up the aisle in search of a seat.

✦ ✦ ✦

Darkness had fallen by the time the train from Naroulia arrived in Vilnius. Semyon Ginsberg, the friend Lewin had contacted, was waiting at the train station. Lewin spotted him on the platform before the train came to a stop.

When Lewin alighted from the railcar, the two men embraced and quickly caught up on the major events of their lives since they'd last visited, because it had been a while. Later, after they'd made their way to Semyon's home and eaten supper, Lewin sat with Semyon and his wife, Leah, at the dining table and talked.

"We were surprised when you contacted us," Semyon finally said.

"That I should contact you, or that I am on my way to America?"

"Both," Leah offered.

"I am sorry it has been so long. Life has a way of distracting one from the things that matter most. And many have expressed their surprise that Michla and I would make this move."

"We were not surprised by the move," Semyon added. "Nor that we had not heard from you in a while. But rather that you would come through Vilnius on your way."

"It is on the way to Klaipėda," Lewin noted.

Leah had a puzzled look. "You were intending to leave through Klaipėda?"

"I was told to go that way. That everyone had gone that way before. Is that not the way?"

"That is old information," she informed.

"Everyone used to go that way," Semyon added. "It used to be good, but now it is not."

A troubled frown wrinkled Lewin's forehead. "Then what should I do?"

"You should leave through Libau," Semyon replied.

"In Latvia?"

"Yes."

"Agents there are much more sympathetic to our cause," Leah noted. "And most of the passenger lines have moved there."

"The Russian American Line sails from there?" Lewin asked.

Semyon shook his head. "There is no Russian American Line now."

Lewin had a sinking feeling in his stomach. As Katznelson and others had suspected, Chernigov had been advising with outdated information. Too much pride. Not enough contacts. "Then what should I do?" he asked.

"Use the Baltic American Line."

Lewin sighed. "I was told to use the Russian American Line because they will not allow their crews to abuse us."

Semyon had a sympathetic smile. "That was true in the past," he explained, "but after the revolution the Russian American Line ceased to operate. It has been out of business for several years."

"The ships were transferred to Libau," Leah added. "They are now part of the Baltic American Line."

Semyon reached across the table and gave Lewin a reassuring pat on the back of his hand. "Do not worry, my friend. This will work well for you. The Baltic is a good line. We have heard no complaints from those who have used it."

After a light breakfast early the next morning, Lewin and Semyon walked back to the train station. They waited together on the platform until the train for Libau arrived. When it was time for Lewin to board, they shook hands and gave each other a hug. "We shall not see each other again," Semyon said. "But I would like to know that you arrived safely in America. So please write to us."

"I will," Lewin replied.

The ride to Libau seemed to last a lifetime and as the train clattered on its way, Lewin wondered what the city might be like. He'd never been to Libau and did not know anyone who had. In fact, he had never been to Latvia at all, and as he looked out the window a sudden realization came to him. *This is the farthest from home that I have ever traveled.*

It was late when the train pulled into the station at Libau. Lewin left the railcar with a crowd of tourists on a holiday to the beach to enjoy the Baltic Coast. He asked about where they were staying, hoping to find a place for the night, but when he learned they were booked in an expensive hotel, he turned aside and asked the rail clerk for directions to a boardinghouse.

What Lewin found was a hostel—a three-story building filled with rows and rows of rickety, well-worn cots. A night's rent was affordable but there was no space for storing his belongings, and Lewin was unwilling to deposit his luggage with the clerk at the desk on the first floor—the only supposedly secure place in the building—so he spent the night with his luggage resting atop his torso, eschewing supper for the sake of his belongings.

The next day, he located an office for the Baltic American

Line where he purchased a ticket for passage to the United States. However, the ship was not scheduled to leave for two more days, which forced Lewin to return to the hostel. This time, he went out for meals, taking his luggage with him everywhere he went.

On the day of the ship's departure, Lewin arrived early to board. His ticket was the cheapest passage offered, which gave him a spot on the lowest deck. Being early, he was ahead of the crowd and found a rack of bunks near a porthole that gave him a view of the horizon. A locker at the foot of the bed gave him a secure place to put his luggage and he stored it there, then chose the bed on the lowest level and lay down, awaiting the assigned time for the first meal.

As he stared up at the ceiling, he became aware of the stale air that already filled the room. By the time it was filled with passengers he knew it would become a stench. Instead of brooding over it, though, he decided to take stock of his financial situation.

Train fare from Vilnius to Libau had been an unanticipated expense, and the room for the previous three nights cost more than he'd expected. As well as the extra days of food. Still, he was on board now and there would be no further payments until he arrived in New York. If nothing else unforeseen occurred, he would arrive in America with enough to see him through, provided he could find a job quickly.

Satisfied his finances were in order, Lewin closed his eyes and tried to nap. But as the hours passed and the ship remained moored at the dock, he began to wonder if they would actually leave. And if they left, would he make it all the way across the ocean? Would he reach America and find the life he hoped, or would this grand venture come to a very bitter end?

CHAPTER 4

In the United States, news of negotiations among world leaders at the Paris Peace Conference dominated the media. Newspapers and radio broadcasts seemed to talk of nothing else, as did neighbors and co-workers in their daily conversation. Everyone had an idea of what went wrong with the war—the underlying events and decisions that caused it in the first place, the poor way it was executed, the people who failed their duty to the soldiers, those who knew how to fight but were denied the chance, those who didn't and wouldn't get out of the way, and an endless array of ideas about what ought to happen next.

Bryce Mullins turned twenty-six that year. Tall, broad-shouldered, and good-looking, he grew up in Schenectady, New York. After graduating from high school, he went to work as a machinist's apprentice at Alco, a Schenectady company that manufactured steam locomotives for the railroad. He was a quick learner and easily mastered the rudimentary elements of the trade, becoming a journeyman machinist in only two years. Stratification in the shop, however, meant he would be stuck in that position for the next five years, something he neither appreciated nor understood.

During a trip to western Massachusetts to visit a cousin who lived in Springfield, he heard about a job opening in the shop at Boatwright Thread and Twill, a textile firm that operated a mill in the adjacent town of Indian Orchard. Feeling he had nothing to lose, Mullins applied for the position and was hired on the spot.

Two weeks later, he moved to Indian Orchard and rented a room at a boardinghouse owned by Sally Smithson, a seventy-year-old widow who had lived her entire life in the house she now rented by the room to strangers.

At work, in the bar up the street, and even at the boarding-house, discussion of events surrounding the war was a topic of interest to many. Everyone, it seemed, had an opinion, but not many were interested in acting on their beliefs or in putting feet to their opinions.

Mullins was not like the others. For him, the war and the peace now being discussed were very much a personal matter. He shared many of the interests expressed by others regarding the Great War, but not because of a prevailing fascination with politics or out a sense of duty arising from his own military service. His interest was, quite literally, much closer to home.

American politicians had done their best to keep the United States out of the war. But after German U-boats sank US merchant vessels, and after agents of the German government attempted to induce Mexican officials to attack the US along its southern border, many of those same politicians who'd resisted the war became ardent supporters of US intervention.

In anticipation of joining the fight, Woodrow Wilson, the US president, issued a general mobilization order that instituted the draft. However, American involvement came late in the fighting, and by the time Mullins was called up for service, the war was almost over. His induction occurred only a few months before a cease-fire ended the bloodshed. He was still in boot camp. Two weeks later, he was discharged and sent home, having spent less than a year in the service. His older brother, Harry, however, was not so blessed.

Harry had joined the army a year before the mobilization order was issued. Bryce remembered him saying, "We're going to get in this fight. There's no avoiding it. Sooner or later, the politicians will see we have no choice. As Americans, it's our duty to go over there and end this thing. And besides, it'll be fun. I always wanted to see Europe and this way I'll get to go for free." Henry was among the first troops dispatched to Europe after the United States formally entered the war.

A few weeks after they arrived in France, Harry's unit was deployed to the Vosges Mountains of France. Not long after taking their appointed position, the German Army launched a surprise nighttime attack. Harry died shortly before midnight on a warm summer's eve.

Because of the distance and the time and the number of casualties—thousands died on both sides that night—Harry's remains were interred at a cemetery near Thann, a village located not far from the site of the heaviest fighting. His parents, too distraught over the loss of their oldest son, refused to hold a memorial service for him. "He was ours," they later explained. "We didn't want to share his life with the world when he was alive. We certainly weren't sharing him with anyone else after he was gone."

Mullins understood his parents' grief, but it left him without a chance to say good-bye to his brother. Since then, he had been plagued by a hollow sense of incompletion, as if the final note of his relationship with his brother was waiting to be played, struggling to be heard. And it was that incompleteness that drove his interest in the war.

In the months following the end of the war, images of the battlefields where the heaviest fighting took place, initially censored from news reports, began to surface. Magazines ran special issues that included photographs of dead bodies, some of them torn in half by machine gun fire, and of landscapes stripped bare of vegetation by barrage after barrage. Rolling hills, once the sight of lush green meadows and deeply wooded forests, seemed like images one might imagine from another planet. Earth freshly plowed by the footsteps of soldiers and the tracks of newly-invented armored vehicles that ranged back and forth, grinding and churning for four long years. Here and there, were rain-soaked, blood-soaked, muddy bogs created by miles and miles of trenches. And worst of all, the bloated bodies of the dead, their faces turned upward, their eyes fixed in a look of empty, hopeless desperation. Mullins viewed those pictures, imagining the moment the bullets tore through his brother's body, the hot shrapnel lodged in his torso, the gas sucking the air from his lungs. And each time he wept.

Gradually, Mullins came to understand the enormity of the conflict. "The whole world was at war," he said more than once. And he began to sense the entire affair had been a total loss for victor and vanquished alike. A waste of men, money, and time. But why? Why were the countries fighting? Why did the United States enter the war? Why did his brother have to die?

Of course, no one had any answers, only opinions. But in the quest to resolve the matter, Mullins began to read the Springfield newspaper every day, hoping to find an article or a comment that would point him toward the truth. Articles in the paper provided a rehash of the issues that had led to the four-year conflagration, but none of them seemed adequate to support a valid cause for the fighting. As his questions remained unanswered, he continued to read. But as the weeks passed, the emptiness inside, the incompleteness of his brother's life, the glaring stupidity and obvious ignorance of those in charge, all of it fermented into anger over what appeared to be the capriciousness of European monarchs and the complicity of the American government. "They should all be thrown out," he often said to himself. "Thrown out or run out. Or, better yet, shot."

Mullins tried to talk about it at the boardinghouse, but few were interested. A man who frequented the bar down the street told him it was just the way things worked. "The older men use the younger men to play army, like they did when they were kids. It's nothing more than that. When they were young, they used toy soldiers. When they grew up and got elected, they used the real thing."

One Tuesday during a lunch break at work, Mullins raised that idea with Tom Kugler, a co-worker in the machine shop. "Do you think that's true? Are they just grown-up children playing army with live men?"

Owen Fletcher, who was seated nearby, chimed in. "The world is their sandbox." Everyone laughed in response. Everyone except Mullins.

Kugler realized the question meant something to Mullins and responded with a serious tone. "I think the entire fiasco was orchestrated by the Jews."

Mullins frowned. "The Jews?"

"They planned it, found a way to get it started, and made a ton of money off it. The Rothschilds have been doing that for centuries."

"They're really like that?"

"They're the ones who fund the roads and dams and railroads. And they're the ones who start the wars."

"They're also the ones who end them," Fletcher added. "Usually as soon as the money runs out."

"And," Kugler added with a flourish, "they do it just to make money."

"He's right," an older guy spoke up. "The Jews manipulate everything—which countries go to war, which ones don't. What gets built, what doesn't."

"International Jewish bankers," Kugler continued, "are the ones behind the Communist revolution in Russia, too."

Jerome Gilbert, another co-worker, spoke up. "Jews are coming here to do the same thing."

"They're already here," Fletcher responded. "Right here in Indian Orchard."

"One comes, then he brings his brother," Gilbert explained.

"Then they bring their sister. Then the parents and the cousins."

"Then they start having kids," Fletcher noted.

"And when they get a job, they do the same thing," Kugler huffed. "Shuffle everyone up the job ladder as they arrive."

"All in an attempt to take over." Gilbert gave Mullins a knowing look. "You watch 'em. You'll see what we're talking about."

Mullins had never heard this kind of discussion at work. Maybe in the bar or the diner but not at the shop. Usually everyone ate in silence, but when he brought up the topic that day it was like dropping a match into a container of flammable liquid. Everything erupted and most of what was said found a place in him. "Doesn't anyone try to stop them?" Mullins asked.

"Some people are talking about it," Kugler replied.

"Lots of people are talking about it," Fletcher added.

"Not nearly enough," Gilbert noted.

"Who?" Mullins asked. "Who's talking about doing something?"

"There's a guy who comes on the radio," Kugler replied. "He talks about it."

"Just more words," Gilbert answered. "Just more talk."

"No," Kugler replied. "I think this guy is actually trying to do something."

"Who?" Mullins repeated. "Who is it?"

"I can't remember his name. His show comes on Wednesday nights."

"What time?"

"I heard him last week after dinner."

✦ ✦ ✦

Mrs. Smithson rented her rooms furnished. The price was higher than most places in town, but her rooms came with breakfast and dinner included at no extra charge. She had rules, too, some of which Mullins had found unnecessarily restrictive at first, but rather quickly he came to appreciate the meals almost as much as the room and bed.

That same Tuesday evening after dinner, Mullins walked outside to the front porch and took a seat on an old kitchen chair that sat near the wall between the door and first window. He leaned it back on the rear legs, propped his head against the wall, and relaxed. A few minutes later, Bobby Rankin, a fellow boardinghouse resident, joined him on the porch.

Rankin worked as a mechanic at a garage located not far from the mill. He and Mullins often traveled to the boardinghouse in the afternoon on the same bus. Through conversation during their commute they became friends.

That evening on the porch as they sat talking after dinner, Mullins mentioned the radio program he'd heard about at work. "The show sounded interesting but the guy I talked to couldn't remember the person's name."

"That's Walter Jones," Rankin said.

"You sure?"

"Yeah. Reverend Walter Jones."

"A preacher?"

"Yeah."

Mullins shook his head. "I don't think that's the one. The guy at work said the show was about politics."

Rankin nodded. "This show is about politics. But the guy who does it is a preacher."

"It's not just preaching?"

"No. It's politics."

"Where's he from?"

"Somewhere in New York, I think. Calls the program the Golden Hour of Power. Talks about the stuff you're always talking about. You know. . .the war. What caused it. The global conspiracy that was behind it."

Mullins's eyes brightened. "He talks about a conspiracy?"

"Yeah. Rich people. Rich Jews, actually. How they manipulate everything and everybody. You would like what he has to say."

"When does it come on?"

"Wednesday nights."

"Hmm. That's what the guy told me."

"I'm sure it's the program. Can't remember the station, but I think it's one here in Springfield."

Just then, the door opened and Sidney Gardner, another boardinghouse resident and one of Mullins's co-workers in the shop at Boatwright, came outside to the porch. Unlike his appearance at work, he was clean, neat, and wearing a suit. He overheard part of the porch conversation and as he came through the doorway he said, "If you boys are interested in what's really going on, you should come with me tonight."

Mullins gave him a disapproving expression. "I'm not going to a union meeting."

"Yes, yes, I know," Gardner spoke with a cocky tone. "You're like all the other followers out there. You'd rather talk about change than do something to make it happen."

Mullins had a sarcastic look. "They'll never let a union form in the mill."

"We'll see about that. When we hit them in the wallet, they'll come around." Gardner looked over at Rankin. "What about you? You want to come?"

Rankin shook his head. "I don't work at the mill."

"Doesn't matter. You work at that garage up on Sixteenth Street, right?"

"Yeah."

"You could organize that shop. We could help."

"Not interested."

Gardner straightened the lapel of his jacket and started across the porch toward the steps. "Suit yourself. You want to be a slave all your life, don't blame us."

"I'm not a slave," Rankin replied.

"You work for a wage, right?"

"Of course I work for a wage. I'm not working for free."

"Then the people who own that shop are stealing your time."

"They pay me."

"But whatever they're paying you, it's less than what your time is worth."

"They pay me what I'm worth," Rankin retorted.

Gardner paused when he reached the steps. "Think about it. The only way they make a profit is to pay you less than what you're worth."

"They wouldn't be in business if they didn't make a profit."

"Well, you'll see. We're going to make them pay at the mill." Gardner stepped from the porch to the walkway with a confident jaunt. "The mill. The shop. The foundry. All of them are going to pay."

Sitting on the porch and talking with his fellow residents was the way Mullins spent a typical evening, but the following Wednesday he avoided the others and went up to his room after dinner. He had a desktop radio that sat on the table in the corner—one of the few luxuries he enjoyed—and after the tubes had warmed, he turned the dial until he found a broadcast. After listening for a moment, he realized it was only the farm report.

Searching a little further, he came to a station playing "Swanee," an Al Jolson song, and then the next one was playing a dance tune. He kept going and finally came to a program on WBZ(A), the Springfield radio station that Rankin had mentioned. The announcer had a pleasant voice and was giving information— something about an address, maybe—but the broadcast was fuzzy and he couldn't quite understand. Mullins adjusted the dial and the static went away, then a second voice came through, loud and clear. "This is Reverend Walter Jones coming to you from

Rochester, New York, with the Golden Hour of Power."

Mullins settled into a chair to listen as Jones said, "If you're like me, you've listened to the news this week from Washington, D.C., and you've been angry. Perhaps angrier than you've ever been in your entire life."

"This must be the one," Mullins decided.

For the next thirty minutes, he listened to Jones talk about how officials in Washington sounded good—they said the right words and talked about the right ideas—but had proven to be too friendly with bankers, big-city moneymen. Jewish moneymen.

"They are the ones who control and influence US policy," Jones continued. "They are the ones who convince the politicians to make laws that apply to you and me but not to them. Have you noticed the laws always exempt the moneymen? Many of them have Communist beliefs, too. They don't tell you up front that they're Communists, but that's what they believe. And they have a track record, too, if you know where to look. They're the ones who brought down the Russian Empire—Communists—Communist Jews—now they're setting us up for disaster right here in America. Acting like kings. Acting like the monarchs who plunged the world into the Great War."

Like the discussion Mullins heard at work the week before, Jones's ideas found a place in him that night. As if Jones was opening a door for him to something bigger and more important than himself. An invitation to a select group of people. Those who were capable of recognizing the truth and strong enough to act on it. To do something. To make a difference. To count.

When the show ended, Mullins made a note of the time and station for the program so he could tune it in the following week. And as he continued to think about what Jones had said, in the desk drawer he found a notebook that he used as an address book and began making notes in it, jotting down the things he remembered from the broadcast.

CHAPTER 5

A t work the next day, Mullins told Kugler about listening to Jones's radio program the night before and about the things he'd heard during the broadcast. IIe attempted to bring up the topic at lunch that day, too, but the discussion was focused on the union and a meeting that had been held the night before.

"Somebody needs to stick a sock in Sidney Gardner's mouth."

"Did you see him last night?"

"Running his mouth off about union this and union that."

"Well, it was a union meeting."

Mullins looked over at Kugler. "Did you go to the meeting?"

"No," Kugler replied. "Not last night. I went to one a few nights ago. Have you been?"

"No."

Kugler reached inside his lunchbox for a sandwich. "I'm a little suspicious of what they actually intend to do."

"I'm a *lot* suspicious," Gilbert offered.

"Yeah. They're right about the owners and the influence they have over us. But the union idea is collective, which bothers me."

"It bothers me, too," Kugler agreed. "I don't know why, but it does."

Fletcher spoke up. "I don't like being tied in with everyone else. I like dealing with things on my own. Seems like that one-for-all, all-for-one approach never quite works out like they say."

"Except for the guys in charge," Gilbert noted.

"The reason it bothers you," Mullins suggested, "is because the collective approach is rooted in Communism."

"Communism?" Kugler frowned. "You think so?"

"Absolutely," Mullins insisted. "'Workers of the world unite' is straight out of the *Communist Manifesto*."

Fletcher glanced in his direction. "You've read the *Manifesto*?"

Mullins shook his head. "No, but I've heard people talk about it. And besides, whether I've read it or not, the collective idea is Communism at its core."

"Yeah," Fletcher continued. "And it never works out too good for the worker. They get all of the workers to work together and pool everything, then the people at the top hand it out as they see fit. Only, they hand more out to themselves than to everyone else. Just ask the people in Russia. They're living in misery, but the guys at the top are living like fat cats."

"And that's how the union will do it, too," Mullins said. "That's why you don't like it."

A voice called out from the far side of the shop, "Hey, Mullins. Shut up."

Mullins looked in that direction to see a man standing near the bolt bin. Someone he'd never seen before. "Or what?" Mullins shouted back.

"Or I'll come over there and shut you up."

Mullins stood. "Then come over here and give it a try if you can."

The person who'd been talking took a bolt from the bin, slipped it into his pocket, and walked away. When he was gone, Mullins looked over at Kugler. "Who was that?"

"Frank Brewster. He's a big union supporter."

"New man on the grounds crew," Gilbert explained. "Comes in here for screws and bolts to keep the cleaning equipment working."

"Just another loudmouth," Fletcher added.

"I don't know," Kugler cautioned. "Union guys play rough sometimes."

"Well, I might join the union one day," Mullins offered, "but I'm not joining just to avoid a beating." The others laughed in response.

✦ ✦ ✦

A few days later, Mullins relented in his opposition to the union enough to attend a meeting with Kugler. It was held in the Masonic Lodge building not far from the mill. It was crowded and noisy when they arrived and as they made their way toward two open seats, Mullins caught sight of Sidney Gardner. "Here comes trouble," he growled as Gardner started toward them.

"Relax," Kugler urged. "Don't start looking for trouble."

"I'm pretty sure it's looking for us."

When Gardner reached them, he couldn't resist needling Mullins. "Finally saw the error of your ways?" he chided.

"Just came to see what all the fuss is about," Mullins replied.

"Well, for whatever reason, we're glad you're here." Gardner gave him a slap on the back and then moved on, working his way through the crowd, greeting others in a similar fashion.

"Hail fellow, well-met," Kugler said with a sarcastic tone.

"Glad-hander," Mullins responded.

In a few minutes, Erwin Beal and Charlie Bagley, two of the primary union organizers in the region, took the stage. Beal, however, seemed to be in charge. He came to the podium and began addressing the crowd about the collective power of the American worker. "Facing ownership alone, we are weak and vulnerable. But together we have the power to make a difference. When workers unite, capitalists lose their power. They can't profit without your back to do the work." Shouts of approval went up from the audience. "You can break the chains of economic slavery, but we can only do it together." The crowd roared and Beal continued, alternately whipping them into a frenzy and bringing them to hushed attention.

Some of what he heard that night appealed to Mullins—Beal's comments about the way employers used their position of power to keep workers in a subservient position was particularly poignant to him—but he also heard themes that were very similar to the ones he and Kugler and others at the shop had discussed earlier. The same themes he'd heard Walter Jones address in his weekly broadcasts. Namely, the parallels between collective bargaining and Communism.

When the time came for questions from the audience, Mullins stood up and Beal called on him. "I'm just wondering," Mullins began, "how much do the men at the top of the union intend to take?"

A murmur swept through the crowd, but Beal motioned for silence. "What do you mean?" he asked.

"How much do you get out of this?" Mullins pressed.

Beal smiled awkwardly. "I'm here for the union."

"I know," Mullins rejoined. "And the union is a collective effort. Which means it's a Communist effort." Murmuring in the crowd grew louder. Mullins forged ahead. "Leadership in the Communist Party always takes more than it gives. Just look at the people in Russia. They live in misery while their leaders live in luxury."

Across the hall, the murmur grew to a chorus of boos and hisses. Someone shouted, "Sit down!"

"Yeah," another said. "Shut up and sit down."

From the corner of his eye, Mullins saw two burly men moving toward him. One of them was Frank Brewster, the man who had confronted him at the shop a few days before. Mullins continued to make his point with Beal. "So, I ask you again, if the union gets recognized, how much will union leadership take from our dues? We *will* have to pay dues, won't we?"

"As I have said before—"

Just then, Brewster reached Mullins and took him by the collar. "I told you before to shut up," he snarled.

"And I told you before to make me," Mullins retorted.

Brewster drew back his arm to punch Mullins in the face but before he could swing, Mullins head-butted him in the nose. Instantly, Brewster let go of Mullins's collar and clutched his face with both hands, writhing in agony as blood dripped from his chin. Seeing the advantage, Mullins struck him with a right hook to the jaw. Brewster staggered backward and collapsed onto Kugler's lap. Kugler shoved him aside, and Brewster toppled to the floor.

Not to be outdone, others lunged toward Mullins to take up the fight. Kugler leapt to his feet in Mullins's defense and in a matter of seconds the meeting hall erupted in a brawl. Some on Mullins's side. Some for the union. Some just enjoyed the fight.

Eventually, guards hired by the union to keep order waded through the melee, shoving people aside and forcing them back to their seats. As they made their way from row to row through the crowd, Kugler took Mullins by the shoulder. "Come on."

"I'm not done here," Mullins responded angrily.

"Yes, we are." Kugler pointed over his shoulder toward the guards. "See those sticks?" The guards carried heavy nightsticks, which they wielded without regard for the consequences. Already three men lay face down on the floor, unconscious from the blows the guards inflicted.

"The police will be here any minute." Kugler shoved Mullins toward the end of the row. "Let's go."

Reluctantly, Mullins did as Kugler said and they started toward the aisle together. When they reached it, they elbowed their way past those who still were fighting and made for the exit.

As they came from the meeting hall, a squad of police officers arrived. Mullins glanced over his shoulder in time to see the police breaking up the last of the fighting, arresting those who continued to resist.

✦ ✦ ✦

After escaping from the union meeting, Mullins and Kugler went to the Starlight Café and had a beer. They sat at a booth by the window and talked about what they'd heard at the meeting and about what Mullins had heard on the radio.

"Both are right about one thing," Kugler declared.

"What's that?"

"We are little people in a very big picture. And it feels like there is nothing we can do about it."

"Walter Jones talked about that the other night. Did you hear it?"

"I don't listen to him. I heard him that one time I told you about, but most of what I know about him comes from my brother."

"Jones says that the notion that we're too small and insignificant to make a change is part of the lie told to us to keep us in our place. He says that every change ever made in history has come from a single person."

"You mean like Jesus?"

"Yes. But others, too. Lincoln, for instance."

Kugler grimaced. "I hate that Lincoln. Should have never let the Negroes out of their place."

"Maybe so, but he was *one* guy and he made a big difference."

"The South would have won if it hadn't been for Grant and Sherman."

"You make my point." Mullins gestured for emphasis. "Grant, Sherman. Key people. That's what Jones is talking about. Key individuals have made a huge difference. Sometimes *the* difference.

And the suggestion that we can't change our circumstances is just a lie used by those who want to dominate us and keep us down."

Kugler smiled. "You're really excited about this guy, aren't you?"

"It's as if I have been asleep all of my life and suddenly just woke up."

"Well," Kugler sighed, "someone needs to do something. The Kikes are taking over."

Mullins grinned. "Jones talks about that, too. Just like we were saying the other day in the shop. The Jews control everything. They're coming here in droves. Reproducing like rabbits. They mean to take over. Destroy America and put us all to work for them."

"Can't be much worse than the people at Boatwright." Kugler took a sip from his beer. "Maybe the Jews *are* the people at Boatwright." Mullins laughed in response. "Undercover Jews," Kugler added.

"Hey, you laugh but—"

Again Kugler cut him off good-naturedly. "I've had enough of Jews and conspiracy for one night. We need another beer." He waved the waitress toward their table. "Two more," he called to her.

CHAPTER 6

Schleman Lewin sat on the edge of his cot and looked out the window between the steel bars that covered the windows. He arrived in New York eight days earlier and since then had been confined to a room at the processing center on Ellis Island. Through the window he could see the city, and when gusts of wind blew against his side of the building he could also smell the city, but he could not reach it. Not yet.

In the other direction, he had a commanding view of the Statue of Liberty. He'd read about it once in a newspaper someone brought to Naroulia from Odessa. The article talked about how big it was and that it was made entirely of copper, and he'd wondered how such a thing could stand. Now, seeing it up close, he understood. It was gigantic. Broad enough at the base to withstand almost anything. *Surely it must be an engineering feat that rivals any other,* he thought.

Three days before he left Naroulia, he sent a letter to Esther and Isador telling them of his plan. Before boarding the ship in Libau, he had posted a second letter telling Esther the name of the ship on which he was traveling and the time it was scheduled to arrive. Knowing the way mail service worked, the letter might very well have traveled on the same ship as he. But it might not. Which meant it wouldn't arrive for another week after he sailed. And that meant the letter might just now be reaching Esther. He hoped so. Staying in that center—being held there—was not

MIKE EVANS

a pleasant experience. But Immigration authorities would not allow him to leave the facility unless someone came to get him and stated to them that he had a place to live.

Lewin looked out the window again at the buildings in Manhattan, just a short distance away. So close, in fact, it seemed as if he could swim right over to them—if he'd only learned to swim. His uncle, Isaac, tried to teach him once when he was young. They'd gone to the lake north of the village. It was summertime and the whole family was present. Isaac thought every boy should know how to swim and he was determined to teach Lewin, but in spite of the warm July afternoon, the water was cold and Lewin spent most of the time complaining and devising ways to end the lesson and escape Isaac's attention. Now, sitting on the edge of the cot, calculating how far it might be across the water to the city, he wondered if he'd made a mistake by refusing Isaac's help so long ago.

"It's much farther than it seems, though," he told himself at last. Then he noticed a ferryboat leaving the island and watched to see how small it became as it chugged toward the Manhattan shore. He smiled as the boat grew smaller and smaller in the distance. *Only an athlete could make that swim. And I'm no athlete.*

Still, the city was close. Freedom was close. So close he could almost touch it. A new life for himself and his family was at hand. He had only to escape the processing center and he would be on his way.

After a few minutes, he grew tired from sitting and lay on his back. He imagined Michla at their house in Naroulia. At that time of day, Michla would be in the kitchen. It seemed she was always it the kitchen. Perhaps he could change that in their new life. In America. He smiled at the thought of it. He was in America. Maybe confined for right now, but he was here in the land he'd dreamed of for so long.

Slowly, Lewin's eyes grew heavy and drowsiness overcame

58

him. He had not wanted to sleep. At least not during the day. During the day was when the guards called people to the front for processing. For discharge. During the day was when family members came for their loved ones and took them away to live and work and enjoy American life. He didn't want to sleep . . . Didn't want to miss Isador . . . If he came . . . When he came.

✦ ✦ ✦

Isador didn't arrive that day. Or the next. But the day after that, a guard came to Lewin's cell and rapped on the door. "Lewin!" he shouted. "Schleman Lewin!" They never pronounced his name correctly and after the first day he had given up trying to teach them. "Let them call me whatever they will," he said to himself. "I shall answer to anything as long as they come to get me and let me go from here."

At the sound of the guard's voice, Lewin jumped from the bed, crossed the room in two steps, and banged on the door with his fist in reply. "I am here!" he shouted.

A moment later, Lewin heard the clank of keys in the lock, then the clatter of the tumblers. Seconds later, the door swung open and the guard gestured with a sweep of his free hand. "Come, and bring your things. They are calling for you."

Without a moment's hesitation, Lewin took hold of his satchel by the handle, snatched it from the floor, and started toward the door. "That's all?" the guard asked.

"Yes," Lewin replied. "This is everything."

To Lewin, the guard seemed to walk slower than anyone he'd ever known. The walk from the cell through the hallway and up to the main room took an eternity. As if he'd grown older by a dozen years in the length of time it took to reach the main desk. But at last, there he was, standing before the processing clerk. And there was Isador, his brother-in-law, standing to one side, grinning from ear to ear. Lewin was so excited he wanted to grab him and hug and kiss him right there, but he knew better than to make a scene and forced himself to concentrate on the clerk at the desk and the task of the moment.

When Lewin stood before him the clerk shuffled through the pages of a file that lay on his desk, and then looked over at Isador. "You know this man?" He gestured in Lewin's direction as he spoke.

"Yes," Isador replied. "He is my brother-in-law. I am married to his sister."

"Does he have a place to live?"

"Yes, he will stay with us."

"And work?"

"They have a job for him at the grocery store where I work. They have assured me they will hire him." Isador took a letter from the pocket of his jacket and unfolded it. As he did, Lewin saw that it was written on Hennig's Grocery Store letterhead. The name and address of the store were engraved along the top of the page. The body of the letter was neatly typed. Lewin was impressed.

Isador handed the letter to the clerk, who scanned it quickly, then handed it back. With a practiced, perfunctory motion, he stamped the pages in Lewin's file, stamped and initialed a card, then handed the card to Lewin and waved him aside.

Lewin held the card with both hands and stared at it, then looked over at the clerk. "That is it?"

"Move along," the clerk ordered.

"I can go now?"

A guard took him by the elbow. "Move along. You can catch the ferry outside."

Tears filled Lewin's eyes and he looked over at Isador. "I am here?"

"You are here!" Isador draped an arm over Lewin's shoulder and gave him a hug, then ushered him toward the door.

"That is all there is to it?"

"Yes. A lot of waiting for not much at all."

"Oh no," Lewin replied. "This is the biggest thing that has ever happened to me. In all of my life, this is the biggest."

Lewin and Isador walked to the dock and boarded a ferry for the ride across the harbor to the Battery docks at the lower end of Manhattan—one of the same boats, across the same water, that he'd watched from his window. Isador dealt with the ticket clerk and paid for the passage, then guided Lewin upstairs to the second deck and a place along the railing. "We can see out from here," Isador told him. "And the air is cleaner than down below."

Isador seemed to know what to do. But more than that, he seemed at ease with it. Something Lewin wondered if he would ever find again. The ease and comfort of home. The unconscious knowing of a place. The way things were done.

A few minutes after boarding, the engines rumbled, and Lewin felt a shudder beneath his feet. He glanced around nervously, wondering what would happen next. Isador noticed and smiled at him with an amused expression. "We are leaving now. The boat is moving away from the dock."

Lewin glanced up to see a plume of black smoke belch from the boat's stack. When he looked out on the water again he saw that they already were free of the dock. The island where the processing center was located was receding in the background. The skyline that had seemed majestic and elegant from his room now loomed ahead as a tangled jungle of steel and concrete. People and vehicles, invisible before, appeared like swarms of insects, scurrying this way and that. And all at once he felt a sense of panic.

How would he learn his way around? A place to live on his own? And the language. He could read and speak English, but the words he heard at the processing center. . .they came so fast and seemed to swim in the soup of a thick, strange accent. How would he make his way?

Once again, Isador seemed to notice Lewin's consternation. "Bigger than you imagined?"

Lewin nodded. "Yes." He looked over at Isador. "How can I ever do this?"

"Do what?"

"Make a way for Michla and the boys to come here. This place is so . . ."

"Overwhelming?"

"Yes."

"I know that feeling. It is so big. You are so small."

"You felt this way?"

"Esther laughed at me."

Lewin grinned. She would. That was her way.

"It is big," Isador continued. "Big and loud and people moving in every direction. All in a hurry to get somewhere. But I assure you everything will be okay. We will help you—Esther and I and all the others."

"The others?"

"We have many cousins here already. And friends. Everything will work out."

✦ ✦ ✦

When the ferry from Ellis Island docked at the lower end of Manhattan, Isador led the way to the street and flagged down a taxi. He and Lewin piled into the rear seat of the car and rode across town. Ten minutes later, the car came to a stop in front of a building that was taller than anything Lewin had ever seen before. "We are here?"

Isador grinned. "This is our building."

Lewin's mouth fell open in a startled expression. "You own the building?"

"No," Isador laughed. "This is where we rent an apartment."

Isador paid the taxi fare, then he and Lewin stepped from

the car, crossed the sidewalk, and started up the stairs. "We are on the sixth floor."

Lewin glanced up at the stairwell. The stairs were arranged in flights, each one covering half a floor's height. It was dark up above and he could see only a single bare electric lightbulb hanging from a cord in the ceiling many floors above. "That is a long way!"

"You get used to it." Isador led the way up the stairs.

A few minutes later, after more than one stop for Lewin to catch his breath, they arrived on the sixth floor. Down the hall from the stairwell, past many doors to many apartments, they stopped and Isador looked back at him. "Are you ready?"

Lewin felt nervous. "This is the apartment?"

"Yes, Esther is inside. As are many others by now. They are waiting to see you. She will grab you and hug you."

"I know."

"You are ready for that?"

Lewin nodded. "I am ready."

Isador grasped the doorknob with his hand. In a single motion, he turned it and pushed open the door. "Schleman is here!" he shouted.

As Lewin entered the apartment, his sister rushed toward him, arms outstretched, tears streaming down her face. "Schleman," she whispered. "It's really you." Before he could respond, she grabbed him with both arms and pulled him close against her. Her skin was damp, but Lewin didn't mind.

"Yes," he sighed. "I am here at last."

After a moment she let go of him and they took a seat at the dining table that was positioned in one corner of the room. For the next twenty minutes they talked of family and friends from back home as she pumped Lewin for information about everyone she could remember. When they had exhausted the list, Lewin glanced around and saw the room was filled with relatives who were there to greet him. Many of them he'd forgotten were in America and some he had never known. Isador came to the table and rescued him from Esther, then led him around the room, introducing him one by one. With each one there were words of remembrance—the time they did this or that, most of which Lewin did not remember at all—and hugs, more hugs than he'd received in all of his life, he thought.

Before long, neighbors and friends arrived and the process began all over again. Soon the apartment was packed and noisy. So much so that those who lived on that floor came to complain. They arrived angry at first, only to be welcomed into the crowd. Which necessitated another round of introductions and more hugs.

Before long, however, Esther and the women who'd been helping her in the kitchen brought out bowls and trays of food. Then they ate. And while they ate, they talked.

"Schleman says New York is overwhelming," Isador offered.

"It is as first," someone noted. "But it's like a tangled string. You find a place to begin and that is where you start."

"You work your way from one thing to the next and sort things out from there."

Someone else spoke up. "The first thing you need to do is find a way to fit in."

Lewin frowned. "How do I fit in? What does that mean?"

"It means you become an American."

"And how do I do that?"

"You could begin by changing your name."

Lewin was astounded by the suggestion. "Change my name?"

Albert Gilman, a neighbor from down the hall, spoke up. "You need a name that doesn't sound so foreign."

"I can do that? I can just change my name?"

"Yes," Gilman answered. "In America, you are the person you claim to be."

Lewin found that hard to believe. "But what do I change it to?"

"Samuel," someone suggested. "Instead of Schleman, you'll be Samuel."

"And not Lewin," another added. "Use the American version."

"And what is that?"

"Levine," someone called from down the table.

"Yeah," another agreed. "Call yourself Samuel Levine."

"Okay," Lewin responded with a sense of disdain no one noticed. "I am Samuel Levine. Anything else you would like me to change? My nose? My eyes?"

Those seated at the table exchanged glances and knowing looks, then someone piped up. "Your accent."

Lewin was taken aback. "My accent?"

"Yes. Lose the accent."

"But it is a part of me. As much a part of me as my nose. Why do I need to change myself? What's wrong with the way I am?"

"You're Jewish," someone said.

"I will always be Jewish." Lewin gestured to the room. "*We* will always be Jewish."

"Yeah. But don't let the Americans know that."

They all laughed, but Lewin did not understand their humor. "The Americans don't know we're Jewish? What's the problem with them knowing we're Jewish?"

"They don't like Jews."

"Americans don't like Jews?" Suddenly everyone fell silent, and Lewin glanced around at them with a frown. "What does this mean?"

"It's a problem for some of them," Isador explained. "Not everyone. But some of them."

"Yeah," someone added. "Not everyone hates us. Just the white ones."

Suddenly the table erupted in howls of laughter.

CHAPTER 7

Esther and Isador lived in an apartment with two bedrooms. When they were the only ones there, Esther and Isador slept in a room together and their three children shared the second room. After Lewin arrived, the youngest child slept in the room with her parents, while the other two slept in the main room—a room that served as both living room and dining room. The oldest made a place for himself beneath the dining table. The middle child—a girl—slept on the sofa. It was an awkward situation, and having an extra adult made it seem crowded, but they accommodated each other and got along well.

In spite of the recommendations from his relatives and friends, Lewin did not change his name and continued to call himself Schleman Lewin. He was chided for it by some. Harassed by others. But he refused to give in and thought it a matter of personal pride that he did not follow their advice.

The day after he arrived at Esther's apartment, Lewin went to work with Isador at Hennig's Grocery Store, stocking shelves and making deliveries. Yitzhak Hennig, the owner, kept a close eye on him but seemed to be glad to have him around.

"He has not changed his name," Lewin noted as he and Isador walked home from work one day.

"What do you mean?" Isador asked.

"He still uses his name. Yitzhak isn't very American."

"That's the name he told you?"

"Yes," Lewin replied. "Why?"

Isador grinned. "He uses that name with some of us. To the public, though, he's known as Michael."

"Michael?"

Isador nodded. "That's what he calls himself."

"But why? Yitzhak is a wonderful name. My uncle has that name."

"To us, it is a name rich with history and meaning. To the Americans, someone named Yitzhak is just another dumb Jew."

"So, they like Michael?"

"Very much so," Isador assured.

Lewin enjoyed working at the store and he especially liked putting things back in their proper place at the end of the day, restoring order to the chaos that had ensued from a day of taking orders, assembling them on the counter, and delivering them on foot. But the pay he received wasn't what he'd wanted.

Lewin paid his share of the rent and contributed to the food budget. He did his best not to burden the others in his daily routine, but as the weeks went by he came to think that he was not saving money fast enough, especially after letters from Michla began to arrive with accounts of how much she and the boys missed him. He wanted to get them to America as soon as possible and began casting about on his own for a different job that paid more, or an additional job he could squeeze into his schedule at night and on weekends. His efforts didn't get far, though.

"I'll ask around for you," Isador assured. He understood Lewin's desire to bring his family sooner rather than later, but he was skeptical. "Jobs are not easy to find right now, but something might turn up."

"This is America. Surely there are jobs."

"I'll check," Isador assured him once more. "In the meantime, maybe you should ask Albert Gilman."

"Who is he?"

"Tall guy. He was at the apartment the day you arrived."

Lewin frowned. "There were many people at the apartment that day."

"Yeah." Isador chuckled. "It was kind of crazy. I'll point him out to you. He knows everyone and keeps a hand in everything."

A few evenings later, Gilman appeared in the hallway as Lewin returned from work. Isador pointed him out and Lewin ran to catch up with him. Gilman seemed glad to see him and when Lewin mentioned he was looking for work, Gilman was ready with a suggestion. "There's a position for a carpenter on Second Street. It's hard work but I'm sure it pays more than the job you have with Isador at the store."

"Great, I will inquire about it tomorrow."

"Ask for George Sutton. Tell him I sent you."

The next day, while making a delivery from the grocery store, Lewin walked up to Houston Street and crossed over the imaginary line between the Lower East Side and the rest of Manhattan. To his surprise, the line wasn't merely imaginary. There really was a different world on the other side. For one thing, the streets were cleaner and the smells were different. But even more striking were the people. They were all white and he noticed they all seemed to be looking at him.

On Second Street he had little trouble locating the construction site. It was a renovation project for a multistory building. He asked for Sutton and was directed to a muscular man who had broad shoulders, blond hair, and stood about six feet tall.

At first, Sutton seemed disinterested. "I got a lot of work here." He gestured to the apron Lewin wore. "Not much need for grocerymen and butchers."

"I am an accomplished carpenter," Lewin told him. "Albert Gilman sent me."

At the mention of Gilman's name, Sutton's attitude changed. "All right. There's a guy over there cutting joists for the third floor.

Give him a hand and let me see what you can do."

Lewin made his way through the site to a man who was sawing lumber that lay across three sawhorses. He removed the apron he'd been wearing, draped it over a toolbox, and began assisting the man who was using the saw. Before long, Lewin was measuring and marking the boards while the man made the cuts, then they switched places and Lewin took the saw.

After a while, Sutton came over to where Lewin was working. "Okay, I assume you need to tell your current employer about this?"

"Yes," Lewin replied.

"You can start in the morning. Be here at seven. What's your name?"

"Lewin. Schleman Lewin."

When he'd finished with Sutton, Lewin hurried from the job site and walked quickly back to the grocery store. Hennig was waiting for him when he arrived. "Where have you been?"

"I made the delivery," Lewin replied, hoping for more time to formulate a truthful answer.

"It was a simple matter," Hennig replied. "You've been gone for hours. Did you take the groceries to her?"

"Yes."

"What took you so long? Did you get lost?"

"No. I did not get lost."

"Then, what was it?"

Lewin felt intimidated. Nervous. His gaze fell to the floor. "I. . .I found a new job." He stammered the words.

Hennig's eyes were wide with surprise but not in a good way. "A new job?" he blurted.

"Yes," Lewin replied.

"You go out to make a delivery for me and come back working for someone else?"

"I haven't started yet."

Hennig seemed to relax. "When do you start this new job?"

"Tomorrow."

Hennig's expression turned angry again. "Tomorrow?!"

"Yes."

"That is all the time you give me to prepare?"

"It is all the time they gave me," Lewin explained.

"Who are you working for? That guy with the store on Houston?"

"No." Lewin shook his head. "It's not a grocery store."

"Then, what is it?"

"A foreman on a construction crew wants to hire me as a carpenter."

"Carpenter? You know how to be a carpenter?"

"I know enough. They had me try a few things. That is why it took so long to come back."

A scowl wrinkled Hennig's face as he moved toward the cash register. "I took you in when you had nothing," he grumbled. "And this is how you repay me?"

"I am sorry," Lewin said. He really meant it but felt he had no other option if he wished to see his family soon. "It pays more than this job and I need the money to bring my family from Russia. I can work for you the rest of the day."

"No." Hennig sighed. "If you're leaving, go ahead and leave." He opened the cash register, glanced up at the clock to calculate the hours Lewin had worked, then handed him the money he was due.

✦ ✦ ✦

The next day, Lewin arrived at the new job site shortly before seven. Sutton, the foreman, was standing near a makeshift work-table in an alley behind the building. He looked over at Lewin with an odd expression. "What are you doing here?"

"You said I should start work today?"

"You're late."

"I'm not late. I'm early."

"Yeah, well." Sutton turned back to the work at hand. "I didn't know if you were coming or not."

Lewin felt his chest sink into his stomach. Could this really be happening? "I told you I would be here."

"It's too late for that." Sutton made a dismissive gesture without looking up. "I filled the job with someone else."

Other workers who were standing nearby laughed. "Go away, Jew," someone chided. "We don't want no Kikes working here."

Lewin ignored them and stepped closer to Sutton. "You promised me a job."

Sutton shrugged. "What can I say? Someone else beat you to it."

"But you told me yesterday that I had the job."

"These things happen."

Lewin was beside himself. "I quit my job at the grocery store because of your promise."

"Look," Sutton glared at him, "you don't like it, sue me."

Lewin was puzzled. "What does that mean?"

The men standing nearby laughed again. "This Jew is so stupid," one chortled. "He doesn't even know about the court."

Another chimed in, "Go back to where you came from."

Sutton waved them off. "Get back to work," he growled. As they moved away, he took Lewin by the shoulder and pushed him up the alley. "You gotta get out of here. You're disrupting the crew."

Lewin pulled free. "But I—"

"If you don't leave now," Sutton threatened, "I'm gonna call the cops."

Finally, reluctantly, with a sense that he had no other choice, Lewin turned away and started up the alley toward the street.

When he reached the corner, he turned and wandered aimlessly down the street, his mind reeling from the way he'd been treated.

For the next half hour, Lewin walked the streets, traveling in no particular direction, brooding over the manner that he'd been treated. The lie. The deception. The laughter. The ridicule. Over and over again, the sights and sounds of that morning in the alley repeated in his mind. It set him on edge to think about it, but he couldn't stop.

After a while, his mind eased enough for him to turn to the problem of what to do next. He thought of returning to the grocery store and asking Hennig for his old job back. Even begging him for it, if necessary. "But Hennig was mad when I quit," he whispered. "He would *really* be mad if I came back now." And besides, going back there might create trouble for Isador. Which would mean trouble for Esther. And he didn't want that at all. But what could he do? How would he pay Esther to stay in her apartment? How would he have the money to send for Michla and the boys?

An hour after leaving the construction site, Lewin passed a building where the door was open and he could see inside from the street. Beyond the doorway, he saw rows and rows of tables with sewing machines atop each one. Workers sat at most of them, busily sewing pieces of fabric together in long, fast runs through the machines. Lewin paused there and watched, amazed at the sound and the apparent ease of the work.

Just then, a man appeared from inside. "You the one they sent?"

Lewin frowned. "Excuse me?"

"Are you the one they sent? For the job?"

The man spoke with an accent and Lewin did not quite understand what he said, but he heard him mention something about a job. "Yes," Lewin answered quickly. "I need a job."

"Good. Come with me, I need workers." The man motioned for him to enter the building.

Lewin followed the man inside and saw that there were many more rows of machines sitting atop many more rows of tables. More than he had seen from the doorway. The air was cool but the lint that rose from the machines tickled his nose. Lewin stifled a sneeze and concentrated on keeping up as they made their way through the room.

"This is your machine," the man pointed when they reached a table on the back row. A box of fabric sat on the floor. He pointed to it. "Take these pieces. Sew them together like the way she's doing." He pointed to a worker seated nearby. "Then put the finished pieces over here." He took an empty box from a stack to the right and placed it on the opposite side of the table, then gestured to it for emphasis. "Finished pieces in here. Got it?"

Lewin wondered what to say and as he thought about it he glanced around at the others who were busy at the tables near his. One of them, a woman who looked to be about twenty, smiled at him and nodded as if to indicate how he should respond. "Lewin took the cue. "Yes, I am ready."

"Good," the man said. "We have timecards in the front to note your attendance, but we pay by the finished piece. I'll make a card for you and clock you in. What's your name?"

"Levine," Lewin said confidently. "Samuel Levine." He had tried his Jewish name at the first place, which didn't go so well, so he decided to try it the way Isador and the others suggested.

"Call me Saperstein and get busy," the man turned to leave. "No talking. And don't get up from your place until we knock off at the end of the day."

As Saperstein moved away, Lewin took a seat at his machine. The woman seated next to him reached into the box beside his chair and took out two pieces of cloth. "They go together like this." She held them to indicate the correct position. "Only overlapping a little. Then you run them through the machine like this." She placed the pieces on her sewing machine, locked the needle into position, and pressed a pedal that lay near her foot. The fabric flew through the machine. When the run was finished, she raised the needle, clipped the thread, and held the completed pieces for him to see. "Now you try it."

Lewin did his best to repeat what she had shown him, but his hands fumbled with the fabric and the needle and the machine. Work went slowly, but gradually he got better at it and by noon he was moving along at an acceptable pace. He was not able to empty the box by the end of the day, but when Saperstein came by to count the pieces, he nodded approvingly. "Not bad for a first day." Lewin felt a sense of accomplishment well up inside and he beamed with pride.

When Lewin returned to the apartment that evening, Esther and Isador were there when he arrived. Esther gestured to his appearance as he entered the room. "You don't look like a carpenter. You're supposed to be filthy."

"I'm no longer a carpenter."

"What happened?"

"That part was terrible," Lewin related, then told them about what happened. About getting fired before he got started.

"This is what we meant earlier," Isador noted, "when we told you that Americans don't like Jews."

Lewin nodded. "And I spent more than an hour wandering the streets trying to figure out what to do next. Then I stopped to look inside a building. The door was open and I could see inside and there were all of these sewing machines in there. And a man came to the door and asked if I wanted a job. And so I worked all day."

"Sewing?" Esther blurted.

"Yes."

"You have never sewn before in your entire life."

"I know. But they told me, 'Sew these two pieces together,' and that is what I did." Isador burst into laughter and they joined him. "God is helping me," Lewin declared.

"Yes." Isador nodded. "I think he is. By the way, where do you attend *shul*?"

Suddenly the laughter died and Isador turned away. Esther had a look of embarrassment. "We have not attended since the first week we arrived."

"We must go," Lewin insisted. "This week. We must attend."

Isador looked over at him. "Do you really believe? After all that happened in Naroulia. After all that has happened to our family. Do you still believe?"

"Yes," Lewin replied. "I still believe. And I do not blame Him for the actions of evil people. None of this happened by chance. God is at work."

Isador chuckled. "We shall see."

"Yes," Lewin said confidently. "We shall see."

CHAPTER 8

Mullins sat in his room at the boardinghouse in Indian Orchard after a long day at work and glanced at his watch to check the time. It was Wednesday evening. Almost time for the Golden Hour of Power on the radio. He hoped he could stay awake long enough to hear the program.

A moment later, his head nodded forward. As his chin reached his chest, he jerked up, checked his watch again, then turned on the radio to let the vacuum tubes warm up. When the speaker crackled with static, he tuned it until the radio station came through clear and sharp.

"Here we go," he muttered. "Maybe I can stay awake long enough to hear it all."

After a series of commercials, the program began with a spokesman who gave the usual introductory remarks, followed by Jones. "Good evening, fellow patriots and believers," he announced. "Tonight, I bring you another thirty minutes of important news. Not the news you hear on your regular broadcasts. Not the news you read in the newspapers that are brought to your door every morning. But the kind of news you can only hear on this program. I bring you, ladies and gentlemen, the truth. Unvarnished. Straightforward. Truth."

For the next ten minutes, Jones sketched through human history, touching only the points that supported his position that most of the world's problems had been caused by the International

Jewry. "A group of Jews who dominate world banking and finance," he explained, "and who use their position to accumulate great wealth. More than any other group in the world. They do not merely accumulate this wealth to live a life of ease. No. They use their wealth to influence world political leaders. Manipulate leaders into starting wars so they can make money from everyone else's misery. That's what happened in the Great War. It was started by Jews. It was financed by Jews. And Jews profited from it mightily.

"At the same time leaders are sending your sons off to fight in some distant land," Jones continued, "the Jews sit at home, safe and sound, because they have caused laws to be passed in most places exempting them from serving in the military. Even outright prohibiting them from serving in some countries, like Russia and England, where they are particularly strong in exerting their influence. They don't have to fight. Their sons don't have to fight. Their mothers don't cry bitter tears of grief over their children who have become the casualties of war. War that the Jews created for you and me to fight. No. While we're out there fighting and dying, the Jews are sitting at home counting their money. And it happens every time. Whenever there's a war, they enjoy the comforts of life while our sons die."

Mullins was wide awake now. Wide awake and thinking of his brother. Of the day the taxi came to the house with a telegram. *The* telegram informing his parents their oldest son was dead. Killed in action somewhere in France. The details didn't arrive until later, but the grief and agony arrived immediately.

"And not simply wars between nations," Jones' broadcast continued. "But wars within nations, too. Civil wars and revolutions of a kind now rumbling through Europe. A cabal of International Jews conspired with radical political elements in Russia to start the Russian Revolution. They are agitating to do the same in France and Spain, continuing their conspiracy with liberals to spread the oppression of Communism throughout Europe. All for the purpose of making it easier for the Jews to make more money."

Jones made it clear he was opposed to Communism—in all of his broadcasts he went out of his way to make that point—but he blamed capitalist greed for making it attractive. Capitalists—taking advantage of every competitive moment, every edge, every vulnerability—to rob, steal, and coerce helpless workers into working for slave wages. He said that many times during his shows.

"We simply must not let this happen here in America," Jones warned. "Not now. Not ever. And the only way to do that is to limit immigration from countries with large Jewish populations. They come here in droves. Steal our jobs. Steal our money. Take over our country. And destroy our American way of life."

As the broadcast came to a conclusion, Jones mentioned a book known as *The Protocols of the Elders of Zion* that supposedly supported his ideas. A book that provided the details of the very conspiracy he saw at work in America right then. "We already are feeling the effects of the Jewish effort. Men returning from the Great War maimed and in need of assistance—men who incurred the scars of war while the Jews lived a life of ease. Others who survived and are able but left without jobs because the Jews have crept in and stolen them away. We need to stop them now! We need to put an end to the great conspiracy that seeks to destroy Americanism and all that we stand for. This is a time, like no other before, when we must come together to keep America great."

When Jones had finished, the spokesman returned with information about the *Hour of Power* newspaper. "A subscription can be yours for the small sum of one dollar," he announced, then he gave the details about how and where to write to subscribe. Mullins jotted down the address and made a note of the title of the book Jones had mentioned.

After the program ended, the radio station switched to music from the Empire Ballroom in Boston. Mullins listened while he found paper and envelopes in a drawer and wrote a letter to subscribe to the paper. When it was ready, he laid it on the dresser next to his lunch box so he wouldn't forget it in the morning, then stuck the note about the book in his pocket to remind himself to locate a copy.

At breakfast the next morning, Mullins asked about where he could find a bookstore. "Hinkle's," someone said as they sat at the dining table. "Great store."

"Where is it?"

"Main Street in Springfield. You can take the trolley from work."

Mrs. Smithson overheard the conversation and gave Mullins the address for the store, which she had scribbled on a small note card. "Anytime one of my boarders asks about books, I get excited," she exclaimed.

"Don't get too excited," Mullins cautioned. "I'm not sure how many books I'll actually read."

"Still, it's a start," she said with a smile.

✦ ✦ ✦

That afternoon, after work, Mullins rode the trolley to Springfield and made his way up Main Street to Hinkle's. It was located near the bank and not far from Nash's Drugstore. He found it with little difficulty.

As Mullins entered, a man spoke to him from behind the counter. "May I help you?"

"I'm looking for a book," Mullins replied.

"Well, you've come to the right place. What book did you want?"

Mullins took the note from his pocket and glanced at it for the title. "It's called *The Protocols of the Elders of Zion*."

The man smiled. "Ah, a very important book." He came from

behind the counter and gestured for Mullins to follow. "It's right over here."

They crossed the room to a row of shelves on the opposite side, and the man took down a copy of the book. Mullins took it from him and turned through the pages. As he scanned the book, the man kept talking. "I assume you're interested in that book because you're interested in the topic—Jews and the influence they have on the nations of the world."

"I'm interested in knowing if it's true," Mullins explained. "I heard about this book from a guy on the radio." He looked up with a smile. "You can hear anything on the radio."

"You must have been listening to the Golden Hour of Power."

"Yes," Mullins replied. "Walter Jones."

"If you're interested in race and how it affects a person's proclivities, you might like this one." He reached behind him and took down a copy of *Race and the Excellence of Society* by Claus Ploetz. "The writer is a German," he noted. "The Germans really understand the differences between the races." He handed the book to Mullins.

Mullins avoided taking the book from him. "I'm not really interested in the German race. Just the Jews."

"But the Jews are a race. A race of people. And this book talks about how the people of the world are divided by race. Some, naturally, are superior to others. Just as some cows are better than others. And some horses. It's genetics and it's incumbent on those of us from a dominant race to understand these things. It's the same idea behind that *Protocols* book you're holding."

Mullins gestured with the book in his hand. "Let me read this one first, then I'll see about the other."

✦ ✦ ✦

It was late when Mullins returned to the boardinghouse. Mrs.

Smithson was waiting for him as he came into the foyer. "I saved you something for dinner. Come on back to the kitchen."

Mullins followed her through the house and took a seat at the kitchen table as Mrs. Smithson set a plate of food before him. "I kept it warm in the oven."

"You didn't have to go to all of this trouble."

"It wasn't any trouble at all. Did you find the bookstore?"

"Yes, ma'am."

"And you bought a book?"

"Yes, ma'am."

"May I see it?" she asked eagerly.

Mullins handed her the book, and a cloud seemed to come over her face as she looked at the title. "*The Protocols of the Elders of Zion*," she read. "I've heard about this book."

"You listen to Walter Jones?"

"Who?"

"Walter Jones. The guy on the radio."

"Oh no. I never listen to those programs." She tapped the cover of the book with her index finger for emphasis. "I read an article about this in the newspaper. There's a dispute about whether it's true or not. A professor at Harvard—I can't remember his name—had questions about the accuracy of the history in it."

"Well, I heard about it on the radio and it sounded interesting. I'm going to read it and make up my own mind."

"Good." Mrs. Smithson laid the book on the table and stood. "I think intellectual curiosity is a good thing." She patted him on the shoulder. "Let me get you a glass of buttermilk to go with your dinner."

When Mullins finished eating he went upstairs and took a bath. Afterward, he dressed for bed but took a seat in a chair by the radio, switched on a lamp, and began reading the *Protocols*. The more he read, the more intrigued he became. It was past midnight before he finally laid the book aside and went to bed.

It had been a long and tiring day, but he fell asleep thinking that all the world's troubles began with the Jews. And he wondered, *Why did we ever let that happen? Why did we ever let even a single one of them come here?*

✦ ✦ ✦

A few weeks later, Mullins arrived at the boardinghouse from work to find the newspaper from Walter Jones's Golden Hour of Power had arrived. Mrs. Smithson handed it to him as he started up the stairs to his room. He took it to his room and laid it on the dresser while he took a bath. Afterward, he sat in the chair by the lamp as he had with the book and read each page carefully.

Articles in the paper contained a few more details than the broadcast but had mostly just more discussion of the same topics— the vast Jewish conspiracy, immigration as their tool of infiltrating the US, and Jewish dominance in the areas of banking, media, and motion pictures. Mullins read them with great enthusiasm and noted some of the articles also mentioned other publications, including the other book the man at Hinkle's had talked about.

The next day after work, Mullins returned to the bookstore. The same man was at the counter and gave a knowing look as he entered. "Back again," the man noted.

"Yes," Mullins replied.

"What did you think of the *Protocols*?"

"It opened my eyes like never before."

"I thought it would. Back for the other book?"

"Yes."

Rather than coming from behind the counter, the man turned to a shelf on the wall behind him. "I put it up here to hold for you. Figured you'd be back." He set the book on the counter and began writing a receipt.

"How much is it?"

"Three dollars."

"Wow."

"Yeah, it's expensive." He flashed a smile. "But worth the price."

"I hope so," Mullins replied. Four dollars was all the money he had left until payday. Still, the book was mentioned in Walter Jones's newspaper and if he mentioned it, it must be important.

Mullins handed the man three dollars, and he in turn handed Mullins a receipt. As Mullins took it from him, the man offered his hand. "Tom Hinkle," he said as they shook hands.

"You're the owner?" Mullins asked.

"Yes. This store has been owned by someone in our family for fifty years."

"That's a long time."

"Yes, it is. But listen, if you're really interested in the ideas in the books you're buying, there's a group of us that gets together to talk about them."

"What kind of group?"

"Just a bunch of men who share the same ideas as the ones you're interested in."

Mullins hesitated a moment but felt obligated. Hinkle had been nice to him, suggesting the books. And the idea of talking with people who held the same opinions—people who might actually do something with those opinions rather than argue with him—appealed to him.

"When do they meet?" Mullins asked.

"Actually, we're meeting tomorrow night. Here at the store." Hinkle gestured in an offhanded manner. "There's a room in back."

"Okay."

"Come about this same time."

"I don't have a car, and the trolley doesn't run after eight."

"If we go that long, I can run you home," Hinkle offered.

"Where do you live?"

"Indian Orchard."

Hinkle smiled. "That's right on my way."

✦ ✦ ✦

The following night, Mullins took the trolley from work and attended the meeting at the bookstore. Three other men were already there, loitering near the front counter. Hinkle introduced them, then guided them toward the back of the store.

Past the rows of bookshelves, they came to a door that opened into a room where a dozen chairs were arranged in a circle. A table stood along the wall. On it were two German flags and a swastika cast in plaster. It was painted red and outlined in black. Mullins thought it was regal in appearance.

Next to the flags were several pamphlets written in German. Mullins pointed to one of them. "What is that?"

"You don't read German?"

"No."

Hinkle picked up the pamphlet. "This is from the Nationalist Socialist Party.

"I'm not sure I've heard of it."

"They're called Nazis," Hinkle explained.

Mullins nodded. "Walter Jones mentioned them, I think. In one of his broadcasts."

"The Nazi Party is more than a political party," Hinkle explained. "It's actually a political movement. Still only in its early stages. Just now emerging in Germany." He flashed a reassuring smile. "But we're going to bring it here soon."

Others arrived and in half an hour their number had grown to ten. Hinkle, who appeared to be in charge, moved to the far end of the room, opposite the door. "We should get started." He paused a moment while they took their seats and when everyone was seated he continued. "Some of you were here last week, but we have a number of new people tonight, so I think I should catch everyone up on who we are and what we're about."

From Hinkle's comments that followed, Mullins learned that the group called themselves the Knights of Teutonia, a name they adopted from a similar organization Hinkle encountered during a recent trip to Chicago. Hinkle liked what he heard from the Chicago group and when he returned home, he told his friends about it. One of them suggested they should start their own group, so they did. The meeting that night was the Springfield group's second formal gathering.

For the next hour and a half, the group discussed one of the pamphlets that had been lying on the table. Decidedly pro-German, the tract was both a propaganda piece for the burgeoning Nazi Party and a defense of its underlying fascist ideals and assumptions. Principally, the notion that some races were superior to others and that Aryans were superior to all, which resonated with those in the room.

Herman Acker, a slender man with graying hair, was one of the first to speak up. "Jews, blacks, faggots, and Italians are already inferior," he noted. "But they make their position worse by choosing an immoral life, which compounds their trouble."

"Yes," Anton Reinhart responded. "And American liberals are empowering those inferior groups solely for political gain."

"And it's costing us dearly," Hinkle added.

Alfred Gable nodded in agreement. "They're destroying our way of life. Jews and liberals."

Julius Moder, a short middle-aged man, had a scowl that wrinkled his forehead. "Jews are the biggest part of that problem. They're just standing back and watching all these other groups competing against themselves and making money off both sides."

"They keep the pot stirred," Reinhart noted.

"While we fight off the liberals and the inferior races," Moder continued. "The Jews scoop up the profits."

Finally Mullins spoke up. "For me, the biggest issue is immigration. Jews are coming here in huge numbers. And once they get here, they birth babies at a tremendous rate. Then they steal our jobs and our money and hoard it for their own kind."

Hinkle chimed in, "And to make matters worse, some of them marry our women."

"They're attacking us from every direction," Reinhart groused. "From within and without."

"We need to stop them," someone added.

"Which means," Mullins reiterated, "we need to limit immigration."

"We need to *end* immigration!" another said adamantly. "We have enough people here already. We need to stop the others from coming."

Mullins liked what he heard and thought the group had the right idea, but the organization had a heavy emphasis on German life and tradition, none of which appealed to him. Still, Hinkle had been nice to him, so Mullins agreed to return for another meeting.

CHAPTER 9

In the weeks that followed, Mullins attended additional meetings with the Springfield members of the Knights of Teutonia, but after two or three sessions with them, he politely bowed out. Not that he had given up on their ideals or changed his mind about the positions they espoused on the important issues of the day. He just didn't care for the Germanic emphasis.

Meanwhile, he continued to read the books he purchased at Hinkle's bookstore and listened regularly to Walter Jones's Hour of Power radio broadcast. In one of those broadcasts, Jones called for the formation of an organization to preserve what he called "traditional views of Americanism."

"What we need," Jones suggested, "is a group of men who will take to the streets and give muscle to our beliefs. Pound the pavement with our determination. Pummel the opposition with our resolve."

Jones left little doubt about the militancy he envisioned, and the message found a ready reception in Mullins. He enjoyed discussing politics and popular culture, but he wanted to do more than merely talk about important issues. He wanted to do something to change the situation; something to address the threat that he perceived America faced. To stymie Jewish attempts at corrupting and changing American values and lifestyle. The organization Jones called for sounded exactly like the kind of group

Mullins felt would be necessary: A paramilitary unit that could put muscle to ideas in an application of physical aggression that brought tangible results.

After hearing Jones's call to action, Mullins considered ways he might implement a response to that call. At first, he wondered if members of the Knights of Teutonia might be shaped into a group that could respond in that manner. But after considering the matter further, he dismissed the idea. Hinkle's group was too focused on its German heritage to be of much use in physically confronting the people who threated Americanism.

Rather than co-opting their group, Mullins decided that forming his own organization provided better opportunities for success. Men who would not shy away from using force to at least put the Jews in their place. And as he thought about it, that option became less and less an obstacle and more and more an opportunity. Maybe he should be the one to lead the effort. That single person Jones talked about who stands up, acts, and makes a difference.

✦ ✦ ✦

A few days later, Mullins and Bobby Rankin went for a walk after dinner. As they made their way up the block from the boardinghouse, Mullins brought up the subject of forming a group to dissuade immigrants from moving to Indian Orchard. To his surprise, Rankin wasn't interested. "I like the idea, it's just too militant for me."

"Why?"

"We can't beat people up for wanting a better life, no matter how frustrated we get."

"We can if they mean to have that life by stealing ours. We have to do *something*."

"Yes," Rankin nodded. "But not what you're talking about. If we did that, someone would get hurt. If someone gets hurt, they're going to file a complaint with the police. And sooner or later, we'd be in trouble."

"Well, we can't just sit around and watch the country collapse because the Jews are stealing us blind."

"I'm not going to jail again. I've been there once. That was enough for me."

Mullins stomped his foot in frustration. "Bobby, they're taking our jobs. Taking our money. Infecting our way of life with their Communist ideas. They aren't like us. We don't need them here."

"Have you considered that your enthusiasm for this might have something to do with your brother and the war?"

"How dare you bring my brother into this! This is about the Jews. The oily, stinking Jews. It has nothing to do with my brother."

✦ ✦ ✦

The next day at work, Mullins broached the subject with Tom Kugler while they sat on the shop floor and ate lunch. "I'm thinking we need to form a group to oppose the Jews."

Kugler had a puzzled expression. "Oppose them?"

"Yeah."

"How?"

"Give them some of this." Mullins balled his hand into a tight fist and gestured with it.

"Fight them? Actually use fists and clubs and all of that?"

"Yeah."

"I don't know," Kugler sighed. "That's going a little too far, don't you think?"

"We have a lot of Jews up here now. And more are coming every day from New York to take our jobs."

"That doesn't sound quite right," Kugler countered. "You

know this for a fact? Or is this something you heard from that guy on the radio?"

"You don't think that's what's happening?"

"I know they didn't get our jobs."

"Not yet."

Kugler shook his head. "We don't have more than one or two Jews working here right now."

"That's because the owners of the mill don't like them," Mullins argued. "They don't like Jews any more than I do. But they're coming. Mark my words, they're coming. If not today, then soon enough."

"They're coming up here," Kugler admitted. "But they're coming because the mills hire them. They don't run people off to get their jobs. To stop that, you'd have to stop the mills from giving them jobs."

"It might get to that."

"I don't think so. The mills are hiring every day. Can't get people fast enough to fill all of the open positions."

"They would stop coming if we made their life miserable enough," Mullins continued. "Eventually word would get back to New York and they'd stop coming."

"And we would be in jail."

"You sound like Bobby Rankin."

"Who is he?" Kugler asked.

"A guy who lives at the boardinghouse," Mullins answered. "He's interested in the topic. And he agrees that the Jews are the cause of our trouble. But he doesn't want to do anything about it except talk."

"Look, I don't like Jews. And I sure don't like Italians. I think they all stink and have a weird way of living. But I don't know of anyone who lost his job to a Jew or anyone else. The ones who lost their job were the ones who weren't working."

"But they're Jews," Mullins lamented. "They aren't like us.

They don't belong here. The only reason they're here is to destroy everything that makes America great."

"Like I said, I would rather none of them came here." Kugler wadded up the wax paper that had wrapped his sandwich and dropped the ball of paper into his lunch box, then closed the lid. "But I don't think beating up Jews in our spare time will change any of that. It'll just get us in trouble." Kugler stood. "Come on. We should stop talking and get to work now."

Mullins rose from the spot where he'd been seated but he felt more frustrated than he had while talking to Rankin the day before. Frustrated and ready to take matters into his own hands.

◆ ◆ ◆

A few days after talking to Rankin and Kugler, the next issue of Walter Jones's newspaper arrived for Mullins at the boarding-house. He read it that evening and found an article that mentioned the recent formation of a group called the Red Shirts—the Crimson Legion of America—taking their name from the shirts they wore, much like the Brown Shirts of the Nazi Party in Germany.

From the information in the newspaper article, it appeared the group espoused ideals similar to those promoted by Jones. However, according to the newspaper, the Crimson Legion was committed to taking action. On the streets. In the courts. In the halls of government. Wherever and whenever possible.

"William Kimball Griffin, founder and leader of the Crimson Legion," the article stated, "intends to take the group's message to the streets. Using Crimson Legion members to apply force where necessary."

Mullins was enthralled by what he read and could hardly finish it fast enough. When he reached the end, he took a piece of paper from the drawer of the table where the radio sat, then scanned through the article again, noting details about the group:

The leader's name. The stated goals.

The article touted the Crimson Legion as a positive response to Jones's call for organized opposition and a direct action to preserve traditional Americanism, and Mullins was convinced this was so. He felt it in his heart. A certainty he'd never known before. This was a solid group. Well organized. And it was led by American people, not German like the Knights of Teutonia. "Good, white Americans," Mullins whispered as he made notes from the article. "Good, white Americans."

The article in the paper included an address for the Crimson Legion's headquarters in Charlotte, North Carolina. Mullins wrote them that evening and was determined as never before to find a way to join their effort.

✦ ✦ ✦

A week later, Mullins received an introductory package from the Crimson Legion that included several pamphlets and an issue of their newspaper. Articles in the paper read much like those in Jones's but with a militant bent, content that fed Mullins's growing sense of urgency toward radical action.

The evening the paper arrived, Mullins retreated to his room, lay on the bed, and read the entire issue in a single reading. On the final page there was an announcement of pending Crimson Legion rallies at cities around the eastern half of the country. Mullins's heart skipped a beat when he saw that a rally was planned for a site in Springfield.

At last I can finally do something besides just talk. He thought, *I can go to the rally. I can meet others who think like I think. Who are ready to take action.*

✦ ✦ ✦

The next morning, as Mullins and Rankin walked to the bus stop to leave for work, Mullins told Rankin about the Crimson Legion and the rally planned for later that month. "I think we should go to it together," he added.

"I don't have time for that sort of thing," Rankin grumbled in response. "It's all I can do to work, get home, and get back to work the next day."

When he arrived at work, Mullins received the same answer from Kugler. As he worked at a stamping machine, punching out a part for a loom, he felt disappointed. He thought they were men of action. Men of vision. Men of determination. Now he knew the truth.

"They're as spineless as all of the others out there," he grumbled to himself, his words hidden beneath the noise of the machine he operated. "They're all lemmings. Followers. Unwilling to do anything that might actually address the problems we face. Unwilling to do anything that might actually change life for the better. Lulled into complacency by their comfortable lifestyle. Bought off by the Jews and the wealthy who only want to keep them in their place."

Mullins finished with the press and stepped over to a grinder. As the machine whirred and sparks flew, he continued to talk to himself. "We can't continue to live by only a minimal effort." He changed sides on the piece he was grinding. "Well, they might," he continued. "But I'm not." Despite the dust and sparks that flew through the air around him, he beamed with pride. "Not anymore." He shook his head. "I'm done with just sitting and talking. I'm gonna find a way to make a difference. They're gonna know it. And the Jews are gonna know it."

CHAPTER 10

Despite the way Lewin had found the job at the sewing factory—or rather, the manner in which it had found him—he struggled with it at first. Sewing was a woman's occupation. At least to him. And he worked each day surrounded by women, though there were a few men at machines on the far side of the room. Still, it took some getting used to. Gradually, he became comfortable with the work, the pace, and the surroundings. Soon, he became one of the fastest operators in the room.

At the same time, Lewin adapted to life in New York and began stopping on his way home in the afternoon to have coffee at a shop a few blocks from where he worked. It was a neighborhood café with a counter along one wall and tables arranged throughout the room. A waitress took his order—always a single cup of coffee—and brought it to him steaming hot, just the way he liked it. Often he sat near the window and sipped the coffee while he watched people passing by outside. He loved to watch them. The expressions on their faces. The way they moved their hands when they walked.

"Cheaper than a ticket to the movie," he had said more than once. "And far more entertaining."

One day, as Lewin sat near the front window, he noticed a newspaper lying on a nearby table. Thinking it was the daily paper, he picked it up and began to read, only to find it was a copy of the *Hour of Power*—the newspaper from Walter Jones—not the *New*

York Times. Lewin read the first two articles of the paper while he sipped his coffee. Soon, however, he became so incensed—both articles described how Jews were out to destroy America—he set the paper aside while he finished his cup. All the while, he muttered to himself about what he'd read.

When he finished drinking his coffee, Lewin folded the newspaper so the front page wouldn't show, tucked it beneath his arm, and strode out to the sidewalk. He made his way briskly down the street toward his apartment, hoping no one asked about the paper.

As Lewin entered the apartment, he called out to Esther, waving the paper in the air for emphasis. "Why do they write these things?"

Isador entered the room. "What are you talking about?"

Lewin unfolded the paper and held it for Isador to see. "This. The *Hour of Power* newspaper."

A frown winkled Isador's forehead. "Where did you get that?"

"I found it in a coffee shop," Lewin answered.

Esther came from the kitchen. "Let me see that." Without waiting for a response, she took the paper from Lewin's hands. As she glanced through it, her expression turned to an angry scowl. "Walter Jones," she huffed in a derisive tone. "Why are you reading anything by him?"

"I found it at a coffee shop." Lewin was puzzled. "Who is he?"

"The man who publishes that paper." Esther tossed it onto the dining table and turned back to the kitchen.

"But who is he?" Lewin insisted.

"He claims to be a preacher," Esther called in response. "He's a heretic, if you ask me."

Lewin looked over at Isador with a blank expression. "What does she mean?"

Isador took a seat at the table and glanced through the paper. "We've been telling you this from the beginning. The Americans don't like us."

"But this is more than not liking us," Lewin argued. "The articles in that paper make accusations against us. As if we are a threat to America and the American way of life."

Esther called out from the kitchen, "The Americans blame us for everything."

Isador nodded. "She is right. Whenever something happens here that they don't like, they blame us for it."

"But that isn't right," Lewin insisted. "They shouldn't do that."

Isador had an indulgent smile. "This is what we've been telling you about."

"There's more." Lewin opened the paper and pointed to an article. "They say they want to stop other Jews from coming here." He tapped on the paper with his finger for emphasis. "They would like to leave Michla and the boys in the hands of the Russian mobs?"

Isador sighed. "I am afraid they do not care what happens to them. Or to any other Jews."

Lewin slouched in his chair. "And we do nothing."

"There is nothing we can do," Isador replied.

Lewin shook his head. "I'm not so sure."

"What are you talking about?"

"There is a man in Belarus named Jabotinsky. I have not met him, but I have heard about him. He says we should fight back."

Isador shook his head vigorously. "That would be a mistake. And it would make things very bad for us. For all of us."

"Why?"

"Because if we fight back," Isador explained, "if we use force, they will respond with force, and there are many more of them than there are of us."

"Then our people should leave Europe now, while they have the chance." Lewin pointed to the newspaper again. "Before this Jones and his supporters do anything to make good on their threats."

"Their threats?"

"To end immigration." Lewin looked over at Isador. "That is what he says should happen. That they should stop any more Jews from coming here." He had a troubled expression. "Do you think they will stop allowing Jews to come to America?"

Isador shrugged. "I don't know. Maybe. Does this bother you?"

"Yes. Because I want to bring Michla and the boys to America."

"They do not do these things quickly."

"Still," Lewin insisted, "I have to get Michla and the boys here now. While they have the opportunity."

"That costs money," Isador noted.

"I need another job," Lewin decided.

"You want to change jobs again?"

"No. I just need an additional job. Two more jobs. As many as it takes."

Esther came into the room. "I will help you."

Lewin looked puzzled. "But what will you do? You have your duties here. With the children. You cannot get a job to help me."

"I have some money." Esther's eyes danced when she said it. "I will help you. You must write to Michla."

"And tell her what?"

"Write to her." There was a hint of laughter in Esther's voice. "Send her the money."

"I would be glad to write her." There was a growing tension in Lewin's voice. "And I would be all too happy to send her money, but I don't have money to send her."

"That's what I'm saying." Esther was insistent. "I will help you. I have some money. Between us we may already have enough. Write to her."

Lewin was overcome by his sister's generosity and leaned forward with his head resting in his hands. "How is it that there is such hatred and division in this country, and yet so much beauty and peace?"

Isador reached over and patted him on the shoulder. "That is a long story."

"And a complicated one," Esther added. "Get some paper." She made an urgent gesture. "Write to Michla. Tell her to join us."

✦ ✦ ✦

Writing to Michla and arranging details for her and the boys to join Lewin in America took an exchange of several letters and multiple trips to the post office, most of which Lewin made on his way to and from work. During one of those stops to mail yet another letter, Lewin saw a flyer pinned to a notice board on the wall near the clerk's window. The flyer was an announcement from an agency in the city advertising jobs at a textile mill in Springfield, Massachusetts. The mill needed workers of all types and promised to pay wages that were higher than any mill works on the East Coast. Lewin had no idea what that meant, but making more money meant he and his family could enjoy a better life.

While he waited in line, Lewin eagerly jotted down the information from the notice on a scrap of paper he found in his pocket. Perhaps this was the answer he'd been looking for. And if it paid more than any job he could find in New York, it would surely provide enough for him and Michla and the boys to have their own place. *What a gift that would be to them—a place of their own as soon as they arrive!*

When Lewin finished at the post office, he continued down the street to his job at the sewing factory. All day long he stitched together pieces of fabric, his fingers feeding the cloth through the machine, his foot working the pedal. But all the while, his mind was on the notice he'd seen at the post office and the dream of what a job like that might be.

At the apartment that evening, Lewin asked Isador about the things he'd read in the job notice. Isador had heard about Springfield. "They have good mills up there. Lots of people have moved up there already."

"Our people?" Lewin asked.

"You mean Jews?"

"Yes."

"Lots of Jews have moved up there. I hear life is better up there, too. Less tension. But most of them work for the armory, not the textile mills."

Lewin looked puzzled. "The armory?"

"They make ammunition."

"Bullets?"

"Yes. And rifles, too."

"Why do people choose to work there rather than here?"

"It's better. They earn more money. And they do not have so much harassment."

"Then, why don't you go?"

"I have a good situation here," Isador replied. "And we like living in New York. But it might be good for you. Maybe you should consider it."

"The notice at the post office said to contact an agency. Is it safe?"

"I don't know. There are many unscrupulous people trying to take advantage of us. Perhaps you should ask Albert Gilman."

"The one I spoke to before. About the construction job."

"Yes."

Lewin looked askance. "His suggestion did not work out so well."

"That might not have been his fault."

"I don't know . . ."

"Gilman has many friends and relatives who have moved to Springfield. He could tell you how they did it. I think he helped several of them go up there."

In spite of Isador's reassurances, Lewin was reticent about contacting Gilman again. He seemed too much like Chernigov back in Belarus—someone who once provided helpful information but had grown out of touch with the latest developments and was too proud to admit it.

✦ ✦ ✦

After an extended exchange of letters, arrangements were made for Michla and the boys to travel to America aboard a ship from the Baltic American Line, sailing from Libau just as Lewin had done. Michla promised to send him a letter a few days before their departure so he could determine when they were to arrive and be ready to greet them without a long delay.

Not long after Michla's last letter arrived at the apartment, Lewin began checking the newspaper each day to determine the time and place that ships from the Baltic line docked in New York. He also traveled to the lower end of Manhattan to determine how and where to board the ferry to Ellis Island so he could make the trip as smoothly as possible when the time came.

Despite his best effort, however, Lewin was unable to determine the precise time of their arrival and he was surprised one day when he arrived at the apartment from work.

"That came for you this morning." Esther had a broad grin as she gestured to a small envelope that lay on the dining table. "You should read it."

"What is it?"

"A telegram."

"You know what it says?"

"Read it for yourself."

Lewin opened the envelope, took out the message, and read out loud. "'We are at Ellis Island. Michla.'" His mouth fell open and his eyes were wide in a look of surprise. "They are here?"

"Yes." Esther cackled with laughter. "They are waiting for you at the processing center."

Lewin grabbed her and hugged her tightly. "They are really here?"

"Yes." She pulled free of him. "You must bring them to the apartment."

"Can I do that now?"

"Better to go tomorrow. It will be too late to go now. Can you get off work?"

"Not all day."

"Ask your boss in the morning if you can leave at noon."

"I will."

✦ ✦ ✦

When Lewin arrived at the sewing factory on the morning after the telegram arrived, he asked Saperstein if he could leave at noon. Saperstein looked perplexed, and Lewin wondered if anyone had ever made such a request before.

"What for?" Saperstein asked. "Why do you want to leave early?"

"My family is at Ellis Island. They have just arrived from Belarus. I must go and get them."

"Can't someone else go?"

"Someone must sign for them. This is my duty," Lewin explained. "I must personally go get them."

"Well . . ." Saperstein had a reluctant tone. "Okay. But just for today. I need all of my workers at their machines. The owners require me to keep all of the machines operating all of the time."

Suddenly, Lewin was worried. "I will have a job when I come tomorrow?"

"You'll be back tomorrow morning?"

"Yes. Of course," Lewin insisted. "I will be here tomorrow morning. Same as usual."

"Good." Saperstein smiled. "Then you shall keep your job."

At noon, Lewin rose from his chair at the sewing machine, dusted the lint from his trousers, and started toward the front. Saperstein was waiting for him at the door. "Here," he thrust out his hand. "You will need a taxi to bring your family."

Lewin glanced down and saw that Saperstein had offered him a five-dollar bill. "It will not cost that much," he was unsure whether to accept the money.

"They might need something to eat. Take it," he urged. "It is a gift. From me to you. Not an advance."

Lewin took the bill from him. "That is very generous."

"Coming to America is a big event." Saperstein's eyes were full. "It should be a time of joy."

Lewin acknowledged him with a nod, then stepped toward the door. Saperstein called after him, "Return in the morning."

Lewin replied over his shoulder, "I will be here."

✦ ✦ ✦

From the sewing factory, Lewin walked quickly to the corner and took the streetcar down to the southern tip of Manhattan, then crossed the park to Battery pier. The ferryboat was loading just as he arrived and he made his way on board.

Half an hour later, Lewin arrived at Ellis Island and entered the processing facility. A clerk stopped him as he came into the central room. "How may I help you?" It was more an order than an offer of service.

"I am here to collect my wife and children."

"And what is your wife's name?"

"Michla Lewin."

The clerk checked his registry, then gestured toward a row of chairs arranged nearby. "Have a seat over there," he pointed. "I will have them brought up shortly."

Lewin did as he was told and took a seat. While he waited, he watched as the clerks continued to work, shuffling papers, shuffling people. Scurrying about. Doing this and that. With each passing minute he grew more and more frustrated.

Finally, after what felt like an eternity, a guard appeared with Michla and the two boys in tow. The clerk waved them to his desk, and the guard ushered them forward. Lewin rose from his seat and joined them. Michla appeared nervous and fidgeted with the folds in the fabric of her dress. The two boys clung to Lewin immediately, their arms wrapped around his legs. But none of them said a word and waited to see what would happen next.

As had occurred with Lewin when he arrived, the clerk went through a litany of questions—did the arrivals have a place to live and someone with a job to support them? Lewin answered for them and the clerk stamped their papers, then waved them on.

When they were finished, Lewin and Michla led the boys outside the building toward the ferry dock. Lewin contained himself part of the way but before they were halfway there, he turned to her, took her in his arms, and kissed her.

Michla blushed and at first seemed to resist. "Schleman, what are you—"

Lewin cut her off again with another kiss while the boys watched and giggled. She tried to speak, but once more he stopped her with a kiss.

Finally she relaxed and kissed him in return, then rested her head on his shoulder and whispered, "I have missed you so much."

"And I have missed you," he replied.

Lewin and Michla stood on the sidewalk, clutching each other tightly, crying unashamedly, as others made their way past. Finally, though, it was time to board the next ferry. They straightened themselves and continued toward the dock. Lewin took the boys by the hand and chatted with them while they walked.

CHAPTER 11

nstead of taking a taxi, as Saperstein had suggested, Lewin arranged for Isador to collect them with a truck from the grocery store. They were cramped with all five of them on the front seat, but doing it that way meant Lewin could save the five dollars Saperstein gave him and use it for something else.

When they arrived at the apartment, Esther was waiting to greet them, along with an apartment full of relatives and friends. As with Lewin when he arrived, the greetings were handled quickly, then everyone sat down to eat. Lewin's sons seemed particularly hungry and ate a lot.

After everyone had eaten and all of the guests were gone, Lewin and Michla visited with Isador and Esther, catching everyone up again with events that had transpired between the time Lewin departed and Michla arrived.

Sometime around ten, everyone was talked out and they all went to bed. Lewin and Michla shared a bed in one bedroom with their sons asleep on a pallet on the floor. As they lay together, Michla whispered, "Everyone was calling you Samuel, not Schleman."

"When I arrived, they told me I should change my name to something that sounded more American and suggested I call myself Samuel Levine, but I resisted. Then I saw how people treated me when I used my Jewish name and it was not good. So

I gave Samuel Levine a try to see what would happen, and things worked out better."

"You said *they* told you. Who told you?"

"Everyone who was here today when you arrived."

"So, now you are Samuel Levine?"

"I am Samuel Levine to the world out there," Lewin explained. "But to myself and to our family and friends, I am still Schleman Lewin."

"And I am expected to do that also?"

"You can call me whatever you wish."

"But am I expected to change my name, too?"

"It might be better for you if you had an American name to use in public."

"I thought this was the promised land."

"It is a great place," Lewin replied, "with lots of opportunity. But it is one with problems too."

"Problems?"

"Since coming here, I have learned that many people do not really like us."

Michla nodded in agreement. "They are like the Europeans we fled."

Lewin agreed. "And that means it is better for us and for our boys if we blend in as much as possible."

"You mean become someone else."

"At least in public."

"And who should I become?"

"When we discussed it last night, someone suggested you should use the name Mollie."

Michla's face was contorted in a disapproving expression. "Mollie?"

"Yes, Mollie Levine. But only outside the apartment. With us and with our friends you can still be Michla Lewin. But out there"—he gestured toward the window—"on the street you should be Mollie Levine."

"And that sounds less Jewish than Michla Lewin?"

"It sounds less foreign."

She frowned the way she always frowned when she suspected there was more to the story than he was telling. "You had some trouble?"

"A little, but then I started using my American name and changed jobs and now things are better."

"I don't know about changing my name, but we have to change our place."

"Why? You haven't even given America a try yet. Surely we can—"

"I don't mean change countries again." Michla chuckled. "Just change apartments. This place is too crowded for all of us. And it's not right to put Isador and Esther out for long. We have to get our own place."

"I will see what I can find," Lewin thought of the mill he'd heard about in Springfield but didn't want to bring it up yet. With everything about getting her and the boys to America and figuring out how to bring them from the ferry docks to the apartment, he hadn't had time to talk to Gilman or anyone else about it. "Let me ask around before you say anything."

"What makes you think I would talk about a thing like that?"

Lewin took her hand in his, and leaned over and kissed her. "You talk about everything."

✦ ✦ ✦

A few days later, Lewin returned to the apartment from work a little earlier than normal. With extra time, he stopped to see Albert Gilman. They sat in Gilman's apartment and drank tea while they talked.

"I saw a notice at the post office about jobs that are available at a mill in Springfield, Massachusetts. Isador said you might know something about that."

"He told you that I have relatives and friends who have moved there?"

"Yes," Lewin said. "Was it a good move for them?"

"It was." Gilman nodded his head slowly. "You are thinking of making the move yourself?"

"Do you think that would be a good idea?"

"I think war is coming in Europe. War is always good for the mills."

"We just finished a war."

"That is correct," Gilman noted. "But they're making things worse by the negotiations over the treaty to end it. War will come again. And when it does, Springfield will be an important place, a busy place where you could make a lot of money—if you get there now while property is cheap."

"What kind of work do they have? I think this advertisement was for a textile mill."

"Springfield is home to many textile mills. Most of them offer steady work, which means a steady income. But the future is in the armory."

Lewin had a puzzled look. "The notice didn't mention an armory."

"That's because the one in Springfield is a government factory that makes firearms for the army. They don't advertise like that for employees. And they don't work through agents, either. They do all of their hiring themselves. This work pays very well."

"How do I get a job there?"

"You could write to them, I suppose. But most people just move up there."

"That sounds risky."

"It is risky." Gilman shrugged. "But so is life. You've made it here. You can make it there."

"How do I find a place to live? I have a wife and two small boys."

"I have a friend in Springfield, Morris Altman. He can help you find a place. I will write to him for you."

"That would be very helpful."

"And I have a friend who works at the armory."

"Would he help, too?"

"I am sure he would. His name is Edward Franck." Gilman wrote the name on a piece of paper for Lewin. "Ask for him when you get there. Use my name. Tell him I sent you."

Lewin glanced at the paper and realized Gilman was assuming he had already decided to make the move. He had come to Gilman's apartment only because Isador suggested it, but he had come with grave reservations about whether Gilman could be trusted. Now it seemed as if those concerns were of no concern at all. Still, he had been troubled by the way some things had turned out, so he forced himself to raise the issue. "I went for that carpenter job you told me about."

Gilman shook his head. "That was my fault. After I told you about it I inquired further. The foreman is a racist. And quite devious. We have been directing people away from him lately. I should have warned you. I am sorry for the inconvenience it caused you."

Lewin was relieved. At least Gilman owned up to his mistake. "It is no problem." Lewin stood to leave. "Everything has worked out well."

"I understand you are at a sewing factory."

"Yes."

"Most of those are owned by our people. They tend to be safer places to work."

"This one is good." Despite feeling better about Gilman, Lewin was hesitant to disclose the location where he worked. "They treat me well.".

"I am glad." Gilman walked with Lewin to the door. "If you

go to the armory, be sure to mention Franck's name. And if you see him, tell him he still owes me that dollar. He'll know what it's about."

✦ ✦ ✦

That night, when Lewin and Michla were in bed, he finally broached the subject of moving to Springfield. "I heard about something that might be better for us.".

"What is it?" There was more than a hint of eagerness in her voice.

"I saw a notice about a mill in another town that is hiring."

"What is this other town?"

"Springfield, Massachusetts."

"I have never heard of it. Is it far?"

"Not too far."

"What sort of mill?"

"They make weapons for the army."

She turned in his direction. "And you are good with that?"

"With what?"

"With making weapons to kill people. Haven't we seen enough killing for one lifetime?"

"This would be a good job," he responded with a hint of irritation in his voice. This seemed like an opportunity to him and he thought she would be glad for it. "A good job with good pay and the hours would not be so long."

"Is that all we should think of?"

He struggled to contain his rising frustration. "But it is something to consider. I am working twelve hours a day. I leave in the morning and come home at night."

Her voice softened. "I know."

"And we are sleeping four to a room in my sister's apartment," he continued. "We can't continue like this indefinitely. And I think we can do better up there."

"Is this an actual opportunity? I hear there are many people trying to take advantage of us here."

"You've been talking to Isador."

"Esther too."

"I spoke with Albert Gilman about it."

"Who is he?"

"He lives down the hall. You met him the first night you were here. He knows about these things. Many of his friends and relatives have moved to Springfield."

"He is like Chernigov?"

"No. Gilman is an honorable man. He is trying to do right. He gave me the name of a contact who works there."

"You think we should go?"

"Yes."

"And you would go first, then bring us up later?"

"No. This time I think we should move up there together."

"Then I suppose we should do what you think best." Michla leaned closer and kissed him. "You have brought us this far." She kissed him again. "I am sure you will take us where we need to go next."

CHAPTER 12

Meanwhile, Mullins continued his attempts to get others interested in attending the Crimson Legion rally. He talked to his fellow boarders at Mrs. Smithson's, but to no avail. And those he encountered at the coffee shop down the street were not interested, either. He was reluctant to bring up the topic with Kugler at work, having done so earlier and been rebuffed, but as the time for the rally drew near, he raised the question at lunch one last time.

"I told you," Kugler snapped, "I don't have time for it."

"It wouldn't take any longer than it does to attend a union meeting," Mullins countered. "You've made time for those."

"Not for many of them," Kugler responded.

Owen Fletcher entered with his lunchbox and took a seat on the floor next to Mullins. "What are you two talking about?"

Mullins glanced at him. "Are you familiar with the Crimson Legion?"

"I've heard about them. That guy you listen to on the radio. What's his name?"

"Walter Jones."

"Yeah. He talks about the Red Shirts all the time now."

Mullins was surprised. "You listen to him?"

"Had to give him a try after all you've been saying about him."

"There's a Crimson Legion rally next week."

"Where?"

"Here. In Springfield." Mullins had an expectant expression. "I'm going. You want to go with me?"

Fletcher shook his head. "Nah."

"Why not?"

"I saw a picture of 'em in a magazine. They looked rather silly. Reminded me of men parading around in their mother's blouses."

Kugler laughed. Mullins was aggravated. "At least they're trying to do something about the things they believe in," he snarled. "Not just talking about it."

✦ ✦ ✦

The following Saturday afternoon, Mullins took the trolley to Springfield and attended the Crimson Legion rally. None of his friends were interested in going with him, so he rode there alone. The meeting was held in the municipal auditorium located downtown near city hall, a building that seated about twenty-five hundred. Mullins entered it to find the place was packed shoulder to shoulder with people.

At the far end of the room was the stage, which had been set up with two rows of chairs behind a podium that stood out front near the edge. Behind all of that was a huge American flag that hung as a backdrop.

On the floor of the auditorium, chairs were arranged in rows and divided into three sections by aisles that bisected the hall from back to front. At first glance they all appeared to be taken, but as Mullins scanned over them again, he spotted an empty seat and made his way toward it. It was still open when he reached it and he sat down to wait.

A few minutes later, local politicians appeared on the stage, followed by a group of other notables. They waved to the crowd that responded with modest applause, then took a seat in the chairs that had been placed on the stage for them. Several of them conferred with each other, then one of them rose from his seat and made his way to the podium. After his own brief remarks, he introduced William Kimball Griffin, the group's leader.

Griffin appeared and stepped to the podium as the event's featured speaker. Right from the start, his message was very similar to the message Mullins heard from Walter Jones on the radio, but Griffin's remarks were more strident and to the point.

"This land was settled by Aryan people of a pure race." Griffin's voice and cadence sounded like a preacher. The look in his eyes and the expression on his face were like those of the activists who spoke at the union meetings Mullins had attended. Griffin's fervor and intensity, however, were unlike anything Mullins had ever encountered.

"Those settlers were honest people," Griffin continued. "Hardworking. Honest. White people." The audience roared its approval.

"They built this great nation with their bare hands. Chopped down the trees. Tilled the soil. Harvested the crops. Built the churches and schools that made this country what it is today. Now liberals and their friends—the Communists, the Jews, and the homosexuals—have unleashed the Negroes—an inferior but useful race—to spread corruption everywhere. And they've thrown open the doors of our great nation to anyone who wants to enter." The crowd booed in response. "With the support of those same liberal politicians, Italians and Jews have come here in droves, bringing with them racial and genetic impurities that threaten our very existence.

"I've been excoriated by reporters for saying those things." Griffin was on a roll. "But they seem to have forgotten that many of us lost loved ones in the Great War, a war instigated by Jews, promoted by Jews, prolonged by Jews, and financed by Jews as a means of lining their pockets with gold. Politicians have forgotten those who died because of Jewish greed. But we haven't forgotten!" The crowd leapt to its feet, shouting, clapping and waving in a wild and tumultuous expression of support.

"Now the Jews are coming here to finish the job they started in Europe. To destroy life in America as we know it." His volume increased. "To destroy America as we know it. To destroy the purity of our Aryan race. Are we going to let that happen?"

A chorus of "No!" went up from the crowd.

Griffin continued. "Many of you are already working to oppose the forces that threaten us. Courageous people. Talking to your co-workers. Encouraging and cajoling your friends to join our cause. Some of you are putting yourself in harm's way to further this work. Confronting with force those who attempt to take from us by force. But we need action from our government to complete your effort. Strong action. Action designed to limit immigration and stop Jews from coming here. To stop Italians and Poles from descending on us like the pagan hordes that swallowed the empires of old. And not only to stop new people from arriving but also to send back the ones who are already here and end the intermingling of the races once and for all. And if the government won't do it, we will. They will not destroy us. And we will send them back." The crowd roared once more.

"While we pressure the government to impose immigration controls, one way we can make certain, on our own, that none of these groups destroy us is to make Jewish life, Italian life, Negro life in America miserable enough that they will all return to where they came from. Make them pay for the misery they've inflicted on us," he said confidently, "and they will be all too glad to take that misery elsewhere!"

The crowd again leapt to its feet, shouting and clapping and cheering wildly, hands raised in the air. Many of them were jumping up and down with excitement. Griffin backed away from the podium, his remarks finished, and waved back at them, acknowledging them with a smile and a nod and a wave of his hand.

Mullins was thoroughly taken by what he'd heard and seen. Finally he had found someone—a group of someones—who understood. People who were determined to do something about the situation. And a leader who meant to help them do it. He stood there with the others, silently gazing up at Griffin, drinking in the moment, feeling as if he had just stepped out of the darkness into a very bright light. The light of truth and insight.

After a while, Griffin was ushered from the stage, and the audience, though reluctant to leave, began filing toward the exit. As the auditorium emptied, Mullins, equally reluctant, turned to leave as well. When he neared the doors, the area became crowded, and Mullins was jostled from side to side by those around him. He stumbled once and caught himself against the shoulder of a man who stood ahead of him. The man seemed not to notice.

Before he was through the doorway, a woman appeared at Mullins's side, just to his right. A brunette about his height with a slender build and deep, dark eyes. He glanced at her, then looked again with a smile and was about to speak when someone bumped into her and she stumbled toward him.

Instinctively, Mullins reached out to help and his arm went across her back, just above the waist. She leaned against him, her weight pressing against his side and for a moment he felt her relax in his embrace. She caught herself quickly, though, and as she leaned away to stand up straight again, he slipped his hand in hers and deftly pulled her arm back to his side. "Let me help you."

She did not withdraw her hand from his grasp.

Holding the woman close, Mullins guided the way from the building and when they reached the sidewalk, he looked over at her. "Are you okay?"

"Yes. I'm fine."

The moment seemed to end between them but Mullins noticed she still had not let go of his hand, so he said, "Would you like to go somewhere and maybe have some coffee or something?"

She smiled. "I would like that very much."

From the auditorium, they walked up the street to a café, where they sat in a corner booth and talked over their pie and coffee. Her name was Grace Anderson, he learned, and her family was from Virginia where she grew up and attended college. She had come to Springfield three years ago to work as a teacher and lived with her aunt, Rose Willingham. Aunt Rose, in turn, had come there because of her husband's job. The husband had since died, leaving Rose alone in a big, empty house. Both were glad to have each other as housemates.

Talking to her that late afternoon, time seemed to stand still for Mullins. He loved the look in her eyes and the sound of her voice as she spoke and did his best to hold each word in his mind, memorizing every feature, every intonation. She seemed equally enraptured by him and they gazed across the table at each other, oblivious to everyone and everything around them.

Finally, though, the hour grew late and they could no longer ignore it. Mullins paid the tab and called for a taxi to take her home. As they waited by the curb for the car to arrive, they exchanged contact information and promised to stay in touch.

When the taxi came, he held the door while Grace climbed in, then pushed it closed and waved to her as the car started forward. He waited until it was out of sight, then walked to the corner and caught the last trolley to Indian Orchard. It was late when he arrived at the boardinghouse, but despite the hour he wrote a letter to Grace and placed it in the box downstairs for mailing. As he drifted off to sleep, he hoped she would reply.

✦ ✦ ✦

Grace did, indeed, respond to Mullins's letter, and to the ones after that as well. In the weeks that followed, their exchange of correspondence left little doubt she liked him and he liked her. After several weeks, though, he could stand the separation no longer and asked if they could meet again. She agreed and suggested they meet at the same café in Springfield as before. They arranged a time for the following Saturday afternoon.

On the appointed day, Mullins traveled to the café in Springfield. She arrived a few minutes after him and they took a seat in the same booth where they had sat before. This time, however, instead of coffee and pie, they ate lunch and spent the afternoon strolling and talking.

Over the next several weeks they met regularly for lunch, then an afternoon movie. Gradually they began to see each other for dinner during the week, usually on Wednesdays. Dinner and occasionally a movie.

One Saturday, as they were saying good-bye, Grace invited him to go with her to the home of a friend the next afternoon.

"Who are they?" Mullins asked.

"Just friends. They were at the rally. Most of them, anyway. And most of them think like we do." Mullins agreed to join her. Not so much because of the friends, though they seemed intriguing, but because of the chance to spend another afternoon with her.

✦ ✦ ✦

That Sunday afternoon, Mullins came to Grace's house and they walked together to the home of Peggy and Jimmy Clayton, a couple who lived a few blocks away. Both were a little older than Mullins and Grace. Jimmy worked at the bank. Peggy was involved with civic organizations, including a number of groups working to gain the right of women to vote.

Several couples were seated in the living room when they arrived. Peggy made quick work of the introductions, noting that this was Mullins's first time with them, and everyone did their best to put him at ease.

Among those Mullins met that day were Ida Hayes and Pete Lawler, a couple much like Mullins and Grace—very much attracted to each other and were just getting to know each other, too. Ida was a secretary for an accounting firm. Pete worked as a millwright at Gompers Machine, a tool and die manufacturer on the southern side of Springfield. "My cousin works at Boatwright," he informed.

"What's his name?"

"Owen Fletcher."

"Yes," Mullins replied. "He works in the shop with me."

"Nice guy," Pete added. "But he doesn't go in for my kind of politics."

"What kind is that?"

"The Crimson Legion," Pete answered proudly. "I've heard Griffin in person three times now."

Mullins smiled. "No, Fletcher isn't interested too much in the Crimson Legion. But I think he agrees with the politics. Just not the method."

Johnny Farris, who sat across from them, spoke up. "That's the problem. People who say they agree that things aren't right but won't do anything about it."

And with that, Mullins was embroiled in a freewheeling discussion. For the next three hours, they ate, drank, and talked politics. Most of them either read the Crimson Legion's newspaper or listened to Walter Jones on the radio and read *his* newspaper. Their discussion followed the messages of both organizations—racial impurity was the central problem facing America.

Ida suggested that Jews were an example of what happens when impurities run free.

"And they are now introducing those impurities to Aryans through intermarriage," Pete noted. He gestured to Ida. "We've been tested already. Not a drop of Jewish blood between us."

"It's part of the Jewish plot," Ida noted. "To lure us into bearing impure children. I didn't want anything to do with it."

Troy Brooks spoke up. "The government needs to limit intermarriage between Aryans and Jews."

"They're supposed to protect us," Pete added. "They need to get those people out of here."

As the discussion continued, Mullins looked over at Grace and smiled. She smiled back and he felt a sense of satisfaction he hadn't known since the day his brother left to join the army. Friends. Becoming family. And a beautiful woman enjoying it with him.

The hour grew late and the gathering with friends came to an end. Mullins and Grace left for the walk back to Grace's house. She took his arm and leaned against him. At the corner, they paused and exchanged a kiss. "Did you enjoy meeting with them?" Mullins asked.

"Yes, but I liked being with you even more."

"I liked that, too."

They kissed again. "Maybe we could do this again."

"The kiss?" She grinned. "Or gathering with friends?"

"Both," he chuckled.

✦ ✦ ✦

In the months that followed, Mullins and Grace spent more and more time together. Just the two of them during the week and on Saturdays, but on Sundays they gathered at the Claytons' house. New people came and a few drifted away, but the discussions continued to be political in nature.

At first, their conversation was simply more of the same—the latest news from the major newspapers and topics discussed by Walter Jones during his weekly broadcast. Gradually, however, the Claytons moved the discussion away from mere talk toward actually doing something about the situation. They began by suggesting each of them confront their co-workers—perhaps in an engaging way but directly nonetheless. "And find new people to talk to. We need to make sure we raise awareness among a wider group than just ourselves."

And with that it became much like an accountability group, with the Claytons regularly raising the question: "What have you done with the things we've heard and discussed?" This was where Mullins had been when he first arrived and he hoped that his presence had somehow contributed to the change. At least the others were now catching up with him, but he still was not satisfied.

One Sunday he pressed the issue. "We still need to do more."

"Like what?" someone asked.

"I don't know, but we're still just talking."

"At least we're talking to new people. I approached three co-workers just this week."

"But what can we do?" Pete asked. "We can't just go around beating up Jews."

Some of the group laughed, but Mullins was deadly serious. "Why not?" he responded. "If they won't go voluntarily, why can't we force them out?"

"We would just get arrested," someone said.

Mullins frowned. "For beating a Jew?"

"Yes."

Someone chimed in, "Not in Springfield. At least, not in our neighborhood. Cops hate them as much as we do."

Grace joined the discussion. "Well, if not physically confronting them, what else could we do?"

"We could hold a protest rally," Ida suggested.

"Where?"

Ida shrugged. "Why not at a synagogue?"

"Which one?" Grace asked.

Mullins spoke up. "There's one on Fort Pleasant Avenue."

"Temple Beth El?"

"Yes."

That suggestion seemed to strike a chord with everyone and they agreed to gather for a protest outside Temple Beth El. For the remainder of the evening, they made plans about when to meet and what they should do once they arrived.

✦ ✦ ✦

The following Friday evening, Mullins, Grace, and the group gathered with hand-printed signs on the sidewalk across the street from the Beth El synagogue. As worshippers arrived, they chanted in unison, "Kikes go home! Kikes go home!" When the group grew tired of that, they switched to, "Christ Killers!"

Others shouted, "Jews steal our jobs." And others tried, "Bring back Americanism."

Those attending the synagogue service seemed to notice their presence and several glanced in their direction, but no one crossed the street to physically challenge the group. Likewise, the group did not cross the street to confront the Jews.

After an hour or so, the incident ended without trouble and several in the group felt discouraged about the outcome. "We didn't do much to make their life miserable," Brooks groused.

"At least we did something," Mullins responded.

"And it's a start," Grace suggested. "We should look at it that way. A place to begin."

From the synagogue, the group walked to the home of Margaret and Johnny Farris, who lived just a few blocks away, and had coffee and pie while they continued to discuss what else they could do.

"We could smash some windows," Pete suggested. "Burn

down a house."

"Not a house," Margaret said. "There might be children inside. And they didn't have anything to do with this. They didn't choose to come here or be born here."

The group fell silent a moment, then Johnny spoke up. "Aren't we a bunch of polite radicals!" Everyone laughed in response, and the discussion continued.

Pete explained, "I'm not interested in wiping them off the face of the earth. But they *are* to blame for the world's troubles."

Mullins conceded. "It's equally true that the trouble we face is caused by Jews, both here and abroad."

Everyone nodded in agreement. "And don't forget," someone added, "It was the Jews who crucified Christ."

"They've been cursed since then because of it."

"Now they're just trying to lay the trouble of that curse on us."

Someone else spoke up, "Well, until we can think of something else to do, we should go back to the synagogue next week. Make it a regular protest."

"Yeah. That sounds good. Maybe find a way to protest more effectively." Mullins interjected, and with that they agreed to protest again at the synagogue the following Friday evening.

CHAPTER 13

Early in January Lewin and Michla made the move from New York to Springfield. Esther was sad to see them go, but everyone realized it was for the best. The apartment was simply too small for both families, and Michla did not enjoy life in the city.

Having left most of their possessions in Belarus, Lewin and Michla had little in the way of personal possessions, which allowed them to make the trip to Springfield by train. All the way up, Michla was nervous about what they would find, but they arrived to a city with tree-lined streets and residential neighborhoods with individual houses. And, as Albert Gilman had suggested, Springfield had a thriving Jewish community. Michla was elated.

For the first few days, they stayed with Morris Altman, one of the friends Gilman had mentioned, but that arrangement proved even more awkward than staying with Esther and Isador in their tiny apartment. Before the week was out, Lewin succeeded in finding a house—actually, one half of a duplex—for them to rent. The house was located on Coomes Street in a predominantly Jewish neighborhood just a few blocks behind Temple Beth El synagogue.

Lewin showed the place to Michla for the first time on the day they took possession. She was elated at first, but then a troubled look came over her. "You are sure we can afford this?"

"Yes." He was certain they could pay the next month's rent, but after that it would depend on finding a job. And keeping expenses low.

She looked over at him with a skeptical glare. "How? How can we afford such an extravagance as this? The boys have separate bedrooms. You and I have a room to ourselves. How are we able to do this?"

"I have saved money," Lewin reassured. "The extra time we stayed with Esther made it possible."

She shook her head slowly from side to side. "I could not wait to leave that apartment."

"I know."

"But this!" She was exultant. "This is more than I thought we would ever have."

He glanced around at the rooms. "It is nice."

"Nice? What do you mean *nice*? There is space. Almost as much as we had in Naroulia. And a place for the boys to play."

"Yes." Michla was overstating the size, but Lewin did not want to spoil the moment for her.

She looked out the window. "And there are other families for us to know. It feels like we have fallen into the bosom of Abraham." Michla turned toward Lewin, grabbed him with both arms, and kissed him, then kissed him again. "Schleman," she beamed, "you have made me very happy."

✦ ✦ ✦

With Michla and the boys settled, Lewin asked around for help in locating Edward Franck, the man whom Gilman mentioned worked at the armory. A neighbor gave him the address, and Lewin arranged to meet Franck at his house a few blocks beyond the synagogue.

On the appointed day, Lewin went to Franck's house and knocked on the door, then waited patiently on the porch. A moment later, the door opened and Franck appeared. Slender with graying hair along his temples, he had intelligent eyes and a sharp, distinguished chin.

Franck seemed unusually guarded as Lewin introduced himself, until he said, "Albert Gilman sent me."

After that, Franck loosened up and invited him inside. They sat in the front room and talked. "Gilman is a good man," Franck commented. "He and I go back a long way. We come from the same village in Belarus."

"Ah." Lewin's eyes opened wider. "I am from Belarus also."

"Oh?" There was a note of skepticism in Franck's voice. "Where?"

"Naroulia."

"Oh. I know it well." Franck relaxed, as if Lewin had passed a Jewish religious formality of sorts. "I am from Gostov. Gilman is from Rudnya," he added.

"Neither of those villages is far from where I grew up."

Franck smiled. "Practically neighbors, considering the distance from here to there."

Lewin wasn't sure what he meant but nodded just the same. "We are a long way from home."

"Ah, but this is our home now."

"And so it is."

"What brings you to see me? If Gilman told you to find me, there must be something I can do for you."

"I would like to work at the armory. He thought you might be able to help with that."

"Well, the armory is a good place to work." There was a hint of tentativeness in Franck's voice. "The conditions are not that bad. Pay is good. And the supervisors do not allow the other workers to abuse us too much."

Lewin frowned. "Too much?"

"Not all Americans hate us," Franck explained. "But many of

them do, and there are people in the armory who resent having Jews do the same work they do."

"But you work there?"

"Yes."

"Will they hire me?"

"They are hiring, but . . ." Again, Franck had a tentative tone. "It depends."

Lewin ignored Franck's verbal cues and had a hopeful expression. "So, maybe?"

"Maybe. Perhaps." Franck shifted positions uneasily in his chair. "But they are tough on the selection of new employees."

Now Lewin had no option but to address the issue Franck had been hinting at. "And you don't think they will like me."

"I cannot say," Franck replied. "I just don't want you to think that because I like you, they will hire you."

"So, what should I do?"

"The first thing is to fill out an application."

"How does that work?"

"You will go to the employment office at the armory and tell them you wish to apply for a job. They will have you fill out an application and then they might give you a test."

Lewin frowned again. "A test?"

"Yes. An examination. An aptitude test."

Lewin looked worried. "This examination is in English?"

"Yes." Franck appeared puzzled. "Is that a problem?"

Lewin mumbled as he shook his head slowly, "I don't know."

Franck looked concerned. "You do not read English?"

"I read it. But I don't have much confidence with it."

"Well." Franck folded his arms across his chest. "I think an examination will be unavoidable for you."

"Then, I must try."

"If you can pass the examination, I can help you get hired. But you must pass the exam yourself."

✦ ✦ ✦

Two days later, Lewin went to the armory and asked a guard for directions to where he might apply for a job. The guard directed him to the employment office. "Third floor," he informed. "Take a right at the elevator. Can't miss it."

In spite of the guard's confidence, Lewin made three trips around the third floor before he located the office behind a nondescript door with no nameplate. A janitor guided him to it.

Inside the office, a row of chairs sat along the wall next to the door with a counter that extended across the room, directly opposite the door. There was an opening at the end that gave access to the area behind it and a door that led to another room. The door, however, was closed.

Behind the counter were two desks. One of them was clean, neat, and orderly but unoccupied. The other was stacked with files and cluttered with papers. A woman of about thirty sat there. She was of medium height and slender, with dark hair that came just below her ears.

The woman was busy with the papers on her desk but glanced up as Lewin entered. "If you're here about your time card, you'll have to see the timekeeper for that." Her voice was flat with a nasal tone.

"I was wanting to apply for a job," Lewin replied.

"We're not really hiring right now," she answered.

Lewin cleared his throat. "Edward Franck suggested I come see you."

The woman heaved a sigh, set down the pencil with a clatter, and rose slowly from her chair. Moving with a deliberate but measured stride, she made her way to a bin on the wall at one end of the counter that had several slots, each of them filled with preprinted forms. She took one from the top slot and brought it to the counter, then slapped it onto the countertop in front of him. "Fill this out, and bring it back to me," she instructed, and reached beneath the countertop and came out with a pencil that she slapped down beside the application form. "Use this and don't make a mess of it."

Lewin took the form and pencil and moved to the end of the counter, where he filled out the application while standing. When he finished, he returned it to the clerk. She looked it over, then ordered, "Come with me." She gestured for him to come through the access opening at the end of the counter, which he did.

The clerk led him to a room that had a table with half a dozen chairs arranged around it. She pointed and said, "Take a seat." When he was settled into a chair, she handed him an envelope, "There's a test inside that envelope. When I tell you to begin, you should take out the test and answer as many questions as you can before I return. Do you understand?"

"Yes."

"Good." She handed him a pencil. "I'm leaving the room now. Take out the test and begin."

As she started for the door, Lewin removed the test papers from the envelope and began reading. Understanding the questions was difficult at first, but as he continued to work his way through them, he came to understand better what was being asked.

Although reading the questions was initially a challenge, answering them was easy. Simply circle the letter corresponding to the answer. That part he understood very well and he enjoyed making the marks on the paper.

After what seemed like only a short time, the door to the room opened and the clerk returned. Lewin had just answered the final question, and as she came into the room, he announced, "I am finished."

She frowned. "Finished?"

"Yes."

"All of the questions?"

"Yes."

She took the paper from him and glanced through it. "No one has ever finished all of the questions."

Lewin did not respond and after a moment, the clerk returned the test papers to the envelope. "Come with me." He rose from the chair at the table and followed her back to the front office.

"Have a seat," she gestured toward the chairs that sat along the wall by the door. Lewin did as she instructed.

As Lewin waited, a man arrived. He was white, perhaps of Irish descent, and brought with him a teenage boy who appeared to be his son. The man was dressed in denim work clothes and had a badge that identified him as an armory employee. He seemed to know the clerk and she smiled at him pleasantly as he appeared.

"This is my son," the man said. "I spoke with you earlier about getting him a job."

"Oh yes." She came from the desk and handed the boy a form like the one she'd given to Lewin. "Fill this out. I think we can put you in the shipping department."

The boy stood at the counter and filled in the blank spaces on the form. As he did, the clerk prepared employment forms and a notice for the timekeeper. When the boy finished with the form, she came from her desk and took it from him. "You're all set." She handed the boy several forms. "Take these to the timekeeper. When you finish with them, report to the shipping department and ask for Donald Harrison. He's the foreman."

Lewin noticed the friendly manner in which the clerk greeted the man and the ease with which the boy was hired but said nothing about it. Instead, when they were gone, he asked, "Is that all I have to do?"

"Just a minute," the clerk answered. That's when Lewin noticed she was reviewing his examination answers. He was nervous that she was looking for a way to turn him down but after a few minutes she looked up and smiled. "Okay, that's all I need for now. Someone will call you when we have an opening."

✦ ✦ ✦

A few days later, Lewin received a message through Franck that he was to report to the armory. He went to the armory and reported to the clerk in the employment office where he applied. "You've been hired for the press shop," she told him. Lewin had no idea what that meant but it was a job and he was thankful. "Fill out these forms," she said, and she handed him several papers.

Lewin completed the forms and when he was done the clerk instructed, "Go to the timekeeper's office and when you are finished there, report to Vance Welch. He's the foreman in the press shop."

An hour later, Lewin arrived at the press shop and asked for Welch, who assigned him to a press machine identified by the number four on a placard that hung from a support bracket.

"This machine does two things," Welch explained. "It adds a taper to the top of this casing." He picked one up to illustrate his point. "And it crimps the plate for the primer at the bottom."

A man appeared at Lewin's side. He was much older, perhaps sixty, and had a kindly smile. "This is Oscar McManus," Welch said. "He'll show you the details."

Welch stepped aside and McManus stepped up to the machine. "He told you this machine does two things?"

"Yes," Lewin replied.

"Actually, it does three things." McManus grinned. "Tapers the top. Attaches the bottom. And it will cut off your hand if you let it."

"Right."

"Ever run one of these before?" McManus asked.

"No," Lewin replied.

134

"I didn't think so."

"Please do not tell them."

"I ain't telling nobody nothing," McManus insisted. "Besides, it's easy. I'll have you going good by the end of the day."

"And still with both of my hands?" Lewin quipped.

"Yeah." McManus laughed. "Still with both of your hands."

For the remainder of the day, Lewin worked with McManus, learning to operate the press. The next day, he operated it on his own.

Not long after the workday began, a co-worker accosted him. A tag above his right shirt pocket identified him as Luther Bogard. "Look, Kike," he snarled, "I don't care what the front office says; we don't like your kind around here."

Lewin was nervous. "My kind?"

"Yeah, Jew boy. We don't want Communists working in a plant that makes ammunition for the US Army."

"I am not a Communist."

Bogard leaned closer. "You're a Jew, aren't you?"

"Yes."

"That makes you a Communist. Be careful you don't wind up like the last guy that worked this station."

"What about him?" Lewin asked.

"He lost a hand when that press came down on it. And he's thankful it didn't come down on his head." Bogard jabbed Lewin in the chest with his finger. "You cause any trouble, you'll get the same thing he got."

As Bogard moved away, McManus appeared. "Don't worry about him. He's all bark and no bite."

"You think so?"

"I know so. The last man lost a hand because he was careless. Bogard had nothing to do with it."

CHAPTER 14

On the next Friday evening after Lewin started working at the armory, he and his family walked to Temple Beth El for worship. As they came near the synagogue, they saw protestors on the sidewalk across the street from the building. Several held signs with racial slurs. All of them shouted with angry voices.

Michla looked concerned. "What are they doing?"

"It's nothing," Lewin answered. "Don't look at them."

"It's not nothing," she replied. "And you only say that when you want me to be quiet. What are they doing?"

"They don't like us."

"Who doesn't like us?" one of his boys asked.

Lewin pointed, "Those people."

Michla spoke up again. "What did we do to them? We don't even know them."

"They think we are stealing their jobs."

His other son asked, "Did we steal their jobs? Is that how you got your job?"

"No," Lewin responded. "That's not how I got my job. And from what I've seen, *goyim* who want to work could get any job here that they cared to have. We Jews are the ones who must struggle for employment."

Michla flashed a look at him. "From what you've seen?"

"Yes."

"What do you mean?" She spoke with an insistent tone. "What have you seen?"

"I will tell you later." Lewin guided Michla and the children to the front entrance and hurried them inside the synagogue.

✦ ✦ ✦

Darkness had fallen by the time the service at the synagogue concluded. After greeting their neighbors and meeting a few new people, Lewin and Michla emerged from the building with their children for the walk home. The protestors were gone from across the street, and the neighborhood seemed calm and orderly.

As they walked toward home, Michla looked over at Lewin and asked once again, "What did you mean about what you said earlier. . .about what you had seen?"

Lewin responded by telling her about what he had heard and seen when he went to apply for the job at the armory. How he had been required to fill out an application and take an aptitude test. "Then they made me wait a few days before they offered me a job."

"And this other fellow?"

"They hired his son on the spot. That very day. While I was sitting there."

"Had they seen this young man before?"

"I don't think so."

"And they hired him without a test?" she asked.

"No test."

"No application?"

"No application. The only papers he had to fill out were the ones they give you after you are hired."

Michla had a perplexed expression. "And that is what those people were protesting when we arrived?"

"No," Lewin responded. "They were protesting because they think we are stealing their jobs."

"How are we stealing their jobs?" she railed. "You had to beg for that job. You had to get help to even find that job. How is that stealing?"

"We're not stealing anything. But they *think* we are."

Michla shook her head. "I do not understand."

"They don't understand, either."

While they were talking, a group burst from the shadows and rushed toward them. Men and women, their faces twisted in an angry, intense expression of hatred. Two of the men at the fore-front held sticks about the size of baseball bats that they wielded like clubs.

"We don't want Jews here!" one of them shouted.

"Communist Jews!"

"Christ killers!"

All the while, they shoved the boys into the bushes, then swung their sticks at Lewin, striking him about the head and shoulders with blows that produced a sickening hollow thud.

"Run, Michla! Run!" Lewin shouted. He wanted to fight back but all he could do was place his hands over his head and face to shield the blows.

Two of the attackers were women, and as Lewin tumbled to the ground he saw them strike Michla on the back and head with their fists. Michla screamed wildly with a blood-curdling howl, and several men from the neighborhood—members of the synagogue whom they'd only met that evening—rushed to their aid. They confronted the attackers, meeting their aggression with fists of their own, and one had a belt that he used like a whip.

More men came from the houses nearby and joined in the defense of Michla, Lewin, and the boys, and soon the defenders outnumbered the attackers by three to one. Facing defeat, and supposing perhaps that a beating might be at hand, the attackers retreated to the shadows with shouts of, "Go home, Jew!"

"Get out of here, Kike!"

"We don't want your kind around here."

As the attackers dispersed, the men who intervened assisted Lewin to his feet, then checked on the boys and Michla. When no one seemed to be badly injured, Aaron Feldman—one of the responders—suggested, "Let's take them to my house so we can check them in the light."

Feldman's house was located not too far from where Lewin and Michla lived. His wife was waiting on the porch as the men escorted them up the sidewalk. Feldman's wife and daughter patched up Lewin and Michla, while others from the neighborhood doted on the children. When they'd been properly tended to, someone appeared with a tray of small cakes and a pot of coffee.

Not long after that, Edward Talmy entered the front room and announced, "The group that attacked them appears to be from the Crimson Legion."

"How do you know that?"

"They were seen at the Crimson Legion rally earlier this year. They are the same people who were out there before the service began."

Moshe Eckstein spoke up. "My brother recognized one of them. His name is Mullins, from one of the textile mills. Boatwright, he thinks. No one seems to know any of the others."

Feldman looked over at Lewin. "You work at the armory, right?"

"Yes," Lewin replied. "I work in the building next to yours. I only started recently."

"Anyone give you any trouble?"

"One."

"Who was it?"

"The tag on his shirt said his name is Luther Bogard." Lewin told the men about what Bogard said and about the person who previously operated the press.

Feldman seemed to understand. "Bogard hates Jews."

"Why?"

"I'm not really sure."

"No one is," Eckstein added.

"What about the man who ran the press?" Lewin asked. "The one he mentioned."

"That was Fritz Schoenberg. He and Bogard didn't get along."

"What happened to Schoenberg?"

"The machine jammed. He reached in to free it up without turning it off and the press came down on his hand. Cut it off at the wrist. Almost died."

"He's still alive?"

"Yes. They kept him at the armory, too. Moved him to shipping as a supervisor."

"Was Bogard responsible for the accident?"

"No. It was Fritz's own fault."

Talmy spoke up. "He'd been told how to clear the machine and he ignored that instruction."

"I think you will be fine there," Feldman assured. "Just do your work. Don't call attention to yourself, and you'll be okay. I don't think Bogard will come looking for trouble."

"At least not trouble that can be traced back to him," Eckstein added.

"He needs his job just like all the rest of us," Feldman noted. "He wasn't one of the people who attacked you tonight, anyway."

"So far as we know," Talmy added.

"Yes," Feldman conceded. "So far as we know, none of the people who attacked you tonight work for the armory."

Lewin nodded. "So I should be safe at work?"

"Yes," Feldman said. "But be careful and always pay attention."

CHAPTER 15

For Mullins, events of the past months—attending the Crimson Legion rally, meeting Grace, then gathering with her friends on weekends and protesting outside the synagogue—transformed his life, his sense of self, his understanding of who he was and of the things that mattered most. He continued to work in the shop at the mill in Indian Orchard, but now he saw that work in a different light.

Emboldened by the weekend meetings at Peggy and Jimmy Clayton's home, and by the protests they were conducting, Mullins was no longer content to merely work at the mill and collect his pay. He now saw politics in everything—the things he did, the things he thought, the things he read—and he responded with a political perspective on every topic.

As a result, Mullins no longer viewed Sidney Gardner, the pro-union co-worker who lived at the boardinghouse, as merely an arrogant, self-assured pretender. As part of the union-organizing cabal, he was a genuine threat to American life.

Mullins's view of the union role was also transformed. No longer a troubling waste of time, he now saw it as a serious threat. He agreed with many of their stated aims, but after listening to Walter Jones, reading the Crimson Legion newspaper, and listening to Griffin at the rally, the Communist influences that drove the politics and doctrine behind the organizing effort became a problem for him. And having equated Communists with Jews, he found comparing the organizers with both of those groups a logical conclusion, which left him increasingly adamant in his opposition to their efforts.

Not long after the group that met at the Claytons' stepped up to conduct protests outside the synagogue, Mullins decided to express his opposition to the unions, too. That expression came by attending a union meeting—a risky venture, considering the brawl that erupted from his comments the last time he attended. This time, however, Mullins went with the purpose of noting the things that were said by the organizers—Erwin Beal among them—and active employees like Gardner. He had no intention of speaking out that evening.

Mullins arrived at the Masonic Lodge building—the same location where union organizers conducted the meeting before—having come directly from work. He was dressed in the clothes he wore to the shop that day. As he approached the building entrance, several of his co-workers recognized him and confronted him while he still was outside.

"You here to make trouble again?" one of them demanded.

"Not tonight," Mullins replied. "Just here to listen."

"See that you do," another ordered as he passed by. "Or you'll get what's coming to you this time."

"Yeah," another chimed in. "If there's any mouth from you, you won't be able to slink off with your pal Kugler this time."

Mullins did his best to ignore them and continued inside. He found an empty seat about halfway up from the back and was just relaxing when three big, muscular men acting as security for the meeting confronted him.

"You gotta leave," one of them told him in a gruff voice.

Mullins gave him a sullen look. "And if I don't?"

"That ain't an option," the man snarled as he grabbed Mullins by the arm to lift him from the chair while the other two took hold of his legs. Together, they lifted him from his seat and carried him toward the exit. The crowd cheered them all the way to the door, and they continued outside to the sidewalk, where they dropped Mullins on the pavement.

"If you come inside again," the first one growled, "they'll carry you out on a stretcher."

Mullins stood and dusted himself off. He thought about trying again but he was sure trouble would follow. With no one there to help, he thought it best to leave and caught the next trolley headed toward Mrs. Smithson's boardinghouse.

✦ ✦ ✦

The following Sunday, Mullins accompanied Grace to the gathering at Peggy and Jimmy Clayton's house. As they ate, he told the group about his experience earlier that week at the union meeting. Pete Lawler suggested he attend the meetings and speak up.

"I already did that," Mullins said. "Which is why they wouldn't let me stay."

"What happened?"

"I spoke up."

"And tell them the rest," Grace urged.

Mullins grinned. "Some men came over to throw me out—not as big as the ones this last time—and a huge fight broke out."

"The police came and everything," Grace added.

Peggy looked alarmed. "You were there?"

"No. But he told me about it." Grace ran her hand over Mullins's arm and looked over at him. "I was very proud of you. I *am* very proud of you."

"A huge fight resulted," Mullins added. "I was thrown out. They know who I am and won't let me back in their meetings."

"Well," Jimmy said, "you can always stand outside and talk to people as they come for the meeting."

"And as they leave," Pete added. "They can't stop you from doing that."

"I hadn't thought of that," Mullins replied. "I might give it a try."

✦ ✦ ✦

A few days later, notices circulated through the shop about an upcoming union meeting. Mullins made a note of the date and time. On the night of the meeting, he appeared outside the meeting hall. As employees walked by, several of them stopped to speak to him.

"Are you back again?" Owen Fletcher asked.

"I'm back to rescue you," Mullins told him.

Fletcher looked perplexed. "What do we need rescuing from?"

"The Jews who are trying to control your life," Mullins pointed out. "Can't you see that?"

"What Jews? Is this more of what you've been talking about at work?"

Jerome Gilbert walked up. "What has he been talking about?"

"Jews," Fletcher answered.

"I hate Jews," Gilbert spat.

"Mullins does, too," Fletcher noted. "And he's out here telling everyone about it."

"Not content to just tell us at the shop?"

"Nope."

Mullins tried to continue. "Look, all I'm saying is, you need to think about what you're getting into with the unions." As succinctly as he could, Mullins outlined his argument, speaking loudly enough for the crowd that was gathering around him to hear: "Unions are for collective bargaining—all workers joining together to pressure owners for concessions. Everyone working for the good of the whole. A collective idea and collective approach are, at their heart, Communist. Communism proposes that we all pool everything while people at the top divvy it up as they see fit."

Gilbert's eyes were wide in a look of realization. "Is that what you were trying to tell us at work?"

"Yes," Mullins replied.

"Then, what was all that stuff about Jews?"

"International Jews like the ones we're dealing with right here, right now—sponsored the Communist revolution in Russia, which is where all of these collective ideas came from. And it wouldn't surprise me one bit to know that the union organizers who have descended upon us—Erwin Beal included—are Jews."

As Mullins and the others talked, Sidney Gardner came over. He listened a moment, then said, "You're crazy, Mullins. Offering these men nothing but baseless theories and passing it off as genuine insight."

"They're not baseless."

"I'd call them stupid," Gardner added, "except you're not stupid, and I don't want to get in a fight." He looked around at the men. "Pay no attention to him, boys. Mullins is a troublemaker. That's all. Just out here trying to stir things up. They threw him out of the last two meetings for being disruptive. And that's all he's here to do. He just wants to keep you from doing anything to help yourselves."

"They threw me out because I was telling the truth!" Mullins shouted. "They didn't want me in their meetings because they don't want you to know what they are really doing. Unions are a front for Communist Jews who want to take over your life! They only want to place themselves between you and your employer so they can make money off your labor."

Gardner yelled, "No! We're just workers who labor like slaves the same as you do. Only, we're the slaves who want to set you free and get you paid like freedmen."

A few in the crowd cheered. Mullins waved them off.

"We need help," Mullins acknowledged. "But these union guys are Communists and Jews—the kind who are out to take over the world. And to do that, they need you all in one place, trapped in a job that barely pays your bills while offering you no hope of advancement. Think about it. If you join the union, they get the right to bargain on your behalf. They control the conditions under which you work and the pay you receive for it. And they won't do it for free. You'll pay union dues once you join. Every month. Cut right out of your pay before you even see it. That's all the organizers are after. They only want your money. Unions may talk a good game, but all they want is to enslave you to a different master."

Gardner looked over at him and lowered his voice. "What's your solution?"

"Ending immigration is the key," Mullins replied. "We have to stop the Jews and other immigrants like them from coming here. Keep them from bringing their Communist ideas and racial impurities to our country. And keep them from influencing us with their aberrant lifestyle. If they aren't here, they can't attack our American way of life or steal jobs that ought to go to descent, hardworking Americans. And then we should—"

Before Mullins could finish, a group of union security men much like the ones who threw him out of the last meeting shoved their way through the crowd. Behind them came four police officers. The disruption spawned pushing and shoving among the workers who were listening to Mullins and Gardner. The union security men got caught up in the fracas that was about to unfold, but the officers plowed their way ahead, shoving men aside and whacking a few with their nightsticks.

When the first policeman reached Mullins, he got right up next to him and looked him in the eye. "You need to move along. Mr. Beal doesn't want you here."

"You work for Beal now?" Mullins asked sarcastically. "I thought you were city police."

The officer gave him a shove. "I said get moving."

Mullins stood his ground. "Officer, this is a public sidewalk I'm standing on. I have a right to be here and to say my piece, just like anybody else."

The officer took him by the arm. "And I got a right to run you in." He gave Mullins a shove. "But I don't want to take the time to haul you downtown. So get moving. And don't come back."

Mullins stumbled to one side, then twisted free of the officer's grasp and started up the street.

✦ ✦ ✦

Later that week, Mullins and Grace went to dinner with Pete and Ida at a restaurant in downtown Springfield. While they ate, they talked about Mullins's experiences at the union meeting and about what they could do next to express their political concerns.

"We have to do more," Mullins stressed. "Protest more. Get more violent. There must be more we can do."

Grace looked concerned. "Did you see those children last time?"

Ida frowned. "What about them?"

"They were terrified."

"The ones when we confronted those people outside Temple Beth El?"

"Yes."

"They're supposed to be terrified," Pete said. "That's the whole point."

"I know," Grace insisted. "But it looked worse than I thought it would."

"Confrontations like that might be a little too personal. But we have to do something."

Pete grinned. "We could torch the place."

"The synagogue?" Grace asked.

"Yeah."

Mullins shook his head. "That's too drastic. We need something that makes our point—that Jews aren't welcome here—but doesn't risk killing someone. We don't want to get charged with murder."

Pete still seemed amused. "What if we get a load of pigs and run them through the synagogue?" he laughed. "That would be funny. Pigs in a Jewish synagogue."

Mullins's eyes lit up. "I like that idea!"

Ida nodded. "Me too." Grace didn't respond but nodded along with the others.

As they left the restaurant, Mullins took Pete aside. "Don't tell anyone about the pigs-in-the-synagogue idea."

Pete seemed surprised. "Why not? You were really interested in it before."

"That's just it," Mullins replied. "I *am* interested. But I don't want too many people to know about it. Just you and me for now."

"Ida and Grace already know."

"Grace won't talk. And I assume Ida won't, either."

"I'll remind her."

"Good." Mullins gave him a pat on the shoulder. "We'll meet alone later. Just you and me. We'll work out the details between us."

After saying good-bye, Mullins and Grace walked back to Aunt Rose's house. Along the way they talked again about what had happened at the synagogue and about the reaction from the people they attacked. Grace repeated some of what she'd said inside the café. "Those kids were really scared."

"I know," Mullins replied. "But you have to realize, they'll be adults one day."

"But they looked so terrified."

"That's probably a good thing. We want them terrified."

"It just doesn't seem right. I mean, what if we had children and something like that happened with them?"

He looked over at her. "You think we might one day have children?"

"Maybe." She grinned. "You never know."

When they arrived at her aunt's house, Mullins leaned over and kissed her. She smiled up at him. "You want to come inside?"

"Your aunt is probably still awake. She won't mind?"

"She likes you. But she isn't home." She ran her finger over his arm. "She left this morning and she'll be gone all week."

He looked hopeful. "Really?"

Grace took his hand. "Come on." She tugged him playfully toward the house. "Let's go inside."

CHAPTER 16

Although Mullins said little about it at the time, the incident outside the union meeting affected him in ways he had not expected. Most notably, in the form of doubt. Despite the things he'd said on the sidewalk outside the hall, and despite the things he'd said to Pete and Ida that day in the café, doubt began to grow about whether the claims he made against the union were true. Perhaps it was from the things he heard himself say. Or the arguments Sidney Gardner made. Or the questions his fellow employees raised. Maybe the look in their eyes as he spoke or the intensity in their voices. Some indescribable, intangible something made him wonder if the things he said really were true. Or accurate. He still hated the Jews—nothing about that had changed—and he hated the Italians. He hated everyone who had anything to do with the war that killed his brother. But the unions ...Were they really Communist inspired? Were they the threat he perceived them to be? Or was the evidence that pointed in that direction merely circumstantial in nature?

Mullins wrestled with those questions through several Friday protests and Sunday gatherings, but after finding no resolution, he turned to Jimmy Clayton for help. They met at a café after work to discuss the matter.

"So," Jimmy began, "tell me what's on your mind."

"You know the unions are active in several of the mills."

"Yes, everyone knows that. We've talked about that with the others, too."

"They've been particularly busy where I work."

"I'm sure management would agree with you."

"Yeah, but that's just because they think if the unions get organized, they'll have to pay more in wages."

"And that's probably correct."

"I don't mind that part."

"Then, what's the issue?"

"My problem is with the underlying assumption," Mullins explained. "The collective idea."

"All for one and that sort of thing?"

"Yes. It sounds like Communism to me."

"A lot of people would agree with you on that, but it's the only way an individual can have any effective voice. A single employee can't bargain with an employer in a situation like you have with the mills."

"But is it the same thing as Communism?"

"Well, it's not being imposed on you by the government."

"No. But the result is the same," Mullins noted. "If the owners recognize the union and agree to negotiate with them, everyone will be forced to join. We'll all become part of a collective whether we want it or not."

"I never thought about it like that."

"And there's something else bothering me, too. The organizers working with the employees at Boatwright all came here from somewhere else."

"Right," Jimmy nodded. "They're outsiders. There were several articles in the newspaper about that."

"Exactly. The organizers claim to be experienced and credentialed in advocating for worker rights. And they claim to be involved for our sake. But no one really knows much about them. Not actually."

Jimmy had a puzzled look. "And you thought I might know about them?"

"I thought you might be able to find out. Maybe with your contacts from the bank or something."

Jimmy seemed flattered by the request. "Do you have a name?"

"The main one is a guy named Erwin Beal," Mullins said. "But there's a guy named Charlie Bagley, too. And there are others."

"You've mentioned someone named Gardner."

"Yeah. Sidney Gardner. He's a smart guy, but he's just an employee. I've known him for as long as I've worked at the mill. He's just a regular guy who likes being in the know. The people driving this thing are the union organizers." Mullins took a note from his pocket and handed it to Jimmy. "These are the ones I know about."

Jimmy glanced at the list, then tucked it into the pocket of his jacket. "I'll see what I can find out."

✦ ✦ ✦

The following Sunday, Mullins and Grace gathered with the others in the Claytons' living room. They arrived early and while they waited, Jimmy took Mullins aside. "I did some research and asked around about those people on that list you gave me."

Mullins asked, "Did you find anything interesting?"

"Yeah. At least one of the organizers in your mill appears to be Jewish—Max Wikler. Ever hear of him?"

Mullins shook his head. "No, but there are several organizers working the plant. It wouldn't surprise me to know there are some I haven't seen."

Jimmy nodded in agreement. "Apparently that's part of their technique. Send in a team. Divide them up. Send them around to different places. That way they appear to be everywhere."

"Who is he?"

"Wikler came up here from Brooklyn. My people say he's got some muscle behind him."

Mullins was puzzled. "Muscle?"

"Italians."

Mullins's eyes opened wider. "The Mob?"

"Yes."

"So, it's true." Mullins grinned. "Jews and Italians really are causing trouble. And working together, too."

"At least part of them."

"You mean the Mob?"

"Yes."

Mullins chuckled. "Jews for the money. Mob for the muscle."

"Looks like it."

Mullins sighed. "We gotta stop these people. Stop them from taking over and stop them from coming here."

"That'll be tough to do," Jimmy noted. "I know Walter Jones talks about it like it could be done. And it might be possible. But it will be tough to get laws passed to do it."

"Why?"

"Politicians love them," Jimmy responded.

"The Jews?"

"Yeah. They have the money to make big political contributions. And they do it, too."

"Payoffs," Mullins snarled.

Jimmy shrugged, "Well, Jews and Italians know how to grease things with money."

Mullins shook his head. "Politicians who take money like that should be shot."

As more people continued to arrive, Jimmy led Mullins back to the living room and they joined the group that had gathered there. Conversation seemed labored, however, and as they talked, it occurred to Mullins that everyone wanted to talk about something other than politics. As the evening wore on, he thought more about who they were as a group and the manner in which things had developed since the time he joined.

At first, they had been content to merely sit and talk about the issues of the day. Gossip, mostly, but nothing more. With his encouragement, they had conducted protests outside several of Springfield's synagogues, but after showing initial enthusiasm for the work, participation began to dwindle. In recent weeks, fewer and fewer attended. And as he listened that evening, Mullins began to wonder if the group had the heart for the real work that needed to be done to address the ills the country faced. However, as he listened more closely he realized they weren't so much losing heart as they were bored with the sameness of their activities.

In an effort to spur the group toward action, Mullins turned the conversation to a different topic and again raised the issue of union activity in Springfield mills. This time, however, he avoided a direct appeal for their involvement and instead asked for suggestions of things he could do, framing the issue in terms of himself, not the group.

Peggy suggested, "You could make some handbills and pass them out."

Someone else thought Mullins should organize a counter group. "You know. A group of employees at the mill that support change but oppose the unions."

"You could use the handbills Peggy mentioned to promote it. Pass them around to your co-workers."

Ida pointed across the room to Matthew Thorpe, a new member. "Matthew could help you prepare the handbills."

Thorpe, who worked in advertising for the Springfield newspaper, seemed agreeable. "Yeah, get me a piece of paper and I'll sketch something for you now." Peggy found an empty envelope in the trash and brought it to him. While the others continued to talk, Thorpe drew the outline of a handbill on the back of the envelope.

A quick idea for a piece that suggested the union organizers were part of an international Jewish conspiracy determined to impose Communism on the US.

"I'll need a place and time for your meeting," Thorpe informed them. "We'll need to include it in the handbill."

"Okay," Mullins reacted. "I'll figure that part out and let you know."

"I can get them printed for you, too," Thorpe added.

After the gathering ended that night, Mullins walked Grace home. As they strolled along the sidewalk, she glanced up at him. "Are you really going to do this?"

"Do what?" he asked.

"Organize a group at work."

"Yeah. I think I will. Why?"

"It's just that. . .if you do it—if you pass out handbills at the mill and invite everyone to a meeting—it will mark a break with the past."

"A break?" He didn't understand what she meant.

"They'll know what you stand for and they'll see you in a different way."

Mullins was dismissive. "Most of them already know where I stand."

"Still," Grace insisted. "Things are gonna change. They'll see you in a different light."

"So, what are you saying?"

"I'm saying, are you sure you want to do this?"

"Yes," he answered. "I think I must."

"Okay." Grace took his hand in hers. "Then I'll help you. What should we do to make it happen?"

"I guess we should figure out where to hold the meeting."

"I can take care of that," she offered.

Mullins was surprised. "Really?"

"If you don't mind using a church as your first meeting place."

Mullins shrugged. "I guess not."

✦ ✦ ✦

True to what she said, Grace arranged for Mullins to conduct his meeting in the fellowship hall of the Congregational Church where she and her aunt attended. Two weeks later, Thorpe produced the handbills and Mullins passed them around to his co-workers at the mill. He was surprised by the number of positive responses he received.

On the appointed evening, a dozen men showed up at the fellowship hall, and Mullins conducted the meeting. He had examples of the newspapers from Walter Jones and the Crimson Legion for attendees to review, along with a copy of the *Protocols*, which he urged them to read. And he told them where to find Jones's broadcast on the radio. But he spent most of the time making his argument against the union, a position he now held with confidence after talking to Jimmy Clayton.

"The union's basic approach," Mullins began, "is to organize us under their control. Force us to bargain with the mill through them. That, my friends, is nothing but Communism."

Ryan Wilson interrupted. "I've been saying that from the beginning."

"And Communism, which you will find out when you read some of the literature I was showing you, is nothing more than a scam created by the Jews as a tool for taking control of the world."

"I've been telling them that, too," Wilson added.

Mullins continued. "We now have confirmation that at least one of the union organizers is Jewish. And people in a position to know say he has the help of the Italian Mob behind him. If Jews are involved, they aren't interested in anything but the money. And so are the Italians. Jews for the money. Italians for the muscle. Why do they need muscle? Because people are starting to learn the truth. And they don't want you to know the truth. They have no intention of following through on their promises of giving us a better life. All they want is to control the workers as a way of controlling the company and ultimately the economy."

"Hey!" Evan Simpson exclaimed. "That's the truth." He sounded as if he just then realized something that should have been obvious. "Think about what they've said they want us to do. They want us to slow down production, which puts our jobs in jeopardy. And if that doesn't convince the owners to listen to us, they want us to go out on strike."

"Which is something the owners have already said will cost us our jobs," Wilson added. "They'll fire us if we do that."

Someone else spoke up. "And they have people just waiting to take our places. They'll replace us with a whole new crew if they have to. They don't care."

"And why do the union organizers want us to do that?" Evans looked around at those in the room. "Why do they want us to do something they know will get us fired? Have any of you asked yourself that question?"

Mullins once again took control of the moment. "Yes, *why* is the question. *Why* do they want you out? *Why* did these people from outside Springfield come all the way out here to western Massachusetts? They didn't come here out of love for you. They're here for their own purposes. They are Jews sent by Jews and backed by Italians. An unholy faction that means to take over our businesses and destroy our way of life. And all so they can make a dollar off the sweat of your brow and the labor of your back."

When Mullins concluded his remarks, several of the men seemed anxious to help. "What can we do?" someone asked. "We can't just sit around here talking about this stuff. We need to do something."

Simpson spoke up. "We need to stop the takeover of the mill."

Lawrence Jackson, who had been quietly listening, suggested,

"What if we stand outside the meeting hall and confront them." He looked over at Mullins. "Like you did a few weeks ago. They can't stop us from doing that."

"And if the employees see more of us out there," Wilson added, "maybe some of them will start to realize what's going on."

Simpson had a mischievous look. "What if we not only did that but also went inside to the meeting. Then we could speak up and raise questions. If we did that, and backed each other up, some of the guys might be convinced."

"We could at least be disruptive."

"We're good at that."

"We might do that once," Jackson cautioned. "But if we go a second time and try to get inside, they'll have thugs there to beat us up before we get past the door."

"I know a little something about that," Mullins quipped.

The men laughed at Mullins's allusion to his prior experience with the union, then Wilson said, "You could stay *outside* while we take care of what happens *inside*."

Someone added, "A brawl might be just what we need to call attention to the situation."

✦ ✦ ✦

A few days later, Mullins and his men gathered after work and walked over to the Masonic Lodge for a scheduled union meeting. When they reached the corner near the building, Wilson and the others came to a halt. "You stay here," Wilson advised. "We'll go on to the meeting."

"It feels strange not going with you," Mullins said.

"If you go," Simpson offered, "there'll be trouble right from the start. They won't let us anywhere near the door."

"I know. "It's just—"

Wilson cut him off. "It feels like this was your idea and now you're bailing on us?"

Mullins had a sheepish expression. "Something like that."

"Well, it wasn't your idea," Simpson noted.

"Not yours alone," Wilson added. "We came up with it together." He patted Mullins on the shoulder. "Keep a sharp eye out for us."

Mullins lingered on the sidewalk near the corner and watched while the others made their way to the building entrance and confronted workers as they arrived. He was too far away to hear what was said, but he saw the crowds gathered in clusters at the front of the building and knew his men were speaking up. Speaking out. Hoping to make the others think.

Twenty minutes later, the men moved inside the meeting hall, and Mullins moved from his position at the corner to have a closer view of the building. At first, all seemed quiet and orderly and he wondered if anything would come of their effort to raise issues with the organizers inside. Then he heard shouts from inside, faint at first but steadily growing louder and angrier.

A smile came to him as he imagined the scene that must be unfolding. Wilson on his feet, calmly addressing a speaker who stood at the podium. Simpson supporting him loudly and urging the others to do the same. And union supporters arguing back over the shouts from the stage for order.

In a few minutes, three black cars came up the street and screeched to a halt near the building's side entrance. As the cars came to a stop, the doors flew open and a dozen men piled out. Italians, by the look of them. Thugs, Mullins presumed. He was certain they were Mob guys and as he watched, they entered the hall. Many of them carried clubs. All of them looked grim and determined.

With his men in obvious danger, Mullins pushed his way past the guards at the main entrance and entered the meeting hall. Sure enough, Wilson was on his feet, arguing in a loud voice with an organizer who stood at the podium. Simpson stood nearby leading others from the group in support of Wilson. As the thugs poured into the room and charged in their direction, Mullins did, too.

Several of Mullins's men saw what was happening and jumped to their feet, blocking the aisle and preventing the thugs from reaching Wilson or Simpson. The men wrestled, each one trying to gain control of the other, until finally a fight broke out. Soon everyone in the hall was involved, chairs swinging, fists flying, and angry voices shouting curse words.

Mullins joined the fight and managed to land a few good punches—one on Brewster, the worker from the shop, and another on the jaw of a thug who'd come for Simpson—but then the police arrived. Officers waded into the crowd, swinging their nightsticks left and right to break it up. In the confusion, Mullins and his men slipped out a side door and escaped.

✦ ✦ ✦

The next morning, Mullins hopped off the trolley and walked toward the mill, wondering what kind of response he might receive that day from his co-workers. He arrived in the shop to find Kugler waiting for him.

"Don't start on me," he warned before Kugler could speak. "Whatever you have to say about the meeting, I'm sure I'll hear it from someone else. And I—"

Kugler cut him off. "Wait! I don't care about that meeting. In fact, if I had been there, which I wasn't, but if I *had* been there, I would have joined the fight on your side. I hear it was quite a big one."

"Yes, it—"

"But wait," Kugler interrupted again. "Mr. Thompson wants to see you upstairs. They said to send you up as soon as you arrived."

Mullins was worried. Hogan Thompson was the owner of the mill. A third-generation owner. Winthrop Boatwright, the founder of the mill, was his grandfather. "You're sure it was Mr. Thompson who wanted to see me?"

"Yes."

"It's not just Webster or somebody causing trouble?"

"Mr. Thompson's secretary came down here herself."

Mullins took Kugler's hand and shook it. "It's been nice working with you."

Kugler frowned. "What do you mean?"

"I'm sure he's going to fire me."

"I doubt it."

"Why?"

"He doesn't fire people. He has someone to do that kind of thing for him. You'd better go up there and find out what he wants. And don't go in there expecting the worst. Let him tell you what he wants before you start mouthing off."

"Right," Mullins sighed.

For safety, the shop was separated from the rest of the mill by an open lawn about forty yards wide. A sidewalk connected the two buildings. Mullins strode from the shop through the side exit and followed the walkway to the main building, then walked through to the administrative wing. Mr. Thompson's secretary greeted him and ushered him toward the office.

"He's waiting for you."

"Any idea what this is about?"

"Not really. He just said for me to come get you first thing." She led Mullins into the office, then stepped out and closed the door behind her.

Thompson looked up from the work on his desk. "Have a seat," gestured to the chair that sat near the desk. Mullins took a seat and waited. "I heard about the union meeting last night."

"Yes, sir," Mullins replied.

"And I understand you and some of your co-workers have distinct ideas about unions."

"Yes, sir."

"Tell me about that."

Assuming he had nothing to lose, Mullins reported, "I think the unions are an instrument of International Jews. They're Communists and they mean to take over. Not only the workers but the mill, too." Mullins paused for effect and looked Thompson in the eye. "Your mill."

Thompson nodded in agreement. "Jews are a big problem." He took a newspaper from a stack of documents on his desk and tossed it toward Mullins. "Ever seen this?"

Mullins glanced at the paper and saw the masthead identified it as the *Dearborn Independent*. "No, sir, I have not."

An article on the front page appeared to be intensely anti-Semitic, though, and he was immediately intrigued. Still, he wasn't sure what Thompson wanted or why he sent for him, so he leaned forward to return to the paper.

"No, no," Thompson waved him off. "Keep it. I have plenty more copies and I would like for you to have that one."

Mullins laid the paper on his lap. "Thank you."

"I called you up here," Thompson continued, "because I need your help."

A frown wrinkled Mullins's forehead. "My help? What kind of help could I possibly give you?"

"I would like for you to continue your work in opposition to the union."

"That won't be difficult. I'm very much opposed to them."

"Union organizers and the Jews who promote them are out to destroy not only this mill and this town, but everything that is good about America. We have to stop them."

"Union organizers tell the men they can force you to recognize them. Some of them believe it."

Thompson's expression was cold and hard. "I'll never give them a union! I'll close the plant before I let that happen."

"I've tried to tell them that. A few of the men believe it. The ones who are with me. But not many of the others."

"That's what I need from you." Thompson leaned forward to make his point. "I need you to make sure the men know my position. Maybe they'll listen to you."

"I'll do my best," Mullins replied.

✦ ✦ ✦

That night after dinner, Mullins sat in his room at Mrs. Smithson's boardinghouse and read the copy of the *Dearborn Independent* he had received from Hogan Thompson. The articles it contained seemed to speak to him even more deeply than the ones he'd read by Walter Jones or in the Crimson Legion paper. A notice on the last page offered a free subscription to anyone who wrote to the paper's office. Mullins prepared a letter that evening and placed it in the basket downstairs for the next day's mail.

CHAPTER 17

Not long after his meeting with Thompson, Mullins received a pay raise and a promotion to the position of shop foreman's assistant. He continued to see Grace every weekend at her aunt's home in Springfield, and they continued to meet with friends at the Claytons' house on the weekends.

However, most of Mullins's time and attention during the week was devoted to the group of co-workers he'd gathered to oppose the union. In the weeks that followed, he convinced each of them to subscribe to the *Dearborn Independent* and to the newspapers from Walter Jones and the Crimson Legion. They read the books suggested by articles in each of those papers and devoted a portion of their meetings to discussing them. Gradually, Simpson, Wilson, and the others began to see themselves as committed to a much larger purpose than merely opposing the union.

At a meeting a few weeks later, Simpson brought up the question of a name. "We need something to call ourselves."

"A group name?"

"Yeah."

"We began by opposing the union," Wilson noted. "What about the Free Labor Movement?"

Mullins nodded. "That's a good idea. But if we use that name, union organizers will use it against us."

"How so?"

"They'll say we want to work for free," Mullins explained.

"And they'll tell everyone we're just pawns of the owners."

"We're certainly not anti-owners," Simpson blurted out.

"We're anti-*unionists*," Wilson emphasized.

"Non-unionists."

"I'm just tired of being exploited," someone added.

"We're independent."

Wilson's expression brightened. "The Independent Labor Movement."

Mullins deflected that suggestion. "We've actually come to have a bigger image of ourselves than merely opposition to organized labor. Maybe we need a bigger name."

"Not movement," Simpson said, "but what about 'league'?"

"Or 'legion'?"

"The Independent Labor Legion."

Mullins shook his head. "Too much alliteration."

Someone suggested, "What about just calling ourselves the Crimson Legion?"

Wilson shook his head. "I'm not sure we can just take their name."

"Can't we find out?" Simpson asked. "That would be a good name."

Mullins wrapped up the meeting. "I'll see what can be done."

✦ ✦ ✦

Later that week, Mullins met Grace for dinner at a café not far from her house. While they ate, they talked and eventually she brought up the group of co-workers that he'd been meeting with at the church. "Are they still interested in opposing the union?"

"Yes, but they're talking about bigger ideas now, too."

"Bigger?"

"More than just opposing the union."

"That's good."

"But, they need a project to go with it. Something to do besides heckling men who attend union meetings."

"They're interested in something else?"

"Yes," he responded. "They've been reading Jones's and Griffin's newspapers and they're fired up for something bigger. They're interested in a name, too."

"A name?"

"Yeah. For the group. They don't have a name to call themselves."

"Did you ever think about forming them into a Crimson Legion chapter?"

Mullins smiled. "Actually, they brought that up at the last meeting. We were tossing around ideas for a name and someone suggested that very thing."

She nodded. "Why don't you?"

"I don't think we can just use it," Mullins replied. "Wouldn't we need permission?"

"I suppose you can ask."

"I told them I would contact the Crimson Legion office and see if it's possible."

"Have you?"

"Not yet."

"I can help you write a letter," she offered.

"I would appreciate that. But who should we contact at their office?"

"Do you need a name? Can't you simply write to the organization?"

"I think it would work better if we had a name."

"Then you should write to Mr. Griffin himself," she suggested.

"Do you think he would read it?"

"Probably. I'm sure if it's addressed to him, someone would take the time to read it."

"We could get the address from their newspaper."

"I have that at home."

As the hour grew late, Mullins suggested they call a taxi to get her home. She looked over at him. "Why not just walk me home?"

"I need to catch the trolley back to Indian Orchard, so I can get to work tomorrow."

She grinned in response. "I can wake you up in time for that."

He was puzzled. "Wake me up?"

"My aunt has gone to see a friend in Boston. She won't be back until the end of the week. We can have the place all to ourselves."

"I came here straight from work," Mullins said apologetically. "I'm rather dirty."

"We have a bathtub," she smiled seductively.

"Do you think it's okay for me to use it?"

"Why wouldn't it be?"

"I don't know."

"Besides," she added with a wink, "we might even have time to work on that letter you're wanting to write."

✦ ✦ ✦

With Grace's help, Mullins composed a letter to William Griffin, asking for official recognition for the Indian Orchard group. A few weeks later, he received a favorable response in a letter signed by Griffin himself, offering to officially recognize the Indian Orchard group as part of the Crimson Legion. The letter included an invitation for Mullins to meet with Crimson Legion leaders and suggested they do that following a rally scheduled in Charlotte a few weeks later.

Mullins and Grace were excited by the news and shared it with the group of friends that gathered at the Claytons' house. Someone suggested Mullins and Grace should attend the rally together, and everyone chipped in to help defray the cost of the trip.

Three weeks later, Mullins and Grace departed Springfield for the trip by train to Charlotte, North Carolina, to attend the Crimson Legion rally. It was an adventurous ride southward along the western edge of the Appalachian Mountains.

Eventually, the train crossed through a mountain pass and arrived in Charlotte late in the afternoon of the following day. They checked into a cheap hotel a few blocks from the station, posing as Mr. and Mrs. Gray and attended the rally that evening. As with the rally they attended in Springfield, the event began with local politicians who made short speeches to warm up the crowd. William Kimball Griffin—the Crimson Legion's founder and leader—was the featured speaker.

The following day, Mullins and Grace took a taxi from the hotel to the Legion's office where they were greeted by Dorothy Miller, a woman about Grace's height but easily ten years older. She was attractive, forthright, and obviously used to being in charge. She seemed immediately attracted to Mullins, laughing at his offhand comments and finding every opportunity to touch him on the arm or hand. None of which went unnoticed by Grace.

The office suite was cramped, every inch of space filled with desks, filing cabinets, and stacks of boxes that held Crimson Legion pamphlets and brochures. Dorothy guided them past the clutter to a small conference room that looked out over the street five floors below. They sat at a conference table that occupied most of the room and chatted a few minutes before being joined by Bradley Edwards and Kenneth Frost, junior staff members who seemed to hold nothing more than functionary roles. Just as everyone got comfortable, Paul Nesbit, a strikingly handsome young man, joined them and took a seat next to Dorothy. She seemed to have quite a bit of confidence in him and more than a little familiarity, placing her hand several times on the top of his thigh as she told a story about this or that.

The six of them talked about life in Charlotte, the differences between North Carolina and the places they'd come from—all of them, it turned out, were from somewhere else—and the challenges of working in close proximity to one another. Everyone seemed nervous and awkward, and Mullins wondered why until the door opened and Griffin appeared.

Tall and regal looking, with a commanding presence and an authoritative voice, Griffin was the kind of person who would take charge wherever he went. He'd enjoyed a successful career as a writer and had been in great demand as a featured speaker long before he thought of forming the Legion. As he entered the room, Mullins knew instantly why the others had been nervous.

Without waiting for introductions, Griffin reached over to Mullins and shook his hand. "You must be the man from Springfield."

"Yes, sir," Mullins replied.

Almost before the words were out of Mullins's mouth, Griffin turned to Grace. "And you came with him?"

"Yes," she answered.

"This is Grace Anderson," Mullins offered.

Griffin smiled at her but nodded his head in Mullins's direction. "I assure you, young lady, he is more delighted to have you with him than he shows. But not as glad as I am to make your acquaintance."

Grace smiled. "Thank you."

A single vacant chair sat near the end of the table and Griffin took a seat in it, as if he'd known all along it had been reserved for him. "So," he turned to Mullins, "you would like us to formally include your group as our chapter in Springfield."

"That is correct," Mullins answered.

Griffin looked over at Dorothy. "I don't believe we've ever formed a chapter in this manner, have we?"

"No sir, not officially. All of the others have been our idea from the beginning."

Griffin looked over at Grace. "You think this is a good idea?"

"Yes, sir," she replied. "I do."

He gestured toward Mullins, but his eyes were focused on Grace. "This young man you brought with you can do the job?"

"He formed the group on his own," Grace said proudly. "Educated them on the issues. And brought them to you. I think he's done an admirable job."

"Admirable." Griffin glanced at Dorothy. "That's a good word. You should use it, too."

"Yes, sir." Dorothy smiled. "That's an admirable idea."

Griffin ignored the pun and turned back to Mullins. "On a serious note, we're all very impressed by your work."

"I appreciate that."

Griffin continued. "We have been working loosely with a group in Springfield calling themselves the Knights of Teutonia. Are you aware of them?"

"I have met with them a few times."

"Oh?" Griffin seemed surprised. "What do you think of them?"

"They have some good ideas, but they're too German for me."

Griffin nodded. "That was our assessment as well." Dorothy seemed to acknowledge that point of view with a grin. "Not exactly a group with a broad appeal," Griffin continued, "but we didn't know about you when we were planning the rally."

"I think they are more interested in the Nazi cause than in the American one."

"Yes." Griffin had a serious expression. "But we would be pleased to have your group as a Legion chapter."

"Thank you, and we would be pleased to join you."

"You will, of course, come under our oversight," Griffin noted. "But that isn't a heavy-handed thing. We just want to make certain that all of the groups under our banner hold to the accepted line."

"And that's perfectly understandable," Mullins nodded.

"Good. Dorothy will prepare a certificate for you to show

you're now one of us. Something you can frame and hang on the wall."

Mullins grinned. "We're delighted to join the Legion."

"There's a lot of work to be done, Mr. Mullins. And I'm afraid we don't have much time to get that work accomplished. Jews are coming here by the thousands every day, and the politicians we have in Washington seem to think nothing of it. If our country is to be saved, we'll have to save it ourselves."

"I couldn't agree with you more," Mullins replied.

"Good." Griffin stood and the others in the room followed suit. "If there isn't anything more to do here, I suggest we all go to lunch."

✦ ✦ ✦

With their new designation as a Crimson Legion chapter, Mullins and the men he'd recruited to oppose the union expanded their reach to include several new members. One of the most motivated was Billy Cole, a store owner from Chicopee who had been searching for a group that identified with his political views. Pete Lawler and Johnny Farris from the Sunday-night group joined them as well.

A few weeks after the trip to Charlotte, Mullins moved their monthly meetings to a garage behind Johnny Farris's house. The first of those meetings also included Wilson, Simpson, Cole, and Lawler. As they gathered that evening over beer and sandwiches, Mullins declared, "We need a new action."

"What kind of action?" Simpson asked.

"One of the things the Crimson Legion is trying to do is to make life here miserable enough for Jews that they will choose to leave."

"And you think we should increase their level of misery?"

"Some of us have been going around to the synagogues on

Friday evening," Mullins explained. "Conducting protests. Others have continued to confront the union crowd down at the mill and at their meetings at the Masonic Lodge. But we need to do more."

Pete seemed beside himself with glee. "You know what we could do?"

"What's that, Pete?"

"We should do that pigs-in-the-synagogue thing I told you about earlier."

Johnny looked perplexed. "What are you talking about, Lawler?"

"We get a herd of pigs and turn them loose in the synagogue."

"Which synagogue?"

"The one over there—" He seemed to struggle to remember the name.

"Temple Beth El," Mullins added.

"Yeah." Pete's eyes were wide with excitement. "On Fort Pleasant Avenue." Everyone laughed except Pete. "I'm serious. We should really do it."

Mullins was noncommittal. "Where would we get the pigs?"

"We would need more than a few," Wilson chimed in. "If we're going to make a statement with them."

"I know a farmer who has pigs," Billy spoke up. "We would have to buy them, but I think he would be glad to sell them to us."

"If we put them in the building on a Sunday night," Simpson suggested, "there won't be anyone there. They could roam around in there for at least a day, maybe longer, before anyone found them."

"How much would it cost?" someone asked.

"I'll find out," Billy replied.

"We would need a truck to haul them with," Mullins added.

Pete spoke up. "I can get a truck. My uncle will loan me his. How many pigs are we getting?"

"As many as we can afford," Simpson suggested.

Billy shook his head. "No, only as many as Pete's truck will hold." They all laughed and had another beer.

✦ ✦ ✦

A few evenings later, Billy came to the boardinghouse. It was dark and Mullins was sitting on the porch talking to Bobby Rankin when he arrived. Billy stood near the street and waited while Mullins excused himself and joined him. "I found out the price of the pigs."

"How much?"

"A hundred fifty to two hundred pounder will cost us about ten dollars apiece."

"Cheaper than I expected."

"We'll need to get up some money to pay for them. I can front the whole thing if you need me to, and the others can pay me back."

"Nah, we should get them to pay up before we do this."

Billy had a puzzled look. "Are you having second thoughts?"

"No, I just don't want you to get stuck with it."

"Okay."

The next day, Mullins contacted Pete and put him in charge of asking the others for donations. Four days later, Owen Fletcher came to Mullins in the shop at the mill.

"My cousin—Pete Lawler—said to give this to you." He took an envelope from his hip pocket and handed it to Mullins. "He said you'd know what it was for."

"I know exactly what to do with it." Mullins took the envelope and slipped it into his front pocket.

Fletcher seemed concerned. "Are you sure you know what you're getting into?"

Mullins frowned. "What do you mean?"

"Pete talks a good game, but he's crazy as a loon. I'm about the only person in our family who still has anything to do with him."

Mullins grinned. "He can be a little excessive. I'll give you that."

"Just be careful." Fletcher turned away. "You never can tell with that guy."

✦ ✦ ✦

Shortly before noon the following Sunday, Pete arrived in Indian Orchard with his uncle's truck. Mullins waited for him on a street three blocks from the boardinghouse. As he climbed into the cab, Pete asked, "Did anyone see you?"

"I don't think so. That's why I chose the spot." Mullins slammed the door closed, and Pete steered the truck forward toward the next corner.

From Indian Orchard, they rode across town to Billy's house and picked him up, then continued toward the east side of town. Billy sat in the middle. Mullins rode with his arm propped on the window ledge.

As the truck started forward, Mullins turned to Billy. "How well do you know this farmer?"

"Well enough.'

"Will he keep quiet about what we're doing?"

Billy looked over at him. "What do you mean?"

"I mean is he going to brag about selling us a load of pigs?"

"I don't think so."

"What did you tell him?"

"I told him I was interested in buying a few pigs and that I had a couple of friends who would help me haul them."

"He didn't ask what the pigs were for?"

"No, and I don't think he will. Are you worried about something?"

"It's just that two dozen pigs rambling around inside a

building for a couple of days are going to create a big mess. There might be trouble from it and when people get mad, they sometimes call the police."

"He's a good guy," Billy offered. "He won't say anything. It'll be all right."

With Billy providing directions, they made their way to a farm located about two miles outside of town. The farmer had the pigs already separated and waiting in a pen. Mullins counted the money from the envelope and paid him. Loading them onto the truck took less than ten minutes, then they rode back to town.

When they arrived back in Springfield, Pete found a street on the south side with plenty of shade and parked the truck at the curb while they waited for it to get dark.

"That didn't take as long as I expected," Mullins commented.

"No," Billy agreed. "It didn't. We have more time than we need."

"Too much time," Pete suggested. "Someone will see us."

An hour or two later, there was a tap on the passenger window. Mullins leaned out to see a man standing beside the truck. "May I help you?"

"How long are you planning on sitting here?" the man asked.

"Does it matter?"

"Your pigs stink," the man answered. "I can smell them inside my house. My wife is beginning to complain."

"Okay," Mullins replied. "We'll move. Sorry. Didn't think about that."

Pete looked over at him. "We don't have anywhere else to go."

"I know," Mullins conceded. "But if we sit here, more people will notice. Someone will remember."

"He's right," Billy agreed. "That guy has already seen us. When news gets out about what we did with the pigs, someone will start connecting the dots." He gestured toward the street. "Let's go. I know a place where we can park."

From the south side, they followed a circuitous route that led to a warehouse in Chicopee. Pete leaned forward to look around. "Where can we park? I don't see a place."

"We can park inside." Billy pointed to the building. "Pull up to those doors."

The building was quite large and sat at a right angle to the street, with double doors on one end. Pete looked puzzled as he brought the truck to a stop in front of them. "Do you know the owner?"

"I *am* the owner," Billy replied.

Mullins and Billy climbed from the truck and opened the warehouse doors, then Pete drove the truck inside. When the truck came to a stop, Pete switched off the engine and crawled from the cab with a smile. "This is a good spot."

"I should have thought of this first," Billy replied.

Mullins took a seat on a crate. "All we need now is a beer."

"I would be satisfied with a nap," Pete yawned. He made his way to an empty pallet and took a seat, then lay back and closed his eyes. "Not exactly a bed," he complained. "But I'm not that particular." A few minutes later, he was sound asleep.

✦ ✦ ✦

An hour after dark, Mullins and Billy awakened Pete, who drove the truck to an alley behind the Beth El synagogue. The back door of the building was locked but Pete found a pry bar in the truck and used it to break open the lock.

Working as quickly and quietly as possible, they herded the pigs from the truck to the doorway and shooed them inside. When the last one was in, Billy pushed the doors closed and held them in place. "The lock's busted," he whispered. "We need something to fasten it with."

Mullins glanced over at Pete. "Look in the truck. See what

you can find."

A minute or two later, Pete returned with a length of rope and used it to tie the door handle to a post that held an awning in place. "That'll hold for a little while. But I don't know for how long."

"It won't take long," Mullins assured. "I think those pigs will make a big mess really quick." By the time they returned to the truck, all of them were laughing at what they'd done. Thoroughly satisfied with themselves, they climbed into the truck and drove away.

Caution, perhaps, might have suggested that they disband their collaboration and recede separately into the night. But none of them had much experience with mischief of the kind they'd just perpetrated. They also were quite satisfied with themselves for what they had done and the thought of going quietly away never crossed their minds.

Instead, they drove the truck to a diner not far from Indian Orchard, went inside as if they were regular customers, and took a seat in a corner booth. Customers stared at them as they walked by, and Mullins noticed one or two pointing in their direction but thought nothing of it and sat with the others while they waited for service.

A waitress soon appeared at their table. "You guys smell like a pig farm."

Billy looked up at her. "You noticed?"

"Noticed?" she laughed. "I couldn't miss it." She pointed to a couple seated at a table near the door. "Neither did they."

Mullins looked in that direction and saw the couple looking back at him. "They complained about us?"

"Yes." The waitress grinned. "And for good reason."

"Why's that?"

"You stink."

"Does that mean we have to leave?" Pete asked. "I'm really hungry."

"What'll you have?" she asked.

They ordered quickly, and when the waitress was gone, Mullins looked over at Pete. "So much for not being noticed."

"Don't worry about it," Pete laughed. "Ain't nothing going to come of it."

Mullins wasn't so sure about that. He didn't like being noticed by the customers and he was certain they'd made an impression on the waitress, too. Still, he had a deep sense of satisfaction over what they had done. Finally they were doing something. Something big. Something important. Something that mattered. And not just standing on the sidewalk across from the synagogue and heckling Jews. *Pigs in the synagogue.* The thought of it and the mess that surely would follow put a grin on his face. He couldn't wait to tell Grace. She would be as excited as he.

✦ ✦ ✦

One of the people in the diner that evening was Raymond Fry, an employee at the Boatwright mill who had been helping Charlie Bagley, one of the union representatives who was present at the first union meeting Mullins attended. Fry worked upstairs in one of the weaving rooms and had no interaction with the shop. But he recognized Mullins from having seen him during the brawl at the first meeting Mullins attended.

Fry finished eating quickly and left the diner while Mullins and the others still were in the corner booth. He went straight away to a cottage that Charlie Bagley had rented on Tyler Street in Old Hill and told him what he'd seen. "They're up to something," he suggested.

"Like what?" Bagley wondered.

"I don't know. But I've heard rumors about Mullins and attacks on Jews."

"What kind of rumors?"

"People say he and some others have been going to the synagogue on Friday night. They stand outside heckling Jews as they come to worship, then attack them and beat them up when they leave to go home after dark."

Bagley nodded thoughtfully. "And you think this pig smell Mullins and his friends brought into the diner had something to do with that?"

"I don't know. I'm just saying it's suspicious. And Mullins was with Pete Lawler."

"That means something?" Bagley asked. "Him being with Lawler."

"Lawler's stark-raving mad, sir. His own cousin says so."

"You talked to his cousin?"

"Yeah. He works at the mill."

"Well . . ." Bagley began slowly, "Maybe it means something. Maybe it doesn't. But I don't see what good it would do us either way."

"I was thinking about that. Mullins has been causing a lot of trouble for us. Disrupting the union meetings and all. Those men who were with him tonight have been in on it, too. Maybe this doesn't have anything to do with the Jews. Maybe it has to do with the unions."

"How so?"

"I don't know. But we have a meeting coming up this week. I've been wondering if there is any way he plans to use those pigs to disrupt our meeting."

Bagley seemed skeptical. "I've heard those stories about attacks on Jews, too. Has anyone reported them to the police?"

"I doubt it. Would you if you were in their position?"

Bagley smiled. "I'd think twice about it, that's for sure."

"And I suspect a Jew living in Springfield would think about it more times than that," Fry noted. "Reporting a thing like that to the police could bring someone, especially a Jew, a lot more trouble than it solved."

"Well," Bagley sighed. "I know one or two officers on the police force. I'll find out if they know anything about any of this. Thanks for telling me."

"Maybe you could tell the police to watch the Masonic Lodge a little closer this week, just in case those pigs are meant for us."

"Yes," Bagley nodded. "I'll tell them to do just that."

CHAPTER 18

On Tuesday afternoon, Lewin exited the armory at the end of his shift and started toward the corner to catch the trolley. He rode to the stop on Belmont Avenue and got off. From there, he still had twenty blocks to walk to reach the house on Coomes Street, but he didn't complain. Despite the challenges he and his family had encountered—the employees at work who didn't like Jews, the people who accosted them each weekend when they attended shul, the regular slurs and indignities visited upon them in the course of their everyday routine—life in Springfield was much better than it had been in New York. And far better than it had been in Naroulia, though he missed his family terribly and thought about them every day. Especially during the walk home from work.

As he turned onto Coomes Street, Lewin noticed his neighbors standing outside in groups of three or four along the sidewalks or in their yards, clustered together and talking. They paid him little attention as he made his way past, but when he arrived at home he said to Michla, "Something has happened. What's the matter? What is everyone talking about?"

"Oh, Schleman." Her voice trembled. "It is so awful."

"What?" he implored. "What is it?"

"Rabbi Tabick found pigs in the synagogue." She seemed on the verge of tears. "They say it is awful."

Lewin had a pained expression. "Pigs?"

Michla sighed. "Pigs."

"In our synagogue?"

"Oh, Schleman. It's happening here, too." She began to cry and he put his arm around her shoulder. "No," he soothed. "It is not like that."

"Then, why?" she wailed.

"Bad people live everywhere. This is not like the mobs back home in Belarus. We will take care of this."

She looked up at him. "Rabbi Tabick seems at a loss for how to clean it and put it right."

Lewin held her a moment longer, then pushed away. "I must go." He turned away and started toward the door.

Michla called after him, "Where are you going?"

"Where do you think I'm going?"

Lewin heard her call after him once more, "But what will you do?" By then, however, he was out the door and headed down the steps toward the street. He didn't bother to reply.

From the house, Lewin walked quickly up to the synagogue, approaching it from the side. The doors in back were open and even without walking up the alley for a close look he could smell the stench that wafted from inside. And through the open doorway he saw a pig move slowly past, its hips waddling from side to side.

Three men from the congregation were gathered with Rabbi Tabick on the walkway by the side door. Two of them—Edward Talmy and Aaron Feldman—he already knew. The third man was a stranger. Lewin joined them. "Is it as awful inside as it smells out here?"

"Worse," Talmy replied.

"Someone put pigs in the building," Feldman added.

"How many?"

"It looks to be about two dozen," Tabick answered. "But I

didn't stay inside long enough to count them."

"We must get them out," Lewin said. "I will help."

"Moshe Eckstein knows someone he thinks will come and take them. A farmer," Feldman explained. "He has gone to contact them."

The awfulness of seeing the synagogue defiled reminded Lewin of the way he, his family, and his village were attacked in Belarus. And the attack he and his family had endured just a few weeks earlier. "Has anyone called the police?"

"Not yet," Tabick replied. "That is what we were discussing when you arrived."

"We should report this!" Lewin declared emphatically. "How do we contact the police?"

"But what can the police do?" Feldman said. "We must not make trouble."

"But how can reporting such a thing make trouble?" Lewin wondered.

The man who Lewin did not know said in a dismissive tone, "You are new to America. You do not understand."

Being chided like that made Lewin even angrier than he'd been before. "I do not understand?" Lewin blurted. "I have felt their fists against my back. And against my head. I have been the victim of their discrimination in the workplace. And I dare say you have, too. Does that not give me experience enough to understand what is happening to us?"

Feldman rested his hand on Lewin's arm. "It's okay, Schleman. Zvi was not present when they attacked you and your family."

Talmy spoke up. "Schleman is right. First they shout at us. Then they attack us. Now this." He gestured toward the building to make his point. "If we do not stand up to them, they will only do something worse."

"Show me how to contact the police," Lewin offered. "I will file the report."

"Come on," Talmy said. "We will go together." And they started up to the corner at Fort Pleasant Avenue.

✦ ✦ ✦

An hour later, Lewin and Talmy returned with Patrick McNair, a police officer, in tow. McNair listened to their description of what they found inside the building and made notes to incorporate into a formal report.

"I spent Monday attending to other business," Rabbi Tabick explained. "Today I arrived here at two in the afternoon and noticed the back door had been tied closed."

"The back door?"

"Yes."

McNair pointed to the side door. "Not this one?"

"No." Tabick gestured over his shoulder. "The back door. Come, I will show you."

Tabick led the way and everyone followed him to the alley, then up to the back door of the building. "This is the door."

"And this door was open when you got here?" McNair asked.

"No," Tabick replied. "I could see that it had been tampered with. A rope was tied around the knob and it was secured to the post." He gestured to indicate. "We never do that."

"So, this is just as you found it?"

"It's open now. It was closed when I arrived. I untied it and went about one step inside."

"But these marks." McNair pointed to gouges on the door and doorframe. "These were not here before?"

"No."

"And they are just as you found them?"

"The gouges?"

"Yes. You haven't done anything to them?"

"I have not touched them." Tabick pointed to a length of rope that lay on the step. "That is the rope that was holding the door closed."

"And you untied it?"

"I untied it and opened the door. But even before that, I could smell the odor. I made it just one step inside the rear hallway. Mud and feces littered the floor. The odor was awful."

"And you saw the pigs?"

"Yes. Two pigs came walking down the hall toward me. I backed out of the building and went to Aaron Feldman's house." He gestured in Feldman's direction. McNair glanced over at him. "You live nearby?"

"Yes," Feldman replied. "Just around the corner."

McNair jotted down several more notes, then turned toward the door. As he started inside, he glanced back at the others and saw they hadn't budged. "Are you coming?"

"No," Tabick shook his head. "We cannot."

"But you go ahead," Feldman interjected. "We'll wait for you right here."

✦ ✦ ✦

From the steps by the side door, McNair made his way inside the synagogue and was engulfed by the heavy, musky stench of swine. He gagged and forced himself to choke it down. Then he saw the mess the pigs had created.

A kind of soupy brown slime—a mixture of mud and pig feces—coated the floor along the rear hallway. He felt it beneath his feet, and once or twice he had to brace himself against the wall to keep from losing his balance.

When he reached the sanctuary, he found the slime extended up the center aisle all the way to the building's main entrance. The walls on both sides of the room were smeared with it, too, forming a grimy stripe at a height level with the tallest pig's back. Four pigs lounged on the dais near the podium, oblivious to his presence.

McNair did his best to take note of what had happened, but he had difficulty keeping his emotions in check. He was a lifetime member of a Methodist Church in Springfield and, unlike many who attended church merely for the sake of belonging, he actually believed the tenets of the Christian faith and held great affinity for the Jews. Seeing the destruction and desecration of the synagogue left him horrified.

Pigs—in a synagogue. Swine, an animal synonymous with all that Judaism opposed. Synonymous with all that it was not. It brought to mind the desecration of the temple in Jerusalem that he had read about. The pogroms of Russia that had been reported in the newspapers. And every indignity the Jews had ever suffered. And it was happening right there in Springfield. In the town where McNair had grown up. Where he worked as a police officer. Where his wife and children lived.

"How could anyone do this?" he wondered aloud. "What could they possibly hope to achieve by it?"

After a few minutes inside, McNair could stand it no more and made his way back outside to where Rabbi Tabick and the others were standing. "I'm sorry," he apologized as he approached them. "Will you need help cleaning it up?"

"We can manage," Tabick assured. "Do you think you can find the people who did this?"

"I don't know," McNair replied. "But I'm gonna try. That's a lot of pigs. They would have needed a large truck to haul them. And one person couldn't put them in there by himself. A job like that would have required two or three, at least."

"Perhaps someone saw them," Talmy suggested.

"Yes." McNair nodded his head. "And perhaps the people who did this will talk."

Feldman appeared skeptical. "You really think so?"

"People who do this sort of thing are trying to make a

statement. They want people to notice," McNair explained. "They're also the kind of people who like to brag. I don't think they'll be able to keep it to themselves for long."

✦ ✦ ✦

The next day, McNair asked to be assigned to Forest Park Heights, the area around Temple Beth El. For two weeks, he walked the streets of the neighborhood stopping in cafés and shops along the way to ask about the incident at the synagogue, hoping to find someone who might have seen what happened. At the same time, he tracked down his usual informants—taxi and delivery drivers who regularly circulated through town, trolley attendants who saw and heard everything—and even questioned some of his fellow members at church.

By then, almost everyone had heard about the pigs and the mess they'd made of the synagogue, but no one knew anything specific about the incident. He was on the verge of giving up when, one day at lunch, McNair stopped at the Starlight Café—a café-by-day, lounge-by-night business whose owner was suspected of running an illegal gambling and loan operation from the storeroom. Just the kind of situation that made the diner a place for people who knew things about people.

McNair took a seat at the counter and ordered lunch, then took a long time eating it. As he sat there, slowly taking a bite of his sandwich and a sip of cola, patrons came and went. And as one sat down beside him, he asked them about the trouble at the synagogue. Had they seen anything? Had they heard something? Even a rumor?.

No one offered any substantive information and he was about to leave when a man came from the far end of the counter and sat down beside him. "You're McNair, right?"

"Yes," McNair replied.

"Tell me something. Why are you doing this?"

A frown winkled McNair's forehead. "Doing what?"

"Why are you making all this fuss over some Jew trouble?"

"Jew trouble?" McNair found the term offensive but did his best to avoid an argument. "What are you talking about?"

"I've heard you today, asking your questions. And I've heard from others that you've been asking the same thing all over town. Asking about that synagogue."

"It's my job to investigate."

"It's Jew trouble," the man repeated. "Whatever happened— pigs in the synagogue, people getting beat up on their way home, and whatever else they're complaining about—they probably did it to themselves just so they could blame one of us."

"Us?" The frown on McNair's forehead deepened.

"Yeah. *Us.* Working people. People who still have a job the Jews haven't stolen yet." He tapped the countertop with his index finger for emphasis. "Those are the people you should be looking after. Not some bunch of Jews."

McNair wanted to say more, but instead he asked, "Aren't they people also?"

"Look, all I'm saying is you used to be one of us before you turned Kike."

McNair had heard enough. "Do you know who you're talking to?"

"Yeah. I'm talking to a cop. A cop who has the job of keeping us safe. *Us.* White people. Working people. Not *them.* And certainly not running around town like some errand boy for the rabbi."

"My job is to enforce the law," McNair countered sternly. "Your job is to tell me what you know."

"I don't gotta tell you nothing about nothing," the man responded. "And that's real easy to do in this case because I don't know nothing."

McNair took a deep breath. "You're Mitch Mantello, right."

"Yeah." Mantello seemed surprised. "What of it?"

"I know who you are. And I know where to find you. And if I find out you had something to do with what happened at that synagogue, I'm gonna haul your sorry tuchus to jail."

Mantello had a snide grin. "Ain't no law against calling a Jew a Jew."

"But there's laws against destroying private property."

✦ ✦ ✦

Sidney Gardner, Mullins's co-worker and fellow boarder at Mrs. Smithson's, was in the café when McNair questioned Mantello. He overheard McNair asking about the synagogue and, although he was seated across the room near the windows, he did his best to listen, picking up snippets of their conversation over the clatter of dishes and the rumble of passing traffic outside.

Synagogue. Pigs. Mullins. He'd heard more than enough to pique his interest. News about the incident broke with the morning paper the day after the pigs were discovered. Almost immediately, rumors began circulating around the mill that Mullins was involved. He'd also heard that Bagley, one of the union organizers, was asking people who knew Mullins about the incident.

When McNair left the diner, Gardner moved from his table to the counter and took a seat beside Mantello and feigned a look of concern. "I overheard some of what you were saying to that cop. Why was he interested in what happened at that synagogue?"

Mantello gestured with a dismissive wave of his hand. "Ah, that's just McNair being McNair. There's nothing to it."

"That's the officer's name? McNair?"

"Yeah. McNair. I can't remember his first name."

"But you know him?"

"Sort of. He arrested me once or twice for fighting. Why?"

"Just curious. He's been asking about that synagogue since he came in here today and I wondered who he was and why he was so interested in something with the Jews."

"We are, too," another customer chimed in. "Wasn't nothing but a few pigs in a synagogue, from what I heard."

Gardner turned in his direction. "You know about that?"

"Just what I heard." The man looked at him askance. "Why are you interested in it?"

"Heard rumors at work. Just wondered what was going on."

"It ain't right," Mantello said. "Him asking us about the Jews. He's got plenty to see after without worrying about them. Besides, they take care of their own kind."

✦ ✦ ✦

Later that evening, Gardner went to see Erwin Beal. "Are you aware of the pigs someone put in a synagogue the other day?"

"I heard about it," Beal replied. "Everyone's heard about it by now. Not sure what the fuss is about. Why are you bringing it up?"

"Bagley's been asking at the mill about it."

"Yeah. I heard. Is that a problem?"

"Not really. I just thought if he was asking, he was probably doing that for you, and you might be interested in whatever we've heard."

"Why are you talking to me and not Bagley?"

"I prefer not to deal with a middleman. If something happens, the fewer people involved, the better."

"So, what do you know about it?" Beal asked.

"Just what I've heard."

"Which was?"

"I was at the Starlight Café today. And a police officer came in asking questions about the pigs in the synagogue and if anyone knew anything about it."

"Well, that's what policemen do, isn't it? Something happens, they investigate."

"I suppose," Gardner concurred. "But there are rumors going around the mill that Bryce Mullins was involved."

"I heard something about that. Did you hear something specific about him?"

"No." Gardner shook his head. "But while I was sitting there in the diner, listening to the policeman, it occurred to me that we could use this situation to our advantage anyway."

"Oh?" Beal seemed interested. "How so?"

"This officer seems rather intent on finding out who's responsible for the damage to the synagogue. And Mullins has been one pain in the neck to us and the union and now he's got a group with him who are making even more trouble. If we could get him tangled up in an investigation, we could get him out of the way. At least for a while."

"You got something in mind?"

"The officer investigating the incident is named McNair. I don't know him but he seems like a decent guy. Trying to do a thorough job. He's been going all over town trying to investigate and it's been two weeks since they found the pigs. So he seems intent on doing his duty."

Beal arched an eyebrow. "And that's good for us?"

"I think all I would need to do is to tell McNair about the rumors at the mill. Mention Mullins's name. Suggest the names of one or two of his friends. And McNair could do the rest."

"Have you talked to anyone else about this?"

"Just you. Right now. But I'm saying maybe we could use the information to help us, even if we can't prove Mullins actually did it."

Beal thought for a moment. "Okay, find this Officer McNair and tell him what you've heard about Mullins and the others. Make sure he knows it's a rumor, though. And don't ask around to see if anyone knows more about it. Just tell him what you already know or suspect and that's all."

Gardner nodded. "Okay."

Beal continued. "I don't mind if Mullins gets caught in something like this. It would serve him right. You're right, it would be a good thing for us. But *we* don't want to get caught in it, either."

"Right."

"So don't say too much."

✦ ✦ ✦

The next day, Gardner found McNair walking the beat in Forest Park Heights. He approached him on the corner outside Butenschoen's drugstore. "You're the officer asking about that trouble with the pigs in the synagogue?"

"Yes," McNair replied. "Do you know something about it?"

"I heard a couple of guys talking about it at work."

"What did they say?"

"Something about pigs and a truck and I think they got them from a farmer on the east side of town." Gardner revealed more than he actually knew, repeating the rumors as if they were facts.

"Any names for the people involved?"

Gardner nodded. "One of them was Bryce Mullins. I don't know the other one."

"Tell me again. What did they say about the incident?"

"They were describing what happened and bragging about it. Got the pigs from a farmer. Some guy named Billy knew the farmer. Someone else got the truck. Loaded the pigs up and brought them to the synagogue."

"Three of them?"

"Yeah."

"And when was this supposed to have happened?"

"Sunday night. About two weeks ago."

"Where do they work?"

"Boatwright Thread and Twill."

"And you work there, too?"

"Yes."

"Okay," McNair decided finally. "I'll look into it."

Gardner acted concerned. "But if you talk to Mullins, don't mention my name. I have to work with him and I don't want any trouble."

"Right. I'll do my best to keep you out of it."

CHAPTER 19

As McNair continued his investigation into the desecration of the synagogue, Mullins arrived home one evening after work and made his way toward the stairs to go up to his room. Mrs. Smithson came from the dining room and handed him an envelope. "This came for you today." He took it from her and scanned the return address to see that it was from William Griffin at the Crimson Legion. *Probably from Dorothy. Or one of those guys we met with. Certainly not from Griffin himself.*

Mullins still was thinking about what the envelope might contain and who might actually have sent it, when he entered his room and tossed his jacket onto the bed. He pushed the door closed and sank into a chair that sat beside the table with the radio. Using his thumb and forefinger, he tore open the envelope and found inside a letter that was from William Griffin himself, offering a job with the Crimson Legion.

"We would like you to join our effort to organize Crimson Legion groups in every major city throughout the nation," Griffin wrote. "The work would be much like what you have done in Springfield, only as a member of our permanent staff. You would, of course, receive a salary as detailed on the formal offer accompanying this letter. I'm sure that salary would be less than what you are currently making at the mill but you would have the chance to shape the course of our nation's future." The letter made clear that should he choose to accept the offer, he would be working from the Crimson Legion headquarters in Charlotte.

Mullins was excited about everything Griffin proposed except the part about moving from Springfield. To say that he and Grace had grown close would be an understatement. Just that day, on the way home from work, he had wondered what it would be like to be married to her, and how many children she might want. He wasn't sure he wanted any. Wasn't even certain he wanted to be married. But he was wondering about it. He didn't want to be all the way down in North Carolina and her still in Springfield.

After dinner and a bath, Mullins returned to his room and again sat in his chair to read and re-read the letter. Finally, as the hour grew late, he put the letter aside and thought about the opportunity. His mind traveled back to the evening that he heard Walter Jones on the radio for the first time. Listening to that broadcast led him to Jones's newspaper and that led to the Crimson Legion, then to the rally where he met Grace. From that seemingly accidental meeting, their relationship had blossomed into a romance. She had been the one who brought him to the meetings at the Claytons' house and it was through her that he found a place for the group he wanted to organize against the union. That, in turn, led to the meeting with Griffin in Charlotte, and the incorporation of the anti-union group as the Springfield chapter of the Crimson Legion. Which resulted in the letter he'd just received offering him a job with them.

What a chain of events, he thought. *And none of them planned or arranged to bring me to this point. It's so happenstance and disconnected and unintentional. It must be God.*

✦ ✦ ✦

The next day, Mullins took the letter from Griffin with him to work. Afterward, he went to Grace's house. She was surprised to see him. "Is something wrong?"

"No," he answered. "And yes." He took the letter from his pocket. "This came yesterday. It was waiting for me when I got home."

Grace read the letter quickly, then looked at him with a smile. "This is great." She threw her arms around his neck and kissed him, then noticed the look on his face. "What's the matter? Isn't this what you wanted?"

"Yes. But I would have to move to Charlotte."

"I know." She kissed him again. "But we can work all of that out." There was a teasing look in her eyes. "But can you keep away from Dorothy?"

"What are you talking about?"

"She likes you."

"That was nothing."

"I'm not sure it was nothing to her."

"So, you don't want me to take it?"

She swatted him on the bottom. "Don't be silly. It's a great opportunity. You have to accept the offer."

"But I want to continue seeing you." He pulled her close. "To be with you."

"But you don't want to work in the mill all your life."

"No. I don't. I used to be satisfied with that. Now, after all we've done and all that has happened, I want more. To do more. To accomplish something big."

"I could always move to Charlotte, too."

"But what about school?"

"What about it?"

"You can't just leave in the middle of the year."

"No," she said. "I'll stay here to finish the term and in the summer I will join you in North Carolina."

Mullins was excited about that. They talked awhile longer about the position and what it would mean to work for the

Crimson Legion, and in the end they agreed that he would accept the offer, she would join him when she finished the school year, and they would continue their relationship in North Carolina.

The following day, Mullins sent a telegram to William Griffin accepting his offer of employment in a permanent position with the Crimson Legion staff. Just to be sure, he sent a letter reporting that, too. A few days later, he gave notice at work that he intended to quit.

✦ ✦ ✦

Two weeks later, Mullins stepped from the train at the station in Charlotte expecting to see one of the staff members from the Crimson Legion office. Or maybe even Dorothy. Instead, he found a platform with a few passengers from the last train of the evening, a cart loaded with luggage, and a porter.

"You look lost," the porter noted.

"I assumed someone would be here to greet me," Mullins responded.

"Lots of people make that assumption. But come on." The porter gestured for him to follow. "We can find your luggage inside and then I'll get you a taxi."

With the porter's help, Mullins retrieved his luggage and made his way toward the exit on the street side of the building. "Now," the porter suggested, "you white folks like to stay at the Windsor Hotel." He led the way to a taxi that was waiting at the curb. "Charlie!" he called out to the driver.

The driver leaned out the window. "What is it, Earl?"

"Take this young man to the Windsor."

"Very well."

Mullins watched while the porter loaded the luggage into the car, then tipped him and got in. "Don't worry about a thing," the porter assured as he pushed the door closed. "Your driver knows the way. And he don't get lost more than once or twice a year." He was still laughing at his own joke as the car started forward.

At that time, Charlotte had a population of about forty thousand people. Not much for places along the Eastern Seaboard but quite large for North Carolina. Much larger than he remembered from his trip there with Grace, though they hadn't had much time to see the city on that trip.

As they made their way to the hotel, Mullins looked out at the buildings and wondered what Grace was doing back in Springfield. *Probably asleep by now.*

The Windsor was an elegant hotel—much nicer than the one where he and Grace had stayed—and Mullins was certain he could not afford more than one night there. Still, he hadn't thought to plan ahead and, with no one to meet him at the station, he had to adapt as best he could. The Windsor, with its beautiful lobby, soaring ceiling, and intricate chandelier, seemed just about right. A bellman took care of his luggage, and directed him to his room. Mullins was asleep before he had time to worry about how to pay for it.

The following morning, Mullins had coffee in the hotel lobby, then walked up the street to the Crimson Legion office which was only a few blocks away. As he'd seen on his previous visit, the office was crowded with filing cabinets and boxes shoved into every open space between the desks that lined the walls. People, some of whom he'd met but most of whom were strangers, scurried about in every direction, talking loudly to be heard above the clatter of typewriters. Mullins stood just inside the doorway and stared in disbelief at the chaos.

At first, no one seemed to notice him, but then Dorothy appeared. She looked surprised, and Mullins was beginning to wonder if this had all been a mistake, then Dorothy smiled, "I thought you were coming tomorrow."

"No. You said to be here today."

Dorothy glanced at a calendar that hung on the wall, then looked back at him. "So I did." She clapped her hands and called out in a loud voice, "Listen up!" Instantly the room was quiet and still. "This is Bryce Mullins. He just arrived to join us. He'll be in charge of setting up new chapters. Bryce says he can get us a chapter in every major city." She flashed a smile in his direction. "Make sure you give him all the help he needs."

Office personnel stared at Mullins a moment, as if sizing him up, then as if on some unspoken cue, they started back to work. The din of conversation and the rustle of activity rose once more. Dorothy rested her hand on his shoulder to guide him. "Your desk is in here." She maneuvered him through the main room to an office that held three desks. Two of them were occupied and he recognized the faces of the men who sat there, but he didn't remember their names.

"You remember Bradley Edwards and Kenneth Frost," Dorothy said. "You met them when you were here before."

"Yes," Mullins answered, glad for the mention of their names. "I remember you both." They were busy stuffing envelopes for a mailing and only acknowledged him with the slightest wave.

"This is your desk." Dorothy pointed to the empty one in the corner. "I think the three of you will get along fine. If you have any trouble, let Paul know."

Mullins had a puzzled look. "Paul?"

"Paul Nesbit. You've met him before."

"Oh, right." Mullins nodded.

Just then, Nesbit appeared at the door. "Here he is now," Dorothy said. "He'll help you find a place to stay if you need one."

"Good," Mullins smiled. "I can't afford the Windsor much longer."

Everyone turned to look at him, and Dorothy arched an eyebrow. "You stayed at the Windsor?"

"Just last night. Someone at the train station recommended it."

"The porter," Nesbit offered. "I think he gets a commission on everyone he sends there."

"Nesbit will help you find a room you can afford." Dorothy made her way to the door. Nesbit stepped aside to let her pass, but only just enough. She brushed against him as she moved past, and from the way Nesbit seemed to enjoy it Mullins was certain she had pressed herself against him intentionally.

"You can take the rest of the day to get settled," Dorothy instructed. "Be here in the morning at eight."

Mullins looked over at Nesbit. "Was she talking to me?"

"Yes," he replied. "Come on. Let's get your stuff from the hotel and I'll show you a good place to stay."

Nesbit led the way downstairs to the street where a Model T Runabout was parked at the curb. "This is yours?" Mullins asked.

"Not really," Nesbit replied. "But I get to use it."

They drove down the street to the Windsor to collect Mullins's things, then continued to a boardinghouse not far from the office. "This place is owned by Harvey Renfrow," Nesbit advised as he brought the car to a stop near the walkway. "He's a little grouchy but he's a good guy. Won't give you much of a hassle."

"Does anyone else from the office live here?"

"Not right now. But we've had several who lived here in the past."

The house was a rambling three-story structure that appeared to once have been an elegant residence. Now it was a boarding-house with some obviously needed maintenance—the concrete walkway was cracked, the steps needed cleaning, and the porch needed paint. And those were only the things Mullins noticed as they reached the front door.

Nesbit introduced Mullins to Renfrow, and after a brief discussion, Mullins rented a room on the top floor. Like the one he had in Springfield, breakfast and dinner were included. "No visitors after ten," Renfrow noted "And it's a dollar a night for anyone staying with you."

"Okay," Mullins replied.

"But," Renfrow added, "they can't stay longer than five days. After that, they have to rent a room on their own."

Nesbit and Mullins returned to the car for his belongings, then carried them upstairs. With three flights of stairs to negotiate, Mullins was glad for the help.

The room was situated in a corner on the back side of the house at the end of the hall, farthest from the stairs. Being in the corner, it had a window on two walls. One looked out on a backyard with rhododendron bushes sprawled beneath tall, mature trees. On the side there was a flower garden that was surprisingly well maintained and beyond it, the house next door.

The room was furnished with a bed that sat directly opposite the door, the headboard beneath the window on the side. To the left of the door was a large wardrobe and to the right was a chiffonier that doubled as a washstand. A chair sat in front of the wardrobe, beneath the window that looked out to the backyard. Next to it was a table large enough for Mullins's radio.

"This will do just fine," Mullins assured him with a satisfied smile.

"Good." Nesbit turned to leave. "I'd better get back to the office. They tend to need me a lot, and if I'm not there things get a little out of control."

Mullins stopped him before he left. ""Let me ask you, what's the office like?"

Nesbit grinned. "Usually, it's about as confused as what you saw this morning. That's a typical morning. But surprisingly, a large amount of work gets done there."

"You and Dorothy work well together?"

"Yes." Nesbit couldn't help but glow at the mention of her name. "She is an excellent administrator."

"Good," Mullins replied.

"You'll see." Nesbit turned again toward the door. "It's a great place to work."

As Nesbit moved down the hall, Mullins pushed the door closed and glanced around the room again. It really was a nice room. Much nicer than he'd had in Springfield. And being located at the end of the hall, away from the stairway, there would be fewer people to disturb him.

After a moment to consider his situation, Mullins unpacked his clothes and placed them in the wardrobe and chiffonier. When that was finished, he brought out his radio and set it on the table beside the chair, then found an electrical outlet and plugged in the cord. He turned the tuning dial until he located a station and listened long enough to hear the call sign. "WBT, broadcasting from atop the Bon Marche building in beautiful downtown Charlotte."

When his belongings were arranged and the radio was in place, Mullins found paper and an envelope and wrote a letter to Grace describing his trip, the things he'd done since arriving, and the arrangement at the office. "I think this will be a greater challenge than we imagined," he wrote. "But I think it will be fun. And for once, I will be doing something big with my life."

✦ ✦ ✦

After dinner that evening, Mullins went out to sit on the front porch. Apparently, that was not the custom at this boardinghouse, and he had the space all to himself. He'd been out there about twenty minutes when a car—a Model T Runabout, the same one Nesbit had used earlier—came to a stop at the end of the walkway. The driver's door opened and Dorothy stepped out. She smiled, "Come on, let's go for a ride."

Mullins was glad for the chance to get away and joined her in the car. "I thought you might want to see some of the town," she told him. "Before you start work."

"That would be great," he replied.

She steered the car away from the curb, "After tomorrow, I don't think you'll see much of it."

"Why's that?"

"You'll be on the road. Establishing Crimson Legion groups in every major city in the country. To do that, you'll have to get out there and visit those cities." She reached over and patted his thigh. The touch of her hand felt good and he did nothing to discourage her. "But don't worry." She patted him again. "It'll be fun."

Dorothy moved her hand from his leg to shift gears as they turned a corner, then glanced in his direction. "So, you've been working as a machinist and organizing on the side?"

"Something like that."

"How did you end up at the mill?"

"My first job was in New York," Mullins explained. "At a company that manufactured locomotives."

"What took you to Massachusetts?"

"I went out to Springfield to visit a cousin. I liked the place and got a job at a mill."

"Your cousin worked there?"

"No, but a friend of his helped me get the job."

"And how did you get interested in politics?"

"My brother died in the Great War," Mullins replied.

"I'm sorry. That must have been awful. And it made you angry?"

"It just seemed so stupid. No," he corrected himself. "It *was* stupid. The whole thing was just a bunch of kings playing games with human lives."

"And that got you involved?"

"It got me talking to anyone who would listen, and someone

told me about Walter Jones. Listening to his broadcasts on the radio and reading the articles in his newspaper led me to the Crimson Legion. Then I attended a Crimson Legion rally and heard Mr. Griffin."

"And it opened your eyes."

"Yes. It did." He smiled at her. "I'm sure I'm not the first to say that.

"No. I've heard it thousands of times. So you went looking for others of a similar persuasion."

Mullins nodded. "I went to a bookstore to get a couple of the books that Walter Jones and Mr. Griffin mentioned. The owner of the store was German and he invited me to attend a meeting of that Knights of Teutonia we talked about when I was here before."

"Right. The ones who were too German for you."

"Yes." Mullins was impressed that she remembered. "Grace, the lady who was with me when I came before, was already meeting with friends for informal discussions about the issues, and I joined them. Working with them led me to form a group to work against the union."

She seemed genuinely interested. "What happened with the union?"

"They were trying to organize workers in the mill," Mullins explained. "After reading all of those books and newspaper articles and listening to Walter Jones, I realized the union organizers were Communists. So I started a group to work against them."

"That is great!" she beamed.

"Yes, it was." Mullins looked over at her. "But I've been doing all the talking. What about you? You have an accent. You're from here in North Carolina?"

Dorothy shook her head. "No, I'm from Atlanta. Mr. Griffin found me when I was working with the Southern Freedom Party, an organization that tried to maintain the political integrity of the 'Old South.' It was a large group with numerous local chapters.

The kind of organization Mr. Griffin wants to build for the Crimson Legion. He recruited me to come up here and help him. Which is where you come in."

"I've been wondering about that," Mullins said. "Any idea what he's expecting me to do?"

"He wants to change the way we've established local chapters."

"How has it been done in the past?"

"When the Crimson Legion was first formed, Mr. Griffin's rallies were rather spontaneous events. Planning them was not a very sophisticated operation. Now that he's become more popular, the rallies have become more complex. Work in advance typically involves selecting local leadership, helping them gather volunteers to publicize the event, man the information tables, act as ushers, that sort of thing."

"Sounds like a great basis for local chapters."

"It is, but until now we haven't had the staff or the resources to capitalize on that."

"Which is where I come in, I assume."

"Yes," Dorothy replied. "Mr. Griffin likes doing rallies. So we're going to send him to as many as he can handle. He wants to take advantage of that and form those local volunteers into chapters at each of the sites where he does a rally." She pointed for emphasis. "Which is what you'll be doing."

Mullins nodded. "Who does the advance work for the events?"

"Right now it's Bradley Edwards and Kenneth Frost."

"The guys I'll be sharing an office with."

"Yes. We'll have one other person doing what you do. His name is Chester Monroe. You haven't met him yet. He's stays on the road almost all the time."

"How will it work, with both of us doing the same thing?"

"You and Chester will leapfrog each other," Dorothy replied.

Mullins frowned. "Leapfrog?"

"Edwards and Frost get the rallies organized. You show up maybe a day or two before the rally and meet everyone. Mr. Griffin comes in, does the rally, and leaves that night or the next morning. You stay behind to make sure the local leaders get the volunteers organized into a chapter. We think that will take two weeks."

"And maybe some return visits," Mullins added.

"Yes," she conceded. "But right now we're thinking two weeks. While you're doing that, the team will have moved on to do a rally in the next city. Chester will be there and he'll stay after the event to get *those* volunteers organized. Meanwhile, you'll leave where you are and catch up with Mr. Griffin in time for the next rally."

"Sounds like a brilliant idea." Mullins didn't really think it was workable, but didn't want to create a problem for himself before he even got started.

"Thank you." She smiled. "I came up with most of it." Mullins was glad he'd kept quiet.

CHAPTER 20

As Dorothy had predicted, Mullins rarely saw his room at Mr. Renfrow's boardinghouse. After a week to get familiar with the office and staff, he went with Griffin as part of his entourage for a trip to Rochester, New York, where Edwards and Frost had scheduled a rally. While on the train, Mullins and Griffin met privately. "I understand Dorothy explained your role," Griffin said.

"Yes," Mullins replied. "We went over it in detail."

"You'll be setting up chapters in the cities where I speak."

"Right."

"You and Chester Monroe will be doing the same thing, just not together."

"She mentioned that."

"I doubt you've met Chester yet."

"No, I haven't."

"He's a good man," Griffin explained. "Stays on the road most of the time, though. Just as you will."

"I understand that now more than ever."

"It's not a bad life," Griffin offered. "You get to see the country—though you'll see most of it through the window of a train car."

"I don't mind," Mullins smiled.

"You and he will be leapfrogging each other," Griffin continued. He was repeating things that Mullins and Dorothy had discussed, but Mullins didn't dare interrupt him. "Catching every other city on the schedule. Organizing Crimson Legion chapters using people we identify in the work we do to organize the rallies."

"I think that's a good strategy," Mullins replied.

Griffin paused to look him in the eye. "But I detect a hint of reservation in your voice."

Mullins smiled awkwardly. "I think it won't quite work out as simply as you might like."

"Working with people is never simple."

"Precisely," Mullins agreed. "Doing the rallies requires a volunteer force. I understand that. Continuing to work with them beyond merely the single event and shaping them into an ongoing organization is an excellent idea. I just think that training leadership for those groups and making sure that they do what they are supposed to do will require an ongoing relationship."

Griffin nodded. "I'm sure it will."

"And that will require return trips to those chapters."

Griffin shrugged. "No argument from me on that point."

"I just want to make sure we manage our expectations about my role."

"That's good." Griffin leaned forward and smiled. "We're all still growing with this. When we first started, things just sort of happened and everyone was satisfied if only two or three people showed up for an event. Now our rallies are like one of those tent revival meetings. They appear to be spontaneous when, in fact, they are orchestrated down to how many people man the information table at the venue."

"And you're drawing more than one or two people now, too."

"Yes." Griffin had a satisfied look. "We're getting huge crowds now." He smiled at Mullins. "And we want to take advantage of it." Griffin stood, indicating their visit had come to an end. "We're expecting big things from you." He gave Mullins a pat on the shoulder. "I'm sure you'll do just fine."

✦ ✦ ✦

The rally in Rochester was a big success, and afterward Mullins remained in town to meet with a group of people interested in creating a Crimson Legion chapter. Rustin Steed, who had been the volunteer coordinator for the rally, wanted to keep the volunteers together in a permanent chapter of the Legion. During one of their meetings, Mullins mentioned his admiration for Walter Jones—the preacher he heard on the radio way back at the beginning—and the influence he had on him.

"I know him," Steed commented.

"You know Walter Jones?"

"Yeah. He lives right here."

"I knew he lived here but I didn't really think about it."

"Would you like to meet him?"

"Sure. Do you think I could?"

"I'll set it up. We'll have dinner."

The following evening, Mullins and Steed met Walter Jones for dinner at a restaurant near the hotel where Mullins was staying. Mullins was impressed at meeting someone with celebrity status like Jones, but he and Jones didn't really hit it off.

Afterward, as they walked back to the hotel, Steed said, "Well, what did you think?"

Mullins chuckled. "He's not really the warmest guy I ever met."

Steed laughed. "He's quite different in person from what you hear on the radio."

"Does anyone ever get close to him?"

"Not really. He came from a rough background," Steed added. "His family was very poor. Ministry was as much a way out for him as a calling to something higher. But he has become a rallying point for people of like mind in the effort to oppose those who want to ruin America."

"He had a tremendous impact on my life."

"That's what I mean. He has reached many lives."

✦ ✦ ✦

Mullins remained in Rochester for two weeks after the rally, working with the fledgling organization he hoped to establish there. Once he'd covered the basics, however, he took leave of Steed and the others and boarded a train to Cleveland where he joined the team with Griffin for another rally.

Griffin arrived a few days early and spent the time conducting meetings with wealthy donors and Ohio politicians. Most of those were appointments he handled by himself. Mullins spent the time with Edwards and Frost, going over details for the rally one last time. However, for his meeting with Jonas Fisher, the junior senator for Ohio, Griffin took Mullins along. "I want you to meet Fisher," he explained. "I think we may be working with him quite a bit in the future and you'll need to know him and his assistant, Marvin Parsons."

The meeting with Fisher took place in a small conference room in the offices of a law firm in Cleveland's downtown business district. As the meeting began, Mullins and Parsons were seated in chairs along the wall while Griffin and Fisher sat at a conference table and talked. It wasn't long before their conversation turned to the topic of immigration.

"We have to do something about the Jews, Jonas," Griffin said. There was an obvious edge to his voice.

"I know," Fisher replied. "You've been telling me that for the last three years."

"I keep telling you that," Griffin insisted, "because you don't do anything about it."

"I know."

"Have you been following developments on this issue in other countries?"

"Probably not as closely as you would like."

"The Germans have several groups that seem to have some good ideas. We've been tracking them for some time now."

"What are they suggesting?"

"Several of their scientists have done some interesting work in eugenics. Are you familiar with that concept?"

"Something to do with race, I think."

"Not merely race, but genetics. The fundamental characteristics endemic to the peoples of the world."

Fisher grinned. "You know you lose me when you use those big words."

"We face big challenges, Jonas. We must meet them with equally big responses."

"Jews have been looking for a home for a long time."

"Yes, and while they've been looking, they've been a major thorn in the side of humanity."

Fisher seemed mildly interested. "So, these other countries are addressing the Jewish issue?"

"They are determined to deal with the Jewish problem. The international Jewish conspiracy. And they are serious about opposing the Communists."

"Maybe we need them to help us over here," Fisher opined.

"Perhaps so. But one thing we could do to help ourselves is to control immigration," Griffin said. "We need to keep out the International Jews. They are nothing but Communist spies."

"Communists," Fisher chuckled. "My people tell me they are the ones stirring up all of this union business."

"Your people are telling you the truth. We are in a battle for control of our labor force."

"Against the Communists?"

"Yes. But those who are leading that battle against us are being funded, inspired, and controlled by some very powerful and very wealthy people."

"Jews."

"Primarily." Griffin squinted with an intense look. "Do you believe what I am telling you?"

"I believe we have an immigration problem."

"But you are not convinced that the Jews themselves pose a threat."

Fisher shook his head. "Not entirely."

"The Germans are way ahead of us on this."

"Perhaps."

"There are several new organizations over there that you should take a look at."

"Such as?"

"One of them is the German Workers' Party. Someone sent me a transcript of a speech given by one of their members. Hitler, I think was his name. He makes a lot of sense. I can send you a copy of it if you'd like."

"Sure."

"They have an associated organization here in the US. The Sons of New Germany. And another called the Knights of Teutonia. They're all part of the same basic organization."

"I've heard of them. They're associated with your friend Walter Jones."

"Loosely," Griffin acknowledged. He gestured over his shoulder. "Mullins has been to some of their meetings."

Fisher looked over at Mullins. "Which group was that?"

Mullins stood. "The Knights of Teutonia. I went to a couple of their meetings."

"What did you think of them?"

"They're a little too German for me."

Fisher and Griffin laughed. "Interesting way of putting it," Fisher smirked.

"Yes, sir."

"But you've had firsthand experience in this."

"Not really."

Griffin rose from his place at the table and moved toward a coffeepot that sat on a stand at the far end of the room. While he poured himself a cup, Fisher came and sat next to Mullins. "But you know about these groups."

"Yes, sir," Mullins replied. "I know of them."

"What do you do for William Griffin?"

"I organize members for him."

Fisher seemed genuinely interested. "Setting up local chapters?"

Mullins realized Fisher was more interested in the work he did—recruiting members and establishing local chapters—than the issues Griffin had been trying to discuss. He wondered why, but instead of raising that issue, he simply said, "Yes."

Fisher smiled. "Walter Jones mentioned you to me."

Mullins was caught off guard by the comment. "Reverend Jones?"

Fisher nodded. "You were with him in Rochester a few weeks ago."

"Yes. I had dinner with Reverend Jones."

"He told me about it. He was very impressed. You should find a place to share your own opinions, too."

Mullins was impressed, but he responded with a deferential tone. "I'm just a journeyman, sir."

"Nonsense! You have more organizational ability than anyone I've met. Jones thinks the same thing." He gestured over his shoulder. "Bill does, too. That's why he brought you onboard."

When Griffin returned to his chair, he excused Mullins from the room. Fisher sent Parsons out as well. The two of them wandered up the hall together. "What do you suppose they're talking about?" Mullins wondered.

Parsons smiled. "Probably something we don't want to know about."

"I suppose so." But Mullins didn't really mean it. He wanted to know everything and especially everything about the issues that interested Griffin. Above all, he wanted to know more about the people and organizations from Germany that Griffin had mentioned. He'd heard bits and pieces about them from Hinkle and the men he'd met through the Knights of Teutonia, but he wasn't familiar with the eugenics research, and it seemed fascinating to him.

✦ ✦ ✦

After two weeks in Cleveland, Mullins had organized a Crimson Legion chapter that was functioning and already planning its initial operation—a demonstration in favor of tighter immigration restrictions.

The next rally wasn't scheduled until three weeks later, so Mullins decided to take the opportunity to return to Charlotte and catch up on details there. Early in the morning, he boarded a train in Cleveland and arrived in Charlotte late that evening.

At the boardinghouse, he found a stack of mail waiting for him, but instead of reviewing it he placed it on the chiffonier and went to bed. It was late the next morning when he awakened and, rather than rushing off to yet another meeting, he spent the day lounging in his room while he sorted through the mail and caught up on correspondence.

The following morning, Mullins arrived at the office early. A stack of mail awaited him there, too, and he spent the morning sorting through it. A little before noon, Dorothy suggested they go out to lunch, and they walked to a café on the corner.

While they sat at a table in back, she told him they had decided to hire another person to help with the office work. Mullins frowned. "You have space for another person?"

"We're expanding the office," she explained.

"That's a good idea."

"I was wondering if your friend Grace might be interested in the new position."

"I think she might."

He felt Dorothy's foot against his. "I wouldn't want that to cause a problem, though."

"What kind of problem would that cause?"

"I don't know." She had slipped her foot out of her shoe and he felt her toes against his calf. "Jealousy can be a powerful enemy."

Mullins shook his head. "She's not that type."

"Good. Then maybe you should contact her and see if she's interested."

When Dorothy first mentioned the idea, Mullins had been overjoyed at the thought of having her in the office. Now, having received what he was sure was a romantic overture from Dorothy, he wasn't so sure how good it would be to have them both in the same location. But he felt uncomfortable saying all of that, so instead, he said, "What kind of salary do you expect to offer?"

"I'm not sure yet." Dorothy's toes ran over the top of his foot. "We're just now creating the position."

"Details to work out?"

"Yes. I'll let you know when the details have been finalized." Dorothy moved her foot farther up his leg. "Maybe you shouldn't say anything to her until then."

CHAPTER 21

Back in Springfield, Officer McNair continued to investigate the desecration of Temple Beth El. Using the tip from Gardner, McNair questioned the shop steward at Boatwright and learned that Mullins no longer worked at the mill. "He quit about a month ago."

"Where did he go?"

"Took a job in North Carolina, I think."

"Any idea who he works for down there?"

"Something called the Crimson Legion. I think it's a political group. They tell me he'd become very interested in that kind of thing."

"You didn't know him?"

"Not very well."

"Anyone here who knows him well?"

"You might ask Tom Kugler. They worked together."

Rather than confronting Kugler at the mill, McNair located a home address for him and went to see him that evening. Kugler suggested they talk in the backyard. "I'd rather my wife and kids didn't hear us."

When they were outside and away from the house, McNair said, "I understand you know Bryce Mullins rather well."

"We're friends."

"Close friends?"

"We worked together every day, so, yeah, we were close."

"I understand he no longer works at the mill."

"No. He moved to North Carolina."

"To work with the Crimson Legion."

"Right." Kugler frowned. "Why are you interested in him?"

"Someone released about two dozen pigs in the Beth El synagogue. You heard about that?"

"Yeah." Kugler seemed unconcerned. "Wasn't that about three or four months ago?"

"Does it matter how long ago it was?"

"No. But that's a long time for the police to spend on something like that."

"Like that?"

"Yeah," Kugler shrugged. "You know. I'm sure it was just a prank."

"It desecrated and ruined a religious sanctuary."

Kugler frowned. "Those pigs did that much damage?"

"They were in there two days."

"I guess they would," Kugler conceded. "And you think Bryce had something to do with it?"

McNair kept pressing. "Did you ever hear him mention anything about something like this?"

"No."

"See or hear anything suspicious? Maybe at work."

Kugler looked away. "Not really."

The tone of his voice said he knew more than he was saying, and McNair caught the look in his eyes. "What was it you saw?"

Kugler shrugged. "I'm sure it was nothing."

"Tell me," McNair insisted.

Kugler sighed. "About the time of that pig thing, a guy came to the shop to see Bryce. He handed him an envelope and I overheard him asking Bryce if he knew what he was getting into."

"Did he say what it was that made him concerned?"

"Something about his cousin."

"Whose cousin?"

"Fletcher's. The guy who came to the shop."

"What else did they talk about?"

"I don't know," Kugler replied. "That's all I heard."

"Who was this person? You referred to him as Fletcher. What's his whole name?"

"Owen Fletcher."

"Does he work at the mill?"

"Yes. He works in the shop with us.

"I thought you said he *came* to the shop. Like it was unusual for him to be there."

"It was his day off. That's why I noticed it."

"Do you know how I could find Owen Fletcher?"

"Yeah. I have his address inside." Kugler started toward the door to the house. McNair followed.

✦ ✦ ✦

With the address supplied by Kugler, McNair had little difficulty locating Owen Fletcher. "I gave him an envelope," Fletcher admitted. "That's all I did."

"Where did you get it?"

"From my cousin, Pete Lawler."

"Why did you ask Lawler for the envelope?"

"I didn't ask for it. He came to me. He knew I worked with Mullins. Asked me if I would give him something. I said okay. He handed me the envelope."

"And you took it to him."

"I was down that way anyway and I didn't like doing it, so I wanted to get rid of it as soon as possible."

"What made you not like it? Pete's my cousin. And I'm about the only one in the family who has anything to do with him. That seemed more important than getting into it with him about what was in the envelope or what it was for. I just took it and gave it to Mullins."

"Did you know what was inside the envelope?"

"I didn't look, but from the feel of it I would say it was money."

"And that's all you did?"

"That's all I did. I don't know what they were up to. I don't know what they did with the money. I just know I got it from Pete and gave it to Mullins."

"Has Pete talked to you about it since then?"

"No."

"Where could I find Pete? And I would rather you didn't tip him off before I get to him."

"I won't."

✦ ✦ ✦

Talking to Pete Lawler proved more difficult than the others. At first he seemed amicable and invited McNair to sit on the back porch. But as McNair's questions homed in on the synagogue incident, Pete grew more reticent. Finally, he refused altogether and told McNair to leave.

Not to be outdone, McNair spent the next few days following him and succeeded in tailing him to the home of Peggy and Jimmy Clayton. McNair knew Jimmy. They went to church together and had worked together on a project for the college. Jimmy had convinced the bank's board to contribute to the policemen's benevolent fund, too. So, rather than barging in that Sunday night, McNair waited in the shadows, noted those in attendance, and approached Clayton at the bank the next morning.

Clayton was seated at his desk when McNair approached. "Patrick," he smiled. "What brings you here?"

McNair scooted a chair up to the desk and took a seat, then leaned closer so he could speak quietly. "We need to talk."

"Okay," Clayton replied. "What about?"

"Pete Lawler. Bryce Mullins. Maybe a few more."

Clayton glanced around nervously. "Do we have to do this here?"

"I don't think there would be an easy place or an easy time for this. Don't you have a conference room?"

"Yes." Clayton seemed to welcome the suggestion. He gathered up a file from his desk as a pretense for their meeting and ushered McNair across the lobby as if he were a client. When they were in the room and the door was closed, he looked over at McNair. "Okay. What's this about?"

"I'm still investigating the incident over at Temple Beth El and I...."

"Ah, come on, Patrick," Clayton groused. "Can't you let that go?"

"If you'd seen the inside of that building, you wouldn't say that." McNair jabbed his finger in Clayton's direction. "I can't believe you'd say it anyway."

Clayton lowered his voice to a hushed growl. "It's Jew business. Give it a rest."

McNair was startled. "I can't believe you. I expect that kind of talk from some lowlifes like Mitch Mantello. But not from you. You're an officer of the bank."

"I'm saying it. The preacher's saying it. Everybody's saying it." Clayton glared at him. "Maybe it's time for you to listen more and ask fewer questions."

"I saw the people who were at your house last night."

"So. It's not a crime to have friends over."

"Pete Lawler was there."

"Yeah. Pete and Ida have been in our home many times."

"Bryce Mullins has been there, too. Hasn't he?"

"Maybe. But he doesn't even live here now."

"He did when those pigs were loosed in the synagogue."

"And that makes him guilty?"

"Pete Lawler. Bryce Mullins. They were at your house on many occasions. They've been to every synagogue in the city, harassing people as they come and go. I'm starting to wonder if you and Peggy weren't with them, too."

Clayton reached for the door. "I think it's time for you to leave."

McNair grabbed Clayton by the forearm to stop him. "No. Not until you tell me what you know about this."

"I don't know *anything.*"

"We both know that isn't true."

"Look," Clayton swallowed, "it's true that Pete and Ida come to our house with several other couples on Sunday afternoons. And yes, we sit around and eat and talk politics. But there's nothing illegal about that."

"And then you go out and harass people as they come and go from the synagogues."

"Not me. That's something Pete and Ida got into. With Grace and Bryce."

McNair frowned. "Grace?"

"Grace Anderson. Rose Willingham's niece."

"The schoolteacher?"

"Yes."

"She was in on it?"

"I've told you all I know," Clayton opened the door, stood aside, and gestured for McNair to leave.

After talking to Clayton, McNair eventually made his way to Mrs. Smithson's boardinghouse and talked to her, but she didn't know much and what she knew she wasn't interested in disclosing. He also talked to Bobby Rankin, the mechanic, at the garage where he worked.

"I never heard him say nothing about that synagogue business, one way or the other," Rankin demurred. "But I know this. When he came home that Sunday night . . ." He paused a moment. "It was a Sunday night that somebody let those pigs loose, wasn't it?"

"Yes."

"When he came home that night, he smelled like a pigpen."

"Awful?"

"Awful ain't the beginning of it. Awful would be polite. The way he smelled wasn't nothing near polite."

✦ ✦ ✦

McNair had begun the synagogue investigation and he talked to everyone he uncovered along the way. All of them, until there was no one else to question. In the course of that investigation, he learned that several people from the group that met at the Claytons' were involved in a number of anti-Semitic activities. And he'd learned enough to convince himself that Lawler and Mullins participated in the release of the pigs in the synagogue. But his supervisor, Richard Long, wasn't satisfied.

"I know you believe they did it," Long explained. "But that isn't enough to charge someone with a crime."

"What if I—"

"No!" Long snapped. "You've done as much as humanly possible on this case. The whole town knows what you've done, and everyone's impressed. But it's time for you to put this aside and move on to other matters."

McNair returned to his desk, placed his notes in the file, and put the file in the bottom drawer. And that's where the matter lay until about a month later when Long called him into his office.

"You still have your notes and things on that synagogue business?"

McNair was unsure where the conversation was headed but he had no choice than to tell the truth. "Yes. Why?"

"The chief received this." Long handed him a memo from the Justice Department. "Seems someone in Washington has fallen victim to the whining Jews. Justice is asking for reports on fringe dissident groups. They're particularly interested in ones engaged in anti-Semitic activity."

McNair smiled. "At least someone is listening."

Long seemed not to notice the slight as he leaned back in his chair and chuckled. "Pigs in a synagogue. Whoever did that has a sense of humor."

McNair cringed. "It wasn't funny to the rabbi or his congregation."

Long sat up straight. "Yeah. Well, the folks in charge around here want us to respond to that memo. So type up whatever you have on that synagogue issue and send it to the chief's office. Maybe we can get them off our backs long enough to do some *real* police work for a change."

McNair returned to his desk, took his file on the synagogue from the bottom drawer, and began working on a report, summarizing as best he could the things he'd learned during his investigation. Four days later, the report was completed, and he sent it to the chief of the Springfield Police Department. A few days later, he received a note from the chief's office thanking him for his assistance and indicating they had forwarded the memo to the Justice Department's Boston office. McNair assumed nothing further would come of it, but he was glad that someone had at least noticed the matter.

CHAPTER 22

Although destined to become the most powerful law enforcement entity in the country, The Agency then called the Bureau of Investigation still was in a fledgling state. Director William Flynn, however, was intent on shaping it into a thorough and efficient service, essential to the proper function and safety of a democracy. Since taking office, he had received a steady but increasingly vehement number of complaints about organized anti-Semitic activity, and saw confronting that activity as a means of demonstrating the Bureau's indispensable nature. As a result, reports of violence against Jews received particularly close attention.

The report McNair prepared about the incident at the synagogue in Springfield arrived at the Bureau's office in Boston where it was flagged for follow-up and assigned to Graham Hawthorne and Roy Martin, veteran investigators who'd come over to the Bureau from the Treasury Department's Secret Service. They reviewed the report, noted the people mentioned therein, and submitted their names to the Bureau's indexing department. Only Grace Anderson came back as a person with a file known to law enforcement.

Hawthorne requested the file on Anderson and reviewed it, then he and Martin traveled to Springfield. They found McNair walking a beat in Indian Orchard and, after a brief conversation, convinced him to let them see his original notes from the investigation.

As they sat at McNair's desk in police headquarters, Martin pointed to a page in the file. "I notice that you didn't talk to Grace Anderson."

"No."

"Why not?"

"I knew her aunt." McNair looked away.

"Rose Willingham."

McNair nodded. "She and my mother were good friends."

"Did you know Miss Anderson?"

"No, just her aunt. But by the time I learned of her association with this, I was convinced Mullins and Lawler were responsible for the pigs in the synagogue. I didn't think she had anything to do with putting the pigs in there."

"So you focused on Mullins and Lawler."

"Yes, do you plan to talk to her?"

Hawthorne spoke up. "We can't really tell you about what we'll be doing. But we're taking a wider view of this."

McNair frowned. "A wider view?"

"Considering additional possibilities."

Hawthorne and Martin took extensive notes, then returned the file to McNair. "I'm sure we don't need to tell you this," Martin advised. "But don't talk to the witnesses anymore."

"Right." McNair nodded. "I won't mention this to anyone."

"Good," Hawthorne replied.

"Not even to Mrs. Willingham," Martin added.

"Or her niece," Hawthorne concluded.

+ + +

The following Friday, just as Grace Anderson was ending her day at school and looking forward to the weekend, Hawthorne and Martin appeared at the door to her classroom. They identified themselves as federal agents, then Hawthorne said, "We would like to talk to you."

"What about?"

They came farther into the classroom and Martin said, "We'd like to know about the group you've been meeting with."

Grace looked puzzled. "What group is that?"

"The one that meets at the Clayton residence on Sunday afternoons."

Grace turned her back to them and straightened a stack of papers on her desk. "What about it? "We're just friends getting together."

"We know about the protests outside the synagogues."

Grace continued to avoid their gaze. "I'm not sure what you're talking about." There was a hint of nervousness in her voice.

"Yes, you are." Hawthorne was firm, but not rude. "We're particularly interested in an incident that happened outside Beth El synagogue."

"I didn't have anything to do with that." Grace busied herself with straightening things on her desk.

"We heard differently."

"Look." Grace stopped what she was doing. "I've shouted at Jews coming and going from there. I've confronted them face-to-face on the sidewalk and in the street. But I never had anything to do with those pigs."

Martin raised an eyebrow. "We didn't mention anything about pigs."

Grace looked back at them, her cheeks glowing with embarrassment. "That's not what you were asking about?"

"No," Martin answered. "We were asking about the night you and some of your friends assaulted a family as they were walking home from the synagogue."

"At the corner of Coomes Street," Hawthorne added. "Behind the building."

Tears formed in Grace's eyes. "They identified me?"

Martin ignored her question. "Tell us what happened."

Grace turned to face them and leaned against the edge of the desk. "We'd been talking about things that we thought were wrong today. Political things, mostly. And Bryce was saying we should do something about it. Someone suggested we protest outside the synagogues. So we went over there and heckled them as they arrived for their service."

"You mean beat people up."

"No." Grace shook her head. "At first it was just about shouting at them and waving signs we'd made by hand. But Bryce still wanted to do more."

"Bryce is Bryce Mullins?"

"Yes."

"So, *he* wanted to do more," Martin prompted, "And that's when things got rougher?"

"I was only there one time for that," Grace insisted. "Just once."

"Once for the protesting? Or once when the beatings started?"

Grace began to cry. "What do you want from me?"

"You know Pete Lawler?"

Grace wiped her eyes. "Yes."

"You mentioned someone named Pete. That would be Pete Lawler?"

"Yes."

"And Ida Hayes—you know her?"

"Yes."

"They were with you at the synagogue?"

"Yes."

"What do you know about the incident with the pigs?"

"All I know is Pete approached Bryce with the idea months ago. Bryce put him off at first."

"At first?"

"Yes."

"And then later?"

"I heard them talking about it. But I didn't hear what they said. And, frankly, I didn't want to know."

"We understand you're in a relationship with Bryce Mullins."

She shrugged. "Sort of."

Hawthorne showed her a photograph depicting her leaving the Claytons' house, arm in arm with Mullins. "Care to revise that statement?"

"We've been seeing each other."

Martin spoke up. "Miss Anderson, we have more questions to ask you, but I think we should continue this somewhere else." He gestured toward the door. "We need you to come with us."

She looked scared. "What else could you possibly ask me?"

"I think you'll understand when we get to that." He gestured again toward the door. "Come with us, please."

Grace picked up her purse and started toward the hall. Just then, Lance Smith, the principal, appeared in the doorway. "Grace?" He looked concerned. "What's going on?"

"It's okay," she told him. "They just want to ask some questions."

Smith glanced at the agents. "Who are you?"

Hawthorne flashed his badge. "Bureau of Investigation. Justice Department. We only want to talk to her."

"Then, why not do that right here?"

"We would prefer to talk to her in a location more conducive to a full and frank discussion." Hawthorne and Martin elbowed their way past Smith and, with Grace between them, escorted her down the hall and out to their car.

A few minutes later, they arrived at their office building in the business district. They took the elevator to the eighth floor and placed Grace in an interview room. The room was small, with a single light overhead and a table beneath it. Three chairs were positioned around the table. Hawthorne and Martin directed her to one and she took a seat. They remained standing.

After reviewing the questions they'd asked earlier and displaying the photographs once more, Hawthorne turned the topic of discussion to Mullins. "We understand he has become affiliated with the Crimson Legion."

"He works for them," Grace replied.

"So he formed a Crimson Legion chapter in Indian Orchard and now he works as an organizer for the national organization."

"What of it?" Grace had a sullen tone. "That's him, not me."

Martin produced a photograph of her at the Crimson Legion rally in Springfield. "I believe that's you right there." He pointed to the picture.

Grace looked away. "It's not illegal to attend a rally."

"But it *is* illegal to plot to overthrow the government."

"I've done no sort of a thing," she retorted. "And neither have they. The Crimson Legion doesn't want to overthrow the government," she argued. "They just want to stop some of the things that are happening."

"Like Jewish immigration?"

"Yes." Her eyes went cold. "What does the government care about the Jews anyway?"

"Truthfully, Miss Anderson," Martin stressed, "we're not so worried about the Jews as we are about radicals like Griffin and others who lead the Crimson Legion."

"He's hardly a radical," she scoffed.

Martin produced more pictures. "These men are leaders of a group known as the Sons of New Germany." He gestured to the photographs. "They are related to people involved with the Knights of Teutonia."

Grace looked away. "I've never heard of them."

"They have a chapter here in Springfield. Bryce Mullins was part of it."

She shook her head. "I didn't know that."

Martin placed another photograph on the table. "Members of both of those groups are friends with these men." He pointed to a group of men wearing what appeared to be military uniforms.

Grace looked at the photo. "I don't know them. Who are they?"

"They are members of a radical fascist organization in Germany and they have direct ties to these two men." He pointed to another picture, this one of Griffin on stage at a rally flanked by a man at each shoulder. They appeared to be friends and were waving to the crowd.

She stood. "That has nothing to do with me. I would like to leave now."

"I'm sure you would," Hawthorne said smugly. "Sit back down and take a look at this. Does this have something to do with you?" He slid a dozen photographs from an envelope and dropped them onto the table. The pictures showed images of scantily clad women at a brothel in Norfolk, Virginia. "These were taken at a house located just outside the naval base."

Grace glanced at the pictures, then leaned back in her chair and closed her eyes. "What do you want from me?"

Martin took a seat in a chair across from her. "Does Mullins know what you were doing before you came to Springfield?"

"That was a long time ago."

"Not that long ago. You do remember there are charges pending against you in Virginia, don't you?"

She opened her eyes and glared at him. "Like I said, what do you want?"

"We want you to keep us informed about Mullins. What he does. Where he goes. What you hear."

"If you know all of this"—she gestured to the pictures on the table—"then you already know as much about him as you do about me. I can't give you anything on him you don't already have."

"There is one thing you can give us."

"What is that?"

"Time."

She looked puzzled. "Time?"

"Yes," Martin said. "You can tell us what he's going to do before he does it."

"Maybe in the past," she answered. "But not now. He's in Charlotte now. Though I'm sure you already know that."

"We understand you're planning to join him there."

She looked away. "That's the plan."

"You're wavering?"

"It's just that he's not there very much now. He's on the road constantly. I would just be in Charlotte waiting for him to return. I'm not sure what good it would do either of us for me to be there."

"It would do *us* a lot of good," Martin replied.

And," Hawthorne added, "it would do *you* some good, too."

"How so?"

"You help us," Martin inserted, "we'll help you."

"What does that mean?"

Hawthorne, still standing, leaned close. "It means help us with Mullins and we'll make the charges in Virginia go away. And we'll make sure Mullins never hears about it."

"And if I agreed to help," Grace replied, "what would I do next?"

Hawthorne leaned back. "In a week or two, you are going to receive an offer from the Crimson Legion to work in their Charlotte office. When that offer arrives, accept it. Move to North Carolina. We'll be in touch after you do that."

"And that's all?"

"We would have an ongoing relationship," Martin said.

"Ongoing?" Grace frowned. "For how long?"

"As long as you do what we say."

Grace was silent a moment but finally asked, "And Bryce will never know about this?" She pointed to the photographs.

"Not from us," Martin replied.

A few days later, Grace received a letter from Mullins telling her details about a job at the Crimson Legion office. He'd mentioned it in an earlier letter but this time he had details—office work, reporting to Dorothy, mostly secretarial duties, no travel. And the salary was enough for her to live on. Not quite what she was making as a teacher, but enough.

At first, Grace was astounded at the timing. The agents mentioned this, and there it was. As if they knew it was coming. But as she read and reread the letter, she realized the Bureau of Investigation didn't merely know about the job offer, they had also infiltrated the Crimson Legion organization.

Grace was worried about Mullins. Worried about her secrets. And worried about what might happen if Mullins found out about her past. The investigators knew a lot about her, but she was not certain they knew everything. *But if they do know everything,* she thought, *they will ruin more than my relationship with Bryce by disclosing it.*

After thinking about the situation for a night, she decided to go along with the plan Hawthorne and Martin had outlined. At least for now she would keep quiet about her suspicions, accept the job, and let events unfold from there. That evening she wrote a letter to Mullins telling him that she was delighted about the job and asked if she should wait for a formal offer before accepting the position or assume it was hers already.

CHAPTER 23

Meanwhile, Mullins went back on the road to continue the Crimson Legion rally schedule, returning by train to the city of Columbus, Ohio. He enjoyed life on the road, living from one hotel room to the next, meeting new people at every stop. Initially, he had thought of Grace often and wondered how suited she was to the hectic lifestyle he had adopted. But as the schedules continued and he rolled from one location to the next, he thought less about her and more of the tasks at hand and the adventure unfolding before him.

As had become his custom when circumstances permitted, Mullins arrived in Columbus a few days before the rally. Edwards and Frost already were there and he joined them in coordinating the tasks that led up to the event itself. He'd learned that getting involved early was a good way to get to know the volunteers. From experience he'd learned that rally participation was a crucial indicator of interest in the organization's work. Those who participated in the tasks necessary for the rally had proved to be the most loyal chapter members.

While he worked to ensure the event was a success and to position himself for the effort to organize each Columbus Crimson Legion chapter, Mullins also staffed Griffin for a series of meetings with important Ohio politicians. The mayor of Columbus was first, due in part to the fact that the rally was being held in his city and no one wanted to risk offending him. Support from police and other city employees was crucial, with attendance at the rallies having grown to be quite large.

After the mayor, Griffin met with several state legislators already identified as sympathetic to the Crimson Legion cause. Over the previous twelve months, they had been recruited and wooed in a specific and deliberate fashion. It was a ploy to gain support for immigration control and other policies curtailing the influence of persons having ties to those Griffin identified as International Jews. Griffin was convinced that state officials had more influence over national policy than they realized and he intended to capitalize on that by bending them to his point of view, then showing them ways to exert their power.

"It's a collateral attack on the issues," Griffin openly admitted, "but they can control much of what happens in their state. Projects that get funded. Banking and insurance regulation. Use of infrastructure. Elections and the right to vote. They can make life miserable for anyone they choose. We just need to focus attention on the Jewish threat and making life miserable for them." Griffin planned to convince them he was right and bring them to his cause by any means necessary. Most notably through hefty political campaign donations.

When those meetings were finished, Griffin met with the governor, a man whom he considered a minor influence in the work he hoped to accomplish. "Governors—particularly this one—usually react. They rarely get out in front of an issue and lead. The real power is in the state legislature," Griffin explained to his lieutenants. "We can make better progress with the legislators than with the governor. Legislators enact laws. The governor merely goes along or not. And most of the time, his decision depends on the sentiment of the people, which legislators can influence at a local level, where it counts." The governor was not a great fan of Griffin, nor was Griffin of the governor, but neither could afford to ignore the other. The meeting took place in a conference room on the campus of the state university and, by all accounts, it was short, tense, and stilted.

In between meetings, Mullins made sure Griffin had time for phone calls and plenty of opportunities to drop in on meetings that Edwards and Frost conducted with the volunteers. Mullins's job in that regard consisted primarily of whispering the names of volunteers in Griffin's ear as he worked the room and keeping Griffin moving. He'd learned very quickly that strategic use of Griffin's presence was an important tool in membership recruitment. But only a strategic presence. A little of Griffin energized the foot soldiers—those who were stuffing envelopes, handing out leaflets, and preparing to work the crowd at the rally. Too much, however, exposed the volunteers to the more abrasive aspects of Griffin's personality, which had the opposite effect on volunteer interest in the cause.

On the night before the rally, Griffin and Mullins met again with Senator Fisher and his assistant, Marvin Parsons. This time they gathered in a private dining room on the second floor of the Hotel Savoy. While they dined on steak, Griffin kept the conversation focused on the issue that mattered most to him—immigration. "It is the single most important issue we face," Griffin spoke between bites. "This is the heart of the matter. Everything else turns on this."

"Our people tell me there are some powerful forces gathering in the economy," Fisher noted. None of them bode well for us. Maybe not right now, but this post-war boom isn't going to last forever. By the time the next presidential election will be held, we could have serious problems on our hands. You don't think the economy is an important issue?"

"The economy is being negatively affected because of immigration," Griffin argued. "Particularly, Jewish immigration. They come here to steal our jobs, our money, and destroy our way of life. We could have far more robust growth if it weren't for them."

"Jews?"

Griffin nodded. "Jews. We can address our economic issues only if we eliminate—or, at the very least, seriously curtail—further immigration of Jews. They are the driving force behind the disintegration of Americanism. And, I assure you, whatever negative forces your advisors see as acting on our economy, it's all attributable to the Jews."

"I'm not sure how much support there is in Congress for immigration control," the Senator commented. "Many of the people who ought to be against it—folks from New York, Philadelphia, places like that—see immigrants as the key to their success. Not economically, but from the standpoint of elections. They're out there signing them up to vote as fast as they can get volunteers to do it."

"That's what I'm talking about," Griffin railed. "Merely by their presence they are corrupting our nation. Turning our own people into little more than what they are themselves. At the rate they're going, by 1920 we'll be little more than a nation of power-hungry, greedy Jews."

"All the same," Fisher insisted, "a new immigration law would be an uphill struggle. Not exactly a fight. Just a difficult thing to sell."

"Then we will have to find a way to convince your colleagues to act. If we do not address immigration," Griffin responded, "we will face the total and complete collapse of American society as we have known it. And how many of your fellow congressmen will have a job in Washington when that happens?"

Fisher seemed unconvinced. "Do you really think it's that much of a threat?"

"Yes," Griffin answered adamantly. "And you still do not?"

Fisher shook his head. "It's not a big issue in Ohio."

"I think it's bigger than you realize," Griffin countered. "The

Jews are out to rule the world and they are well on their way to doing so."

"This is an issue for some in the northeast—New York and places like that," Fisher said. "Despite what I said earlier about some of my fellow congressmen using it to their advantage. But here in Ohio—"

"They're not just in New York," Griffin snapped, cutting him off. "Los Angeles is under siege, too."

The Senator had a puzzled expression. "Los Angeles?"

"The motion-picture industry." Griffin sounded frustrated. "The entertainment industry in general. They're under enormous pressure from the Jews."

"But how important is that? I mean, does it really matter who makes the movies?"

Mullins found the tone of Fisher's questions rather curious. Did the senator really not know this argument? Was he really so out of touch with popular culture that he didn't see the strategic importance of entertainment as an influence on the lives of ordinary people?

Griffin also seemed perturbed by the question. "The typical American citizen is *heavily* influenced by the entertainment they enjoy." The look on his face showed how little he cared for explaining the mundane aspects of the issues. To him, anyone of common intelligence should grasp the importance of the issues immediately, without the need of extensive explanation. "Jews know this better than anyone," he continued. "They have their people firmly in place at the heart of the motion-picture industry, the music industry, the theater. Newspapers and radio, too. And they use their influence in those positions to very subtly shape and mold the way we think and feel."

"I've heard you talk about Jews and their involvement in banking and finance. And I've seen for myself what they can do with that. But movies?" Fisher shook his head. "I don't know."

Griffin took a condescending tone. "If you would look into the matter even a little, you would see the truth of what I've been telling you."

Fisher seemed to ignore the point. "There *are* lots of Jews in the money business."

"But what I've been trying to get you to understand is they aren't only after the money. They have bigger goals than just that."

"They're coming here in large numbers as immigrants." Fisher nodded, finally understanding. "And that makes immigration a national issue."

"As I've been telling you over and over for the past two years."

"But does it have the reach?"

Griffin frowned. "You mean does it attract the kind of interest that would make it useful to a politician with an eye toward national office?" Griffin smiled for the first time that evening. "Well, I can tell you this. We are organizing chapters in every state and working to educate our people on the threats we face. And we're educating them on which politicians have their best interests at heart. Politicians with their eye on the long term and the ones who are only interested in short-term success."

Fisher smiled at him. "Are you making any progress with that effort?"

"You've seen the size of our rallies." Griffin gestured toward Mullins.

Fisher observed, "You've been drawing quite the crowd. But can you keep them interested long enough to accomplish something?"

Griffin gestured toward Mullins. "Our staff has been doing excellent work in using that response to develop Crimson Legion chapters in the cities where we've held meetings. We have an extensive reach now, with our newspaper and with the endorsement of others like Walter Jones. And that reach is expanding every day. A person with his eye on a bigger office than the US

Senate might benefit from a network like the one we have and the one we're developing."

"Yes," Fisher grinned, "He might."

The conversation struck Mullins as odd and when they were alone in Griffin's hotel room, Mullins asked, "Do you think Fisher really was that poorly informed on the issues?"

"What do you mean?"

"Does he really not understand the way Jews use entertainment to shape and influence public opinion?"

Griffin smiled. "No. He knows better. He was just trying to goad me into a rant."

"Why?"

"It's just the way he is with me."

Mullins was not convinced. "Is he serious about the presidency?"

"I think he seriously wants to be president. I don't know if he's committed to actually doing what it would take to win an election. And I'm not certain he understands just what a campaign like that would require of him."

✦ ✦ ✦

After the rally, Mullins remained in Columbus to continue the work of organizing Crimson Legion chapters. By then he had identified several people who were interested in a long-term association with the Legion and he worked closely with them to get a group formally organized.

One of the people who seemed key to that effort was Dawson Campbell, a mortician who owned Dryden Funeral Home on East Broad Street. Over the next several days they spent quite a bit of time together, getting rally volunteers committed to the group and shaping it into a formal entity.

Late one evening, Mullins returned to his hotel from a meeting with Campbell and as he came through the lobby, a clerk at the front desk waved him over. "You have a message." He took an envelope from beneath the counter and handed it to Mullins.

Mullins made his way to the elevator and opened the envelope to find a message from Senator Fisher. Apparently written in his own hand, the note asked Mullins to join him for dinner the next evening.

✦ ✦ ✦

As scheduled, Mullins and Fisher dined alone the following evening at a restaurant on Grant Avenue. "I've been hearing good reports about you," Fisher began.

"Oh? Who would that be from?"

Fisher smiled. "Dawson Campbell."

Mullins was surprised. "I didn't realize you were acquainted with him."

"Dawson and I go back a long way. In fact, I don't believe I can remember a time when I didn't know him."

"That's a long friendship."

"He was my campaign manager for my first senate election. He thinks you're a first-rate organizer," Fisher continued. "A great motivator of men. And I'll just cut to the chase with you." Fisher put down his fork and looked over at Mullins. "I want you to join my staff."

Mullins was taken aback. "I'm not sure I know what to say."

"We're assembling a team to do big things. I want you to organize offices for us in some key states."

"You're serious about the presidency?"

Fisher leaned forward and lowered his voice. "Not so loud."

Mullins grinned. "We're in a private room."

"I know. But I'm still self-conscious about this."

"But you're interested."

"Woodrow Wilson is done. Even if he runs again, he can't win."

Mullins nodded. "And we should be glad of that."

Fisher smiled. "You're not a Wilson fan?"

"No." Mullins could never be a Woodrow Wilson fan. Wilson was the one who dragged the United States into the Great War. The one who caused his brother to die. And the one who ruined the peace afterward. But he didn't say any of that. Instead he said, "There might be a crowded Republican field for the primaries."

Fisher waved him off. "That won't be an issue. We can take care of that. Half of them will be gone before the first primary occurs. And besides, Warren Harding is the only one with any heft."

"And you think you can defeat him?"

"I think he's vulnerable." Fisher took a drink from his glass. "But let's talk about you working for me. What do you think about it?"

"I'm flattered that you asked. But I'm working for the Crimson Legion. I can't run out on them. If you're putting together a campaign, you need someone who can get to work on it quickly. I can't leave Bill like that."

Fisher had a knowing smile. "He said you'd say that."

Mullins was startled. "You talked to Mr. Griffin about this?"

"The other night. After dinner."

"And what did he say?"

"He said he would hate to lose you, but he's agreeable to releasing you to join me."

Mullins arched an eyebrow. "He is?"

"Yes."

"Even so, I need to finish what we're doing here in Columbus. And I need to work out the remainder of the rally schedule."

Fisher nodded. "I know."

"We're on a seven- or eight-city run right now," Mullins explained. "It's all set up. There's no way for someone else to step into it now."

"We talked about that, too. He's agreeable for you to join us without a lengthy delay. To give you enough time to finish the immediate details. Then you'll join us in Washington."

CHAPTER 24

Afew days later, Mullins boarded a train in Columbus for a return trip to Charlotte. What he had told Fisher was true; they were on a seven-city rally schedule. However, not all the events were back-to-back and his next rally wasn't for three weeks, which gave him time to return to Charlotte and discuss his situation with Griffin. He really was flattered that Fisher wanted him to join his staff, but he didn't care for the fact that they had discussed the matter before talking to him—as if they were the ones making the decision about his future.

Still, Mullins was glad for the offer to join Fisher's staff. And he had no regrets about accepting the position. But something else about the situation left him uncomfortable. It wasn't that he'd accepted without talking to Griffin—he'd been unsettled about that, but not after he learned Griffin and Fisher had talked. It was something else. Something he hadn't . . . And then it hit him. *Grace.* She was the one he hadn't considered. He hadn't even thought of her until just then.

As the countryside moved past the railcar, Mullins began to wonder if things had run their course with Grace. She was a good person. A nice person. Fun to be around. They had enjoyed many experiences together. But now . . . He'd moved on from heckling Jews outside synagogues. And from juvenile acts like the pigs. A grin spread over his face at the thought of it. The pigs. It seemed so silly—Jews don't eat pork. Pigs in the synagogue! He'd seen Jimmy Goldberg eat a ham-and-cheese sandwich more than once. Jimmy was Jewish. Pork wasn't such a big deal for them anymore. Not all of them. "They probably didn't even notice," he mumbled to himself. And his mind wandered back to that day with Pete and the truck and the farmer. A lot of people knew about the pigs. But surely no one cared about that now. Not even Grace.

Perhaps he and Grace had gone as far together as they should. Or could. Working for Fisher would be a big move. A senator. A presidential campaign. Didn't get any bigger than that! Grace would just be stuck in a job in Washington. That was a long way from Springfield. But not very far from Virginia, where she grew up. Where her family still lived. He wondered about her family. Grace had never said much about them. What happened back there that she didn't want to talk about? Why had she come all the way to Springfield for a teaching job?

A job. *Oh no!* The sinking feeling stabbed him in his stomach again. Dorothy had mentioned a job opening at the office in Charlotte. She had wondered if Grace might be interested. He'd written to Grace about it and hadn't received a response. *But what if . . .*

At the time Dorothy mentioned it, having Grace in Charlotte sounded like a good idea. But not now. Not after all of this. Surely Dorothy wouldn't actually offer Grace a job like that without talking to him first. He had to get to Dorothy as soon as he arrived. Go to her house. Tell her that things had changed. Tell her to not make that offer. Things would be much easier that way. He could tell Dorothy to find someone else. And tell Grace they filled the opening without telling him. And then he could maneuver her into staying in Springfield, leaving him to take the job in Washington without worrying about her. Without being entangled with her. Without being tied down.

By the time the train reached Charlotte, Mullins had sorted things out in his mind and convinced himself that everything would work out fine. He'd have to move quickly, but as long as he did that, things would all fall into place. Grace would remain in Springfield. He would finish his work with the Crimson Legion, then leave for Washington. And he might get an evening alone with Dorothy in the process. Follow up on the interest she'd showed him.

Just then, the Charlotte train station came into view and up ahead he saw the platform. It was empty except for one person. A woman. Not too tall. Slender, with a pleasant shape. A shape he knew all too well—Grace, waiting expectantly for him to arrive.

Once again, the sinking feeling stabbed him in the pit of his stomach—this time as the carefully laid plans he'd spent hours constructing came crashing down around him.

When the train came to a stop, Mullins rose from his seat and made his way up the aisle to the exit. Grace was standing at the bottom of the steps and he made his way toward her. "What are you doing here?" he asked with a laugh.

She wrapped her arms around him and squeezed him close, then kissed him deeply. After a moment, she looked up at him and smiled. "Dorothy offered me a job, and I accepted."

"But the school term isn't over yet, is it?"

"No, but they thought I should go ahead and accept. So I did." She kissed him again. "I've only been here two days."

"Where are you staying?"

"At Renfrow's." She leaned forward and whispered in his ear, "Just down the hall from you."

"How is it working out with Dorothy?"

She stepped back and took his hand in hers. "Well, I've only just started, but I think she and I will get along well." They started up the platform toward the crossover to the station. "She has been very helpful in getting me settled."

From the station, they took a taxi to the boardinghouse. Mullins did his best to say all the right things, but her appearance in

Charlotte made him noticeably tense. When they arrived at the house, she stopped him on the walkway before they reached the steps to the porch. "What's wrong?"

"We need to talk."

She looked stricken. "What about?"

"Let's go inside first."

Mullins took his suitcase to his room while Grace waited for him in the parlor downstairs. When he returned, he took her by the hand and said, "Come on. Let's go for a walk."

From the boardinghouse, they walked up to the corner in silence, then turned. A little way down the block he finally had the courage to begin. "Do you remember I mentioned Senator Fisher from Ohio in one of my letters?"

"Yes."

"He offered me a position on his staff in Washington."

She grinned. "Are you going to take it?"

He glanced down at the pavement. "I already did."

Grace smiled. "That's great."

"I wanted to talk to you first." He worked at sounding apologetic. "But I—"

She cut him off. "No. It's okay. I understand."

"He wanted an answer right then and I didn't think he would wait."

"I understand." She placed her finger against his lips and spoke softly. "I'm not angry." She kissed him again. "This is a wonderful opportunity for you."

"It just happened so suddenly. I didn't expect it at all."

"What does he want you to do?"

"The same thing I'm doing now, except for him."

"Then, he must be interested in running for something big. Something that would require a large network of people. Something like . . ." She looked over at him. "President?"

Mullins leaned closer. "Don't tell anyone."

Her mouth fell open in a look of amazement. "This is unbelievable!"

"Yeah. I was rather amazed by it, too."

"Not that." she went on, "The way your life has opened up. Like we've talked about before. One thing to the next. Coming to the mill in Springfield. Listening to Walter Jones on the radio. And that led you to the Crimson Legion. And that led you to this."

"Then, you really aren't angry that I accepted without talking to you first?"

"Not at all."

"Will you come to Washington?"

"I'll have to set things right here. I've only just begun. Seems a terrible thing to just leave after only accepting the job."

"Let me talk to them first. After I've settled with them about me, I'll talk to them about you."

"Okay." She slipped her arm in his. "This is exciting." She grinned from ear to ear. "I can't believe it."

✦ ✦ ✦

The next day, Mullins went to the office and met alone with Griffin. They reviewed the results from the Columbus rally and the meetings they held in association with it. Then Mullins gave him a report on the effort to organize a Crimson Legion chapter there. Finally, he came to the matter of Senator Fisher. Mullins outlined the senator's offer—organize support groups for him in key states, mostly along the East Coast but a few out west.

Griffin smiled. "He's really serious about this presidential bid?"

"Yes. I think so. He said he talked to you about me."

"Yes, "we talked about you joining his staff when we were in Cleveland. Then he mentioned it again before I left Columbus. I wasn't sure he was going to make the offer, though."

"Well, he did."

Griffin changed positions in his chair and propped against the armrest. "This will be a good thing, actually. For both of us."

Mullins was puzzled. "What do you mean?"

"You get to ride up the ladder of political success on Fisher's coattails. And I get to ride along with you."

Mullins frowned. "I'm not sure I follow."

"Take the job. Do good work for him, but steer him toward our priorities—you know them as well as anyone. And keep me informed. That way, I can help you smooth things out from time to time and you can help us."

"Like your inside man."

"Exactly like my inside man."

"Okay." Mullins wasn't sure how that would work out, but he didn't want to argue. "He wants me as soon as possible but I said I would stay here to work through the end of the current schedule."

Griffin nodded approvingly. "That would be good. Gives us a few months to get someone else in here to take your place."

They talked awhile longer, but as the meeting came to an end, Mullins added, "There is one more issue. We're just friends."

Griffin grinned. "You mean the girl?"

"Yes, I would like for her to come to Washington, too."

"I see why you like having her around. I like her, too. We all do."

"I need her with me." Mullins wasn't sure he actually needed her but he didn't like the idea of someone else telling him what he could and couldn't do with his life.

Griffin thought for a moment, then nodded. "Okay. She can join you. But not until the fall. We need her here until then."

"I need—"

"We just hired her, Bryce." There was an unmistakable coldness in Griffin's voice. "And besides, you won't be finished here for a few more months." He looked Mullins in the eye. "She can come in the fall."

They stared at each other a moment, neither man blinking. Then Mullins relaxed and muttered, "Okay."

✦ ✦ ✦

A few days after his meeting with Griffin, Mullins once again boarded the train and left Charlotte, this time for a rally in Chicago. Grace remained behind to work at the Crimson Legion headquarters. The next Saturday, she worked half a day and then walked up the street to Belk Brothers department store, located a few blocks from the office. It was a pleasant, sunny day and she enjoyed the time away from her co-workers.

While shopping in the women's section of the store, Graham Hawthorne, one of the agents from the Justice Department's Bureau of Investigation, slipped up beside her. She was startled by his presence but before she could speak out, he placed a finger to his lips in a gesture for silence. When she'd collected herself, he instructed in a low voice, "Go to the dressing room as if you are trying on a dress. Leave the dress in the first room, then walk to a door at the end of the hall. Go through that door and make your way to the loading dock behind the building."

"I don't know where that is," she whispered.

"You'll find it," he directed. And then he disappeared.

Feeling she had no other option, Grace did as she was told. She selected a dress from the nearest rack, made her way into the dressing-room area, and hung it on a peg just inside the door of the first room. At the end of the hall she came to the door Hawthorne described. She pushed it open and stepped into a utility area of the building where extra equipment was kept. Picking her way carefully, she came to a door marked EXIT in plain block letters. She opened that door and stepped out onto a loading dock. A truck was parked to one side but there were no employees in sight.

Just then, a black sedan came to a stop a few feet beyond

where she stood. Stairs at the far end of the dock led down to the pavement. She walked down, then started toward the car.

As she approached, the driver's door opened and Roy Martin, the other agent she'd met in Springfield, stepped out. He opened the rear door of the car and held it while she got in. When she was seated, he closed the door and got in behind the steering wheel.

Following a circuitous route, they came to a warehouse in an industrial part of the city. The doors to the building were open and Martin drove the car inside. As it came to a stop, workmen closed the doors behind them, cutting them off from the outside.

A moment later, Martin opened the rear door of the car and gestured for Grace to step out. As she rose from the back seat, Hawthorne approached and gestured for her to follow. "Right this way, Miss Anderson." She started in that direction and the two men fell in beside her.

Hawthorne and Martin escorted her across the building's main floor to a windowless room off the central storage hall. In it, a single light hung above a plain table with four chairs arranged around it. Martin gestured to one. "Have a seat."

Grace took a seat and waited while they did, as well. When everyone was comfortable, Martin began. "We're glad you took the job and made the move here to Charlotte."

Grace shrugged. "I'm not sure what I can do for you. Things are changing."

Martin raised an eyebrow. "What do you mean?"

"Bryce has been offered a job on Senator Fisher's staff."

"Jonas Fisher? From Ohio?"

"Yes," she acknowledged with obvious pride.

"Will he accept it?"

"He already has. Plans to move to Washington, D.C., in a few months."

Both agents appeared surprised by the news. Hawthorne spoke up. "When did the senator make the offer?"

"While they were in Columbus a few weeks ago."

Hawthorne continued. "What will Mullins do?"

"He'll be organizing groups of the senator's supporters. Much like what he's been doing for the Legion."

"Organizing? In Ohio?"

"I'm not sure I can tell you that."

"I would remind you," Martin reiterated, "that we have a deal. And you are hardly in a position to be difficult."

"As I understand it, he'll be working in most of the eastern states and several key cities."

"And you're certain he'll be doing this with supporters for the senator?"

Grace nodded. "That's what he said."

"Why does Fisher need supporters anywhere except Ohio?"

Grace looked amused. "You tell me. You're the federal agents."

Hawthorne frowned. "Is Fisher planning to run for president?"

Grace smiled. "I believe that is the plan."

"Have they talked to you about a job?"

"No. But Bryce and I are planning for me to move to Washington, too."

"And do what?"

"That hasn't been decided."

"Does William Griffin know this?"

"They talked."

"And Griffin agreed to it?"

"Yes."

Martin spoke up again. "And he'll agree to let you go, too?"

"I'll go whether he says so or not. He can't keep me here against my will."

"For now, though," Martin warned, "we need you to stay put and keep up your normal routine at the Crimson Legion."

"We've already discussed me leaving."

"But we need you to stay there," Hawthorne reiterated.

She looked over at him. "Will you be joining me for more shopping trips?"

Hawthorne smiled. "We'll be in touch."

"How?"

"We'll find you."

"And what if I need to find *you*?"

Both men were silent for a moment, then Hawthorne asked, "Do you like hats?"

"Sometimes, but not always. Why?"

"If you need to talk to us, wear a hat to work in the morning."

She gave them a look. "I don't usually wear a hat. Won't it be obvious if I do?"

"Obvious to you," Hawthorne pointed out, "but not to anyone else. Women wear hats all the time."

"Not me."

"You can make an excuse for it." Hawthorne sounded frustrated. "You can tell them anything you think you need to. Just wear a hat to work when you need to talk to us. We'll know what it means."

She glared at him. "You're watching me all the time?"

"Just wear the hat," Hawthorne snapped.

"And if you can come up with a better signal," Martin added with a pleasant voice, "we'll be glad to use it. But for now wear the hat."

CHAPTER 25

Two months after accepting Senator Fisher's offer, Mullins arrived in Washington, D.C., to take his position with the senator's staff. With Grace's help, he had packed his belongings into two suitcases and three boxes, then boarded a train from Charlotte headed north to Washington.

Late the following afternoon, the train arrived at Union Station, not far from Capitol Hill. He was met at the station by Travis Fielding, one of the senator's assistants, who took him by car to a boardinghouse a few blocks away.

As the car came to a stop at the curb in front of the house, Fielding glanced over at Mullins. "This place is owned by Truman Taylor. His wife died a few years ago. Since then he's been renting out rooms, mostly to people new to town like you. Lots of new staffers on the Hill room with him."

"Sounds like the place to be."

"It's a good place," Fielding replied. "But don't get too chatty with your fellow residents."

"Might be talking to an opponent's staffer?"

"Yeah." Fielding had a sly grin. "It's also a good place to pass along information you want someone to repeat."

"Right." Mullins nodded. "It's all about who and what you know."

"In this city," Fielding continued, "everyone talks. The trick is to figure out what they're telling you that's the truth and which part is something they want you to *believe* is the truth."

"A shell game," Mullins noted.

"Precisely."

Mullins rented a room from Taylor and brought his things from the car, then went to dinner with Fielding. Mullins was interested in knowing as much as possible about how the office functioned before he arrived there for work.

"The real power in the office," Fielding explained, "is with the senator and his chief of staff, Robert Gilmore. Have you met him?"

"No, I've only met Marvin Parsons."

"Parsons is a good man. And he's the senator's favorite of all the staff. Takes him along everywhere he goes. But Gilmore is the one who runs the place. He's in Ohio right now, but he'll be back soon. He and the senator control most of what happens with the staff."

"How does Gilmore feel about Parsons? Seems like they would be rivals."

Fielding laughed. "Lots of tension between those two. But Gilmore is shrewd. He knows that the senator won't let him do anything with Parsons. And Parsons seems to recognize that Gilmore is in charge."

"But they don't care for each other."

"No. They don't." Fielding grinned. "Gilmore will be up here in a day or two. You can see them together for yourself."

When he returned to his room at the boardinghouse, Mullins busied himself putting away his belongings, then wrote a letter to Grace. Despite the way he'd felt about her before, he decided that ending things with her would be too disruptive right then. And besides, she'd been useful in the past. Perhaps she would be useful in his work for the senator. He made sure the letter sounded the same as all the others, giving no hint of how he truly felt, then took it downstairs for the outgoing mail.

✦ ✦ ✦

For the remainder of the week, Mullins concentrated on getting acquainted with Parsons, Fielding, and other members of the staff, including Ann Aldridge, a writer hired by Fisher to help craft his speeches, and Emma Hart, his secretary.

On Thursday, Gilmore returned and the staff, most of whom were considerably younger than Mullins, became noticeably tense. Mullins kept to himself, though, and observed them from a distance.

Late in the afternoon, Gilmore called Mullins into his office. "Are you getting settled in?"

"Yes, I think I'm situated for the time being."

"Did Fielding take you to Truman Taylor's?"

"Yes."

"That's where he takes everyone new. I wonder sometimes if he doesn't get a referral fee for the business he brings that old man."

"I'm sure Mr. Taylor appreciates it."

"I suspect so." Gilmore leaned back in his chair. "Do you have any questions about the details of your job?"

"Many," Mullins nodded.

"Such as?"

"I know what the senator told me I was to do—organize support groups in various locations—but I was wondering what *you* expected me to do. You're the person who directs the actual work around here."

"I'm sure my expectations are the same as the senator's," Gilmore replied. "We want you to organize support groups in key states and cities. That's the important distinction. There are strategic locations we want you to concentrate your efforts on."

"Which places did you have in mind?"

"Well," Gilmore began, "as you are aware, we are preparing

for a presidential campaign."

"Right."

"The way the election process works, the first thing we have to do is win the party's nomination."

"How do we do that?" Mullins knew, but wanted Gilmore to tell him as a way of gaining insight into Gilmore's expectations. He was certain Gilmore expected more than he would ever say in a forthright manner.

"Some states have primaries, but not all. For those that don't have primaries, we work the state party officials and members. Trade, bargain, cajole—do whatever it takes—to get our people named as delegates to the national convention. The senator can do most of that. What we need your help with is in the states that *do* have primaries."

"So, New York, New Jersey. Places like that."

"Yes. The important ones for us are California, Pennsylvania, New Jersey, Massachusetts, Michigan, and Maryland." Gilmore ticked off the names with practiced precision. "In the general election, assuming we get that far, we'll need support from the usual groups—women, progressives, internationalists, business elite, and corporate interests. But for the primaries, we need party members. Loyalists who are active year in and year out."

Mullins frowned. "Some of those groups you mentioned are part of the problem we face. Immigrants dominate the media, business, banking, and finance."

"You mean the Jews."

"Yes."

Gilmore sat up straight. "Look, the senator is well aware of your ties to the Crimson Legion and the issues William Griffin has been pushing. No matter what he's said or how naïve he might have sounded to you, the senator knows all about your agenda."

"I'm sure you made sure of that."

"My sympathies are not at issue here. It's the senator's

interests that count. And, for the record, he's sympathetic to the issues Griffin has raised, but you were brought on board for your organizational skills. Not to be a policy advisor. We'll handle the political message."

Mullins didn't like the sound of that. "And you don't intend to raise those issues in the campaign?"

"The senator is the junior senator from Ohio. Being from Ohio has its advantages, but he is number two on the list of senators from that state."

Mullins nodded. "And you think Harding is going to run against you."

"That's a very real possibility. And the political reality is, regardless of how we might feel about the issues personally, we need the support of party regulars if we are to have a chance at this." Mullins had the sense that Gilmore thought Fisher's campaign for the presidency was a mistake, but he kept quiet and listened. "So some of those issues you've noted," Gilmore continued, "will have to be toned down in the senator's speeches. In my opinion, he's already said too much about them, and his association with Griffin and the Crimson Legion has been far too obvious."

"It's been noticed already?"

"Yes. And many in the party already are suspicious of him because of it."

"So, aside from the issues, we need to focus on winning the support of state party regulars."

Gilmore nodded. "We're looking to win the primaries, pick up a key endorsement or two on the way, and roll into Chicago for the convention with a healthy margin of delegates already in our pocket."

Mullins pushed the question of issues aside for the moment and concentrated on preserving a working relationship with Gilmore. "Any idea who you might get to endorse him?"

"We're hoping the treasury secretary."

Mullins raised an eyebrow. "Andrew Mellon?"

"Yes." Gilmore smiled. "Think he'll do it?"

"I don't know," Mullins replied. From the look on Gilmore's face he was sure the idea had been his. "But that would be a big endorsement."

Gilmore grinned. "We're interested in him because he controls the Pennsylvania party. Which means he'll control the delegation to the convention. If we win the primaries in the states I noted earlier and get Mellon's support—or the support of someone like him—we think we can win the nomination on the first ballot."

"Winning on the first ballot would avoid a fight."

"Right." Gilmore seemed less combative. "We don't want a floor fight or multiple rounds of voting."

Mullins nodded. "Sounds like we have a lot of work to do."

"Yes, we do." Gilmore stood, signaling the meeting had come to an end. "The convention is scheduled for next summer in Chicago."

"For a project like this, we don't have much time."

"No. We don't." Gilmore smiled. "So get to work and let's make it happen."

✦ ✦ ✦

After talking to Gilmore, Mullins decided to focus his initial effort on organizing support for Fisher in Pennsylvania. It was perhaps the most important state on Gilmore's list and it was close, which meant he could travel there without incurring great expense. From his experience organizing for the Crimson Legion, he knew his work at the beginning would require multiple contacts with operatives and volunteers in each of the locations. Getting his start in a place that was closest to the office meant he could go there often without much difficulty while he sorted out the complexities of what he was trying to do.

Using contact information for Fisher's existing supporters, Mullins plotted a series of one-on-one meetings in and around Pittsburgh, a location in the state where Fisher had done well in the past and where he was well-known.

After two days of meetings with businessmen and party activists, Mullins met with Sumner Bayless, the mayor of Pittsburgh. Mullins outlined what he was trying to do and asked Bayless for his cooperation in getting it done.

Bayless was hesitant. "I don't know."

"Why not? You've shown your support for Senator Fisher in the past."

"Look, I know you've been meeting with our people on this. And we're all interested in Senator Fisher as a potential president. But most of us are cautious about him."

"Cautious?" Mullins was curious. "Why is that?"

"We think Fisher might be too far to the right to win the general election."

"Too far to the right on what?"

"Immigration. The things he says about Jews."

Mullins hadn't realized how much influence Griffin exerted over Fisher. He didn't think Griffin knew it, either. "Don't get me wrong," Bayless continued. "I've talked to Jonas many times. We go back a long way together. I believe in the positions he has taken on these issues. I even helped him figure out where he stands on them after he's talked to your friend Griffin."

Mullins was also surprised at how much everyone seemed to know about Fisher. "And I believe that issues like immigration and Jewish influence are important," Bayless added. "And the Italians, too. They are taking over everywhere." His disgust for Italians was obvious. "But I'm not sure Fisher can get elected."

"You're not thinking of supporting Teddy Roosevelt again, are you?"

"Some would like to see him make a run at it. But the talk is, Harding is going to run and if he gets into the race, I don't think Fisher stands a chance at the nomination."

"Harding is all talk, though. That's all he has. Just talk."

"We're not so sure," Bayless hedged. "Harding has been building relationships for a long time. Longer than Jonas. And he's known to the public. Fisher isn't known very well outside of Ohio, and where he *is* known, he doesn't have broad appeal."

"Sounds like you've made up your mind."

"No." Bayless shook his head. "I'm just speaking frankly. If you can show some muscle, a lot can change."

"Well, at least don't work for any other candidate."

Bayless shook his head. "I'm not sure I can even promise that at this point."

Mullins knew what that meant. "Who are you working for?"

Bayless looked away. "Harding came through here last week."

Mullins stood. "You're making a big mistake." He did little to hide his frustration. "A big mistake."

"I assure you," Bayless replied, "it won't be my first."

✦ ✦ ✦

That evening, Mullins met with Eugene Felton, a party activist and a known member of the German American Federation, an organization much like the Knights of Teutonia.

"I understand you met with Bayless today," Felton began.

"Yes," Mullins answered. "We had a full and frank discussion."

"Did he tell you he favors Harding over Fisher?"

"Yes."

"Don't worry about him."

"Harding or Bayless?"

"Both. They're the least of your troubles."

"What do you mean?"

Felton gave him a knowing look. "I am aware of your association with the Crimson Legion."

"Not much of a secret. And certainly not here in Pittsburgh."

Felton chuckled. "I work with a similar organization known as the German American Federation. Are you familiar with them?"

"Sort of. I attended some Knights of Teutonia meetings before I found the Crimson Legion."

"Ah, yes." Felton recognized the name. "We share goals similar to them."

"Do you share their German emphasis?"

Felton shrugged. "It's not for everyone." He looked over at Mullins and smiled in an eerie way. "I heard about your protest in Springfield." He lowered his voice. "Pigs in the synagogue! That was brilliant. We laughed about it for weeks." Felton started to chuckle. "We still do."

Mullins was concerned. "Where did you hear all that?" He did his best to ask without admitting anything.

"News gets around. Especially when the feds come around asking questions."

Mullins had a sinking feeling in his chest. "The feds?"

"Yeah." Felton seemed to relish in telling him. "They've been looking into that whole thing." He reached across the table and patted Mullins on the shoulder. "But don't worry. Your secret is safe with me." He winked. "I want you to come with me to a meeting of our local Federation. Meet the guys. See if we can find a way to help you with the senator's dream of being president one day."

"I'm on a rather tight schedule," Mullins replied.

"We're meeting tomorrow night. Surely you can stay over one more night."

✦　✦　✦

Against his better judgment, Mullins stayed over one more night and attended the Federation meeting the following evening. Felton introduced him to the members and he joined in their discussion of the issues—immigration, Jews, the plot to seize control of the economy, to destroy American jobs, and subvert the American lifestyle in Communism. For Mullins, it was like returning home.

Finally, as the evening drew to a close, Felton asked, "What can we do to help Senator Fisher?"

"One thing you can do," Mullins replied, "is to become active in the party."

"The Republican Party."

"Yes. I know you have your opinions about the party and about politics, but Senator Fisher will be running as a Republican and for him to be a success, he needs party support. One way we can achieve that—and one way we as fellow activists in the fight for America's survival can exert our influence—is to become active in the party and work from inside the party structure to support the senator and the causes we believe in."

Someone spoke up. "You mean infiltrate the party and take over."

"That's exactly what I mean. But," he added, "without the party regulars knowing that's what you're doing."

Mullins hadn't thought about his work quite like that before, but even as the words rolled off his lips, the idea resonated with something deep in his soul. He'd formed Crimson Legion chapters across the eastern half of the country. Chapters that now seemed ripe for involvement in a political campaign. He knew those groups. They would be eager to exert their influence and equally eager to accept the challenge of surreptitiously taking over state Republican Party organizations. It was a strategy he was certain could benefit both the senator and the Crimson Legion.

Over the next several weeks, Mullins traveled back to all the cities where he had previously organized Crimson Legion chapters; only, this time he did so as a staff member for Senator Fisher. He met with the chapters, outlined the strategy, and enlisted their help—infiltrate the party, get active, become delegates, vote for Fisher in the primary and at the convention. As he expected, every chapter agreed to do just that.

Despite the reservations of Bayless and others whom Mullins encountered on his first trip, he quickly established campaign support groups for Fisher in Pennsylvania, New Jersey, Massachusetts, Michigan, and Maryland. In each of those locations he relied heavily on Crimson Legion chapters already active in the area. And at each of those chapter gatherings his message was the same: Senator Fisher intended to run for president, and regardless of the outcome he intended to use his campaign to address issues like immigration control and breaking the grip of Jews on American banks and industries. "Get in now," he urged, "and you can play an important role as we put together a coalition of support for a candidate who can effect real change in America."

CHAPTER 26

After multiple trips through the eastern half of the country, Mullins returned to the office in Washington where he met with Fisher and Gilmore to review progress in organizing support for Fisher's presidential campaign. They gathered around Fisher's desk to talk.

"Party regulars are interested in you," Mullins noted. "But they're reluctant."

Fisher had a knowing look. "They think I can't win."

Mullins nodded. "Some say that, but they also think you might be too far to the right on the issues to win in the general election."

"I've tried to tell you that would be a problem," Gilmore said.

Fisher seemed to ignore the comment. "That's interesting.". A humidor sat on the corner of his desk. He opened it and took out a cigar, then lit it while he talked. "Most of the regulars have never heard me express my positions."

Mullins shrugged. "Perhaps, but news seems to be getting around."

"I warned you about that, too," Gilmore chimed in again.

Again Fisher let the comment pass. "And I suppose they think Harding is going to run."

"Yes," Mullins replied. "Most of them do. And they think if he does, he'll roll right over us."

Fisher leaned back in his chair. "So, where do we find our support?"

"We need an issue that will divide Harding's support," Gilmore commented. "It's the only way."

Fisher looked over at him. "And you still think immigration control won't do that?"

Gilmore shook his head. "No, it will only solidify them against you. Harding supporters are progressives. They'll never go for an issue like limiting immigration."

Fisher turned to Mullins. "So if the party regulars won't go for us with Harding in the race, no matter what, then what about the conservatives? Will they go for us?"

"Conservative groups are interested," Mullins noted. "But they're skeptical of you, too, though for a different reason."

Gilmore seemed irritated. "And what would that reason be?"

"They wonder whether you are a true believer."

"A *believer* in what?" Gilmore had a sarcastic tone.

Mullins glared at him. "They're very committed to their causes. They wonder if we are, as well."

Fisher spoke up. "What will it take to convince them?"

"With party regulars, there is no issue you can use to win them over. If Harding is in, they're with him. That's not an issue-related choice. So convincing *them* is a nonstarter. With the conservative side of the party, immigration is your best issue."

Gilmore looked perturbed. "You mean immigration limits."

Again Fisher ignored Gilmore's comment and focused on Mullins. "Immigration is an issue we're both interested in. And it's one supported by many powerful groups. But most of the people in those groups aren't active in the party."

Gilmore spoke up. "And that's a point I've made for a long time. That issue can't take us anywhere with the party."

"Not the party we have right now," Mullins agreed.

Gilmore frowned. "What are you suggesting?"

Mullins leaned forward. "We can't win this election by merely appealing to traditional party members. Traditionalists will go for

Harding rather than you. They've been with him all along, and we can't pry them loose using issues."

"What else is there?" Gilmore scoffed.

"If we can't bring the party to us," Mullins proffered, "we'll have to bring *us* to the party."

Gilmore scowled. "That's a lot of nonsense."

Fisher seemed interested. "I like the sound of this. Tell me what you mean."

"Like I've said, we can't turn party regulars away from Harding. And even if Harding doesn't run, progressives will never agree with us on immigration control. If we let party regulars make the nomination decision, we will lose—either to Harding or to someone else. They'll never choose you. But we don't have to let them do that. We can bring our own people to the party."

Fisher nodded. "Bring our own votes with us."

"Exactly."

"Or," Gilmore sulked, "we could find a way to talk about something else that appeals to regulars."

Mullins shot him a look. "Like what?"

"I don't know." Gilmore slumped in his chair.

Fisher continued. "We use immigration as a way of appealing to conservatives. Let Harding have the progressives. Push him in the direction he's already going. Recruit our own support and bring them into the party. Immigration control is a good issue." Fisher sounded confident. "It's an issue that can become *our* issue. I like it."

Mullins knew Gilmore did not agree with them. And he was certain Gilmore would chastise him later for the way the meeting went. But right then he didn't care. He had analyzed the situation, saw an opening, and steered Fisher in the direction he wanted him to go.

✦ ✦ ✦

That evening, after everyone else left the office, Mullins was still there, sorting through notes and letters and memos on his desk. Gilmore appeared in the doorway. He did not look pleased. "I spent the remainder of my day trying to undo what you did in that meeting."

Mullins did not look up. "Undo what?"

Gilmore folded his arms across his chest and leaned against the doorframe. "Thanks to you, the senator is convinced that limiting immigrants from eastern and southern Europe—people who are predominantly Catholic and Jewish—is the single most important issue we face."

"He's right. It is the single most important issue we face."

"But he can't win on that issue." Gilmore's voice had a hard edge.

"It's the only issue he *can* win with."

"No." Gilmore pushed away from the doorframe and stood. "He has to run just far enough to one side or the other to attract enough votes to win." He gestured with his hands to indicate. "But that's it. Just far enough. Not an all-out commitment either way."

"The middle of the road," Mullins replied disdainfully. "The safe approach that accomplishes nothing."

"It's not nothing," Gilmore argued. "Winning the nomination is not nothing."

"And you think he can do that with your plan."

Gilmore's voice was growing louder by the moment. "Yes. He can."

"Without offending anyone."

"Well, it's certainly not about offending people."

"Especially not the Jews." Sarcasm dripped from Mullins' every word.

"He has to win the nomination without alienating Jews and Catholics," Gilmore retorted. "So, he can still win in the general election. The kind of immigration position you're talking about will alienate both groups. And the progressives. And anyone else who hasn't yet decided whom to vote for."

Mullins spoke in a flat tone.

"Immigrants are the source of all our trouble,"

"You mean *Jews* are the source of our trouble," Gilmore snapped. "And I wish you'd be honest enough when you talk to me to just come out and say it."

"Okay. Jews are the cause of our problems—especially in the northeast—and the senator knows it." His tone was decidedly more combative. "And on top of that, immigration control is an issue he believes in. He's not interested in just winning. He's not interested in offending the least number of people. He's not interested in dancing around the issues to try to out-Harding Harding. He wants to change things for the country's good."

"Look." Gilmore attempted to lower his voice. "You're new to this. You don't understand the way politics gets done. So I'll explain it to you. Jews and Catholics are huge in the northeast. New York, New Jersey, Pennsylvania, even Maryland. Those are states with large Jewish populations. They're also the most populous states. And they are states where party members are most active. We need support from those states in order to have any chance at all of winning."

Mullins had a condescending look. "This is your idea of an election strategy?"

"It's my idea," Gilmore ranted. "It's the party's idea. It's everyone's idea. And, frankly, if it were left up to me, I would fire you for bringing up your ideas in a meeting like the one we had this afternoon without getting my approval first."

"You would." Mullins grinned. "But you can't, can you?"

Gilmore shoved his hands in his front pockets. "No, I can't."

"Then I guess we'll just have to work around each other."

"Listen to me." Gilmore stepped closer and took a seat on a chair in front of Mullins. "The senator gravitates naturally toward your position on immigration. He has always liked the idea of ending immigration altogether. He thinks limiting or ending Jewish immigration would solve many of our problems. And given his own choices, he tends to be very hardline about it. We have spent enormous amounts of time and energy steering him away from immigration, Jews, and Catholics for that very reason."

"We?"

"The staff and I."

"And you think that's a good thing? To steer him away from where he naturally wants to go with an issue?"

"His natural position on those issues would place him too far to the right even for many people in Ohio. He has to be closer to the middle." Gilmore stood and moved the chair aside. "If you want to work here, I suggest you stick to the plan we're already working."

Mullins looked up at him with a cold, unblinking stare. "Or what?"

"Or, regardless of how the senator might feel about the issues, or the Crimson Legion, or your friend Griffin, I'll find a way to move you out. And I'll ruin you in the process."

✦ ✦ ✦

The following day, Fisher called Mullins into his office. They met privately, just the two of them behind closed doors. "I've thought about what we discussed yesterday," Fisher began.

After his discussion with Gilmore the night before, Mullins braced himself for a confrontation. "Robert let me know last night that he really didn't like my suggestions on the immigration issue. So if you need to do something else, just let me know."

"Ahh." Fisher gave a dismissive gesture. "Don't worry about Gilmore. He's been steering me away from the difficult issues for a long time. They all have. They're afraid I'll offend too many people."

Mullins smiled. "Yes, sir."

"But they aren't the junior senator from Ohio. I am. And I think getting control of immigration is the key to the survival of the republic."

"I couldn't agree with you more."

"It might not be an issue that gets me elected to the presidency," Fisher continued, "but it's an issue the country needs to face up to."

"Yes, sir."

"We have to control our own borders," Fisher continued. "And not just the physical border with Canada and Mexico. Anyone could wander across there, but that's not where our issue lies right now. The weakest parts of our border are the ports of foreign entry—the eastern cities with people coming from Europe—Jews and Italians, mostly—and on the West Coast with people coming from China and Japan."

"Yes, sir." Mullins nodded. "But there's one thing about this issue that we didn't discuss yesterday."

Fisher had a questioning look. "What's that?"

"If you run on this issue, you'll have to propose legislation to address it."

"Yes, yes, I know."

"You can't just talk about it. To use it as a way of gaining support for your candidacy, you'll have to show you really mean it. And the only way you can do that is to introduce an immigration-control bill and then seriously fight for its passage."

"I understand."

"Your staff will never draft a bill tough enough to be effective."

"I know that, too." Fisher pointed to him and smiled. "Which is why you and I are going to draft the legislation ourselves."

Mullins smiled, too. "You realize I've never done that before."

Again Fisher made a dismissive gesture. "That's not a problem. I've written plenty of bills and we have copies of bills lying around here that came from everybody else. Read a couple of them to see the format and then let's get busy."

"Yes, sir." Mullins stood to leave.

"But keep this to yourself," Fisher added. "And don't tell Gilmore. Or any of the others."

✦ ✦ ✦

Over the next two weeks, Mullins helped Fisher craft an immigration bill structured around quotas drawn from 1910 Census data, a time when Jewish immigration was lower than the current era. Tying the legislation to the census, without mentioning specific numbers, produced the restrictions they wanted but avoided singling out any particular group by name. Fisher liked the approach. "This will make it easy for people to agree with the details and less resistant to voting in favor of it."

Mullins acknowledged. "On the one hand, we're establishing quotas, but on the other we're merely rolling back the rate of entry to that of an earlier date."

"We might even get some co-sponsors for it."

Mullins was unsure of what that meant. "That's a good thing?"

"Yes. Co-sponsors are people who want to 'me too' on the legislation. Add their name as a proponent. When they do, they're guaranteed votes in favor of the bill."

Once they were certain of the language, Mullins assisted in the approval process by sounding out staff members from the offices of other senators and congressmen. In order to become law, both sides of Congress would have to approve the bill, not merely the Senate.

"We need to work both sides of the process," Fisher stressed. "Passage in the Senate but failure in the House would show me to be a weak leader. We need to come out strong for this and be strong all the way through."

Working carefully and quietly, Mullins gathered a group of co-sponsors in the senate and lined up votes for the bill in the House. Many of the officials he spoke with were hearing calls for immigration reform from among their constituencies at home but were worried that a serious immigration bill could not pass. They were all too glad to have Fisher take the lead in getting a bill through Congress.

Fisher smiled when he heard about the reaction from his colleagues. "They want me to take the lead so that if it fails they can blame me. They need to support the issue because of the voters at home, but they aren't sure if the legislation will pass, so they don't want to get too close to it. But if they sign on as co-sponsors, they're just as much at risk as I am. And if we can get enough to co-sponsor, the others will join rather than being left out, regardless of how they perceive the risk. So get as many co-sponsors as possible."

In working all of that out, Mullins came to know staff members in Congress and at key government agencies—State Department, Justice Department, even one or two staffers at the White House. It was a heady time for him. Long hours. Working with people who, just a year or two earlier, were only names in a newspaper article to him. Now they were seated across from him, listening to every word he said.

With the hectic pace and his concentration devoted to the legislative process, Mullins's contact with Grace dwindled. Even though her letters continued to arrive for him almost daily, he wrote to her with less and less frequency. Once again, his interest in her began to wane.

As Senator Fisher's proposed bill made the rounds, and as more congressional members signed on as co-sponsors, it became more difficult to hide. Before long, Gilmore learned about it from a fellow aide. Predictably, he was livid with Mullins and charged into his office.

"How dare you do this behind my back!" Gilmore waved a copy of the bill. "You were brought here to organize support. Not draft legislation or advise on policy. He had a chance to become president. A chance! And now you've ruined it!"

"His chances aren't ruined," Mullins countered calmly. "Our supporters love the bill. And we have plenty of people lined up to co-sponsor. They'll be glad he introduced it."

"How many times do I have to tell you?!" Gilmore shouted. "He can't win on this issue!"

"He can if he follows through. If this bill passes, immigration will become *the* issue of the campaign."

"No!" Gilmore shouted. "No, it won't!"

Just then, the door opened and Fisher appeared. "Robert," he said in a stern voice, "the bill was my idea."

"Your idea because he guided you to it," Gilmore fumed.

"It was my idea because that's what I believe. If you can't support me in the things I'm trying to do, I think you should find someone else to work for."

Gilmore gestured with the copy of the bill. "If this is what you want, then you'll have to find someone else to help you with it. And good luck finding a job in Ohio next term." He pushed his way past them and left.

When he was gone, Mullins looked over at Fisher. "I'm sorry. I didn't mean for that to happen."

"Don't worry about it. He was always more supportive of himself than he was of me."

"Yes, sir. I think he was."

Fisher ordered, "Get that bill passed."

✦ ✦ ✦

The following day, Fisher appointed Marvin Parsons to be his new chief of staff. Parsons and Mullins worked well together and put the finishing touches to the proposed immigration bill. A few days later, Fisher introduced it in the Senate. Thanks to Mullins's hard work, the bill already had much of the support it needed for passage.

While the bill made its way through the Senate process, Mullins prepared a schedule of nationwide rallies for Fisher to gather more support for his bill and to help him gain broader name recognition. To assist with that, he contacted Dorothy at the Crimson Legion headquarters in Charlotte and asked her about getting names and addresses of their people in key cities around the country. Dorothy was agreeable to help. "But you'll have to come here to get the lists," she insisted. "We're not mailing it to you."

Mullins wasn't sure if she was coming on to him, or if he was reading into her voice the memory of their encounter at the restaurant before he left Charlotte. Nevertheless, he had no choice but to do as she said. He needed Crimson Legion support for the campaign he was building. But traveling to Charlotte meant seeing Grace and he hadn't been diligent about staying in touch with her. Not diligent at all. In fact, it had been more than two weeks since he last wrote to her. There was little time to make amends, so after arranging the details of his travel, he went to the telegraph office and sent Grace a message, delivered to her at the boardinghouse, telling her of his expected arrival.

Later that week, Mullins took the train from Washington. The following afternoon, he arrived in Charlotte. He had no way of knowing whether Grace received his message or how she felt about him, and for much of the trip he was nervous thinking about being with both Dorothy and Grace in the same office at the same time. *What if they both come to the station to meet me?* He wondered.

To his relief, he saw Grace waiting for him on the platform as the train came into the station. Dorothy was nowhere in sight. As he stepped from the railcar, Grace walked forward and kissed him warmly. He was surprised at how excited he was to see her.

"You look great," he whispered as he nuzzled her ear.

"I'm supposed to take you to the hotel," she replied softly. "Then bring you to the office."

"We could always forget."

"Not this afternoon." She pulled away and took his hand. "But tonight we can lose ourselves in each other."

He grinned. "I like that idea."

After collecting his luggage, they rode to the Windsor Hotel where he deposited his belongings in his room, then they left together for the Crimson Legion office. As they walked up the street, he asked, "How is it going with Dorothy?"

"I think I was right," Grace smiled. "She has an interest in you."

He felt his cheeks grow warm with embarrassment. "Yeah?"

"You sound interested."

"No, just amused."

"Then, why are your cheeks red?"

"Because I'm with you." He forced himself to relax. What did he care if she knew? The worst that could happen is she would get angry and break things off. As long as Dorothy didn't get angry, he would be in good shape. He had to have her help with the campaign. He didn't need Grace. Not like that.

"She seemed to think her interest in you was reciprocated," Grace said.

A pang of guilt struck Mullins and for an instant the memory of Dorothy's foot against his calf that day at the restaurant flashed through his mind. He'd thought about that moment many times and the longer he stayed in Washington the more he wished he'd pursued what Dorothy had suggested. No one would have ever known. Not even Grace. Perhaps he could find a moment with Dorothy on this trip. Send Grace off on an errand. Have an afternoon with Dorothy.

Grace tugged at his hand. "Did you hear me?"

"What?" he asked, startled to be brought back to the moment. "I was thinking about you and the hotel tonight. What were you saying?"

"I said, Dorothy seemed to think her interest in you was reciprocated."

Mullins shrugged. "I don't know why she would think that."

"Are you sure?"

"I'm sure." But inside, he felt guilty about lying to her. And about the desire he felt toward Dorothy.

When they reached the Crimson Legion office, Mullins met briefly with Dorothy, then they were joined by Grace and Bradley Edwards in the conference room Griffin had used the first time Mullins and Grace came to Charlotte. Seeing it again left him with a sense of nostalgia and he looked over at Grace. "Remember that first time we came here?"

"Yes, it seems like a long time ago."

"A lot has happened since then." He would have enjoyed reminiscing more but there was little time to waste and he forced himself to focus on the task at hand.

"So," Dorothy began, "how can the Legion assist Senator Fisher?"

"We need the Legion to get behind Senator Fisher's immigration bill."

"That won't be difficult at all," Dorothy replied. "After all, it's pretty much *our* immigration bill."

"Yes," Mullins acknowledged. "We also need the Legion's help with Senator Fisher's campaign for president."

"What did you have in mind?"

"We would like to hold a series of rallies with Senator Fisher and Mr. Griffin sharing the stage."

Dorothy gave him a suspicious look. "He'll really do that?"

Mullins frowned. "Who?"

"Fisher. He'll really get on the stage with Griffin? He hasn't always wanted to be closely associated with us in the past."

"This campaign has changed things. He's over the wall on this now." Mullins sighed. "He has no choice but to support the bill and reach out to those who see the wisdom of it."

Edwards spoke up. "And he'll do that enthusiastically?"

"Yes, this was his idea."

"Okay," Dorothy interjected. "But if we do these rallies, they will be the typical Crimson Legion rally. That's the only way we can do them."

"Right." Mullins nodded. "That's what we want."

"These events can get a little out of hand at times," she cautioned.

"I understand, and the senator does, too."

"Okay, then." Dorothy set a stack of documents on the table. "These are the lists you asked about. We should get started sorting through them so we can figure out where to hold the rallies."

For the remainder of the day, Mullins, Dorothy, Grace, and Edwards scanned the lists of cities where Crimson Legion rallies had been held in the past, comparing information about those rallies to lists of Crimson Legion chapters, trying to identify the best cities with the best chapters.

"Many of these are new cities," Mullins noted.

"Yes," Dorothy replied. "We've been active since you left. And we're getting a lot of help now from ancillary organizations. We work with the Sons of New Germany. We're aligned with Knights of Teutonia. The German American Federation. I believe you know most of those groups. Sons of New Germany and the Knights of Teutonia are very active in promoting ideas about race, politics, and racial purity, particularly in the northeast, which might be good for you."

Mullins nodded. "We need all the help we can get. Harding has a tight grip on the state parties. We need to bring in new people."

Dorothy smiled, and pointed to the lists. "People from our organization would be new. I don't think any of them have been politically active in the traditional sense."

Late that evening, Mullins had dinner with Grace. Afterward, they went to Mullins's room at the hotel and spent the night together. The next morning, as they lay in bed, he rolled on his side to face her. "When will you be moving to Washington?" He asked it in order to know how to handle her in the future, but he made it sound as if he wanted her there with him.

"I wasn't sure you still wanted me to do that."

"Why did you think that?"

"You haven't written me in a while. And when you did, it wasn't very romantic. Just information about where you'd been and who you'd seen."

"I'm sorry. I know I should have written more often. I've just been really busy with this immigration bill—writing it and lining up votes. It's taken every minute of every day lately."

"It sounds exciting."

"It is. And I've met many of the people we've talked about and read about. I've been right there in the room with them, working on the ideas we were talking about back at Peggy and Jimmy's house in Springfield."

"I'm not sure being with me could compare to all of that." She had a pouty voice, and for a moment Mullins felt a sense of empathy toward her.

"Do you *want* to come up there?"

"I would need a job." She rolled on her side and they lay face-to-face. "Where could I work? You said when you left that you would help me find a place."

"I know. I haven't done much about that, either. But the senator's office is building up staff for the campaign. Maybe you could work there."

"Can he win?"

"I'm not sure. Most of the party is with Harding. If he gets in the race, they will all go for him. We're trying to build our own base by bringing new people into the party, which is why I wanted the list from Dorothy."

"You mean bring in new people to take over?"

"Sort of. But we aren't calling it that."

"That sounds like fun." She grinned. "Like what we used to talk about with Pete and Ida and the others. Actually doing something."

The mention of Pete brought back memories of turning the pigs loose in the synagogue and the conversation he'd had in Pittsburgh with Eugene Felton, who knew about the incident. For a moment he wondered if he should mention it to her, but instead he pushed the thought aside. "It's exactly what we talked about. But it's a lot of work and I'll be on the road even more than I was when I was working here."

"But Fisher is really going to do this? He's really going to run for president?"

"Yes. I just said that." Mullins, suddenly curious, frowned at her. "Do the others at the office think he won't?"

"They wonder."

"That's how they've been talking about it?"

"Yes. They wonder if he can win. And if he doesn't, what would that do to the Legion if the Legion is closely associated with him."

"I can understand them asking that." He rolled onto his back and looked up at the ceiling while he spoke. "But whether he wins the election or not, the immigration bill is going to pass and he will have done that and that's a good thing for all of us."

She moved closer and draped her arm across his chest, then rested her head on his shoulder. "But if you're on the road all the time, what's the point of me moving up there?"

"We could be together when I'm not traveling."

"We could do that here."

He shook his head. "Getting down here takes an entire day. I can't do that very often. If we're going to have time together, you need to be up there." He sensed that she was reluctant to make the move and he hoped that by portraying the situation in dire terms she would refuse to join him. But to his surprise she said, "Find a job for me and I'll move."

He forced a smile and turned to kiss her. "Okay, that part will be easy."

CHAPTER 27

The morning after Mullins departed Charlotte for the return trip to Washington, Grace dressed for work as usual, only this time she wore a hat. Nothing fancy. Just a straw garden hat with a bow at the base of the crown. She set it atop her head and stood before the mirror, adjusting it so that it fit just right. "I hate these things," she muttered to herself. "They make a woman look like an object." She shifted the hat slightly to one side. "And they always make me seem so. . .pretentious."

When she was prepared for the day, Grace left the house and made her way out to the sidewalk. She fully expected that Martin or Hawthorne—the federal agents who'd brought her there in the first place—would pop out from behind a shrub or mysteriously appear at her side, then whisk her away to an undisclosed location for questioning about her wonderful weekend at the hotel. But nothing unusual happened.

At noon, she left the office and walked down the street to a café four blocks from the building. It wasn't her usual café but she hoped that by going there she might avoid being seen by people she knew, if the agents should contact her on the way. She took a seat at a table in back, hoping to avoid being accosted by overly-confident men who sometimes approached her in public, and ordered a chicken salad sandwich.

When she'd eaten about half the sandwich, a waiter passed her table and handed her a note that read, "Use the back door.

Come to the alley behind the cafe." She glanced around and saw a doorway that opened to a hall that led to the back of the café. Grace took another bite of her sandwich and followed it with a drink from her glass. They devised this scheme for contacting her. They could wait.

After finishing her lunch, Grace stuffed the note in her purse, rose from her place at the table, and paid the bill. Instead of leaving by the front, she made her way back through the café and continued down the hall as the note instructed. She was nervous about what to say if anyone stopped her, but no one did.

At the end of the hall she came to a door. From the look of it—the lock in the knob and brackets for an extra bolt—it appeared to be a door to the outside. She grasped the knob and gave it a twist, then pushed open the door to the alley that ran behind the building.

A car was parked a few feet away and as she came from the building, the driver's door opened. Roy Martin, one of the federal agents she met in Springfield, stepped out from the car and opened the rear door. Without a word of greeting, he gestured for her to enter. When Grace was seated in the back, Martin closed the door, returned to the driver's seat, and steered the car up the alley.

A few minutes later, they arrived at the same warehouse where she'd met with Hawthorne and Martin before. As the car came to a stop inside the building, someone closed the doors behind them. Hawthorne appeared and gestured for them to follow. Grace exited from the back seat and Martin led her to the room where they'd talked earlier when she first arrived in Charlotte. As before, they sat around a table.

"I understand Mullins was in town this weekend," Hawthorne began.

"Yes," she replied.

"And he attended a meeting at the Crimson Legion office."

"Yes."

"Who was present at that meeting?"

"Bryce, Dorothy, Edwards, and myself."

Martin spoke up. "Edwards?"

"Bradley Edwards. He works in the office."

"What was discussed at this meeting?" Hawthorne asked.

For the next few minutes, Grace outlined Mullins's work for Fisher—developing campaign organizations in key states and, lately, drafting legislation and shaping policy.

"What kind of policy?" Martin asked.

"Immigration."

Hawthorne scowled disapprovingly. "Jews."

"Yes," she agreed.

"These campaign organizations he's establishing, does Fisher plan to run for the presidency?"

"The legislation Bryce worked on is a bill to limit immigration. Fisher hopes to use it as a stepping-stone to win the election."

Martin added "And they plan to use Crimson Legion chapters to establish support in the states where they are active?"

"Yes, that's why he came to Charlotte. To coordinate that effort."

Hawthorne looked puzzled. "Fisher is a Republican. The Crimson Legion has not been active in the Republican Party."

Grace smiled. "Not until now."

"They plan to become so?"

"That's what Bryce wants to do," she explained. "He wants to gather all of the groups—Crimson Legion, German American Federation, Knights of Teutonia, Sons of New Germany—and use them as a base for taking over the Republican Party."

Hawthorne raised an eyebrow. "Win the party. Win the primary. Win the election."

Grace nodded once more. "Yes, but I'm still not sure how this helps you."

Martin tapped the table with his finger for emphasis. "This

is what we were telling you before. You can tell us what Mullins is going to do before he actually does it."

They were silent a moment, then Hawthorne asked, "Anything else you can tell us?"

Grace had a knowing look. "We talked about me moving to Washington," she smiled coyly.

"Oh?"

She grinned. "You sound surprised."

"Well . . ." Martin hesitated. "We. . .were unsure of his. . .interests."

Grace felt smug. "I spent a weekend with him," she informed confidently. "I'd say he's interested enough."

"How would that move work out?"

"Bryce said he would see if Senator Fisher has any room on his staff for me. Apparently, they are adding new people."

"Good." Martin seemed to like the idea. "You should do that."

"In fact," Hawthorne offered, "we'll help orchestrate it."

Grace frowned. "You can do that?"

Both men ignored her question. "Continue with your routine as normal at the office here in Charlotte," Hawthorne ordered. "Do whatever it is you do each day. In a few days or so you will receive an offer of a job from Senator Fisher. When it comes, you should accept it and move up there as soon as possible."

"You can—"

Martin cut her off. "We need you up there. As soon as possible."

Grace felt uneasy. "You seem urgent about this. Has something happened? Is something wrong?"

Hawthorne and Martin stood. "Accept the offer when it comes," Hawthorne told her. "And get up there as quickly as possible."

✦ ✦ ✦

Ten days after meeting with Hawthorne and Martin, a letter arrived for Grace at the boardinghouse. The envelope bore the return address for Senator Fisher's office in Washington. She opened it and found a letter inside offering her a position on his staff. The letter was signed by Fisher himself. "You would be working as Bryce Mullins's assistant," it read. "Keeping his schedule straight, handling correspondence, and the like."

Once again, Grace felt uneasy about the extent of her involvement with Hawthorne and Martin. They had told her she would receive an offer from the Crimson Legion, and she did. That was odd, but not entirely impossible. The Crimson Legion was a private organization and they could easily turn someone, as they had her. But Fisher was a US senator and a potential candidate for the presidency. Was the Justice Department actively involved in deciding which people filled which offices?

Grace was wary about the whole situation—Mullins, whom she secretly suspected of being unfaithful to her—Dorothy, whom she didn't trust for a moment, no matter what she'd said to the contrary—the federal agents, the Crimson Legion, really the occurrences that led her to that moment. She could always run. Lance Smith, the principal at the school in Springfield, would probably allow her to return to the faculty. Maybe. But when she thought of that, she remembered the threat Hawthorne and Martin had made to expose her past.

The things she'd done with Mullins in Springfield—attacking Jews outside the synagogue, the pigs—she'd done more than she had admitted to anyone, and all of it was something she preferred to keep to herself. Not that she was ashamed or anything, but she knew her life, especially her professional career, would go better if no one knew. And she *really* didn't want anyone to find out what had happened in Virginia.

For Grace, going along with Hawthorne and Martin seemed the only way to keep her life under control. And besides all of that, she had come a long way emotionally and professionally from teaching in the classroom. Perhaps too far to go back. Doing that had been exhilarating, but now she felt trapped. As though she had no other option but to continue as the agents demanded—to go to Washington, work with Fisher and Mullins, and give Hawthorne and Martin whatever information they wanted regarding whomever they wanted to know about. . .at least for now.

At noon the following day, Grace walked up the street to the telegraph office and sent a message to Senator Fisher accepting the offer of employment and proposing that she would arrive within the next two weeks. She felt certain that would be soon enough to secure the position, especially if the agents were involved in the offer.

Late that afternoon, she met with Griffin and notified him that she had received an offer from Fisher and that she would be moving to Washington. A strict adherence to protocol would have required her to notify him first before contacting Fisher to accept, but she was certain the job offer had been arranged by Hawthorne and Martin and equally certain that Griffin, for all his persuasiveness, didn't have the kind of information on her that the federal agents did. By then the matter was settled for her and she had no intention of declining Fisher's offer, whatever the outcome with Griffin might be.

They met in Griffin's office—he was seated behind the desk, she on a chair in front—and Grace told him in straightforward terms that she had received the offer from Fisher himself. "I know we talked before about me leaving to go with Bryce. But I think this is somewhat sooner than you had hoped. I apologize if I am putting you in a bind."

"There's no reason to apologize. I talked with Fisher before he sent you that letter."

Grace was intrigued. "Oh?" she replied. "I didn't realize that."

"He and I have a long history together," Griffin explained. "He would never do something like offering one of my employees a job without checking with me first."

Grace wondered whether either he or Fisher realized what was really happening. "You've known him a long time?"

"Yes, a long time."

Rather than allowing the conversation to run its course and end right there, she asked, "Do you trust him?" It was a question the answer to which she cared not one bit but one she thought a woman in her position might ask of a man like him.

"Trust with a politician is a difficult thing," Griffin seemed to relish the opportunity to give her advice and so she let him continue without interruption. "A person can't get elected without placing their interests above everyone else's." He gave her a concerned look. "Are you worried about him?"

She shrugged. "It's just. . .working for a senator in Washington is one thing when it's merely an idea. But when it becomes a reality—or is about to become so—it seems. . .quite different."

Griffin had a fatherly smile. "Well . . ..To answer your question, I think Jonas Fisher is as trustworthy as any of the other senators up there. But I'm not sure that helps you much."

"I'm not sure it does, either. They are quite the eclectic gathering, I'm sure."

"For me," Griffin offered, "it doesn't matter whether he's particularly trustworthy or not. As long as he promotes the issues and policy positions we're interested in."

Grace nodded. "So you're okay with me leaving?"

"Very much so. Soon my entire staff will be in Washington, working to elect officials who support our positions and enacting policies that comport with our wishes. I hadn't expected to find success in that manner, but it's a good thing, just the same."

Grace stood to leave. "Will you need help in finding a replacement for me."

"No," Griffin replied, still seated at his desk. "I think we already have someone in mind for the job."

✦ ✦ ✦

A few days before Grace was scheduled to leave Charlotte for Washington, Ida Hayes, her friend from Springfield, arrived at the office. No one had told her she was coming and Grace was surprised to see her. She also was immediately suspicious and more than a little wary. Ida knew some of Grace's secrets. Having her at the Crimson Legion office, with Griffin and Fisher so closely related, left her worried about what might happen next.

Ida met with Dorothy briefly, then with Griffin. Afterward, Dorothy asked Grace to show Ida around and help her get settled. "I think you two know each other."

"Yes," Grace replied. "We do."

As had been done for her, Grace drove Ida to the boarding-house and introduced her to Mr. Renfrow. "This is a safe place," Grace advised as they looked around. "The men won't bother you too much."

"Too much?"

"Well, you know." Grace smiled. "They're men, so they have to bother us some, but at least these guys are nice about it."

"And if things get out of hand," Renfrow added, "just tell me. I don't mind stepping in to put them right."

After Ida was settled and they were alone in her room, Grace took a seat on the bed and brought up the questions she was certain were on both their minds. "How's Pete?" she began.

"Not so good." Ida looked nervous and uncomfortable. She stood near the window and glanced out at the garden below.

Grace feigned a look of concern. "What's wrong?" She didn't like Pete, but it seemed better right then to act as if she did. "Nothing serious, I hope."

"Pete got arrested for some of that stuff they did." The expression on Ida's face indicated she thought Grace would know what she was talking about, but when Grace didn't respond she quickly added, "At the synagogue." She brought a chair from the corner of the room and took a seat on it. "You know. With the pigs."

"Oh." Grace knew exactly what Ida meant, but didn't want to volunteer anything.

"He wouldn't tell me everything," Ida continued. "And he didn't tell the police everything, either. That's why I'm here alone. He's still inside."

Grace was puzzled. "Inside?"

"Jail," Ida shifted positions in the chair where she sat and glanced around nervously. "He's still in jail."

"Oh. Did anyone else get arrested over that?"

Ida shook her head. "Not from the group we met with at the Claytons'." She leaned forward and looked out the window. "Most of what happened with the pigs seemed to come from the group Bryce formed at work."

Once again, Grace was puzzled. "At work?"

"The group he formed to oppose the union."

"Oh, right."

"Pete went to some of their meetings, but he wasn't really a part of the union opposition. Not that active in it." Ida fidgeted with her hands as she spoke. "I don't know why they singled him out with the investigation."

Grace remembered that putting the pigs in the synagogue was Pete's idea. He was the one who thought of it and who promoted it, but she didn't say anything. Instead, she changed the subject. "How did you get the job with the Legion?"

"They approached me."

The answer surprised Grace. "Oh. Mr. Griffin contacted you?"

Ida shook her head. "No. Dorothy. Said they had heard about

me and wanted to know if I was interested. I assumed you told them."

Grace shook her head. "No, I didn't. I would have if they'd asked me about it, but no one ever said anything about needing help to find someone. In fact, they told me they had someone in mind for the job. I had no idea they were talking about you."

Ida's nervous appearance put Grace on edge and she wondered if Ida had been turned by the Justice Department investigators the same way they turned her. The business about Dorothy contacting her and the offer of a job sounded like the way Grace had come to work with the Legion. It left her curious about what the investigators might have on Ida to make her do as they said. But she didn't press the matter. Grace didn't want to talk about her own involvement with the investigators, especially with Ida in Charlotte and her on her way to Washington.

They continued to visit until mealtime, then went downstairs to the dining room. Grace introduced Ida to the other residents and the typical dinnertime banter began. Ida seemed to fit right in, not minding their flirtatious remarks at all.

✦ ✦ ✦

The train from Charlotte brought Grace to Washington's Union Station. Mullins was waiting for her on the platform. After a warm embrace, they collected her belongings and took a taxi from the station.

"Where are we going?"

"To the boardinghouse."

"Which one?"

"Mr. Taylor's."

"Where you live?" Grace frowned. "Are you sure that's okay, both of us living in the same house?"

He grinned. "It's fine. This isn't Springfield or Virginia. No one cares about that kind of thing here."

When they arrived at the house, Mr. Taylor met them in the front parlor. "You get room with breakfast and dinner," he said. "No noise after ten. Serious people stay here."

Mullins carried the things to her room and then they lounged together on the bed. After a while, they relaxed and she told him, "Ida took my place in Charlotte."

Mullins seemed confused. "Ida?"

"Ida Hayes. Pete's . . ."

"Other," Mullins suggested. "I had forgotten all about them."

"They haven't forgotten about you. Pete's in jail."

The news startled him. "For what?"

"Turning those pigs loose in the synagogue."

Mullins looked away. "Really?"

"I know what happened. You don't need to act like you weren't involved."

Mullins had a sheepish smile. "Did Pete talk?"

"She said he didn't. But she thinks all the trouble came from the Crimson Legion chapter you formed with the men from work. She tended to minimize Pete's involvement and put the blame on you."

"She said that?" Mullins had an incredulous tone. "She said it was all my fault?"

"No. She didn't quite go that far, but I think she wanted to. So I'm not sure how much Pete might have said about you."

"What about the others? Did any of them get into trouble?"

"I don't know. She didn't say."

Mullins stared up at the ceiling. "That whole thing was Pete's idea."

"I know."

"He was right in the middle of whatever happened."

"I know," Grace repeated.

"Did you tell her that?"

"No. I didn't say much of anything."

"You didn't tell her what you knew about it?"

"No." Grace shook her head. "I didn't tell her anything. I just listened."

"Good."

"Have you heard any more about that?"

"I haven't heard anything, but I'm not surprised there was trouble. Jews have a lot of influence over everything. They are everywhere."

They lay together on the bed the remainder of the afternoon and in the evening they ate dinner downstairs with the other residents, then went upstairs to Mullins's room. Grace spent the night there, only returning to her room early the next morning in time to prepare for work.

CHAPTER 28

Mullins introduced Grace to the staff in Senator Fisher's office, expecting everyone to be cordial to her. They knew she and Mullins had a long-standing romantic relationship and he expected that to temper their reaction to her presence. As he expected, the women in the office—Ann Aldridge, the writer preparing Fisher's speeches, and Emma Hart, his secretary—were initially tepid in their response to her.

Much to his surprise, however, Travis Fielding and Marvin Parsons liked and accepted her right away. They showed no hesitancy in helping her get settled, even to the point of being flirtatious. So much so that Mullins bristled at their seemingly instant familiarity with her, a feeling that struck him as odd, given his attitude toward her earlier.

Prior to their most recent meeting in Charlotte—when they rekindled their romance—Mullins had drifted away from Grace, at least in his mind, and had come to think he might be better off without her. And he'd been less than satisfied with her interest in moving to Washington to join him. But seeing how others responded to her—and seeing her reaction to them, which was not at all to resist their advances—he wondered if he shouldn't rethink his rejection of her and try harder to develop their relationship at a deeper level.

Before Mullins could resolve all of that, though, he was back on the road again. This time traveling westward by train across the country, organizing rallies for Senator Fisher in support of the immigration bill. Much like the method he'd used when he worked with the Crimson Legion, only this time in reverse, he worked ahead of Fisher, setting up each event location by identifying key people with the skill and interest to make the rally a success. Organizing the events in advance, then moving on before Fisher and his traveling staff arrived from Washington.

As the schedule permitted, Mullins circled back to cities where Fisher had concluded an event and worked with each event group after the fact, shaping them into a permanent campaign committee. In that manner, he hoped to create a nationwide organization capable of continued political activity in support of Fisher's presidential campaign. The groups were small but skilled and highly motivated to do something about the issues that threatened the nation. Mullins found the effort exhilarating.

Working in that manner, Mullins made his way, one event at a time, to California. He began at the northern end and held planning meetings in San Francisco, then continued down the state to Fresno and Los Angeles before reaching San Diego. Unlike locations on the East Coast, in California Mullins found party officials in each location who were supportive of Fisher's immigration bill and enthusiastic about having him as the party's presidential nominee.

"We think Harding is just more of the same," one person told him.

"And he's beholden to Jewish moneymen," another added. "The very people who are causing us trouble. Most of us are looking for someone else as our candidate."

Indeed, at every stop in California, Mullins heard firsthand accounts about the threat posed by Jewish dominance in the state's most important economic interests—the entertainment industry in Hollywood and the defense industry taking root near

Los Angeles. However, at a meeting in Bakersfield, he heard of a threat to a new area: Agriculture.

Mullins understood the way Jews used the media. And he had no doubt they had infiltrated the nation's defense contractors. But Jewish involvement in agriculture seemed a new issue to him. "They're causing trouble with farmers?" he asked.

"Yes," someone replied. "But it's not about farming. It's about the land."

Mullins shook his head. "I'm not sure I understand."

"Out here, agriculture is all about water. No water, no crops. Everything is irrigated. Those who control the water determine which farms succeed and which ones fail. Powerful men with powerful friends have been using water to ruthlessly eliminate the growers."

"To eliminate them?"

"Yes."

Mullins found that incredible. "But why?"

"People are moving out here in droves. They're building houses as fast as they can cut down the trees for lumber. Those orange groves around Los Angeles and cropland farther up the valley are large tracts developers want to exploit."

"And there's oil underneath most of it," someone else added.

Mullins's eyes opened wider. "And the developers are Jewish?"

"The big ones are."

"And if they aren't in it directly," another said, "they're in it indirectly by loaning the money to make it happen."

In an effort to help counteract the threats he learned about, Mullins redoubled his effort to bring Crimson Legion chapters together with other groups that were similarly oriented. Primary among those was the Sons of New Germany.

Like the Crimson Legion, Sons of New Germany was well organized throughout California and very much aware of the issues affecting state politics. Mullins saw them as the answer to the threats he'd been hearing and a force potentially large enough to change the outcome of the state's primary election. Despite a crowded schedule, he gathered leadership from both groups for a meeting in Sacramento.

"The threat this state faces from Jews and other ethnic groups is also the single most important issue we face as a nation. Perhaps the most important issue confronted by any generation in the life of our country," Mullins related as he addressed the leaders. "We need to end immigration, and Senator Fisher's efforts toward that goal offer the sole piece of legislation standing between us and the barbarians at the gate. We need your help in getting his immigration bill approved by Congress. And we need your help with his presidential campaign. So that he can take the fight all the way to the White House."

"We're with you!" someone shouted.

"Just tell us what to do," another called. "We're ready."

Louis Whitmore, a used car dealer and active Crimson Legion member, spoke up. "There is one difference out here," he noted.

"And what's that?" Mullins asked.

"Out here, it's not just Jews and Italians causing the trouble. We have problems with Orientals and Negroes, too."

"That's right," someone agreed. "Negroes are coming out here as fast as anyone."

Someone else chimed in, "We need to send them all back where they came from."

"If you can get your people active in Senator Fisher's campaign," Mullins replied, "I'm sure we can find a way to let states handle these issues the way they want them."

"That's what we need," Whitmore agreed. "A solution tailored to each state's situation. Not an answer dictated to us by Washington politicians."

Mullins seized the moment. "And that is exactly what Senator

Fisher would propose. We can stop foreign immigration at the federal level. And states can control it as they need at a local level to preserve their traditional values and their traditional way of life."

"I like the sound of that," someone yelled.

Whitmore had a questioning look. "And you're sure Fisher would do that?"

"Senator Fisher is committed to solving our problems." Mullins was on a roll, creating his remarks as fast as they rolled off his lips, but he wasn't about to let them get away without sealing their support for Fisher. "Whatever form that solution must take at a state level, he'll see that each state gets an opportunity to have it." He glanced around the room. "If you and your members get involved now, laying the groundwork for a presidential campaign, you'll be with him early. And you'll have a chance to be part of something big."

✦ ✦ ✦

After organizing groups from the northern end all the way to San Diego, Mullins returned to Los Angeles and remained there, awaiting Fisher's arrival. While he waited, he continued searching for additional opportunities to bring Crimson Legion chapters together with other like-minded groups as he had in Sacramento.

One of those opportunities involved a luncheon with Clive Bailey from the Sana Monica Crimson Legion chapter. Mullins expected their meeting to be a quiet, intimate discussion, perhaps one at which he could acquire particularly helpful inside information on specific individuals he had encountered. Instead, Bailey brought Ernst Haffner with him. Haffner was the leader of a Sons of New Germany chapter that met on the east side of Los Angeles. That chapter had been active in confronting Jews in the Boyle Heights area. Mullins knew of their work and was hoping to meet with them. He was glad for Bailey's foresight in bringing Haffner to the meeting.

Both men were veterans of the Great War and very much dissatisfied with the way the war turned out. Bailey was deployed to the Vosges Mountains of France, the same place where Mullins's brother, Harry, had been killed. They fought valiantly, risking their lives to carry out US policy, only to see that policy forsaken—as they viewed it—at the end of the war and totally abandoned in the peace negotiations that followed.

"None of us wanted to fight in that war," Bailey explained. "We all thought we were fighting someone else's war. But after we got over there, most of us were glad to do it once we saw that the Europeans understood the root problem."

"They knew that aggressive ethnic groups were the cause of their trouble," Haffner added. "And they meant to do something about it."

"And they did," Bailey concurred.

Haffner nodded. "All the other things that went on over there were merely cover for the true purpose of that war. The one the people believed in and the one they wanted to see accomplished."

Mullins was intrigued. "And what was that purpose?"

"To eliminate Jews and Serbs," Bailey replied.

"And Armenians," Haffner quickly added.

"Yeah." Bailey nodded. "The Armenians, too."

"At least as a threat," Haffner noted. "Maybe not to exterminate them all, but most of them."

"At least the troublemakers."

"The Communist Jews," Mullins said. He didn't know that for a fact, but he'd learned about the idea from reading and listening to Walter Jones, then Griffin, and knew the conversational cues that indicated an opportunity to share the thought.

"Yes," Haffner nodded. "International Jews are the ones who caused that war. The Rothschilds and all of them. They had to be dealt with, and that's what people on both sides wanted to do."

Mullins shook his head. "Most Americans don't understand this."

"Well, the Europeans sure do," Bailey commented.

"Yeah," Haffner continued. "But the leadership gave in. They didn't let us complete the fight, though."

"That was Wilson." Bailey groaned.

Mullins rolled his eyes. "Don't get me started on him."

"The Turks were well on the way to eliminating the Armenians," Bailey assured. "And we were about to wipe out the Jews in central Europe. Not sure about the Serbs."

"The Germans would have finished them off, win or lose. They were after the Serbs."

Bailey was exasperated. "But they stopped the war before we could get it all finished."

"We'll go back." Haffner stated the point as if it were incontrovertible. "Mark my words. We'll have to go back. And when we do, we're going to finish it."

Bailey cut his eyes toward Haffner and grinned. "The Europeans might take care of it for themselves before then."

"The Germans," Haffner corrected.

"Yes. The Germans. They have some people over there who'll get them all. Serbs. Armenians. Jews. Homosexuals. Negroes. All of them. They'll wipe them out."

Haffner looked over at Mullins. "You see, we understand the situation. The ones who fought in that war—we understand it. Not many others do."

"I agree," Mullins quickly responded. "And what we need are *politicians* who understand it. A president who understands it."

"There are some politicians in this state who realize what we're facing," Bailey noted. "They are well aware of the Jewish takeover in the entertainment industry. News media. Financial centers."

"Some of them hate the Jews as much as we do," Haffner added. "They just won't say it."

"And that's the beauty of Senator Fisher's immigration bill," Mullins pointed out. "It sets quotas that severely limit immigration from the groups you've mentioned but without naming them as groups."

Bailey looked puzzled. "How does it do that?"

"It uses population numbers from the 1910 Census as the basis for establishing quotas," Mullins explained. In drafting the legislation with Fisher, the idea to do that had been Mullins's own and he was very pleased with himself for thinking of it.

"Ah." Haffner had a knowing smile. "There were a lot fewer of them coming here in 1910."

"Right," Mullins agreed. "And because the bill doesn't single out groups of people specifically, it gives politicians the cover they need to become more active in passing it into law. They can curtail the flow of specific immigrant groups without being on record as opposing any of those groups."

"You need to make certain our officials understand that," Bailey warned.

Mullins smiled. "You men need to introduce me to the local politicians so I can."

Haffner spoke up. "Both of us will help. Between us, we know a lot of people."

✦ ✦ ✦

True to their word, Bailey and Haffner introduced Mullins to key players in the California Republican Party. One of them, Bernard Jordan, was a member of the party's executive committee. He arranged meetings for Mullins with the mayor of Los Angeles, half a dozen state legislators, and two California congressmen. At each of those meetings, Mullins made the case for Senator

Fisher's immigration legislation and outlined his strengths as a presidential candidate.

"Fisher is the only candidate who is actively shaping national policy on key issues facing our nation. Not just talking about the issues but working to form US policy that addresses those issues."

"We need help," the mayor concurred. "Particularly with immigration. California is a major point of entry for immigrants. Not from Europe, but from the Orient."

"And the senator is fully aware of that," Mullins added. "You could be inundated by foreigners in a very short time. From the Orient. From Latin America. Millions of people flooding the state. Stealing jobs that ought to go to real Americans."

By the time Fisher arrived for the Los Angeles rally, Mullins had gathered a sizeable committee of notable politicians who favored not only Fisher's immigration bill but also his presidential candidacy. Once Fisher was settled in his hotel room, Mullins met with him and went over the details of their involvement with him. "They all want to see you," Mullins pointed out.

"We can arrange that?" Fisher asked.

"Yes," Mullins replied. "The rally is scheduled for tomorrow night. You have meetings all day, beginning with breakfast."

"With the mayor?"

"No. State legislators. The mayor is set to see you over lunch."

Fisher grinned. "This is looking good."

"Yes, it is," Mullins replied. "And not just here in California, but almost every place we've stopped as we came across the country."

"The rallies have been going well."

"More than well," Mullins rejoined. "The turnout has been great. But more than that, the committees we formed to work the rallies are holding together as permanent campaign committees. I think people everywhere are worried about immigration. More worried than Harding or anyone else realizes. This is a good topic for you."

"I was thinking the same thing."

"We still face one big problem, though."

Fisher was puzzled. "What's that?"

"Because of the way the party has worked in the past," Mullins explained, "we will need to build, in effect, our own party. To do that, we still have to bring in people from outside the traditional party group."

Fisher nodded. ""I know. We've discussed this situation many times. Are you wondering now if we can do that?"

"No, but this trip has shown me that an operation like that will cost money. And lots of it."

Fisher nodded. "I agree. But I think we're seeing a shift in politics."

"A shift?"

"In the past, elections were all about party organization and working your way up from the bottom to become an elected official and then moving up to become the highest elected official possible. The party supported its people with a complex scheme of precinct captains, ward bosses, block leaders. All of them tightly controlled up and down."

"We can't get anywhere in a system like that." Mullins had a solemn tone. "The party scheme won't allow you to rise any higher than you already are."

Fisher again nodded. "And that's what I'm getting to. For us—and in the future for everyone, I think—money will be the key to a presidential race. Money will replace the party scheme."

"There'll be a lot of people opposed to that. Everyone in the party has a vested interest in keeping it a party plan."

"Yes, but with money, a candidate can buy people to go door-to-door. Pay them to go around getting people to the polls. To pass out leaflets. To put up signs. With money, a candidate could pay for all of that and cut out the party bosses entirely."

"That's something that hasn't really figured into previous campaigns."

"It hasn't figured into it at all. Not in our lifetimes. At least not like that. Many campaigns were decided by backroom meetings where party officials bypassed the scheme and the members and the voters. But no candidate has put together his own way around the party." Fisher looked over at Mullins. "Harding is counting on the party scheme. We could make history by defeating him."

Mullins was excited by the idea of participating in an historic moment but found the practical reality unavoidable. "I can organize, gather, and motivate groups to support you. But I can't solve the money issue. You have to raise the money."

Fisher grinned. "Don't worry about that. I have the money issue under control. I know where to get the money."

Mullins wasn't sure what Fisher meant by that remark, but decided not to pursue it any further. Fisher said he could handle it and Mullins was fully willing to let him do it. He would concentrate on his area of responsibility and let Fisher focus on his.

CHAPTER 29

While Mullins was out west, Grace continued to work at Senator Fisher's office in Washington, steadily gaining a deeper understanding of how Fisher operated. Most of her work was clerical in nature, which meant she decided nothing but saw everything—memos, documents, reports—and she made notes of all that she saw and heard. At night, when she was alone in her room, she used those notes to record her observations and thoughts in a diary that she kept hidden in the train case that sat on the shelf in her closet.

At first she thought she'd been clever and that no one had noticed, but then one day Travis Fielding came to the room where she was working. He scooted a chair close to her and said in a soft voice, "I think you and I have something in common."

Grace was put off by his approach and wondered if he was making a sexual advance—and how much about her he knew—but she was curious, too, and curiosity won out. "What's that?" she asked as cheerfully as she could muster.

Fielding took a lapel pin from his pocket and held it for her to see. The pin was about the size of a quarter and bore the unmistakable insignia of the Crimson Legion—oak leaves arranged in a circle around the edge with a raised L on a black background in the middle.

Grace was unsure how to respond and so avoided the implication they might have a common association with the Legion and instead replied, "How long have you been a member?"

"Three years, officially." Fielding returned the pin to his pocket. "I got in from the start. I'm the one who got you your job. Me and Mullins."

The comment left Grace reassured and yet suspicious. If Fielding was a Crimson Legion loyalist, then they did, indeed, share much in common. But if, like herself, he had been compromised by federal investigators, then he was someone from whom she would like to keep a safe distance. She kept those thoughts to herself, though, and smiled. "Bryce knows about you?"

"Yes. He asked me to help find a place for you. I talked to Marvin Parsons. Didn't take much to convince him we needed another person in the office and not much after that for him to agree that you were right for the job."

Parsons. . .she had wondered about him earlier, thinking perhaps he might be working with federal investigators, too. But she let that notion pass and gestured to the papers on her desk. "I need to get this done."

"Sure," Fielding replied. "Want to get lunch together?"

Grace didn't like the idea but felt unable to refuse. "Sure."

At noon, they walked up the street to a café and sat at a table in the corner by the window in front. Grace felt awkward being there with Fielding when she was supposed to be in a relationship with Mullins, and so visible to people passing on the street. But after a few minutes she remembered she didn't know anyone in Washington except people from the office and soon felt better about it.

As they ate, they talked. Fielding asked, "What do you do on weekends?"

The question sounded like an all-too-obvious approach to asking her on a date, but once again she felt unable to respond directly. "I don't know." She shrugged. "I haven't been here long enough to have a routine." Still, she knew what was coming next.

"I have something to show you that I think you'll find interesting."

"What is it?"

"It's something you have to see to appreciate. Shall I pick you up on Sunday morning?"

Now Grace was *really* uneasy. "I don't know . . ." It sounded too much like a date—even more than merely having lunch with him—and she was worried about how Mullins might take it if he found out she went somewhere with another guy.

Fielding seemed to sense the tension. "Don't worry." He gave a dismissive gesture. "I won't say anything to Mullins about it. And anyway, it's not like a date or anything. Just something I think you might enjoy."

"Okay," she said finally. "What should I wear?"

"Something you might wear to church." He grinned. "I think you'll really like this."

✦ ✦ ✦

That night, when Grace returned to the boardinghouse, she went to her room and took a train case down from the top shelf in the closet. In it, she found the letter that she had received from Fisher offering her the job. She slipped it from the envelope and read it again.

The letter appeared to be signed by Fisher but in the lower-left corner, below the signature block, there were the initials M. P. "Marvin Parsons," she whispered. "Parsons is the one who prepared the letter."

Fisher might have signed it—the signature appeared to be genuine—but Parsons had prepared it and put it before him. Whatever questions Fisher might have raised—did they need someone, was she qualified, had someone looked into her background—Parsons was the one who answered them. If Fisher had needed convincing to sign it, Parsons was the one who convinced him.

Even more than before, Grace was convinced Parsons was an inside man for the feds. If he had been merely a Crimson Legion member like Fielding and Mullins, Fielding would have said so. "Parsons is one of us, too," or words to that effect. But he did not. And the fact that he didn't led her to believe Parsons was not one of them. Yet he went along with hiring her. Became her advocate, even. "He's been compromised," she whispered. "I know."

✦ ✦ ✦

On Sunday morning, Fielding arrived at the boardinghouse in a car he had signed out from the office. Grace was dressed and waiting on the porch. As the car came to a stop, she moved down the steps to the front walkway and made her way to the passenger's door. Fielding remained behind the steering wheel and when she was seated inside with the door closed, he steered the car from the curb.

They rode from the city into the Virginia countryside with the windows down and the air circulating through the passenger compartment. She liked the countryside but entering the state again she remembered the charges still pending against her in Norfolk and wondered if the outing would lead to trouble. She was glad to be out of the city, though, and the change of scenery made her forget about feeling guilty over being with someone besides Mullins.

Before long, a church appeared off to the right side of the road. Just the steeple first, rising above the trees, then the building came into view. It was white with clapboard siding and sat in a grove of oak trees. Cars were parked everywhere around it and wagons too, with the horses tethered beneath the trees for shade. Five or six Negro boys tended them and she wondered why that seemed good and right to her—that Negroes should be the servants of Whites, but not Jews or Italians who, in her mind, should not be in America. Or even alive, for that matter.

Fielding guided the car from the pavement across the lawn and brought it to a stop in an open space near the building, but away from where the horses were kept. Grace smiled over at him. "There is big crowd."

"Yes," he replied.

"Think we'll be able to find a seat?"

He had a confident look. "I'm sure of it."

Grace slid from the car and as she moved around the front fender, Fielding took her by the hand and led her up the steps to the church door. He pulled it open and waited while she moved inside, then followed after her.

As they appeared at the doorway, an usher standing nearby saw them. From the expression on his face Grace was certain he and Fielding knew each other.

The usher gestured, and they followed him up the side aisle. Across the room Grace saw that the pews were filled and she wondered if they would be able to find a place. But the usher paused when they reached the front row and gestured to an open space, as if he knew they were coming and had reserved the spot just for them. Grace made her way onto the pew and Fielding slid in beside her. As he did, the usher gave him a friendly pat on the shoulder, then disappeared toward the back of the room.

A few minutes later, a door to the left opened behind the podium and a choir entered. As they filled the seats reserved for them in the choir loft, the conductor took his place in front. He waited while everyone got into position and, when they were ready, nodded to the pianist. At the sound of the first notes, the congregation stood and soon everyone was singing. Loudly, Grace thought. But on key.

After three or four songs, a door to the right behind the podium opened and a man appeared. From the way he was dressed—dark suit, white shirt, dark tie—Grace knew he was the preacher. The audience was seated while he made his way to the podium.

The preacher carried a Bible that was tucked under his arm like a schoolbook. He rested it on the podium, opened it, and began reading from a place in the Gospels. A passage about the crucifixion of Christ. Grace thought it a curious reading. Easter had come and gone.

When the preacher concluded the reading, he smiled at the crowd, "I know some of you are wondering why I chose that passage for our lesson today. Yes, I know, Easter has already passed." Laughter tittered lightly through the congregation. "As many of you who were here on Easter remember, I told you then that the resurrection is the moment that separates Christianity from all else. Because of the resurrection, Christianity is not merely a philosophy. Because of the resurrection, it is not merely a way of life. Rather, it is the source of life."

"Amen," someone said loudly. "Preach," another added.

"But before there was the resurrection, there was the crucifixion. The awful, terrible crucifixion. An event, an experience, so horrible that words cannot adequately describe it. No matter how many words we might use, we could not reach the depths of the agony and misery that Jesus experienced that day.

"My point today is not to dwell too much on that, but to remind you of the people who were responsible, from the human perspective, for the agony he experienced. Now, I know theologians speak of the agony as the product of our sins. And theologically they are correct. But practically speaking, someone else was responsible for Jesus' death."

"Go ahead on," someone shouted. "Preach the truth," another added.

"As much as liberals would like you to believe otherwise, Jewish leaders were the ones who charged Jesus with a crime. And those same Jewish leaders put him on trial. They offered bribed witnesses, contrary to Old Testament practice, and made sure to find him guilty. And when they did, those same Jewish leaders delivered Jesus to the Romans and demanded his execution."

Members of the congregation shouted in support of what he said. And Grace felt warm inside.

"Jews did this," the preacher continued. "We weren't even here then. Jews, not Europeans; Jews."

"Let them burn in hell!" someone called out.

"Go ahead on," another added.

The preacher lowered his tone. "Now, I'm sure we all know a Jew or two who are just regular people. Not all Jews are bad." The congregation responded with groans and murmuring loud enough that it interrupted him. "No. It's true," he insisted, gesturing with both hands. "Not all Jews are bad, but Jews are the ones who caused the trouble back then. And they are the ones causing the trouble for us now. And not only here but throughout Europe. Jews who forfeited heaven for their misdeeds. Who forfeited their place as the chosen people of God—a position now occupied by the church. By you. By me. They are the ones who are causing our troubles today.

"International Jews—powerful groups of intermarried, interlocking families—control enormous amounts of wealth. So much wealth, in fact, that nations needing financing have no alternative but to turn to them for help. By the 'Yes' of International Jews, canals and railroads get built. And by their 'No,' they do not. By their 'Yes,' countries go to war and prevail. And by their 'No,' others go down to defeat.

"International Jews remain wed to the Old Testament understanding and committed to a communal lifestyle. And as such, they are the natural ally of the Communists. It was the International Jew, with their extensive money connections and their Communist ideals, that brought an end to the Russian Empire. And with that power, they seek to spread Communism throughout Europe and beyond.

"We have our own version of the International Jew living right here in America. We know them as the New York Jew. They control the financial industry. They have politicians in their pockets who do their bidding. And they are breeding day and night with the sons and daughters of ignorant Americans as they introduce inferior hereditary strains from their most depraved members to our pure Aryan race. By that effort, they intend to shape our country to suit their aims and shape our race into a docile people easily malleable to their desires and acquiescent to their control."

The preacher's message was a toxic stew of religion, politics, and racism, but no one in the congregation seemed to notice. Instead, they offered rousing support, standing to their feet at times. Clapping and shouting and waving their hands in the air. Grace found the sermon and the crowd's response unlike anything she'd ever experienced before. Not even at a Crimson Legion rally with Griffin at his best could compare. She was totally exhilarated by what she heard and saw. So exuberant that she wanted to hug Fielding right then and there for bringing her there.

After the church service ended, Fielding said good-bye to his friend who served as usher, then he and Grace returned to the car and started toward the city. A few miles up the road, however, Fielding slowed the car and steered it from the pavement into the parking lot outside a small rural café.

Again, the venture seemed to take on the nature of a date, and Grace became uncomfortable. "Why are we stopping here?" she asked.

"It's lunchtime," Fielding replied cheerfully. "And this is the only restaurant we'll see between here and the city." He brought the car to a stop alongside the building and switched off the engine. "Come on," he urged. "I'm hungry. Aren't you?"

Grace was hungry. And the thought of driving all the way back to Washington without eating was not appealing to her at all. Not only was it a long distance away, by the time they arrived at the boardinghouse lunchtime would have long since passed and she would be forced to wait until dinner for the chance to eat again. So she pushed aside her feelings of guilt, opened the door, and followed Fielding's lead.

Lunch proved more enjoyable than Grace imagined, as did the conversation they enjoyed. A freewheeling discussion of the preacher's sermon, her thoughts about the Negroes tending the horses, and how that conflicted with her opinion that Jews had given up their right to exist—a notion with which the preacher seemed to agree.

By the time they returned to the boardinghouse it was almost time for dinner. Even after a hearty lunch, Grace was ready to eat again and ready to be out of the car. Not because of the sense of guilt she'd experienced earlier, but from the drive itself, which had left her tired and in need of a bath.

As they said good-bye, however, Fielding leaned over and kissed her gently on the lips. "I had a great time today."

The kiss surprised her and she blushed in response, but when he withdrew she leaned closer and kissed him again. "So did I." She then threw open the car door, got out, and bounded up the steps.

As she made her way across the front porch, someone spoke to her and she turned to see Sinclair Norris, one of the boardinghouse residents, seated in a rocking chair. "What happened to you and Mullins?"

Norris's question caught her off guard, but she recovered to say, "Nothing. Why do you ask?"

"I saw you." Norris gestured toward the street. "With that man. Just now in the car."

Grace felt her cheeks grow warm with embarrassment at the thought that someone had seen her with Fielding. His kiss seemed a spontaneous thing of the moment. She was certain hers was, too. But she had not thought beforehand that someone might see her. "What do you mean?"

"I mean that . . ." Norris stopped in mid-sentence and waved her off with a gesture. "Never mind. I'm sure it was nothing."

"What was nothing?" She couldn't let the matter pass that easily.

He shook his head. "It was nothing. And certainly none of my business anyway."

Grace waited a moment longer, trying to think of a way to resolve the matter that would put it completely to rest. To make it as though the kiss had never occurred. As though Norris had never seen them. But she could not find a way and so, at last, she opened the front door and went inside the house.

Now she was not merely worried that she had been seen, nor feeling guilty in a way that she could discount. She had been kissed by another man. And she had deliberately kissed him in return. And she was worried about what might happen when Mullins returned and found out. If he found out. Of course, he would find out. Men always learned of such things. They were bigger gossips than women ever had been. They talked. Always talked. Especially about women.

And she was worried about how she felt about Fielding. He seemed like a nice man. He seemed genuine. He seemed to be many things that Mullins was not. And he was handsome. She smiled. Yes, he really was handsome. And she was conflicted about that, too.

By then she was at the top of the stairs and continued down the hall toward her room, still thinking. Always thinking. About her situation. The things she faced. The choices she knew she would one day be required to make.

Despite all she had experienced with men before, her life and future had become entwined with Mullins. He got her the job with the Crimson Legion. And the job with Fisher. She had followed him a long way from where she began. A long way from the trouble in Virginia. Would she ever be able to put that behind her? And a long way from the trouble in Springfield. All of those had been moves forward, certainly, but she had left a lot behind, too. And she wondered if Mullins might get violent if he learned of her and Fielding. If she broke things off with him. If she simply moved away.

As she prepared for dinner, Grace decided that the best course of action was simply to ignore what happened with Fielding. Ignore Norris's comments on the front porch. Ignore the entire day. Well, not the *entire* day. The sermon had been great. And lunch afterward had been fun. But she resolved to make sure things went no further with Fielding. No more trips to Virginia. No more long and splendidly enjoyable lunches. And no more kisses in the car. Definitely no more kisses in the car. She would apply herself to the work at the office, make herself essential to the office function, to Senator Fisher's presidential hopes, and carve out her own place. Her own role. Then she would see what might happen after that.

✦ ✦ ✦

Although Grace had resolved to limit her time with Fielding, their work at Fisher's office made time together unavoidable. Even so, she declined his repeated invitations to lunch and dinner and avoided being with him in the car or any other place one might consider an intimate setting. Nevertheless, they worked together every day, often in the same room.

One of Grace's tasks was to prepare correspondence for the office regarding fund-raising events. That correspondence included invitations to exclusive gatherings and necessitated her work with Fisher's several campaign-donor lists. As she sorted through those lists, she noticed many of the names sounded familiar. She'd heard them somewhere before.

When she broached the issue with Fielding, he said, "Of course you've heard them before. They are people from major financial businesses in New York. They appear in newspaper articles all the time."

"These are people from Wall Street?"

"Yes," Fielding replied.

"And they are attending the senator's campaign events?"

Fielding gave her an odd look. "Yes, of course. Why wouldn't they?"

"Well, for one thing, they are the source of the trouble he talks about in his speeches."

"They also are the ones who supply the money that makes those events possible. In fact, the money they give makes it possible for him to do *all* of the things he is doing."

Grace gestured to one of the lists on the table before them. "Some of the names on this list sound Jewish."

"They *are* Jewish," Fielding stressed.

Grace was astounded. "Why is he taking their money?"

Fielding grinned. "He can't very well get money from people who don't have it, can he?"

"But what about the sermon we heard at that church?"

"What about it?"

"These are New York Jews, right?"

Fielding shook his head. "Don't read too much into what the preacher said."

"I'm not reading anything into it," Grace retorted. "He singled these people out as the source of our problems. Griffin singles them out all the time. So does Walter Jones. Yet Senator Fisher seems to have no difficulty at all in accepting their money. And neither do you."

"Nothing in Washington is as it seems."

"And why are the Jews giving Fisher their money? Haven't they heard him speak? Haven't they heard Griffin and Walter Jones and the hundreds like that preacher we heard in Virginia? It all seems like a terrible conflict." Fielding chuckled in response and Grace glared at him. "What's so funny?"

"You," he answered.

"What about me?"

"Did you really expect this to be anything else?"

"But this is the very thing we've been talking about eliminating since the Crimson Legion was formed," she argued. "Even before then. This is the problem that lies at the heart of our nation's government. And we condone it. We facilitate it."

"Calm down. It's just politics."

"Just politics?" She was angry. "How can you say that?"

"Listen." Fielding adopted a professorial tone. "If you aren't in office, you can't do anything. And these days money is how things get done in politics. If you have it, you can campaign for office and have a chance to make a difference. If you don't have it, you go home and get a job at a factory."

"And what's in it for the donors?"

"Access," he said flatly.

"Access." She frowned. "Is that all?"

"That's all they need. For them, access is power. It's the way they can make changes. If they don't have access, they don't have power. If they don't have power, they can't make the changes that suit them."

"So, everyone is forced to pay."

"Yes." Fielding nodded. "They choose the person who can give them the most things compatible with their goals, while costing them the least things offensive to their goals."

Grace shook her head. "That sounds like the kind of thing we've said we're opposed to. The kind of thing we wanted to change."

"In theory. But we're not the idealists in this show. Our job is to make sure the senator gets what he wants out of the scheme and hope we can shape events toward the things we believe in. But it isn't going to happen all at once. That's not the way the government works."

Grace took a condescending tone. "It's the way it ought to work, though."

"For that to happen, we would need a different government. The one we have was designed by the Founders to force compromise. And that means both sides. Not just them, but us, too."

"Then, like I said, maybe it's time for a new government."

✦ ✦ ✦

A few days later, Fisher returned to the office with glowing reports of Mullins's success in California. Grace was proud of his work but wondered what else he might be doing while he was out there. She'd seen the way he responded to Dorothy's attention when they were in Charlotte and she wondered what kind of attention he was getting from women while he was on the road.

Later that day, a group of the senator's donors arrived from New York. Grace watched them as they trooped past her desk and noticed they all were white, male, and older. When they were in the office and the door was closed, she glanced longingly in that direction. "I wish I could hear what they're talking about in there."

Fielding overheard her. "Come with me," he gestured.

Grace rose from her chair and followed him, thinking she was about to get one more lecture about "It's just politics." Fielding led her to a supply room that adjoined Fisher's office and, with his finger to his lips, he pointed to a heat register in the wall near the floor. She shrugged and asked, "What do you mean?"

Fielding gestured again for her to keep quiet, then leaned close, cupped his hands around her ear, and whispered, "If you kneel by that register, you can hear every word they say in the office. But be very quiet. They can also hear you."

Grace's eyes opened wide in a look of realization and she knelt near the register. As Fielding suggested, she heard every word that was said in Fisher's office.

"Your immigration bill has some of us worried," one of the men said.

"I wouldn't worry too much about it," Fisher replied.

"Many of us have important business ties with Europe," the first man continued. "We would hate to see those ties imperiled by a policy that asserts your idea of Americanism in a restrictive manner."

"Flourishing Americanism does not play well with our associates," another added.

"I suspect Jewish sympathy doesn't play well with them, either," Fisher responded. There was a caustic bite to his tone, which Grace was pleased to hear.

"No." Someone chuckled. "Most of our people hate the Jews almost as much as your friends at the Crimson Legion, but we would remind you that we do business with Jews here in America."

Grace felt angry about that comment. How could they do that? How could they hate the Jews, see the Jews as a threat, yet continue to do business with them? Every transaction only added to the Jewish fortune.

"We need their money," someone spoke up.

"*You* need their money," another added.

Grace realized that comment was directed at Fisher and she

was surprised when he didn't respond.

"As you know," a new voice began, "although they won't meet with you personally, they continue to send money for you through us—in spite of all you've said against them."

"Yes," Fisher replied. "I am well aware of the arrangement we have with them."

The first man spoke up. "The Jewish bankers with whom we deal are concerned that you have grown too chummy with conservative extremists. They don't mind the immigration restrictions, but some of your friends actually mean to do them harm."

"In fact," another spoke up, "many of the Jews are privately glad for your restrictions. They are very comfortable with life in America and want to keep things just as they are. Your bill does that—"

"And eliminates potential competition for them," someone interrupted.

"But that's where the problem is," the first man continued.

"And what's that?" Fisher asked.

"The kind of people who promote the anti-Semitic rhetoric you seem to embrace are anarchists. In the business world—the world in which we live and move and operate—anarchy means unlimited risk, and *that* we cannot abide."

"I think you're wrong about my supporters," Fisher responded. "They are not anarchists. In fact, they are far from that."

"And how do you see them?"

"They are fascists." Fisher spoke in a matter-of-fact tone. "That's all. Plain-and-simple fascists."

A collective gasp seemed to rise from the room, and Grace was delighted at the sound of their discomfort. Men like the ones in Fisher's office needed to be shocked. Deserved to be shocked.

The room was silent for a moment, then someone said, "You can't possibly mean that you agree with them."

"Aren't we all fascists?" It was a rhetorical question but one

Fisher seemed to relish asking. Before anyone could respond, he continued, "When you think of a successful America, do you envision one with a Negro president?" There was a shuffling sound as the men shifted positions uncomfortably.

"Or how about a Jewish president?" Fisher continued. "When you think of a successful America, do you think of a Jewish man in the White House?"

"We'd all be wearing yarmulkes," someone quipped.

"Exactly," Fisher agreed. "When you think of a successful America, you think of a successful *white* America with only *white* leaders. And that, my friends, is a fascist idea." There was a creaking sound, and Grace imagined Fisher leaning forward in the chair that sat behind his desk. "Listen, when I talk the way I talk in my speeches, I am only telling them what they want to hear—what they need to hear in order to support my campaign. You can understand that, I'm sure."

Grace was appalled by the comment. She wanted to shout in response but forced herself to keep quiet.

"Once we're in office," Fisher continued, "we can change the rhetoric and dial down the heavy-handed talk. And as for the disruption you called anarchy, we need the other side off-balance. We need them on the defensive. Talking about issues they aren't comfortable in addressing—like immigration and Jewish influence on American life—accomplishes that. It keeps them off-balance and on the defensive."

"You're referring to the Harding crowd as the other side," someone suggested.

"Harding, among others."

The first man spoke up again. "And you think you can keep these conservative groups under control once you're in office?"

"Some of them are becoming quite adamant in their hatred of the Jews."

"And Negroes."

"And Italians," someone added.

"If my strategy plays out," Fisher responded, "those conservative groups you're worried about will be rolled into my political organization. We'll involve them, incorporate them, syphon off their leadership, and divert their money. In the process, we'll convert them from their current agenda into promoting our own agenda. If we do this right, they will never know they're being compromised. And over time, they will simply cease to exist as separate entities."

With that comment, Grace could take no more. She rose from her place by the heat register and returned to her desk. Upset beyond all ability to concentrate, she sat at her place with her arms folded across her chest, her eyes staring blankly at the desktop, while the conversation from Fisher's office played over and over in her mind.

Fielding noticed her disposition. "What's the matter?"

"That." She gestured toward the office door. "How can you work for a man like that?"

"It's my job."

Grace looked over at him with a pained expression. "Your job?"

"Yes."

"It's your job to work for a man who deceives the people behind that lapel pin you carry in your pocket?"

Fielding leaned back in his chair and lowered his voice. "Those people behind that lapel pin are the ones who put me here."

Grace frowned. "They know about him?"

"Some of it."

"You mean they know as much about Fisher as you tell them."

"I am not the only one giving information to the Crimson Legion from this office. But look, as we discussed before, this is the reality of the world in which we live. Everyone is angling for something they want. Everyone is paying a price to get it. Everyone is making a compromise, giving up something to get something else. The senator. His donors. His constituency. Me." He pointed his index finger toward her. "And you."

Grace shook her head. "Not me."

"Don't kid yourself. We're all angling for something and paying a price to get it."

Fielding's words hit too close for comfort and Grace needed space to think. She grabbed her purse and started toward the door. "I'll be back in a few minutes."

From the office, Grace made her way to the corridor and then down the stairwell to the first floor. The doors at the entrance were propped open and a breeze blew through the doorway. She lingered there, enjoying the fresh air while her mind cleared.

Fielding was right. She had made compromises. Many of them. She'd compromised when she was in Virginia and wanted to live on her own. She'd compromised when she met Mullins and wanted to be with him. And at every step along the way. Not major things. Not at first. Just little things that seemed to be not so bad at the time. But here she was, living in Washington, telling the investigators whatever they wanted to know in the hope of keeping her compromises a secret. *This wasn't how I wanted it to be.*

As she stood there thinking, worrying, and wondering what to do next, the delegation of donors from Fisher's office began to leave. They did not seem to notice her and continued to talk as they made their way toward the building exit. Grace listened to their conversation as they moved past her position.

"If he is playing the conservatives," one of them said, "isn't he also playing us?"

"Of course," another replied. "Aren't we all playing each other?"

They laughed, then the first one pressed the point. "But why is he appealing to conservatives like Griffin?"

"You heard what he said. He thinks they will vote for him."

"And get others to do the same," someone added. "He can't win against Harding and the establishment crowd in a traditional fight. He has to look somewhere else for votes."

"And he thinks the Jews will give him the money to run such a campaign."

"Rather audacious, isn't it? Thinking the Jews will pay for the campaign of a candidate with an anti-Semitic message."

"Is he really that stupid?"

"Are *they* really that stupid?"

"Or just that naïve?"

"I don't think either side is naïve at all."

"Well," the first one cautioned, "we just need to make certain we get what we're paying for."

A car arrived at the curb and as they made their way toward it, the conversation faded. Grace watched as they drove away and realized how correct Fielding's comments had been about them, too. At this level, politics was nothing more than a business deal. And no one—not the senator, or his supporters, or his fellow office holders—was anything like the image they portrayed of themselves in public.

CHAPTER 30

Having heard Fisher talking with donors in the office, and having overheard the donors talking about him afterward, Grace was disillusioned, angry, and suspicious of Fisher and everyone at work. And she wondered what else might be going on that she didn't know about. To find out more about Fisher, she started working at the office later than the others, searching through files and offices after everyone else had left.

Late one evening she went to Marvin Parsons's office and began reviewing files in a cabinet that sat near his desk. In it she discovered folders containing background research on various people—other senators, cabinet officials, agency directors, staff members, Mullins. And even a file on her.

The file on Mullins contained notes from the Springfield police investigation into complaints about attacks on Jews and notes from their review of the incident with the pigs. It also held notes from federal investigators who followed up on Mullins's activity against the unions and his association with the Crimson Legion.

Information in the files was nothing new, but the fact that the files existed was a shock to Grace. She was also struck by the fact that Fisher knew about what they did in Springfield—the attacks on the people outside the synagogue, the pigs in the synagogue, the trouble at the union rallies—and yet he hired them both anyway.

Reading further, she came to records from conversations that federal investigators had with Pete and Ida. Grace had been suspicious of Ida's sudden and unexpected appearance in Charlotte. Now she was certain Ida had been turned by investigators. Probably the same ones handling her. *They moved me up here, then brought her to Charlotte to take my place. They controlled the entire process, which means they control the Crimson Legion and Fisher.*

After returning the file on Ida to the cabinet, she took out the one on her and took a seat at Parsons's desk. It was surprisingly thin, with notes regarding the incidents in Springfield but nothing about the trouble she faced in Virginia. And nothing from the interviews she had given Hawthorne and Martin. She was relieved that there was so little on her—and particularly glad there was nothing about Virginia or her cooperation with federal investigators—but she was deeply troubled about the way she and Mullins had apparently been manipulated.

It was late when she left the office, much too late to catch a streetcar. So she took a taxi to the boardinghouse. On the way, she sat in the back seat of the car and thought about her situation.

Fisher was playing both sides against the middle, hoping he could win the Republican nomination and have a chance at becoming president. He talked like a Legion member, but he cared nothing for their cause. He'd compromised their values so many times, Grace wasn't sure he believed in anything. And Mullins had reduced their relationship to little more than a night together in bed—on the occasional night when he was in town.

Hawthorne and Martin were not much better. They had approached her as honest, upfront investigators. Just trying to do the right thing. But they had used her past to manipulate her into doing their bidding. Yet of all the people in her life, Hawthorne and Martin had one advantage. They had the power to make her life miserable as well as the power to free her from the web in which she now found herself hopelessly ensnared. And then she knew what she must do next.

✦ ✦ ✦

The following morning, as Grace prepared for work in her room at the boardinghouse, she took a hatbox from the shelf in the closet and set it on the bed. From the box, she took a red cloche hat, moved in front of a mirror, and carefully positioned it on her head before leaving for work.

At noon, she wore the hat to lunch and made sure to dine alone, thinking Hawthorne or Martin would mysteriously appear at her side and hoping no one from the office would see her with them. Lunch passed without incident, however, and Grace was beginning to wonder if they had decided to leave her alone after all. She would like that very much, she thought. To be left alone. By them, Fisher and Mullins. To go back to her life in Springfield without any of the entanglements she had acquired since that day she first saw Mullins at the Crimson Legion rally.

Late that afternoon, Grace left the office with everyone else and walked to the corner to catch the streetcar. The others from the office went in the opposite direction and she was there, waiting in a cluster of staff members and office workers whom she did not know. While she waited, a man appeared at her side and murmured in a low voice said, "There's a bakery in the middle of the next block. Walk to it and go inside. Make your way to the back. Someone will guide you."

No sooner had he spoken than he turned away and started up the street. Grace watched him a moment, wondering who he was and where he'd come from, but then the traffic signal changed and she crossed the street in the direction he had said.

Grace came to a bakery near the center of the block. As the man had instructed, she went inside and walked to the rear of the store. A clerk noticed her and gestured with a nod toward a door in the corner. She opened it and found a hallway that led to still another door. Beyond the second door she came to an alley that ran behind the building.

An automobile was parked there and as she appeared in the doorway, Martin stepped from the driver's seat. He opened the rear door and held it while she got inside. When she was in position, he returned to his seat up front and they started up the alley. She caught his eye in the rearview mirror. "You know, if we keep meeting like this every time, someone will notice." Martin did not reply but kept his eyes focused on the street ahead.

From the alley behind the bakery, they made their way through town to a house in a remote section of Georgetown, then little more than a village on the western side of the city. The car came to a stop between the house and a large outbuilding that appeared to have once been a barn. She expected Martin to slide out of the front seat and open the rear door of the car for her, but he did not, and instead they sat in silence.

Presently, the back door of the house opened and Hawthorne stepped out. He came down the steps, opened the front door on the passenger side of the car, and took a seat beside Martin. When he was inside, both men turned sideways to face her.

"You wore a hat today," Hawthorne observed. "I assume that means you have something to tell us."

For the next ten minutes, Grace recounted what she'd seen and heard in Fisher's office. The donors from New York. The method they used to funnel donations to Fisher from Jewish businessmen. And the way all of them—Jewish and Caucasian alike—seemed uncomfortable with the tone and content of Fisher's speeches.

"I'm sure his Jewish friends want to keep their involvement a secret," Martin suggested. "As does Fisher."

"Yes," Grace agreed. "Both of them have something they want

and both of them are willing to pay to get it."

Hawthorne smiled. "You're really enjoying this political business, aren't you?"

"Not really. I wish I were back in Springfield and had never heard of any of it. Or of either of you."

"I don't doubt that Fisher's Jewish supporters are uncomfortable with his rhetoric, but what about the men you saw in the office? How do they feel about it?"

"They don't really care for his association with groups like ours but—"

Martin interrupted. "Ours?"

"No matter where I go or what I do, I will always be a member of the Crimson Legion."

"And these businessmen are not?"

"No. They don't like groups like ours, but it's not because of what we stand for."

"If not for that, then because of what?"

"They see us as disruptive of the system and they perceive that disruption as increasing their risk. I suppose our activity adds uncertainty to their business projections."

Hawthorne caught her eye. "Do they think Fisher can win?"

"I don't think so, but the men from New York are afraid of what might happen if he does and they weren't already with him. So they are funding him anyway rather than taking the risk of being left out."

Martin spoke up. "And there were no Jewish men with them when they met?"

"None that I could tell." She had a sour look on her face. "But, like I said, they have Jews from New York who are participating behind the scenes."

"You don't like the Jewish involvement?"

"I don't like Jews," she sneered in a nasty tone. "So, no. I don't like their involvement in his campaign. Even indirectly."

"Anything else?" Hawthorne asked.

"Fisher told the donors that he plans to use fringe groups—and by that I'm sure he means the Crimson Legion and others like us—for his political purposes now, then dissolve those groups once he's in office."

"How does he propose to do that?"

"Drain off their leadership and find a place for them in the system. Move the rest out. I don't think he can do that—at least, not with the Crimson Legion—but that's what he's telling them."

Martin shook his head. "I don't think he can do it, either. Fisher isn't that smart."

Hawthorne changed the subject. "What about Mullins? Where is he in all of this?"

"He's still in California. I haven't seen him in several weeks."

"We've heard things about Crimson Legion activity out there that we don't really like. Especially the support they're building for Fisher in California even among Republican members."

Grace smiled. "That doesn't surprise me. Bryce is great at what he does."

"They also seem to be joining forces with groups that are even more radical."

"Glad to know you don't see us as the worst threat."

Martin glanced in her direction. "Ever hear about a group called the Sons of New Germany?"

"Only that Bryce has met with them. I know he is bringing them into the senator's campaign effort. Fisher intends to use this immigration bill as a base to run for president. The Sons of New Germany is very interested in the legislation."

"When will Mullins return?" Hawthorne asked.

"I'm not sure. I haven't heard from him in a while."

Hawthorne raised an eyebrow. "Are things still okay between you?"

Grace took a sarcastic tone. "Do you mean will he still want to sleep with me when he gets back?"

Hawthorne shrugged. "We're just asking."

She glanced out the window. "Things are fine between us, as far as I can tell."

Hawthorne seemed to let the matter drop but took a slip of paper from the inside pocket of his jacket and handed it to her. "These are some people we're interested in. Keep an eye out for anything that comes through the office about them." Grace took the paper from him and saw that it contained a list of names. Several of the people on it were donors to Fisher's campaign. "Let us know if the senator has anything on them," he added. It wasn't a request and Grace felt she had little choice but to give them the information they requested.

"I'll see what I can find."

When they finished talking, Hawthorne opened the passenger door and stepped from the car. Grace watched as he moved up the steps and into the house.

Martin started the car and drove her to a street three blocks from the boardinghouse. As he brought the car to a stop at the curb, he said, "You should get out here. That way no one will see you with me and ask questions." After the issue with Fielding that day when he brought her home and Norris saw her kiss him, she was glad for Martin's forethought.

As she made her way home, Grace thought about what she'd told them. She didn't like being a snitch. But she didn't like what Fisher was doing. Not now. Not after hearing the way he talked about the Crimson Legion and others like them. And certainly not after learning that he took money from New York Jews. She hadn't told Hawthorne and Martin all she knew, either. That made her feel a little bit in control of the situation. Not much. Just a little. But it would suffice for now.

CHAPTER 31

Two weeks after Grace met with Hawthorne and Martin, Mullins returned from California. Grace met him at the train station and on the way back to the boardinghouse they stopped at a restaurant for dinner. While they ate, he brought her up-to-date on what he had been doing with groups in California. Most of what he told her she had already learned from her conversation with Hawthorne and Martin.

"That's great," she exclaimed. "But we have a situation you need to know about." Then Grace told him what she had learned about Fisher, the donors from New York who were financing his campaign, and the plans Fisher had for the Crimson Legion and other similar groups once he took office.

Mullins grimaced. "That's not right."

Grace was taken aback by his apparent challenge. "I heard them with my own ears."

"No. I don't doubt what you heard. I'm saying he can't treat us that way."

"He has files on us."

Mullins frowned. "Who has files on us?"

"Fisher."

"I'm sure he does. Seems reasonable that he would have someone check us out before hiring us."

"It's more than that," she said. "He knows about what we did in Springfield."

Mullins looked puzzled. "In Springfield?"

Grace lowered her voice to a whisper. "The attacks on the people outside the synagogue. The pigs."

Mullins's eyes opened wider. "How did he find out about that?"

"I think Pete told the police about it."

He had a troubled expression. "Pete talked?"

"Yes, and I think that's why Ida showed up in Charlotte to take my place just as I was leaving."

"You think Ida showing up in Charlotte is linked to Pete talking to the police in Springfield."

Grace knew she couldn't tell him everything she'd learned or come to suspect without also telling him *how* she came to know it. And that would mean telling him she had been cooperating with federal investigators—something she knew she could never admit. So, instead, she made up a story. "I think Mr. Griffin gave Ida a job as part of a deal to keep her quiet and to keep Pete from saying more about what happened."

"That means Griffin knows, too."

"Yes."

"And you think he arranged things to protect me?"

"I think he likes you a lot. And I think he had bigger plans for you."

"Really?"

"He admitted as much when I told him I was taking this job. Said he hadn't realized when he began that having his people on the staff of a senator would be the way he made changes in the government, but that it was okay with him if that's how it turned out. I think he orchestrated all of this." She didn't tell him that the real people in control were federal investigators. That part of the story she kept to herself.

"Mr. Griffin said that?"

"Yes."

Mullins was obviously pleased to know that Griffin had taken an interest in him. "He must have big plans for us."

"I think so." Grace was pleased that she had avoided telling him the truth. "But Pete knows a lot, and that would threaten everything."

"Yes, it would be bad if he talked. Does Fisher have a file on you, too?"

"From what I can tell," Grace responded, "Fisher has people investigating everyone. The people he thinks he'll run against. The staff. You. Me. Everybody. And he has the money to find out anything he wants to know."

"He has the money," Mullins admitted.

"And something else. Fielding says he's a member of the Crimson Legion and that you know it. Is that true?"

Mullins looked away. "Yes. He's a member."

"He also said he helped you get me this job."

Mullins seemed uncomfortable. "He talked to Marvin Parsons about it. I talked to the senator. Somewhere between us, they agreed to hire you. Why?"

"Just making sure I know where I stand. That's all."

They continued to talk through dinner and then went to the boardinghouse. Grace spent the night in Mullins's room.

✦ ✦ ✦

Two months later, Senator Fisher's immigration bill was approved by Congress. Reluctantly, President Wilson signed it into law. The night that his signature was made official, Fisher held a celebration party at a restaurant a few blocks from the Capitol. The following day, Fisher, Mullins, Parsons, and Fielding gathered in Fisher's office to discuss how to make the most of the bill's passage and what to do next.

"I'm rather at a loss," Fisher grumbled. "Two days ago it

seemed like a good thing, getting the bill approved and enacted into law. But winning takes an issue off the campaign agenda that we had been building all of our efforts around and now I'm not quite sure how to proceed."

"I was wondering that same thing," Parsons acknowledged. "As we were working so hard to get the bill approved, I kept thinking it would be good to have that issue throughout the campaign."

"I don't think it's a problem," Mullins replied. "I think it's an opportunity."

Fisher looked puzzled. "How do you see that?"

"First of all, the bill was approved and you're the one who got it approved. You won. So you can say that from now until the end of the campaign. 'That's the kind of person I am. If I see a problem, I don't stop until I get it fixed. The other candidates only talk. I act.'"

Fisher grinned. "I like the sound of that."

"The other thing I see as an opportunity is the bill itself," Mullins went on. "The version of the law that was enacted isn't strong enough to satisfy the groups I've been working with the most. The Crimson Legion, Sons of New Germany, Knights of Teutonia—none of them are satisfied with this bill."

Parsons's face wrinkled in a scowl. "They don't like it?"

"They like it as far as it goes. They just don't think it goes far enough."

Fielding spoke up. "What makes you think that's an opportunity? We can't explain the weakness by saying we conceded to Jewish interests and let them water it down."

"No. And we won't say that."

"Then, what *will* we say?"

"We'll say the Jews took control of the legislation through their liberal puppets and watered it down."

"Not just the liberals," Fisher added. "But the establishment, too. We have to include the Harding crowd."

"Better yet," Parsons added, "we say that Harding's supporters conspired with the liberals to do it in an effort to make us look weak. And that kind of gambling with America's future is the very reason Harding should not be elected to the presidency or any other office."

Fisher grinned. "Oh, that's good. I like that. Can you get that to Ann Aldridge and have her work it into my speech?"

Fielding stood. "I'll get her started on it right now."

When Fielding was gone, Parsons commented, "That kind of language will work for a campaign speech and we can probably draft it into legislation, but what will we do when people start asking for the proof of what we're saying? About Harding and his supporters."

"Ignore them," Mullins replied.

"We can't just ignore them," Parsons argued.

"No." Fisher looked over at Mullins. "He's right. We can't just ignore them. It'll look like we have something to hide."

Mullins reached over to the corner of Fisher's desk and picked up a couple of newspapers. "Take a look at these. I had someone send these to us from California." He opened the newspapers and spread them over the desktop. Fisher and Parsons leaned over them to have a look.

On the front page of each were articles describing a recent increase in the movement of Jews out of Germany and the growing refugee problem that movement created in neighboring countries. "Talk about this," Mullins stressed. "When reporters ask for details, tell them, 'Listen, Jews are leaving Europe as fast as they can. They are flooding the borders of neighboring countries, straining the capacity of governments to handle them. Many are of a criminal element with dubious documentation. They devour everything in sight. And soon they will be here. They're already coming in droves.' And cite recent immigration statistics. Tell them, 'I am the only one doing anything to address the threat we face. The recent immigration bill was a first step but only a first step. We need to do more. We must do more. And we need your help to do it.'"

Fisher seemed intrigued. "Will people buy that message?"

"They will," Mullins assured, "if you deliver it."

Fisher seemed interested but noncommittal, and Mullins realized he was thinking about the people Grace mentioned—his financial backers from New York and their wealthy Jewish colleagues—and whether they would continue to support him with campaign donations if he gave a more strident version of his campaign speech.

Parsons seemed to sense Fisher's mood, as well. "Actually," he suggested, "the State Department could help."

"What do you mean?" Fisher seemed confused. "How could they help?"

"They can control the way the process works," Parsons explained. "By adjusting the way they issue visas, passports, and refugee applications. They have to follow the law and implement the prescribed processes, but they have a tremendous amount of latitude in the regulations they promulgate to do that."

"That's a good idea." Fisher's mood lightened immediately. "We could get them to tighten up on the enforcement side of what we just enacted. Get them to make the process more difficult."

"And," Mullins added, warming to the topic, "if we're asked about that by reporters, we could say that we've been working with State Department officials to make sure enforcement of the law follows a strict view of Congress's intent. As a measure to take in the meantime while we work on amending current law."

"That would be easier and faster than trying to pass a new immigration bill." Fisher leaned back in his chair. "Especially since we just enacted one."

"I know some people over at the State Department from our work on the bill," Mullins recommended. "I can sound them out and see if this will be possible before we start talking about it in speeches and with reporters."

"Good." Fisher nodded. "See if that idea has any appeal. And see where they stand on a new immigration bill, too."

✦ ✦ ✦

The next day, Mullins met with his State Department contacts and reviewed Fisher's proposal to tighten enforcement of existing immigration law while working to amend the recently enacted legislation. They liked the idea and introduced him to Langston Tammet, the undersecretary for immigration administration, for further discussion of the matter.

After hearing Mullins on the issue, Tammet leaned back in his chair and smiled. "I was wondering when you would get around to talking to us about this."

"You are not opposed?"

"Opposed?" Tammet chuckled. "I've been doing my best to slow the process all along. Your new bill gives me room to do things I've been trying to do for years, but Wilson and the liberals wouldn't let me. Now, thanks to Jonas Fisher, I finally have the tools I need."

"So, you can do it? You can tighten immigration to the margin allowed by law."

"Even below," Tammet replied confidently.

"That would be great."

"But I must say I don't like the limited number of immigrants allowed under the newly enacted law."

"What's wrong with them?" Mullins asked.

"They're much too high."

"That's why we want to introduce another immigration bill. To lower the numbers further."

"If you had worked more closely with us on that bill, we could have provided you with a more accurate estimation of its effectiveness, before it was introduced."

"Well," Mullins vowed, "this time we will."

"Good. Don't get me wrong," Tammet added, "it's better than the way things were before. And with the enforcement latitude in the current law, we can slow this process down to a trickle administratively."

"How long will you need to make that take effect?"

"We can do it immediately."

"Good."

"There's just one thing, though."

"What's that?"

"I want to meet with Jonas Fisher."

"Okay."

"Privately," Tammet added.

"I'll set it up."

When he returned to the office, Mullins arranged a meeting between Tammet and Fisher for later that same afternoon. Grace showed Mullins the heat register through which he could listen to their conversation.

"Langston," Fisher began, "it's always good to see you."

"Yes," Tammet replied as he took a seat. "We really should talk more often."

Mullins heard the familiar squeak of Fisher's chair. "I understand you might have some questions about addressing our immigration situation."

"That's not why I wanted to see you," Tammet apprised with a dismissive tone.

"Then, what is it?"

"My sources tell me that you may have some trouble coming your way."

"Oh?" Fisher sounded surprised. "What kind of trouble?"

"I'm sure you must have done a thorough job researching your man Mullins before you hired him."

"Is he in some kind of trouble?"

"You're aware of the issues he faced in Springfield?"

Fisher's chair squeaked again. "Yes, we looked into that. Didn't seem to come to much."

"My sources tell me that Justice Department investigators have widened their inquiry."

"Into Mullins?"

"They're now deep into a full investigation of the Crimson Legion."

"I know Griffin has been under their eye for a long time."

"This is more than that."

"Really."

"Apparently, investigators have an inside person at the Crimson Legion headquarters in Charlotte. And it looks like others may be cooperating, too."

"Others?"

"That's all I know. But there is something else."

"What's that?"

"William Griffin may act like he's your supporter, but my people tell me he doesn't think you have what it takes for the office. He wants to be president himself. If I were you, I would find a way to contain him."

"He talks a lot," Fisher smirked. "But he doesn't have the heft for that sort of job. Not really. Not the depth it requires."

"My people tell me you want to co-opt his organization. Bring it into your campaign operation, then ease them out of existence."

"Think it could work?"

"I think you could get killed in the process."

"I'm not worried about that. You can help us with immigration?"

"Yes," Tammet answered. "We're already working on it. But we need your people to consult with us this time. To get the numbers right on a new immigration bill."

"Yeah. About that. . .I've been thinking about that some more since I sent Mullins to see you and I'm not sure I can get a bill passed right now. Not after just passing this one so recently."

"You'll find a way." Tammet spoke as if they both knew more than they were saying. "For old time's sake, if nothing else."

There was silence for a moment. "Okay." Fisher's response made it seem as though he had some obligation to follow Tammet's suggestion. "But it won't be easy," Fisher added.

"If it were easy," Tammet said, "I would have asked someone else to do it. We need to move back the quota year to one with fewer people from Europe. That's all. Just amend the law to use an earlier reference year. One with even fewer Eastern Europeans."

"I'll need some help getting it through Congress," Fisher responded. "If I introduce it, I can't afford for it to fail."

"I'm sure you can find co-sponsors who would help with that."

"Does anyone come to mind?"

"Try some of the Southern senators," Tammet replied. "I think one or two of them would be eager to work with you."

"I'll need your help, too."

"Of course," Tammet said. There was a rustling sound, as he stood. "When you're ready to introduce the bill, let me know and I will see to it that recalcitrant senators fall in line behind it."

After the meeting with Tammet, Fisher called Mullins to his office. "I've decided to explore the introduction of a new immigration bill."

"Okay. Do you want help drafting it?"

"I don't think I'll need much help. We're going to propose this as a fix for the current law by moving back the reference year."

"You think that will work?"

"Yes. And it will be much easier to get it approved. But I need you to find co-sponsors for it."

"Any ideas about where to look?"

"Check out these two." Fisher handed him a card with two names on it—Lawton Newbern and Penrose Forsyth. Both were senators—Newbern from Alabama, Forsyth from Georgia—who had painted themselves as racists in every respect. That made them appear on the surface as natural allies in a battle for passage of yet one more racially motivated immigration bill. But both men were ardent Southerners who loathed the idea of another president from up north, which posed a challenge that was patently obvious to Mullins.

"Are you sure they will work with us?" he asked.

Fisher ignored the question. "Make some inquiries at the staff level. I think they might be interested."

"Tammet gave you these names?"

"Don't worry about Tammet. Just find out what kind of support a new immigration bill will have." Fisher gestured toward the card in Mullins's hand. "And talk to those two first."

"Perhaps we should concentrate on the language of a bill first, then look for sponsors."

"Just make the inquiries." Fisher sounded irritated. "I'll do the heavy lifting on the language."

✦ ✦ ✦

Of the two senators Fisher suggested as potential supporters of a new immigration bill, Senator Newbern seemed the most likely. To see if his hunch was correct, Mullins arranged a meeting with Newbern's chief of staff, Kirby Pittman. They met in Pittman's office.

"Let me get this straight," Pittman summed up Mullins's proposal. "Senator Fisher just obtained passage of an immigration bill and now he wants to amend that bill?"

"Yes," Mullins replied. "To further restrict the number of European immigrants."

"And why do you think Senator Newbern would be interested in supporting it?"

"He supported the one that just passed."

Pittman nodded. "And I think he told you then that it wasn't restrictive enough."

"And now I'm asking if he would like to make it more restrictive."

"I'll talk to him about it."

"Will he work to get it passed?"

Pittman grinned. "You mean will he work to get it approved knowing that if it is enacted it will strengthen Fisher's presidential hopes?"

Mullins smiled. "Yes. That's the question on our minds."

"I think he will like the bill," Pittman replied. "And I think he will work to win passage for it. But he doesn't like the idea of Fisher as president."

Mullins frowned. "Why doesn't he—"

Pittman held up his hand to interrupt. "Don't get me wrong. Senator Newbern likes Fisher. They get along well on a personal basis. But Fisher is a Yankee and we're all very tired of having one more Yankee president shoving the Constitution down our throats."

Mullins was puzzled. "I'm not sure I understand. That sounds like a reason *not* to support the bill. It would clearly help Fisher's chances at becoming president."

Pittman shook his head. "But that's just the point. It won't matter."

Mullins's forehead wrinkled in a deep frown. "Why not?"

"Fisher can't win a presidential election. A new immigration bill might strengthen Fisher's position, but even if it did, it won't be enough for him to win against Harding or whoever the Republicans dig up to run. The party is against you."

"The party won't matter."

"No one's ever done it that way before, Pittman noted. "And I hear you might face a wide-open fight for the nomination. Some say Teddy Roosevelt might even get in."

"We're not worried about Roosevelt."

"But you are worried about Harding. And either way—Roosevelt or Harding—your man can't win."

Mullins stood. "You'll talk to Senator Newbern about the bill?"

"Yes." Pittman stood, too, and they shook hands. "But you need to take a serious look at your man Fisher."

"Why is that?"

"You're a Crimson Legion man. I'm sure you can figure out where you stand without my help."

A meeting later that week with Senator Forsyth's chief of staff went much the same. Forsyth would be willing to support the bill and work for its passage primarily because he favored further immigration restrictions. But Forsyth saw little chance of Fisher winning the presidency, and for that reason he would work diligently to win a new bill's passage.

From those conversations, Mullins sensed that, although Fisher's strategy of changing the party by bringing his own supporters seemed sound, and although conservative groups seemed interested, support for Fisher even among his friends was soft. Yet after all he'd learned from Grace and from listening in on Fisher's meeting with Tammet, Mullins was reluctant to pass that information on to Fisher and instead decided to keep it to himself. When Mullins reported to Fisher on the meetings, he reported only that both senators would agree to co-sponsor new legislation and that they would work for its passage. He made no mention of their feelings about Fisher's presidential candidacy.

At the same time, Mullins was troubled by Pittman's cryptic remark and his apparent reference to his Crimson Legion connection. Did everyone know the things Tammet had mentioned when he was in Fisher's office? Was the ground about to collapse under his feet? Mullins was concerned, but felt he couldn't say much without making the situation worse. Rather, he resolved to pay closer attention to Fisher and to discern for himself what might lie ahead, hopefully in time to make his next move before trouble could destroy all he'd worked to build of his life.

CHAPTER 32

Not long after the immigration bill became law, Mullins returned to the road, once again traveling the country, organizing campaign committees and rallies for Fisher's all-but-certain presidential bid. At each of those locations, Mullins brought together the coalition of groups that had been effective during their swing through California. Groups like the Crimson Legion, Sons of New Germany, and the Knights of Teutonia. All of them further to the right politically than the established Republican Party. And, as he did in California, Mullins used them to bring additional members to the local party apparatus.

Fisher, for his part, seemed invigorated. Fresh off a major legislative victory, he gave rousing speeches, most of them filled with racist, anti-Semitic invective. Somewhere in each of those addresses he found a way to repeat the lines they'd crafted that night in his office. "In our recent effort to address the threat of uncontrolled immigration, Harding's supporters conspired with the liberals to frustrate our efforts at every turn. Gambling with America's future to court favor with New York Jews and Communist sympathizers—the very people who want to destroy our country—all for the sake of gaining political office. A man like that, my friends, should never be president of the United States."

And, as Mullins suggested, when reporters questioned him afterward about the reference to Harding, Fisher said, "Listen, Jews are leaving Europe as fast as they can, and are flooding across the borders of neighboring countries. Many of them are of a criminal element, newly released from a failing prison system and traveling with dubious documentation, and devouring everything in sight. And soon they will be right here in America." Usually, he paused there to cite immigration statistics—some of it factual, some of it not—then always added, "I am the only one doing anything to address the threat we face. The recent immigration bill was a first step, but only a first step. We need to do more. We must do more. And we need the help of the American people to do it."

During a trip to New York in advance of still more campaign rallies, Mullins met with Anderson Burke, chairman of a Sons of New Germany chapter in Hempstead, a village on Long Island about twenty miles east of Brooklyn. Burke had agreed to help coordinate volunteers for the campaign. They met over dinner and as they ate, Burke asked, "Aren't you friends with William Griffin?"

"Yes," Mullins replied. "Do you know Bill?"

"Quite well. He was out here the other day."

Griffin was scheduled to appear with Fisher at a rally in Newark, New Jersey, later that week but Mullins was not aware he already was in town. "What was he doing out here?"

"He visited the Eugenics Record Office. Stopped by to see me on his way through."

Mullins was puzzled. "What is the Eugenics Record Office?"

"You don't know about that? Their work is in keeping with many of the things you, Fisher, and Griffin discuss."

"The Eugenics Record Office is actually a laboratory," Burke explained. "Scientists who work there are exploring the apparent connection between race and ability."

Mullins remembered the books Tom Hinkle had sold him when he was at the bookstore in Springfield. "That sounds fascinating. We've known for a long time that not all races have equal ability."

"That's what they're trying to confirm."

"And when they do, what will they do about it?"

"Well, that's the big question, isn't it? Humans are the one group of animals in the kingdom that can, to some extent, determine its own evolution."

"And that's what they want to do? Guide the advancement of the human race?"

Burke had a sinister smile. "Perhaps not advancement for *all* of the races. Some of them we might like to keep as a permanent underclass."

"And these are actual scientists?"

"Yes. Top of the class. Their work is being supported by the Carnegie Institution."

Mullins was intrigued by the work and by the fact that it was supported by Carnegie. Many of the claims Fisher and others had made about the effects of racial impurities from intermarrying had been met by derisive comments from reporters and others. Perhaps the Record Office could help legitimize their claims about the inferiority of Jews, Negroes, and others and add legitimacy to their efforts to confront the rising influence of those groups.

✦ ✦ ✦

With Burke's help, Mullins arranged a tour of the Eugenics Record Office. Irene Dunham, an administrative aide, escorted him through the building and explained their operation. "Most of our work from this location consists of surveying the population through questionnaires about their ancestry and family background," she clarified. "We then compile that information by race and country of origin."

"Do you conduct experiments?"

"Our supporting institutions do that, but not here. Our purpose here is to compile and disseminate the work being done by our array of institutions and scientists from around the world."

"And what do you hope to accomplish?" Mullins asked.

"Basically, we hope to winnow from the human race those with undesirable traits."

"Physical defects?"

"Yes, as well as cognitive and personality. They all are a threat to us."

Mullins smiled. "And I suppose for that to be effective, you'll need government support?"

"That's why we were eager to see you today." Dunham continued, "We can do a lot with education, but to be its most effective the program would need government action."

"And how would you envision that occurring?"

"Prenatal testing to identify problems before delivery. Sterilization for those deemed an immediate threat. One day, genetic modification could make all of that unnecessary, but in the meantime, we would need to be. . .aggressive."

Mullins was surprised to learn the facility was part of an international effort but not surprised at all that application of their discoveries might involve the use of government power and authority. "When you say sterilization, I assume you are talking about forced sterilization."

"Primarily. But I'm sure you know already, there has been some resistance to that practice."

They talked awhile longer, then Dunham escorted him toward the exit. As they passed through an office on their way to the front hall, Mullins noticed a copy of Walter Jones's newspaper lying on a desk. He paused to pick it up and flipped through it. "You are familiar with Walter Jones?"

Dunham smiled. "Reverend Jones is a big supporter of our work." She opened a desk drawer and took out an older issue of the paper. "This one has an article about our work. He has mentioned us on his radio show, too."

Mullins glanced through the second issue. "I used to read this paper all the time."

"Why did you stop?"

"Time. Just not enough time in the day."

Dunham opened the desk drawer again and took out a third copy. "This one came a few days ago." She handed it to Mullins and he turned quickly through the pages. On the back cover he noticed Jones was promoting a rally scheduled for later that month at Madison Square Garden. He made note of the details, then returned the paper to her. "Thank you for your time."

✦ ✦ ✦

When Mullins returned to the office in Washington later that week, he met with Fisher and suggested that involvement with the Eugenics Record Office might be a way of expanding Fisher's connections to academic circles. "Eugenics is the latest craze in the scientific community," he related. "And it's attracting a lot of publicity."

"But not all of that publicity is good," Fisher responded. "Some of my colleagues in the senate are genuinely alarmed by the ideas many of these eugenics enthusiasts are discussing."

"What do you mean?" Mullins knew already, but he wanted to hear from Fisher.

"Every time they talk about eliminating negative traits. People hear them proposing forced sterilization, forced pregnancy termination, prohibition of marrying. No one likes that idea except people like those in the Eugenics Record Office."

"They have a worldwide group of scientists working with them," Mullins countered. "Some of the greatest minds on the planet are working on this."

Fisher nodded. "I know, but it has a lot of problems and I'm not sure we need that right now."

"You could use some heft in the academic area," Mullins suggested.

Fisher's eyes were intense. "Are you saying I'm perceived as not being intelligent?"

"I'm saying," Mullins stressed, "that's an area where you lack credentials. The academic credentials of their researchers would be a way of adding legitimacy to your candidacy and your political claims about the threat posed by inferior races."

Fisher appeared to be unhappy with the way the conversation was going. "I've made the case for our arguments." His voice had a strident tone. "And I've used some of the most explicit language yet. Jews have convinced Aryans it's okay for them to marry Poles and Italians. . .and Negroes. But when they do, it produces an inferior version of the white race. I've said that. People either believe it or they don't."

"I think eugenics scientists would agree with you. And I think they would agree that something must be done to stop it. That evolution can be used to our advantage. Breed out the unwanted influences. That sort of thing."

"Maybe." Fisher sighed and seemed to relax. "Perhaps we could help them obtain funding for their work. Do you have anything on them for me to read?"

Mullins handed him several pamphlets he'd picked up on his recent tour at the Eugenics Record Office. "These should give you an overview of what they're trying to do."

Fisher took them. "I'll look at it, but I'm not promising anything."

✦ ✦ ✦

Seeing Walter Jones's newspaper and the brief discussion he'd had with Irene Dunham about Jones during the trip to the Eugenics Record Office reminded Mullins of the questions he'd had at the death of his brother, the route he'd taken in the pursuit of answers, and how far he had come since that first night he heard Jones on the radio. From Jones's broadcast, to the newspaper, to the Crimson Legion, to his job in Fisher's office staff.

Along the way, he had accomplished much, but now he was concerned that Fisher might not be as committed to the Aryan agenda as he first seemed and that concern changed the way Mullins viewed his work, his role, and himself. That change was slight at first but almost every day since he'd returned from California, he felt himself drawn further from the agenda he'd embraced with the Crimson Legion—of confronting the threat of an immigrant horde—and toward an agenda designed only to place Fisher in office. An outcome that Fisher had already suggested more than once would spell the end of the Crimson Legion and similar groups.

In his room at the boardinghouse that night, Mullins searched through the boxes in his closet and found several old copies of Walter Jones's newspapers. He sat in the chair in the corner and reread them, then returned to the closet and searched again until he found the books he had purchased at the shop in Springfield—the first one, *The Protocols of the Learned Elders of Zion*, and the other, a copy of *Race and the Excellence of Society* by Claus Ploetz. With those books in hand he returned to the chair.

Even before the end of the first page, he felt his soul renewed with a sense of purpose and commitment to the cause of the Crimson Legion and their fascist vision for America: a vision of a land inhabited and governed by a pure Aryan race. And then he thought of the people he'd encountered in the corridors and halls of the Capitol. Men and women committed to a process that could not adequately address the ills that plagued the nation. True, they had drafted and won approval of a bill that restricted immigration, but his meetings with Langston Tammet from the

State Department had shown him how easily the permanent government could frustrate efforts to reform from within. If a conservative undersecretary in the State Department of Tammet's stature could tighten application of the law, a liberal could loosen that application just as easily.

Remembering Tammet brought to mind his meeting with Fisher and the conversation he had listened to through the heat register. What did Tammet's vague references mean? Even more unsettling, why had Fisher reacted with immediate deference? Those questions and more rattled around in Mullins's mind as he read, and it was late in the night when he finally turned out the light and went to bed.

Reading late into the night meant Mullins overslept. By the time he awakened, breakfast was over and Grace already had left for the office. He was late, but he did not regret reading Jones's newspaper or the books he'd brought from Springfield. Encountering those again brought a sense of clarity and by the time Mullins left the house, he had decided to travel to New York and attend Walter Jones's rally at Madison Square Garden. He needed to hear again Jones's message. To be uplifted by his fiery oration. To be swept up in the cause anew. And he wondered if Grace might like to go, too.

When Mullins reached the office, he took Grace aside and told her about Walter Jones's rally planned for New York later that month. She seemed to understand he wanted her to go even before he asked. "I don't know." Her tone was tentative, as was the look on her face.

"Do you want to go with me?" Mullins implored.

"I would love to attend that rally. But how can we manage time for it with the office schedule? The campaign schedule? The legislative calendar? We have a lot going on."

"I know. But New York isn't that far away. We can leave early on the day of the rally, take the train up, and then come back that night after the rally is over. It won't take more than four or five hours each way."

Grace looked doubtful. "I don't know . . ."

"We'll tell the office that we're going up there to. . .to meet with supporters," Mullins suggested. "New York is an important state. I've been up there several times already. No one will suspect anything."

"Not about you," she responded. "No one ever raises any questions about what *you* do. But they will about *me*."

Mullins shook his head. "They won't ask about you, either. Not if you're with me."

"I don't know," she sighed again.

"Come on, Grace," he pleaded. "It's Walter Jones. In New York City. You know what this means to me. To us. To you."

"Well," she decided finally, "okay. It'll be a long and tiring trip but if you want to go, I'll go with you."

CHAPTER 33

A few weeks later, Mullins and Grace traveled by train to New York City and made their way to Madison Square Garden for the rally that had been advertised in Walter Jones's newspaper. The building was packed with people when they arrived and not long after they entered, police began turning people away at the door. "The building is full," they called out, and then repeated. "The building is full."

From a window on the mezzanine level Mullins saw those who'd been prohibited from entering had not dispersed but had gathered outside. Many of them were chanting Crimson Legion slogans. Some confronted passersby with angry taunts. The sight of it made his spine tingle and he realized he hadn't felt that way in a long time. Not since. . .the night they confronted Jews for the first time outside the synagogue in Springfield. And the night they released those pigs. A broad grin turned up the corners of his mouth at the thought of it.

Several of the men working the floor recognized Mullins from their involvement with his campaign efforts. Chairs were brought and a place was made for them at the front of the crowd. Not long after they were seated, representatives of the several groups participating in the rally appeared on stage.

Like similar events, this one began with speeches from lesser-known people. Heinz Rudolf, an official with the German American Federation, went first. He was followed by a rousing delivery from Albert Herman, a representative from the Sons of New Germany. Finally, Walter Jones delivered the keynote address.

"As many of you are aware," Jones began, "Jews have dressed themselves in the fine clothing of what passes for respectability. They have washed their hair. They have augmented their accent. And they have learned to carry themselves with an air of apparent dignity. But make no mistake about it. The Jews you see today on the streets of this city and on the streets of your hometown are the same pagan reprobates who killed Christ."

The auditorium erupted in applause and cheers.

"The church—the Christian church—is the new Israel. *We* are God's chosen people. Destined to become a powerful nation. A nation that rules the world in righteousness and in purity. Racial purity."

The crowd cheered wildly.

"Free from the taint of Negroes, Italians, and from the putrid corruption of the International Jews."

More applause and more cheers followed.

Jones, continued, "But that purity is a status that will not come easily to us. Communists and their American liberal allies have infected our once great and pure society with the stench of foreign immigrants. Brown skinned. Black skinned. The so-called olive skinned. They have allowed them into our country in very great numbers, for the specific purpose of neutering the very soul that makes this nation great. And for that, the Communists and the liberals must be made to pay.

"Because of the imbecilic manner in which this country has been run, the racial purity we seek will come to us only by a fight. And that fight is a conflict from which we will not shrink."

A shout went up from somewhere, "Kill them all!" And then it became a chant repeated in unison.

Jones let the response continue a moment, then gradually brought the audience under control. "We must fight for racial purity in our homes," he continued. "Some of our fellow Aryans have been misguided by the liberals and the Communists into thinking it is acceptable to marry from among the pagan horde. We must fight by educating them about the error of their ways."

"We must fight for racial purity in our neighborhoods. In our towns and in our cities. In our counties and in our states. We must purge this nation of every impurity. Racial, moral, and political impurity." He paused for effect, leaned close to the microphone, and lowered his voice to a dramatic whisper. "And no Jews."

Again the auditorium erupted in cheers as everyone stood to their feet, shouting and waving their arms wildly. Then from somewhere another chant arose. "Jews burn best! Jews burn best!" It swept across the crowd like a wave and as it died away another rose in its place. "Send them back!"

Jones spoke for almost an hour. Afterward, as the crowd began to file from the auditorium, Mullins and Grace made their way backstage. "What are we doing back here?" Grace asked.

"I want to see Jones," Mullins replied.

"Will they let us?"

"I think we can find a way."

At first, policemen guarding the rear hall of the auditorium intervened and blocked their way, but Mullins caught sight of someone he knew and waved them over. When he explained what he was trying to do, the friend brought him to the holding rooms where dignitaries had gathered. They found Jones seated along the wall on the far side of the room, sipping from a drink.

With Grace in tow, Mullins made his way toward Jones and introduced himself. "I work for Senator Jonas Fisher," he explained. "We met once before and I just wanted to thank you for that speech today. Your radio program got me started and had a lot to do with where I am now."

Jones smiled. "We met once before in Rochester." He stood and they shook hands. "I wasn't feeling well that night we had dinner together. I don't think I made a very good impression."

"I was just glad to see you," Mullins replied.

"I know Senator Fisher quite well. We have been friends for a long time. You're helping with his campaign, right?"

"Yes," Mullins replied. He was surprised Jones knew or remembered anything about him.

"Jonas is a likeable guy," Jones added. "But I don't trust him at all. And you should know, no one else in the movement does, either."

"We've been working hard to correct that."

"His immigration bill helped some, I suppose," Jones noted. "But most people think he did that only because you goaded him into it. They think all he really wants is to get into office." Jones had a knowing look. "And there is no way Fisher can win the presidency, no matter what he's telling you."

"I think he means to try."

"If Harding doesn't enter the race," Jones added.

"That is a factor," Mullins conceded.

"And there's something else. I've been trying to find someone to tell about this, so I guess you're that person." Jones waited, apparently for Mullins to respond, but when he didn't, he continued. "Many of us wonder if Jonas doesn't mean to destroy this movement we're building."

Although Mullins had heard that before, he was taken aback that similar ideas were circulating through the Aryan movement. "Who is saying that?" he asked, knowing full well the comments came from participants at the meeting Grace described for him earlier.

"Various ones." Jones bypassed the opportunity to name names. "I personally think he means to destroy it from the inside. He's been working closely with many of our groups, supposedly for their political support, but I think he's been trying to take away our best people. Are you aware he's been meeting with prominent members of the Federation and some of the others, offering them jobs in his political organization?"

"No." The comment caught Mullins by surprise. He had heard that Fisher wanted to do that, but he had not realized it already was happening. "I know he meets with many people." Mullins struggled to push aside his thoughts and concentrate on the moment. "I'm traveling most of the time, so it's entirely possible he has met with them and I don't know it."

"Wasn't it your idea to draw us into the campaign?"

"Not to destroy the movement," Mullins countered quickly. "I wanted to bring voters into the party. New people. Our people. People who agree with our views. Bring our own support with us. It's the only way Fisher can win the nomination."

"That's a good strategy," Jones noted. "But first we must have a candidate who agrees with our ideas. Not one who merely mouths the words to get our votes."

"Politics is a trade-off," Mullins countered.

Jones nodded. "Yes, but there must be something on both sides for that trade to work. Our people have a natural instinct toward doing something, taking action to protect their own interests. Not merely handing out political leaflets and voting for Jonas Fisher."

"Is there any evidence that he means to destroy us?" Mullins asked. "Other than rumor?"

"I have heard reports that he told his supporters that very thing. Right there in his office. That once he is elected, he will take our best people, push the rest aside, and dismantle our organizations."

"Which supporters said that?"

"That group of Wall Street men who finance his every move." Mullins' heart sagged but Jones's eyes flashed. "And that's another thing," Jones continued. "Word is going around that those money-men have ties—deep ties—to wealthy Jews. Those International

Jews we've been warning about. The very same people we oppose."

Mullins wanted to ask questions. To get to the bottom of the issue. But doing that would force him to admit, at least to himself, that he might have been duped by Fisher. That he might be complicit in Fisher's intentions. That what he thought was helpful to the movement had really been working all along for its destruction.

"This is not good," Jones continued. "It's even said that those New York supporters receive campaign contributions from Jews and funnel the money to Jonas's political efforts. A scheme devised by Jonas himself."

Mullins looked away. "Politics sometimes forces one to make difficult choices."

"I think you know much more about this than you are saying. In fact, your lack of defense or explanation tends to convince me that what I've said is true. And I think you should consider your position very carefully. Compromise of one's integrity does not come in a single swoop. It comes incrementally. One small decision at a time."

✦ ✦ ✦

By the time they left the auditorium and started toward Penn Station for the train ride back to Washington, Mullins' mind was in turmoil. As they walked in that direction, Mullins ignored the sights and sounds of the city and thought only about the things he had seen and heard that day.

Most of what Jones told him was information he had already heard from Grace. And from people on the campaign trail—though he thought he had addressed the campaign concerns. Still, the fact that comments about Fisher's intentions for the Crimson Legion and similar groups, his ties to New York financial interests and

New York Jews were making the rounds left Mullins angry, confused, and worried.

Grace looked over at him. "What did you think of what Jones said?"

"I don't know." Mullins shrugged.

"It's the same thing I told you about what I heard when they were in his office."

"I know," Mullins sighed. "I know."

Grace sensed his mood. "Don't get mad at me, I didn't do anything."

"I know." He took her hand. "It's just. . .I feel like I've been deceived."

"We all have been."

"Do you think I should quit?"

"What else would you do?"

"I think I could go back to Charlotte. Mr. Griffin would take me. I think."

"I think he would, too. But I can't tell you what to do. This was a big dream for you."

"Yeah, but I think it has turned out to be a nightmare."

She smiled and pulled him closer as they walked. "But on the bright side, we heard some good speeches today."

"Yes, we did," Mullins responded. "Hard to believe Jones is a preacher."

"He's good at it."

"I have never heard a preacher who preached like that. "In fact, if there was a church with that kind of preacher in Washington, I'd attend every Sunday."

"Actually," Grace perked up, "there is."

Mullins glanced at her. "Really? Where?"

"In northern Virginia."

He was puzzled. "How do you know about it?"

"Fielding took me there."

"Fielding?"

"Yes. While you were in California."

Suddenly the frustration Mullins had felt while talking to Jones—frustration that had been building for weeks over Fisher, his financial ties to Jews, his statements about dismantling the Crimson Legion erupted inside him. He jerked free of Grace's embrace and turned on her. "You went out with him behind my back?!"

"Nothing happened," she insisted. "We just went to church. That's all."

"I'm out there working and trying to do something, and you're back here going out with other men and having a good time." Mullins flayed the air with his hands while he continued to shout. "I can't believe you would do that to me."

"I haven't been out with *other men*," Grace retorted defensively. "I went to church with Fielding. That's all. And I didn't . . ."

Mullins didn't wait to hear the rest. By then he was several strides ahead of her and lost in his own anger. When they reached the station, he bought a ticket for them both, handed one to Grace, then waited for the train at the opposite end of the platform from her. When the train arrived, he took a seat at the opposite end of the railcar.

They reached the station in Washington a little before midnight and took a taxi to the boardinghouse. Although they sat together in the back seat, Mullins said not a word. As they entered the house, Grace stopped in the hallway and turned to face him. "Look," she said. "Nothing. Happened. Okay?" She spoke in a soft voice and touched him tenderly. "Fielding knew about a church he thought I might like and offered to take me. We went there and came back. That's all."

Mullins, still was in a black mood, sneered, "Do you really expect me to believe that?"

Her face became hard with anger. "Don't call me a liar!" she snarled and stormed up the steps.

As Grace disappeared down the hall on the second floor, Norris, the man who had been on the front porch the evening Grace and Fielding returned, sauntered from the kitchen. "Is this about what I think it's about?"

Mullins frowned. "You were eavesdropping on us?"

"Kind of hard to avoid hearing you," Norris replied.

"You know something about it?"

"About that guy she went off with a few weeks ago?"

Mullins had an angry scowl. "What about him?"

Norris had a sly grin. "It didn't happen exactly like she said."

"You saw them?"

"Yeah. I was on the front porch when they came back. Parked up the street but I could see them. He leaned over and kissed her. She said something, then kissed him back." Norris raised an eyebrow. "I'm pretty sure it was more than just a ride to church."

Despite the lateness of the hour, Mullins hurried upstairs to Grace's room and knocked on the door. When she opened it, he pushed past her and stood near the center of the room. "I know what you did with him."

"What are you talking about?"

"He kissed you." Mullins moved closer and pointed with his finger near her face. "And you kissed him."

"Yes," she admitted. "He did kiss me. And I kissed him. But it was only a friendly gesture."

Mullins had a mocking tone. "Friendly gesture—"

"I have no feelings for him other than friendship."

"Some kind of friendship."

"He's our co-worker," she argued. "We went to church together. I couldn't stop him from leaning over and giving me a peck on the lips."

"You could have turned your head and given him a cheek."

She gave a wry sort of chuckle and turned away. "Don't be silly."

Mullins was livid. "Don't make fun of me!" he shouted and he gave her a shove in the back with both hands, then started toward the door.

Caught off-balance, Grace stumbled forward and collided with the chair that sat in the corner. She caught herself with a hand against the wall. Mullins felt bad about what he had done and moved to help her. "I'm sorry." He took her by the arm to help her stand. "I didn't mean to—"

Grace shrugged free of his grasp and, without warning, landed a backhanded slap against the side of his face. "Don't ever touch me again."

✦ ✦ ✦

The next morning, Mullins rode the streetcar to work with Grace. They sat in silence the entire way and kept their distance at the office. At noon, he convinced her to have lunch with him and as they sat at the window in a Capitol Hill café, he apologized again for the way he had acted the day before. She grudgingly accepted.

They ate in silence awhile, then Grace said, "The way you erupted on the street, there must be something else wrong besides me going to church with Fielding. What is it? What's bothering you?"

"Working for the senator," he replied.

"What about it?"

"When we started, it seemed good and right. Now it doesn't feel right. And it doesn't seem good, either. That rally," she whispered. "It made a huge difference in both of us."

Mullins nodded. "Maybe it was seeing Walter Jones. Maybe

it was the eugenics people I talked to a few weeks ago. Or maybe it was what you told me about the things you heard when Fisher met with those people from New York."

"That's the same group that Jones was talking about."

"I know."

"It sounded like the word is out on Fisher."

"And it's that word that bothers me. Not that people are talking about him, but that they know the truth about him."

"You couldn't know everything before you started. And you were relying on his relationship with Griffin as an indication that he was one of us."

"When we were with the Legion, it seemed like we were actually trying to change things. To confront those issues that threaten the country. Now it seems like all we're doing is promoting Fisher. It all seems only about him."

"I think you're right."

"Jews are a problem. We can't just dance around it or soft-pedal it the way politicians do. This is a serious problem for America, and it has gotten so far out of hand that we can't fix it with polite rhetoric, which is all we'll ever get from politicians."

"Do you think he'll even offer a new immigration bill?"

"I think he might. And I think we can get the support of Southern congressmen. But they're only supporting it because they think he can't get elected president."

"They don't want him as president?"

Mullins shook his head. "No. Because they think he's not one of us." Mullins laid aside his fork and looked over at Grace. "Do you think we could try again?"

She had a puzzled expression. "With the immigration bill?"

"No. With us. I'm sorry I got so mad last night. And I'm sorry I shoved you. I shouldn't have done that." He'd already apologized but he still felt guilty. "Do you think we could start over and get things right between us?"

"Yeah." She smiled at him. "Sure."

But inside he knew that something had changed between them. Something that was irreparable. And a sense of sadness swept over him.

CHAPTER 34

A few days later, Mullins met with Fisher in Washington to update him on the New York rally, and his meeting with Walter Jones. As usual, they gathered around Fisher's desk.

"How was Walter?" Fisher asked. He took a cigar from the humidor on the corner of his desk and lit it.

Mullins sat with his legs crossed and an elbow propped against the armrest of a chair on the opposite side of the desk. "He's concerned about your efforts to restrict immigration further."

Fisher grinned. "He's against another immigration bill?"

"No, he wants you to shut it down altogether."

Fisher frowned. "End immigration?"

"Yes."

"Yeah. Sounds like Walter. I'll give him a call. Maybe we can arrange a time for me to meet with him. He gets like this sometimes, but he'll come around. What else?"

"Some of the groups we're working with think the masses will never understand the threat we face from the Jews."

"That might be right." Fisher leaned back in his chair and puffed on the cigar. "Who is that coming from?"

"Primarily people in the German American Federation."

"And what do they want us to do about it?"

"I don't think they want us to do anything about it. They think we're part of the problem."

Fisher looked over at him with a pained expression. "They think *I* am part of the problem?"

"Yes." Mullins nodded.

"So they want to move me out?"

"No. They want to take over the country."

Fisher smirked. "Griffin, Jones, those guys from the Federation, they all want to be president." He took another puff from his cigar. "Perhaps not this election but possibly someday. They all want to be king."

"I suspect they think they could do a better job than what we have," Mullins opined. "I don't know if they think they could win an election."

"All the same, we need to find a way to contain them. Griffin in particular. He doesn't have the heft for this sort of job, but he's the strongest of the bunch. Strong enough that he could convince the others to withdraw their support, make it difficult for us to win."

Mullins didn't like the comment about Griffin, but he forced himself to remain calm and respond without giving away his view. "How do you suggest we contain him?"

Fisher set the cigar in an ashtray, then rested his hands in his lap and gazed thoughtfully at the ceiling. "We need to make ourselves the only game in town on immigration. Make the other groups see that they have no option but to deal with us. Box out Griffin on immigration."

"To do that, we really need another round of immigration restrictions," Mullins suggested. "Or some decisive new action on that front."

Fisher glanced at him. "Can we speed up work on that next bill?"

"Yes."

"Are the Southerners still on board?"

"Yes," Mullins replied. But he failed to tell Fisher why they were willing to support his legislation.

"And I want you to explore what it would take to oust Griffin from his position with the Crimson Legion." Fisher gave Mullins a serious look. "You can do that?"

Mullins felt as if the air had been sucked from the room. Oust Griffin? Was Fisher out of his mind? Was he that far over the edge that he could not see that it was Griffin who could oust him, not the other way around? Walter Jones had warned him of this. Said others were talking about it. Now he'd heard it from Fisher's own mouth.

"I'm not sure how to proceed," Mullins managed to say.

"Maybe we could at least splinter the Legion. Divide them before they divide us. Got any dirt on Griffin? Women trouble? Money?"

"Neither of those options seems workable," Mullins was still trying to get past the comment about moving Griffin out. And these accusations?

"Well, whatever works. I'm sure you can get it done," Fisher continued confidently. "And once the Legion is neutralized, we can move against the others. With Griffin out of the way, they'll fall right into our hands. Then we can roll their people into a new organization that we can control. Who knows?" He looked over at Mullins with a smile. "Maybe you'll be in charge of that new group."

Mullins was certain that would never happen. Even if Fisher moved Griffin aside—something he would never allow to happen—Fisher would move Mullins out, too, when he was finished with whatever usefulness he might find in the venture.

✦ ✦ ✦

When the meeting with Fisher ended, Mullins left the office and went for a walk. He needed time to think. Time to process.

Time away from the vacuous and vapid world of Capitol Hill. Without telling anyone where he was going, he made his way to the exit downstairs, crossed Pennsylvania Avenue, and strolled down the National Mall. Halfway to the opposite end, he found a bench and took a seat in the shade of a large oak tree.

When Grace told him about the conversation she overheard in Fisher's office—and even when he talked with Walter Jones—the notion that Fisher wanted to move against groups like the Crimson Legion was merely an idea. He didn't doubt the truth of what Grace told him. Nor did he discount the accuracy of Walter Jones's opinions. But until that moment in the office talking to Fisher, it was all just an idea. A possibility.

Now it was a reality. The unavoidable truth. He had heard it from Fisher's own lips. Nothing Fisher had said or done, nothing he had spoken about in his speeches, none of it meant anything. The only thing that mattered to Fisher was winning and, after winning, to be in control.

"Power. Money. Prestige," Mullins whispered. "That's all the political machine knows. That's all they respect. That's all they value." Loyalty, truth, the best interests of the country—those things meant nothing to them.

Griffin had given Mullins his start. Made him who he was. And even more than all of that, Mullins believed in the Crimson Legion message. For him, it represented the truth about America. Something most people would never consider but if they did, they would think it was right.

And the Legion also was right in its belief that the vast majority of Americans would never understand the threat the Jews posed nor embrace the effort necessary to address that threat. Fisher might understand it, but despite the things he'd said in recent speeches, he would never take the measure necessary to rid the country of that threat.

Fisher would never propose that Jews be detained simply for

being Jewish. Or that they be deported. Or simply that they be herded into the desert and left to die. People from the Crimson Legion would understand that approach. And they would actually do it.

After considering his dilemma at length, Mullins reached a sense of resolve. He had come to the end of his association with Fisher. Perhaps not that day. Perhaps not that month. But he had reached the end.

When Mullins returned to the office, he asked Grace to join him for lunch. "Where would we be going?" she asked playfully.

"I thought we might try Chinese food. There's this new restaurant on E Street."

"Good." She smiled. "We've never been there before."

They walked down to E Street and after a brief wait were seated at a table in back. While they ate, Mullins told her about his conversation with Fisher and about Fisher's statements regarding the Crimson Legion. Grace was astounded. "He actually said that to you? He wants to move Griffin out?"

"Yes. He wants *me* to do it."

"You can't really do that, can you?"

"No," Mullins replied.

"Good," she said. "I like Mr. Griffin."

"I do, too. And that's part of my problem."

She looked over at him. "When the senator said that, it sort of pushed you over the edge with him, didn't it?"

"Exactly over the edge," Mullins replied.

"Then maybe it's time for you to leave Senator Fisher and go back to the Crimson Legion."

"If I do that, I'll have to go back to Charlotte." He looked over at her. "Will you go back there with me?"

She glanced away. "I've moved several times already." There was hesitation in her voice but Mullins couldn't determine if it was because of him or because the move was to Charlotte. "But what's one more move," she shrugged. "I would need to let the senator know."

"Okay"—Mullins gestured with his hand—"slow down. I haven't decided about leaving yet. Not finally."

"But you're going, right?"

"Yes. I think so."

"Well, you make that decision," Grace acquiesced. "And talk to Griffin about your situation first. Then I'll decide what to do."

✦ ✦ ✦

Another rally, much like the one Walter Jones held in New York, was planned for later that month in Pittsburgh. This time, however, the German American Federation served as lead sponsor. The Crimson Legion and Sons of New Germany were relegated to the role of mere participants, as were other similar but smaller organizations. Nevertheless, Griffin was scheduled to deliver one of the opening addresses.

Mullins arranged his schedule from Fisher's office to permit his attendance at the rally and traveled to Pittsburgh for the event. Afterward, he met with Griffin privately in Griffin's hotel room. "I see you are doing well getting Fisher's campaign organized," Griffin ventured. "Is that going as well as it seems?"

"The organization is coming together."

Griffin arched an eyebrow in a questioning look. "But . . .?"

"The success we've had is part of my dilemma. Fisher wants me to contain your effectiveness, fracture the Legion, and siphon its best membership into a separate organization that he can control."

Griffin seemed unfazed. "I wondered when he would get around to that."

Mullins was puzzled. "You're not surprised?"

Griffin shook his head. "He was never really one of us."

"But the two of you are so close."

"Close?" Griffin shook his head again. "Not really. We both recognized that we needed each other. At least for a time. We've drifted apart since he started concentrating on a run for the presidency."

"You are aware of his ties to Wall Street financiers?" Mullins asked. "And through them to a group of wealthy New York Jews?"

"I've heard stories of that." Griffin looked concerned. "Is it true?"

"Yes, I'm afraid it is. Grace overheard him talking about it in his office with the people from Wall Street."

"They must have been upset."

"They weren't too happy. Walter Jones received an account of that meeting from one of the Wall Street group members," Mullins added.

"So, it really is true."

"Yes, Fisher is tied financially to the very group we oppose the most."

Griffin smiled. "We?"

"Yes." Mullins had a serious expression. "We."

"You've always thought of yourself as one of our members." Griffin seemed proud. "I like that."

"And that's my problem. I can't support Fisher any longer."

"I can see this would all be an issue for you."

"It's more than an issue. I've done all I can for and with him."

"What are you planning to do?"

"I would like to work for the Legion again. Full time. Like before. Fisher is only in this for himself. I suppose that's always been the case but now it is patently obvious. And more than that, he is against all of the things we stand for. If I continue working for him, I'll be working against the Legion."

"It hasn't all been a loss. Fisher has helped us with the immigration bill. Griffin took a seat in a chair near the window. "But that immigration bill was mostly your idea."

"I participated in the legislative process," Mullins said. "And I know from that experience that we can't make the kind of changes the country needs merely by legislation. We need a radical new approach. One that confronts the Jewish threat head on. With force."

"And Fisher's presidential campaign? You're no longer interested in that?"

"If he becomes president, we will no longer exist."

Griffin smiled again. "I don't think he can become president as I once did when you first went to work for him. I thought he might actually have a shot at winning. But not now." Griffin shook his head. "I no longer think that is possible. No one else does, either."

Mullins nodded. "You can find a place for me again with the Legion?"

"Certainly. We have an opportunity to establish a training camp in California for just the radical purpose you mentioned. Preparing select members and equipping them to confront the country's problems with force. Direct, physical force if necessary."

"Where in California?"

"Los Angeles. A site called Cleary Ranch. Are you familiar with the Clearys?"

"I met them once, I think."

"They are giving us a piece of property near the Palisades. We need someone to lead that work. It will be a rather rustic setting at first. Might be a perfect fit for you."

"Sounds like a great opportunity," Mullins responded. "And precisely the sort of situation I'm looking for."

"Good. I'll check the details when I get back to the office and let you know about it."

✦ ✦ ✦

When he returned to Washington, Mullins told Grace about the trip to Pittsburgh, the conversation with Griffin, and the training camp the Crimson Legion wanted to build in California. "He offered me the chance to be in charge of it," Mullins said.

Grace's eyes opened wide. "In charge?"

"Well," Mullins corrected himself, "it's not really an offer yet. But it's the suggestion of an offer."

"Wow," she said, doing her best to seem enthusiastic. "This would be an even greater opportunity for you than working for the senator. A chance to do what you've always thought we should do—confront the Jews in a straightforward manner."

He nodded eagerly. "So you think I should do it?"

"I think if Mr. Griffin makes an offer—a real offer—you should accept it immediately."

Mullins slipped his arms around her shoulders and drew her closer. "I don't want to go without you."

Grace shook her head. "I can't go now. And you can't say no to this."

"You will be okay with continuing to work for Fisher?"

"For the time being, yes."

✦ ✦ ✦

Two weeks later, Mullins returned to the boardinghouse in the evening to find a letter from Griffin waiting for him. He opened it and found an offer of a job with the Crimson Legion. "As we discussed," the letter read, "we are working to establish a training center in California. You would be in charge of that center as the director. We will expect you here at the office in Charlotte in two weeks."

Mullins bounded up the steps to Grace's room and showed her the letter. She read it quickly and looked up at him with a smile. "This is it. The offer you wanted."

"It will mean a move back to Charlotte, at least at first. But once everything is set, we would be working and living in California." She handed him the letter, then turned away and sat on the edge of the bed. He took a seat beside her. "Will you come with me?"

Grace looked away. "You're going to Charlotte first. And you might not be there long." There was a distant, rather tentative tone in her voice. "I should stay here until you find out what you will actually be doing."

"We'll be going to California, eventually."

"I know . . ." She glanced down at the floor. "But I don't want to leave here, go there, only to leave again for California. I've moved around a number of times already."

In his excitement about returning to the Crimson Legion, Mullins missed the nuance in her response. He stood and turned toward the door. "I'm going to send a telegram telling them I accept."

She looked up at him. "Right now? Even before you talk to Fisher?"

"Whatever he says won't change anything. I'm going. I'm taking the job in Charlotte." He offered his hand to her. "Want to walk to the telegraph office with me?"

"Sure," she answered as she followed him out the door.

✦ ✦ ✦

The next day, Mullins met with Fisher and told him of his plans to leave his current job and return to work for Griffin and the Crimson Legion. "I came here to get the immigration bill passed," Mullins boasted triumphantly. "And we've done that."

Fisher was not pleased. "You came here to organize my campaign for president. That's not finished yet."

"Well." Mullins glanced down and straightened the cuff of his pants. "I think we both know what will happen with that campaign."

"You think I will lose?"

"I think the people you need to support you in order to win think you'll lose."

"So you're just cutting and running."

"No." Mullins shook his head. "I have your organization built. All you have to do is work it."

Fisher pointed at him. "You were going to work it for me."

"I'll get Fielding ready to handle it."

Fisher shook his head. "Fielding can't do that kind of work by himself."

"Grace can help," Mullins offered.

Fisher's eyes brightened. "She's staying here?"

"For now." He wanted to say more. That she would be joining him soon. That they had come together and were leaving together. But something inside gave him the sense that he should not speak for her and so he said nothing more.

"Very well." Fisher turned his chair to the side and stared out the window. "If you want to go, then go." He gave a dismissive gesture. "Send Fielding in here."

Mullins stood and excused himself, then went to find Fielding.

✦ ✦ ✦

Ten days later, Mullins had done all he could to apprise Grace and Fielding of his work organizing Fisher's campaign and his effort to win passage of a new immigration bill. It was time for him to go. On his last day at the office, the staff held a small reception to mark his leaving. Aides from other senators joined them. Fisher still was angry at Mullins's departure and refused to bid him good-bye.

The next morning, Grace saw Mullins off at Union Station. Mullins, hurt by the snub from Fisher, was in a sulking mood. As they came from the station and walked out to the platform, he said for the third time since breakfast, "I can't believe Fisher wouldn't at least acknowledge that I was leaving."

"Don't worry about it," she replied. "You're going back to the Legion and he's going on to do whatever it is he's going to do."

Mullins smiled at her. "You've changed a lot since we met."

"Yes, I have." She grinned as she pointed at him. "And that's the first time you've smiled since yesterday."

"It's just. . .I had expected more," he sighed.

"Aunt Rose says expectations always get in the way."

"Aunt Rose may be right." His mood seemed to improve. "Do you regret any of it?"

"Any of what?"

"Any of the things we've done."

A cloud came over Grace and she had a distant look. "I still see the eyes of those children, the first time we confronted the Jews outside Temple Beth El. Their fear was so vivid and real." She grimaced. "I regret that."

"You regret confronting them?"

"I regret terrifying them."

A whistle sounded in the distance as a locomotive came into sight. Mullins put his arm around her shoulder and pulled her close, then kissed her gently on the lips. "Maybe those terrified children will remember that night, too, and go back to where they used to live."

"I doubt it works that way."

Steam billowed around them as the locomotive chugged slowly by and the train came to a stop at the platform. Mullins looked down at her. "I'll let you know what happens in Charlotte."

"I look forward to it."

"And you'll join me in California?"

"Let's see how that develops."

"You sound skeptical."

"I've seen a lot since we left Springfield. People aren't the same up close as they are from a distance."

"I think Griffin is."

"When you find out, let me know."

They kissed once more, then Mullins boarded the train. He waved good-bye from the window.

For Grace, this was the moment she had been hoping for. The chance to break free of Bryce without having to endure the trauma she knew would come from breaking up with him. As the train rolled out of the station, she sensed a new chapter opening in her life, and she meant to do everything in her power to seize it. To make the most of it. To build a life for herself outside the boundaries of a relationship with Bryce, or anyone else.

CHAPTER 35

The day after Mullins left for Charlotte, Fisher called Grace and Fielding to his office. Fisher sat at his desk, smoking a cigar. Parsons sat at the end of the desk to his right. Grace and Fielding took seats in chairs on the opposite side.

Fisher began, "Mullins is gone."

Parsons spoke up. "Now we can get down to work."

Despite her relief that Bryce was gone, Grace did not care for the tone of Parsons's comments. Yet, in keeping with her new-found determination to make a place for herself in the office, she kept quiet about her opinions and chose to focus on the moment.

"Mullins had developed ties with people at the State Department," Fisher continued. "We will need State to lean on key senators and representatives as the bill comes up for a vote."

Fielding spoke up. "Are you certain we can get an immigration bill out of committee?"

"Yes, I've talked to the majority leader. He will see that our bill gets to the floor."

"It cost me a few too many chats with him, but it's good."

"Should we approach State about helping?" Grace asked. "I believe Bryce was working with Langston Tammet, the undersecretary for immigration administration."

Fisher shook his head. "Not yet. And leave Tammet to me. I'll call him and set up a meeting when the time comes—after we figure out which senators need help to get on board with the bill."

He gestured in their direction. "You two work on the Senate, then come back to me when you've done all you can do with them and I'll get Tammet to help us do the rest."

"Mullins was also working closely with Forsyth and Newbern," Fielding added. "He mentioned they had already agreed to help."

"He was working with them," Fisher acknowledged. "Not sure how closely. But, yes, both men have agreed to sign on as co-sponsors."

Grace spoke up again. "Could they be helpful with some of the others?"

"Newbern and Forsyth?"

"They are from the South," she noted. "Could they help us with other Southerners?"

"They're supposed to be doing that now," Fisher replied. "Check with Newbern's man. . .I can't remember his name."

"Pittman," Parsons offered.

"Yes." Fisher nodded. "Kirby Pittman. Fielding, check with him and see where we are."

"I'll get right on it. They can—"

"Not you," Parsons interrupted. "Grace is from Virginia. She has a softer accent. Let her take care of it."

For a moment, Grace was flattered by the reference, then she realized what he was really saying. *Send her. She's a woman. Pittman will enjoy looking at her while he agrees to help.*

"Yes," Fisher agreed. "Let's let Grace take care of it."

The following day, Grace arranged a meeting with Kirby Pittman at his office, which was in the same building as Fisher's, and she walked there in only a few minutes. When she arrived, an assistant ushered her from the reception area and she took a seat across from him at his desk.

"I understand you are taking Bryce Mullins's place," Pittman said.

"Picking up where he left off," she replied.

"And you want to know about the immigration bill."

"We need to keep it moving through the process."

"Doesn't Travis Fielding still work in your office?"

"Fielding is handling other assignments."

"Interesting."

"You told Bryce you could bring along a dozen Southern senators."

"They have agreed to sign on as co-sponsors."

"Can you get me a list?"

Pittman opened a file on his desk and took out a list. He glanced at it, as if checking one final time, then handed it to her. "They're awaiting word from Senator Fisher."

"Good." Grace tucked the document into a folder she carried and stood. "We'll be in touch with them."

"I think you should let Senator Fisher do that. Most of them are not used to dealing with a woman on these matters."

"Senator Fisher prefers to assign tasks to his staff himself," she replied tersely.

Pittman grinned to cover the glow on his cheeks. "I'm sure he does."

On the way back to the office, Grace crossed paths in the hall with Fielding, who'd been working other senators. "Having any success?"

"Some," he replied. "How about you?"

"Got a list of senators from Kirby Pittman."

"Firm commitments?"

"He says they are."

"You know, this is all an exercise in futility," Fielding said.

Grace was puzzled. "What do you mean?"

"It won't make any difference."

"The immigration bill? You don't think it will have an effect on immigration?"

"Oh, it will put a stop to immigration," Fielding assured. "For the most part."

"Then, what are you talking about?"

"The election."

Grace argued to the contrary. "I think the immigration bill helps the senator's election chances immensely."

Fielding chuckled. "And I think you're kidding yourself."

"Why are you talking like this?"

"Look, Harding is going to enter the race. He was always going to get in the race. And when he does, the senator's chances of winning will evaporate."

"It will get tougher for him," Grace conceded. "But I don't think Harding is everyone's choice. We've already shown that."

"We'll see." Fielding checked his watch. "You want to get lunch?"

"Sure." Grace was troubled by Fielding's comments and wondered whether he was correct. Would Harding's entry into the election campaign wipe out their work in an instant? She found that hard to believe, but she didn't have much experience in this sort of thing, which left her with doubts. Doubts about herself. About Fisher's chances in the election. And about Fielding's loyalty.

From the office building, they walked up the street a few blocks and got a table in a café. As soon as they were seated, Fielding asked, "Are you interested in returning to the church in Virginia?"

Grace shook her head. "I don't think so."

"I heard Mullins was mad about last time."

"Mullins is in North Carolina, on his way to . . ." She paused mid-sentence with a sense she shouldn't say more. "To who knows where."

Fielding gave her a knowing smile, "Do you want to go?"

She shook her head again. "Once was enough."

Grace had enjoyed the church service, and she would have been glad to spend the day with Fielding, but she didn't want to risk returning to Virginia while the trouble in Norfolk remained unresolved and the federal investigators still were lurking about. The thought of them made her uneasy and she wondered why she hadn't heard from them recently.

✦ ✦ ✦

A few days later, Grace came from the office on her way home at the end of the day. At the corner just down from the building, she boarded a streetcar. As she stepped inside the car, a man seated next to her stood and offered her his seat. She took it and as she moved past him, he pressed a note into the palm of her hand. She glanced at it to see that it read, "Get off at the next stop."

When the streetcar stopped at the next corner, Grace got off and stepped to the sidewalk. As the streetcar moved away, an automobile came to a stop at the curb in front of her. The rear door opened and she slipped inside. Roy Martin was seated next to her. Graham Hawthorne was seated up front at the steering wheel.

As the car started forward, Martin smiled at her. "We haven't heard from you in a while. Did we miss seeing you in a hat?"

"There hasn't been much happening."

"That's not what we heard."

"Oh?"

"We heard your boyfriend is moving to Los Angeles." Martin gave her a knowing look. "And that you want to ditch him. Are you planning to ditch us, too?"

Grace was startled that they would suggest that, especially since it was true. "Who said I was ditching him? Or you?"

Hawthorne turned his head to one side and spoke over his shoulder. "If we figured it out, don't you think he did, too?"

"I can stop seeing him if I want," she snapped. "But I think that's *my* choice."

"Not really," Martin replied.

She glared at him. "You're going to tell me who to date?"

"You can stop seeing Mullins when we tell you to stop."

Grace frowned. "What does that mean?"

"It means," Hawthorne chimed in, "when he moves to California, you move to California with him."

"And if I don't?"

Martin looked over at her. "You remember the deal, don't you? You work for us, we keep quiet. You stop working for us, we tell everything."

"Look, Bryce Mullins is in Charlotte right now but he'll be moving to California soon. If he—"

"Tell us about that," Martin interrupted.

"About what?"

"About Mullins going to California with the Crimson Legion."

"The Crimson Legion is building a training camp out there. In Los Angeles."

"Los Angeles is a large place. Where in Los Angeles are they building this camp?"

"How would I know? I've never been there."

"He didn't mention a location?"

Grace sighed. "I think he said something about a place called the Palisades."

"And does this place have a name?"

"They call it The Ranch."

"How did the Legion acquire this property?"

"Someone gave it to them."

"And does this someone have a name?"

"Cleary."

"Nothing more?"

"I'm sure they have more of a name than that, that but that's all I know. Like I said, I've never been there. I've never seen it. As far as I know, neither has he. All I know is that it's rustic."

"What does that mean?"

"I don't know. Living in tents, maybe. I don't know."

"You don't seem to care for the idea."

She glared at Martin. "I'm not going out there to live in the woods with a bunch of men and be everybody's girlfriend."

"You've been everyone's girlfriend before," Hawthorne sniped.

Grace leaned forward and cuffed him on the side of the head. The force of the blow startled him and he jerked the steering wheel to one side. The car swerved violently, but Hawthorne managed to avoid wrecking. "You hit me!" he howled.

"I would do more than that if I could," she fumed.

Martin grabbed her by the shoulders and pulled her back, laughing. "Okay, okay, calm down."

"We ought to take her in," Hawthorne railed.

"I think you deserved that one," Martin replied.

"Well, keep her under control."

Grace settled onto the back seat again and took a deep breath to calm her nerves. "Look, I've followed him from Springfield to Charlotte. And from Charlotte to here. If you want to know more about what Bryce is doing, ask Ida. She's right there in the Crimson Legion office."

Martin seemed puzzled. "Ida?"

Grace cut her eyes at him. "Don't act like you don't know her."

Martin avoided her gaze. "Miss Anderson, you have helped us a lot. We'll see what we can do in Charlotte and California without you." He turned to face her squarely. "But if we need you, you'll come."

Grace no longer cared what Mullins thought of her, but she liked working for Senator Fisher and was worried that if Hawthorne and Martin talked to the senator about her and told him the details of her past, she would be fired. "Okay," she said politely.

"And," Hawthorne added, "you'll keep us informed about what happens with Fisher. Before we have to ask you about it."

Grace nodded in response. "Okay, but isn't there a law against interfering with his job?"

"We're not talking about interfering with anything," Hawthorne responded. "We just want to know what he's up to before he does it. And with a little more frequency than you've given us lately."

The car pulled over to the, and Martin gestured to the door. "This is where you get off. And remember: keep us informed."

Grace opened the door and stepped from the car. As she made her way to the sidewalk, the car started forward, then blended into traffic and was gone.

CHAPTER 36

As the train carrying Mullins to Charlotte steamed southward through the Blue Ridge Mountains, he stared out the window and thought of the work he'd been doing for Fisher, of what he was about to do for Griffin, and of getting his life back on track.

Opposing the Jews as they gathered at the synagogue in Springfield had been better than merely meeting at the Claytons' to talk about the issues of the day—better in the sense that it more directly addressed the problem posed by Communists and International Jews. Organizing the anti-union group had been a step in the right direction, too—in terms of the way in which it confronted the issues. Working for Griffin the first time had directly proceeded from those earlier periods.

Working for Fisher, however, had been a diversion—a distraction—a development that proceeded only from the relationship between Fisher and Griffin, not as a logical extension of events in Mullins's life. Sure, he used skills honed while working for the Legion to build Fisher's organization, but that was the extent of it. Fisher wasn't interested in building or furthering a cause. All he wanted was someone to organize an election campaign, not someone to help him transform American society.

A detour. That's what Fisher was for me. A long detour.

When the train stopped at the station in Roanoke, Virginia, to take on passengers and water for the locomotive, Mullins got off to walk around for a moment. The smell of steam and coal smoke from the engine seemed to move his thoughts on to other things—like Grace and the way they had left things between them.

By the time he left Washington, Mullins had reached the conclusion that Grace wanted to dump him. The way she responded—eager but not eager—excited but not too excited—seemed contrived. As if she had something else to do and was just waiting for him to leave. And, oddly enough, he'd also determined that ending the relationship might be a good thing.

Things between them had run their course and they seemed to be moving in different directions. He was tired of having her around, too. Tired of having to check with her. Tired of having to remember to write when he was on the road. Tired of having to consider her when thinking of his own life and career. Perhaps there might be a better arrangement with someone else.

And then he thought of Dorothy. She was older than Grace. Older than Mullins, too. The kind of older woman who wasn't really an older woman, just not as young as *he* was. Someone who had seen the world and enjoyed it. Who had experienced the good and the bad and survived both. Someone with fewer expectations. Or different expectations. *I don't know. She's just different. And I think I want different now.*

When the train arrived at the station in Charlotte, Dorothy was waiting for him on the platform at the train station. She wore a copper-colored top, open one button too low, with a maroon skirt and high-heeled shoes. Seeing her there, waiting for him, he was instantly attracted to her in a way that made him forget all else. And from the way she looked—smiling up at him through the window of the car as the railcar came to a stop—he assumed she must be interested in him, as well. After all, she was at the station to meet him. She could have sent any of a dozen people to get him. Instead, she came herself.

From the train station, they rode to Renfrow's boardinghouse.

Mullins got his old room back and deposited his luggage, then he and Dorothy went to dinner. After dinner, Dorothy took him to her house, where he spent the night.

The next morning, Mullins had breakfast with Dorothy, then rode with her to the Crimson Legion office. Griffin was there and put Mullins to work coordinating the planning process for the California training camp. "We want it to establish a paramilitary cadre," he explained. "But part of that training process for the initial recruits will including building the facility."

"Sounds interesting," Mullins replied.

"We have a team working on preliminary plans." Griffin stood and came from behind his desk. "Come on. I'll introduce you."

Griffin made quick work of presenting Mullins, then retreated to his office. As Mullins listened to the others catch him up on their work, he noticed Bradley Edwards and Kenneth Frost were in and out of Griffin's office multiple times that day.

Noticeably absent, however, was Ida Hayes. She had been there when Grace left to work for Fisher. Now she was nowhere to be found, and Mullins wondered what had become of her. Had she really been cooperating with the Justice Department investigators, as Grace suspected? And if she had been, what became of her? Mullins kept those questions to himself for the time being, but he was determined to find out where she went.

When Mullins had worked there before, organizing Crimson Legion chapters in conjunction with Griffin's rally tours, Edwards and Frost had been low-level operatives carrying luggage and coats, retrieving packages, and delivering messages. Now they seemed to be in positions of authority.

Late that first afternoon, Mullins approached Edwards and attempted to strike up a conversation. Edwards responded in a curt tone, "Mind your own business and things will go well for you."

"And if I don't?"

"You won't like the result."

Mullins was put off by the response, but being new to an obviously changed situation, he decided to let the moment pass. But he did not forget it.

✦ ✦ ✦

In his new position, Mullins joined a carefully selected group of former military trainers. Experienced men with extensive military service, they were disgruntled over the war—the way its execution had failed to address the Jewish cabal they imagined had started it. They felt the lack of a meaningful peace had left the US vulnerable to domination by the same International Jews who subjugated Europe.

Among that group of trainers were Stanton Lynch, Ralph Davis, and Charles Gropper. They were recruited by Griffin to design the components necessary to train people to conduct military-style operations in demolition, assassination, and small-group warfare. By the time Mullins arrived, they were well on their way to doing just that. After reviewing the details of their work, Mullins came to the conclusion that the trainers where quite competent and equally committed to their task.

Satisfied that development of the training regimen was in good hands, Mullins chose to concentrate on creating a facility that would allow them to conduct the training course in the most proficient manner possible. To do that, he consulted with Legion-friendly engineers and architects to design the required facility. At the same time, he began the search for an equally friendly California construction company.

Work on the project progressed at a respectable pace. However, not long into the effort, Mullins came to feel that, although he was officially in charge of the project, he was executing someone else's ideas about the facility and the people who would train there.

Though Mullins understood the notion of creating the camp originated with Griffin, he nevertheless wanted it to ultimately produce a result in keeping with his own ideas of direct and dramatic confrontation as a means of permanently transforming American society. To make certain the camp would fulfill that vision, he began searching the Crimson Legion ranks for his own cadre of former soldiers. Men who were as disgruntled with the way the Great War had been conducted as he was but who had a raw edge to their anger that gave them a bent toward the brutal.

Mullins began his search in Rochester, the site of the first Crimson Legion chapter that he helped establish. Rustin Steed, a man recruited by Mullins when the chapter was formed, still was the chapter leader. He contacted Steed and they met for coffee at a diner on Broad Street. After catching up on each other's lives, Mullins asked about the chapter and its recent activities.

"I'm not sure I can tell you about it," Steed admitted.

Mullins was puzzled by the response. "Why not?"

"They said to keep it quiet."

"They who?"

"Edwards and Frost."

Mullins frowned. "They've been up here?"

Steed nodded. "They've been working with us for the past year or so."

"Doing what?"

Steed looked him in the eye. "Things that should not be discussed in a diner."

"Then let's go somewhere else."

Mullins paid the tab, then they walked outside to Steed's car and headed east toward Irondequoit Bay, an inlet along Lake Ontario. When they were on their way, Mullins looked over at Steed. "So, tell me about what's going on."

"Edwards came up here first. Told us we needed to be doing something rather than merely talking about it."

Mullins nodded. "That's what I've been saying all along."

"Right. Only, he wanted us doing some serious stuff."

"Like?"

Steed kept his eyes on the road. "Blowing up houses and burning down buildings."

"Did you?"

Steed shook his head. "Not me personally. I'm not getting into specifics."

"But the others?"

Steed nodded. "Some of them thought it was a great idea. They really got into it."

"These were Jewish properties?"

"Most of them."

Mullins raised an eyebrow. "Most of them?"

"That's what I'm talking about," Steed replied. "That's the part that bothered me the most. I understood going after Jews. But some of the places they wanted us to hit didn't have anything to do with Jews or Communists or Negroes or anybody else that's actually causing trouble. I could have taken them to a dozen places where members of the Communist Party live, but they wanted us to hit these other sites."

"Any idea why they wanted you to hit those places?"

"No." Steed sighed. "I have no idea at all."

"Are Edwards and Frost still working with you?"

"A little, but not like before. Frost was up here a few months ago. Said they were bringing in some new guy to take over most of what they'd been trying to do. He wasn't too happy about it, but he said we'd have to curtail our activities for a while."

"How did you feel about that?"

"We have to hit back at the Jews, but I wasn't sad about leaving the other stuff out. The hits on people who had nothing to do with us. That just seemed like their own business getting mixed in with ours."

The comment struck Mullins as odd. "What kind of business do you think Edwards and Frost might be involved in?"

Steed shrugged. "I don't want to say too much."

"It's just you and me," Mullins responded. "Tell me what I need to know."

"Some . . ." Steed tapped his fingers on the steering wheel. "I don't know if I should tell you."

"Tell me," Mullins urged. "It won't go any further than me."

Steed hesitated a moment longer, then finally said, "Alright, some of the guys say they saw Frost with Anthony Ripepi."

Mullins was not familiar with the name. "I've never heard of him. Who is Ripepi?"

"He's a Mob guy from Pittsburgh. Has a place up here on the lake. Used to come up here just to fish. Now they say he is setting up his own operation here."

"The Mafia?"

"Yeah." Steed glanced over at him. "I'm not saying he is or he isn't. I'm just telling you what the guys are telling me."

"How did the rest of the chapter feel about Edwards and Frost and all of the rest of it?"

"Most of them were willing to go along. And, like I said, one or two of them were very enthusiastic. Too enthusiastic, if you ask me. But Edwards and Frost seemed to like it."

"Who were the ones that liked it?"

"Fred Payne and Vince Stone." Steed looked over at Mullins once again. "Why?"

"I thought it might be good to talk to them," Mullins replied. "Maybe find out a little more about what they've been doing."

"Why are you interested in this?"

Mullins had a thin, tight smile. "I'm the new guy Frost told you about."

Steed's eyes opened wider. "You're the new guy?"

"Yeah."

"But they know you already."

"Yes," Mullins said.

"They came up here with Griffin when you first started with the Legion. You worked with them up here."

"You sound surprised."

"It's just. . .Edwards and Frost didn't seem too happy about the Legion bringing in someone else to take over their work. Like some stranger was moving in on them. But you're someone they know."

"Well, I'm not really taking over. Not the whole thing. Just a part of it. And those two are different now from when I knew them before. Can you put me in touch with Payne and Stone?"

"I can get you Payne. Stoney died last week."

✦ ✦ ✦

Fred Payne turned out to be exactly the kind of person Mullins was looking for. He deployed to France with one of the first units—at about the same time as Mullins's brother—and saw action in some of the worst fighting. When he returned at the end of the war, nothing seemed the same and he had a difficult time fitting in. Most of his friends had remained at home and had moved along with their lives and careers—job, spouse, home, even a family for some. But not Payne. He'd been an apprentice plumber before the war. Afterward, he found it difficult to hold down the simplest job. He also was single.

Joining the Crimson Legion had been a gift for Payne. A place to belong. A place to grow and develop. And a place to fight again, this time against the real enemies of America, not the ethereal, tangential, indirect threats posed by a European conflict. This one was right here at home.

Mullins contacted Payne and arranged to meet him at a diner, this one near the Kodak plant, Payne's latest place of employment. "As you are aware," Mullins began. "I work for the Crimson Legion."

"Yeah," Payne replied. "Steed told me about you. Said you were a straight-up guy. What's this about?"

"We're making plans to build a training camp. And—"

Payne interrupted. "What kind of camp?"

"A place where we can teach Crimson Legion members the skills they need to confront our problems head on."

"What kind of skills are you talking about?"

"The kind of skills one would need to do some necessary things and do them without getting caught."

"What makes you think I would be interested in that sort of thing?"

"You've been working with Edwards and Frost."

"Yeah. What of it?"

"I understand they are involved in some. . .marginal activities."

"What sort of problems are you wanting to confront?"

"The problems we've been talking about at our meetings," Mullins replied. "International Jews. Politicians who back them. Bankers who finance them."

"So, are we going to war?"

"Yes. But not open warfare. We could never win an open confrontation. This will be far more clandestine."

"It's about time," Payne muttered.

"The camp isn't ready yet. In fact, the first groups we send out there to train will be involved in construction as well as training."

"Out there? Where are you building this camp?"

"California."

"When will it start?"

"Probably the first of the year. But for the kind of operation we have in mind. We need explosives, weapons, boots. . .The equipment and clothing used in combat."

"Backpacks, uniforms, that kind of thing?"

"Not uniforms," Mullins replied. "We will be engaged in clandestine operations."

"We can get construction-grade explosives without much trouble. Edwards knows about that," Payne noted. "And we can get civilian-grade weapons—the kind of firearms you'd buy for hunting and target shooting. But to get military-grade stuff, we would need access to military sites. That's the only place you can find it. Bases and National Guard armories."

Mullins smiled. "That's why I want you to be involved."

Payne frowned. "You want me to break into a military base?"

Mullins shook his head. "I want you to find the people who have access to those places and figure out which ones will help us get it."

"Okay, if I find what you're looking for, who's going to move it from here to wherever you're building this place in California?"

"That's the other thing." Mullins paused to look Payne squarely in the eyes. "I want you to move out to California and do your work out there."

"I don't know nobody in California."

"You wouldn't begin at zero."

"You're right. I'd be at less than zero." Payne did not seem at all pleased with the notion. "Here I at least know where to look."

"We need you," Mullins insisted. "We'll rent a place for you to stay. You can circulate among the cafés and bars around the bases out there. And I'll put you in touch with our people out there. You won't be starting from zero. You'll be starting with our own Crimson Legion people."

Eventually Payne agreed, and Mullins rented a bungalow for him in Venice, a newly developed neighborhood at the beach on the west side of Los Angles—just south of Santa Monica. He'd

warned. "Mr. Griffin thinks they're great."

"And you?"

"I'm pretty sure they are only in this for themselves."

"Every time they're around they make me feel like they're up to something."

"They make me feel creepy."

He laughed. "That's exactly how they make me feel."

She reached over and took his hand. "You make me feel very wonderful." She tugged at him and he rolled on his side toward her.

CHAPTER 37

In Washington, Senator Fisher's new immigration legislation was ready for submission to Congress. As Mullins and others had suggested, the bill shifted quota calculations to figures based on the 1890 Census, a time when fewer people from Eastern and Southern Europe immigrated to the United States. That simple change would effectively end the immigration of Jews.

After reviewing the current draft and after tabulating support for it in the Senate, Grace met with Fisher and reviewed the status of the bill. "It's time to contact Tammet."

"We're ready to introduce the bill?"

"Yes," she replied.

"Who are the holdouts?"

She handed him a list of senators who had yet to make their commitment known. Fisher looked it over. "Not that many. Can we win without them?"

"We will likely get the support of some on the list without asking, but that would be risky."

He gave her a questioning look. "What do you mean?"

"We need to make a big statement with this bill," she explained. "You have the lead on this issue. You're known as a strong advocate for immigration reform and limitation. Everyone knows that about you. Now we need to make it obvious that your position commands broad support from your fellow senators."

"For the campaign."

"Yes, sir. For the campaign."

Fisher nodded in response. "I'll make the call to Tammet."

✦ ✦ ✦

A few days later, Langston Tammet arrived at the office. They met alone in Fisher's office. As she had done before, Grace stood near the heating register in an adjoining room and listened to their conversation.

"Langston," Fisher began by way of greeting, "it's good to see you."

"I'm sure it is. And I understand you have an immigration bill ready to introduce."

"You've read it, no doubt."

"My office wrote the bill." Tammet bit back sarcastically. "Of course I read it."

"Just checking," Fisher responded. "You'd be surprised what you can find out with a few questions."

"Have you seen her recently?"

"It's been about a year."

"Does Muriel know about her yet?"

"I don't think so."

"If Muriel knew, you'd know." Tammet chuckled. "She would make sure of it."

Fisher wasn't amused. "I'm sure she would. Why do you ask about her?"

"Just to make certain you don't forget."

"Forget what?"

"That I know."

"And you shouldn't forget, either."

"About?"

"Her sister."

"She was never—"

Fisher cut him off. "Don't even try it."

Tammet changed the subject. "Which ones do you need help with?"

"I'll have my staff provide you with a list before you leave."

They talked awhile longer about nothing nearly as interesting as what Grace had heard in those first few minutes. Now she knew why Fisher had responded to Tammet the way he did before. And she knew something about Fisher she had not known. Everyone, it seemed, had a past. Many of those pasts were as challenging as her own.

After a while, Grace heard a chair scoot back on the floor and Fisher asked, "Is that all?" And she knew the meeting was coming to an end. Moving quickly but quietly, she came from the room where she'd been listening and returned to the chair at her desk. She was seated there as Tammet and Fisher emerged from the office. Fisher asked for the list of senators, Grace handed it to him, then Tammet left.

✦ ✦ ✦

In the days that followed, Fisher introduced the immigration bill and conducted a series of meetings with senators and congressmen, building support for the measure. As before, many members of Congress joined as co-sponsors, although not as many as before, and not everyone was enthusiastic about the vote.

A dozen senators refused to support the bill and held out until just before the end. They were in favor of the bill's effect but refused to vote for it on the grounds that its passage might help Fisher in his bid for the presidency. They detested Fisher and thought he was nothing more than a pretender and a fraud. But Tammet knew things about them, too, and when reminded of it they reluctantly gave the bill their approving vote.

When the votes were tallied, the immigration bill—Fisher's

second—passed by an overwhelming margin. Enough so that he could brag about the success of its passage and went on the road immediately, conducting rallies in each of the key states for the upcoming Republican primaries.

✦ ✦ ✦

As the campaign for the presidency continued, rumors circulated that Theodore Roosevelt was considering the race. A few at first, then too many to ignore. Republican Party leaders opposed his candidacy, primarily because they did not want to lose control of the party, but the suggestion that Roosevelt *might* enter the race was enough to chill Fisher's financial support.

Close on the heels of the Roosevelt rumors, however, came the announcement that Warren Harding, Ohio's senior senator, was entering the race. Overnight, newspaper reporters flocked to him. Soon, glowing articles appeared extolling his intelligence, experience, and ability. And just as quickly, Fisher's name disappeared from the newspapers. Not long after that, the financial support Fisher had received from Wall Street executives moved to Harding, as well.

Fisher sensed the moment slipping away and he called a meeting in his office to discuss what to do. Parsons, Fielding, Ann Aldridge, and Emma Hart joined them. Grace sat near the door.

After a review of the scenario they faced, Fisher declared, "I'm open to suggestions. What can we do to change this campaign?"

Parsons offered little encouragement. "I'm afraid there are no options left, Senator."

"You think we're finished?"

"Yes, sir. We knew Harding would be the end of it."

"We knew he would make it difficult."

"And he has done more than that."

Emma Hart spoke up. "Senator, you still have some campaign

money left."

Fisher nodded. "We're not broke yet. But we're headed in that direction."

"The speeches seem to be working well," Ann Aldridge noted. "I've watched the lines and the crowd responses. We're tracking right on the spot."

"The speeches are fine," Fielding interjected. "And no, the campaign isn't completely out of money. But as anyone can see, Harding is drawing more and more of our support every day."

"And the press is gone from us," Parsons added. "We could say anything anywhere on any topic and it wouldn't get reported."

Grace was appalled at the attitude displayed by Parsons and Fielding, and as they talked, she felt certain they were voicing that opinion at the behest of Griffin and others with the Crimson Legion. There seemed no other explanation. She had dismissed Fielding's reluctant attitude when they were working for the immigration bill's passage, but this display revived her former suspicions. She was about to speak up when Fisher continued. "Parsons and Fielding don't think we have any option but to drop out?"

"That's correct," Fielding added.

Fisher looked over at Grace. "What do you think?"

"Get on the road," she blurted.

Fisher was caught off guard by the remark. "On the road?"

"You've just had a major success with the immigration bill," Grace argued. "Get out there and talk about it." Her voice grew louder. "Talk about the issues. Talk about the things that matter to you. Talk about it like you did when they got you this far."

"Yes!" Emma cried.

"Absolutely," Ann agreed. "Take the message to the people."

Parsons smirked. "Senator, no one will sponsor the big rallies for you now."

"We can sponsor them," Emma offered. "At least for a while."

"We don't have that kind of money," Fielding interrupted.

"We have some," Emma argued. "Enough to do one or two and if those go well, maybe we'll get enough to do some more. But we can't just sit here in the office."

Parsons scoffed. "None of you know what you're talking about. It takes a lot to organize a rally. These are big events. And they require a lot of money to do them."

"Then don't do huge rallies. Take what we can handle." Grace was determined not to give up. "Speak wherever you can. The Rotary Clubs. Over coffee in private homes. At cafés and diners. Get on the road."

Fisher seemed to warm to the idea. "You think it would work?"

Fielding shook his head. "No, Senator. This is the—"

"Yes." Grace interrupted. "It will work."

"We've come this far," Emma added. "We can't concede before a single primary is held."

Despite the protests of Parsons and Fielding, the meeting ended with Fisher determined to fight on. Grace went to work that afternoon scheduling him for events big and small in the key states. Parsons and Fielding, however, huddled together in Parsons's office until most of the staff left for the night, then they left, too.

When they were gone, Grace went to Fisher in his office. Fisher was seated at his desk. She stood near the door. "Senator, may I have a word with you?"

Fisher glanced up from the papers on his desk. "Certainly. What's on your mind?"

"I wanted to talk to you about Parsons and Fielding."

"What about them?"

"I didn't like the things they said in the meeting today."

"Rather pessimistic, weren't they?"

"It's more than that."

"Oh." Fisher had a troubled frown. "How so?"

"Well, sir. Fielding has deep ties to the Crimson Legion."

"I am aware of that."

"And I think Parsons does, too."

"Oh? What makes you think that?"

In order to answer that question, Grace would have to tell him the whole story—the things that happened in Springfield, the Justice Department investigation, Ida and Pete, the way her appointments to positions in Charlotte and in Fisher's office fell neatly into place, and the comments of Hawthorne and Martin about how they did it. She couldn't tell him that. Instead, she said, "I just think it's true. And I think that's why they want you to drop out."

"You think Griffin told them to tell me that?"

"Yes, sir."

"And do you base this on anything more than a hunch?"

"Do you remember telling Bryce Mullins that you wanted him to find a way to contain Mr. Griffin?"

"Yes."

"And you told him you wanted him to come up with a way to bring the best Legion people into the campaign and phase them out so that the Legion and similar organizations no longer existed?"

"He told you about that?"

"Those conversations you had with him are the reason he left."

"Really?"

"Yes. Bryce, Fielding, Parsons—they're all Crimson Legion members and they're devoted to Mr. Griffin first and foremost. When you told Bryce that plan about bringing the Legion into the campaign and ending the organization, he felt like he was being asked to betray Mr. Griffin. I'm sure Fielding and Parsons feel the same. They have greater ties to the Legion than to you."

"What about your own ties to the Crimson Legion? You worked at their office in Charlotte. Aren't you one of theirs?"

Grace slowly shook her head. "I worked there. I was with Bryce. But my ties were never to Mr. Griffin. They might have been to Mullins, but not to the organization."

"*Might have been* to Mullins? Did something happen between you two?"

"He's in Charlotte and probably headed to California. I've had enough. I like it here."

Fisher nodded slowly. "And you think Fielding is one of them, and not one of us?"

"Fielding and Parsons are Crimson Legion operatives. They are not *your* operatives. And they are not helping. Mr. Griffin has decided you cannot be president and he has instructed them to see that you do not. I am certain of it."

✦ ✦ ✦

The following day, Fisher talked to Ann Aldridge and Emma Hart. They told him the same thing. "Fielding and Parsons are not helping. If anything, Fielding is getting in the way." Based on what he heard from them and from Grace, Fisher called the two men to his office and confronted them.

"Yes, sir," Fielding replied. "I am a member of the Crimson Legion."

Fisher looked over at Parsons. "And you?"

"Yes, sir. I am a member, too."

"And is that why you two think I should get out of the race?"

Parsons frowned. "Sir?"

"Did Griffin tell you that I should get out of the race?"

Parsons looked away. Fielding spoke up. "Yes, sir. He did."

"And is that why you said what you did in the meeting?"

Fielding snarled. "I could never support someone who takes

campaign money from Jews. And neither could anyone else in the Legion. Taking their money makes you nothing more than a Jewish whore."

"Well," Fisher responded, "I don't suppose I have to tell you that you're both fired."

Parsons stood. "No, sir. I'll clean out my desk now."

As he started toward the door, Fielding stood. "I hope you go down in the most humiliating defeat possible. And I hope you burn in hell for the way you cater to the Jews."

✦ ✦ ✦

With his staff's support, Fisher took his message of restoring Americanism on the road, speaking to any church, civic, or student group that would have him. Grace, Anna, and Emma set up the meetings and recruited volunteers to advance them, making sure the rooms were filled with people, whether they supported him or not.

At every stop, Fisher gave a version of the same speech he'd given when he first began the fight for immigration control. "Today, we are beset by International Jews, International bankers, and International Communists who intend to dominate American life, control American business, and put an end to the American way of life.

"None of the other candidates think this is an issue, but that's because they take campaign money. They take money from our enemies and tell you those groups pose no threat at all. And all the while American jobs go to immigrants. American businesses come under Jewish control. And American grandeur fades from view.

"People are out to destroy the way of life that you love and enjoy. It will take powerful leadership to keep that from happening. I am the only one doing anything to address this threat. In the past two years, I have introduced and gained Congressional approval of two immigration reform bills that have all but ended Jewish and Italian immigration. I'm fighting every day for you, but I need your help to complete that job."

At first, Fisher's appearances attracted meager interest, but as he continued to make troubling claims about the source of his opponents' campaign contributions, reporters began to pay attention and crowds grew larger. Money, most of it in the form of small donations, began to arrive at the office.

As Fisher's rejuvenated campaign gained ground, he met behind the scenes with party delegates and election officials, shaking hands, talking, doing his best to gain their support for his candidacy.

None of it, however, could overcome the momentum that gathered behind Harding. As states conducted their primary elections, voters gave their approval to Harding, not Fisher, who won only a single contest. With the convention date approaching, he held only a handful of committed delegates.

At the Republican convention that June in Chicago, most expected Harding to win with ease. Delegates, however, seemed to have other ideas and voting went through eleven rounds. Fisher held on through the early rounds, but as the fight wore on, delegations slowly lined up behind Harding and eventually he won the party's nomination.

Fisher was bitterly disappointed by the defeat and retreated to his hotel room. As the convention came to a close, Grace found him in his room, drunk and on the verge of collapse.

"All that work," he lamented, "and nothing to show for it."

"Not nothing," Grace corrected. "We've had great success."

Fisher took a sip of his drink. "Name one."

"Two," she corrected.

He took another sip. "What do you mean?"

"You wrote and introduced two immigration bills that won congressional approval and were signed into law."

Fisher shook his head. "It wasn't enough."

"But think about what you did," she countered. "You are the junior senator from Ohio and you almost single-handedly ended immigration to the US for Italians and Jews."

He turned up the glass and drained the last drops from the bottom. "But was it the right thing to do?"

"What do you mean?"

Fisher rose from his chair and wobbled across the room toward a table where a bottle of Scotch sat next to an ice bucket. "Most of those pitiful little Jews just wanted a better life. And the Italians only wanted a place to have babies."

Grace caught up with him and lifted the bottle from his grasp. "I think you've had enough of that."

"But I didn't get any," he protested.

"You had plenty before I got here." She took him by the elbow and guided him back to his chair.

"I painted myself into a corner." Fisher dropped onto the chair and hung his head. "For the rest of my life I'll be known as the anti-immigration senator."

"Nonsense."

"The anti-Semitic, bigoted senator." He looked at her blankly. "Say that five times fast if you can."

"You need to get some sleep."

Fisher held up an empty glass. "I need another one of these."

"No," Grace replied insistently. "You need sleep."

"What for?"

"You have a term to finish. And in four years we'll have another presidential election." She took him by the arm. "Come on. Let's get you to bed."

He stood and shuffled toward the bed. "I'm not running again."

Grace knew better than to argue with him, but she couldn't let the comment pass without *some* response. "Why not?"

"They will never forget that I lost."

By then they'd reached the bed and she helped him take a seat on the edge. "They'll never remember this race. Especially if we begin now to work toward the next campaign."

Fisher kicked off his shoes and collapsed backward, his head landing on a pillow. "Do you really think that, or are you just saying it to make me feel better?"

"I think we should make the most of the notoriety we've gained and the contacts we've made. You can't stop now." She partly believed that, but mostly she wanted to stay in Washington and thought being definitively on his side would make that possible.

"I don't know," he sighed. "I don't know."

Grace lifted his feet from the floor and swung his legs around to rest them on the bed, then pulled a blanket over him. "You get to sleep. I'm going back to my room to work on the next campaign."

"You do that," he slurred. "Get things organized and I'll . . ." By the time Grace turned out the light, he was sound asleep.

CHAPTER 38

By the time Fisher's presidential campaign came to an end, Mullins had completed as much of the preparation for the Crimson Legion's California training center as could be accomplished from the office in Charlotte. The time had come for him to move from talking about building a camp, to doing so.

After saying good-bye to Dorothy, Mullins packed his plans and belongings and moved to the site in California. He was joined there by the training staff—Stanton Lynch, Ralph Davis, and Charles Gropper. With them came an initial class of recruits—Crimson Legion members who had been singled out for their aggressive action against Jews and other immigrants.

Situated in a remote canyon on the edge of Los Angeles, the training-camp property was little more than a tract of vacant acreage when Mullins and the men arrived. They set up tents for living quarters and large canopies that served as office work space, then went to work creating a facility that could provide the kind of paramilitary training Mullins envisioned.

The first task in developing the site was the construction of a road into the property. Once that was made passable, Mullins and his men began work on a series of interconnected buildings, underground bunkers, and ancillary locations for service equipment—generators, fuel tanks, water storage, and an armory where Mullins planned to store weapons and equipment for the clandestine operations he hoped to conduct. The recruits provided the labor, but actual construction was contracted out to a firm with ties to Griffin.

While supervising and coordinating the components of the project, Mullins contacted Fred Payne, the man from Rochester he had sent to California to begin the task of locating and acquiring weapons and other operation equipment. Items he hoped to store in the armory that was being constructed at the camp. He met with Payne at the house in Venice. They sat at a table in the kitchen and talked.

"Did you have any success in identifying people to help?"

"It wasn't as easy as it seems," Payne replied. "But I found a couple of guys."

Mullins nodded. "Tell me about them."

"The first one is a guy named Jesse Nettles. He lives in Anaheim. A veteran like me. I worked with him and found out how much he hates Jews. He'd been harassing them on his own before joining us. Started out breaking grave—"

Mullins interrupted. "He's a Legion member?"

"Yes. That's where I found him. At a chapter meeting."

"Good. So he agreed to work with us?"

"Yeah. He was a little puzzled when I told him we needed him to join the National Guard, but after I explained what we were doing he agreed to it right away."

"Did he actually join?"

"Yes. He's assigned to the armory right up here in Santa Monica." Payne gestured to indicate the direction.

"And he has access to their weapons?"

Payne grinned. "He's a weapons clerk. They pay him extra to come in a few days each week and maintain the inventory."

Mullins was delighted. "That's great. What about the other one?"

Payne frowned. "Other one?"

"You said you found two men."

"Oh. Yeah. The other one is Allen Waller. He was already in the Guard when I met him. He's a member at the armory in Burbank. I'm not sure how helpful he will be, but I'm working with him."

"Is there a problem?"

"Not really. It's just taking time. He lives with his mother and she keeps a close watch on him. Kind of a strange relationship. It hampers how freely he can go and come, but I'm getting him involved. I think he might like to come out to the camp and work with you."

"We'll have to check him out first."

"It would help him get free to come and go. Make him more useful to us that way. And he might be a good addition to the people training at the camp. You know. Prior experience and all."

"Right." Mullins wasn't convinced, but was willing to consider the possibility. "Are both of these men Legion members?"

"Yeah, like I said, that's how I found them. Their prior experience made the Guard an easy option. And the National Guard is the way to do it," he added quickly. "With the Guard, a guy can pick his own place. Join an existing unit. If we had them enlist in the army, we'd have no control over where they were assigned. They could enlist here and be sent to. . .Florida."

"Good point," Mullins noted.

Not long after Mullins's meeting with Payne, firearms and ammunition began arriving at the training center. Just a few items at first—a rifle, two handguns, and a hundred rounds of ammunition. The camp's armory wasn't ready for it, so Mullins placed the items in a locker in the tent where he slept. Seeing the arms, however, greatly encouraged the recruits and they redoubled their effort to complete the camp's first buildings.

✦ ✦ ✦

As work progressed at the camp, Mullins divided the staff and recruits into two crews and placed them on alternating schedules. One crew worked on construction in the morning, then trained in the afternoon. The other did the opposite. In this manner, Mullins told them, they were being prepared to launch attacks against the enemies that threatened the nation—Jews and capitalists who lived in luxury while the workers lived in squalor—even as they prepared the facility to extend their effectiveness. "We're building for the present and the future at the same time," he assured them.

In conjunction with their labor on the construction projects and the rigors of their training regimen, Mullins periodically took the recruits into downtown Los Angeles where they distributed pamphlets to people passing by on the street. Most of the literature was in a form circulated by the German Workers' Party, which was by then a rising influence on German politics. Those publications placed blame for the horrors of the Great War and the rise of Communism squarely on the Jews and accused Jews of conspiring to bring about the downfall of America.

Though timid at first, Mullins encouraged the recruits to push themselves toward greater and greater boldness in accosting people on the street. Gradually, they became quite brusque in their approach, telling anyone who would listen that America was under attack. "Not from a foreign government," the recruits explained, "but from International Jews who want to take control of our economy."

When one cornered an individual, another stepped up to assist chiming in with something like, "They come here without learning the language, steal our jobs, and want to ruin our American way of life. They control the press. They control the entertainment business."

Then the first recruit rejoined, "They want to control the way you think. And they are supported in their efforts by a conspiracy of Jewish bankers, Communists, and the liberal politicians beholden to them."

For the most part, people either ignored them or listened without response, then moved on. A few, however, argued back, their level of anger steadily rising as they attempted to refute the claims of the recruits. The training staff had instructed the recruits on how to respond in a way that kept the tension in an argument always on the rise, round by round, and as the recruits became more adept at the technique, the street campaigns became increasingly confrontational. At times, those confrontations became violent and on one or two occasions, police were called to break up the fracas.

Although Mullins did not want the attention of the police, the incidents on the street achieved their desired effect. The recruits were inspired and energized almost to the point of frenzy. As a result, their training and work at the camp took on a new vigor. Construction progressed ahead of schedule, as did the proficiency of the men in their military-style exercises.

At the same time, Mullins began to have second thoughts about the use of only slight force. He'd seen the way the police reacted to the men on the street. The kind of force they had at their disposal. The reserves they could call if needed. Overwhelming force, an assault of force against the government was never going to accomplish the Crimson Legion's aim. They had to combine force with a greater strategy. One that included manipulation of those already in power. But how to do that seemed illusive.

✦ ✦ ✦

A few months into the program, Griffin came to California to visit the center. Mullins led him on a tour of the grounds and had the men display some of their skills in practiced drills and exercises. Griffin was impressed and as the demonstrations came to an end, he sat with Mullins under one of the canopies to talk. "You've made great progress with the men and the facilities," Griffin exclaimed enthusiastically.

"Thank you," Mullins responded. "We've been working hard."

"It shows in the result you've produced, and not just here at this facility."

Mullins was curious. "What do you mean?"

"Members from our chapters on the East Coast have heard the news of your work," Griffin explained. "Particularly the incidents downtown that attracted attention in the press."

"Sorry about that." Mullins had a repentant expression. "I hadn't planned for it to get quite that far yet."

"No, no." Griffin shook his head. "There's nothing to be sorry about."

"It was a little too much attention too early in our work."

"Nevertheless, it has had a positive effect on the entire organization. Others have seen what you are doing and have been encouraged by it to replicate your work in their own areas. And many of them are doing it." Griffin smiled at him. "Following your lead, as it were, though without the facility or the formal training."

"We're still in the preparation phase. Preparing and organizing for action."

"I know, but your work is having a positive effect on the entire organization. Several of the chapters back east have come together to explore the creation of their own training facility. Perhaps not as extensive as this one, but helpful just the same."

"Do they have a site chosen?"

"They've tentatively settled on a location in Michigan. Remote. Rural. A place where gunfire would not be noticed."

"That would be more convenient than sending people all the way out here."

"Exactly." Griffin nodded. "They've also formed their own organization. A group within the group."

Mullins frowned. "You're okay with that?"

"Oh yes. I'm quite okay with it. In fact, I'm proud of their personal initiative."

"What sort of group is this?"

"They call themselves the Christian Warriors. They intend to function as a paramilitary organization, just as your group out here."

"We could bring them out here and put them through our course," Mullins offered. "If that would be helpful."

Griffin shook his head. "I don't think so. That might disrupt their esprit de corps. The Warriors will work in the East. You and the staff out here will work in the West."

"Okay," Mullins conceded. "But what kinds of things have the Warriors been doing?" He was interested in how violent they had become and whether his group had been outpaced by this upstart organization.

Griffin shrugged. "Mostly desecrating Jewish graves. Attacks on Jewish businesses. Smashing windows. That sort of thing. But I understand they're planning even bigger operations." He gave Mullins a look. "Though I make it my business to stay out of the details."

"Yes. And rightfully so." Mullins was relieved to know that the others hadn't done even as much as he himself had, but he had a sense that Griffin was telling him to step up the work.

Griffin continued. "These are unsettled times, Bryce, and they are bound to get even more so. Jews are leaving Germany in large numbers. Surging into surrounding countries at a faster pace than ever before. Spreading unrest across the continent. The same thing will happen here if we let them into our country."

"That's what we mean to end." Mullins looked over at Griffin. "It will take a concerted effort from us, though."

"I agree. The masses will never understand the threat posed by Jews. We are the only ones who can save America now."

"I've been thinking about that."

"Oh?" Griffin raised an eyebrow. "Having doubts about the strategy?"

"Not so much doubts as questions."

"What questions?"

"When we move in force, we must be ready to do it with widespread attacks that can overwhelm the government. Not just a few rocks thrown here, or a house burned there."

Griffin seemed interested. "You have something in mind?"

"Think about this: we have Crimson Legion chapters throughout the country. If we can create unrest at each of those locations—unrest on a level that overwhelms local and state police at each of those places—the president might be pushed into declaring martial law for the entire nation."

"And?"

Mullins continued, "Then we can maneuver him into suspending elections, and deporting the groups that caused the trouble. Groups we oppose. Groups we will make sure take the blame for the unrest and violence. The Jews, Italians, and Negroes."

Griffin did not seem to care for the idea. "That sounds a little convoluted, don't you think?"

"Perhaps, but we can't take down the federal government merely by random acts of violence. Whatever we do must have a point. There has to be a plan. The federal government is huge and has lots of resources at its disposal. We are small, by comparison, and need to act strategically. Otherwise, they will simply crush us by brute force."

"That's a novel approach." Griffin folded his hands behind his back. "I'll give it some consideration."

"I don't have doubts about confronting our enemies. And I don't doubt we need to use force in that confrontation. But a head-to-head battle with the federal government would be the end of us. Like I said, they have far more resources at their disposal than we do."

"Speaking of government resources." Griffin looked over at Mullins. "Justice Department investigators have been questioning our people. They've even talked to me. Have they come to see you?"

A wave of panic swept over Mullins. "Have they talked to Grace?"

Griffin frowned. "Grace? Grace Anderson?"

"Yes."

"I don't know, but I would assume so. She works for Fisher now. I'm sure if they know about her, they will want to talk to her. Why?"

"Just curious."

"But have investigators talked to you?"

"No."

Griffin raised an eyebrow. "That's very interesting. You've been at the heart of almost everything we've done. Why would they talk to the rest of us and not to you?"

Mullins felt he was being viewed with suspicion, but before he could think of a response, Griffin said, "Well, I'm sure they'll get to you eventually." He looked Mullins in the eye. "When they do, make sure you are very careful in your responses to their questions. These investigators can be real snakes."

Mullins nodded in response, but his mind whirred as he tried to think of what might have happened. Did Ida Hayes talk? Did Pete talk? If Pete told them what he knew, they might all be in big trouble.

Griffin stood. "Keep working." He shook Mullins's hand. "Get the men ready as quickly as you can. We're working on something big and this center right here is the key."

✦ ✦ ✦

Though Griffin had been encouraging in his review of the camp, the visit left Mullins with the impression that more was expected of him. As if Griffin and the leadership in Charlotte had expected to see quicker results. And for them, results meant action. Confrontation. More than handing out leaflets on the street. More than tussles with detractors on the sidewalk.

A few days after Griffin had gone, Mullins gathered the training staff—Lynch, Davis, and Gropper—in his tent. "We need to move up the pace with our recruits."

"They're working about as hard as they can," Lynch replied.

"I don't mean more labor," Mullins stressed, "I mean we need to step them up in their training. Move them more quickly toward decisive action."

"Interesting you should mention that," Davis spoke up. "We were considering whether to approach you about doing more with them."

"What did you have in mind?"

"There's a Jewish cemetery on the east side of the city," Gropper added. "Off Downey Road. We thought we would take a team out there to desecrate some Kike graves."

"Desecrate them?"

"This would be a training exercise," Lynch explained. "We want them to deface the gravestones. Push them over. Smash them. Deface the stones with paint."

"Some of them have shown an interest in symbols used by the German Workers' Party," Davis put forth. "They hate the Jews almost as much as we do. We thought we might let them try that."

Mullins nodded. "Okay, but this action has to fit into a bigger picture. We aren't just playing pranks."

"This is training," Lynch reiterated. "It would be a step up from what they've been doing."

"Yes, but a step toward what?" Mullins wondered.

"Toward something bigger."

"And what would that be?"

"We haven't come up with that yet," Davis responded.

"But you must have talked about it."

"There's a synagogue on Broadway," Lynch suggested.

"And another on Figueroa," Gropper added.

"Both of those are likely locations we could hit," Lynch said. "But we haven't discussed the particulars of what the men could do there."

Mullins thought for a moment, "When do you want them to hit the cemetery?"

"We're ready to go tonight," Lynch replied. "We can leave as soon as it gets dark."

"We?"

"I'll go with them," Lynch proposed. "Just me and six guys."

"And you're sure the men can do this? Get in, get it done, get away—without getting caught?"

"Yes. But that's one of the things we want to assess. Whether they can do a military-style operation without getting caught."

"We have to take them out to the field at some point," Davis jumped in. "They can't just train."

"I understand." Mullins didn't like the tone of Davis's voice, but he let it pass.

Lynch spoke up. "This is a rather low-risk outing."

"Unless they get caught," Mullins noted.

Lynch smiled. "They won't get caught."

Davis commented, "Most of these men have combat experience in one form or another. They know what it takes to do this kind of thing."

"And more," Gropper added.

Lynch looked over at Mullins. "You seem hesitant."

"It's just that . . ." Mullins had a pained expression. "I've come to see that merely confronting our enemies with force will not accomplish our goal. We need a much larger plan."

"That's not for us to decide, is it?" Lynch responded. "That's something they'll have to figure out in Charlotte. We're just getting these men ready for when they tell us what to do."

"Yes." Mullins sighed. "You're right. It's just that this is our first real operation."

Lynch nudged him on the shoulder. "Relax! Our men are ready. This will go well."

Mullins smiled more broadly. "I'll expect a full report tonight as soon as you get back."

As they turned to leave, Mullins questioned, "Have you selected the people you're going to take?"

"We have four," Lynch replied. "I was thinking of adding one more."

"Who did you have in mind?"

"That new guy. Waller. He's been working hard."

"Okay, but he's in the Guard."

"Yeah. That's why I was wanting him. He has more experience than some of the others."

Mullins wasn't sure that was a good idea, but he'd already raised enough questions about operations and strategy. "Okay. Come find me as soon as you get back."

CHAPTER 39

On Wednesday morning, as was his custom, David Edelman drove out to Downey Road on the east side of Los Angeles and made his way to Mount Zion Cemetery. Edelman, an attorney with a thriving practice in downtown Los Angeles, had a busy schedule that day and he easily could have made an excuse for not making the trip. But his grandfather, Ira Salman, had been an important part of his life; on the day Salman died, Edelman made a commitment to honor his memory at least once each week. And so he put aside the pressing business of the day and made this trek.

A wall surrounded the cemetery, obscuring it from view, but as Edelman turned the corner and started up the driveway, he saw people milling about the grounds, many of them pointing and crying. All of them looking grim and serious. Then he saw the graves.

Across the cemetery, headstones had been splattered and swabbed with black and white paint. Many of the tallest ones lay face down, cracked in the middle from the force of the fall. The more ornate monuments lay in pieces on the ground.

Edelman brought the car to a stop, threw open the door, and climbed from the front seat. He slammed the door behind him as he rushed toward Grandpa Salman's grave, his heart pounding against his chest with every step. "What have they done?" he muttered. "What have they done?"

Reports had circulated for weeks about roving gangs of men,

vandalizing graves in Jewish cemeteries. And there had been rumors of at least one attempted fire-bombing at the home of a prominent Jewish community leader. But Edelman had been unable to uncover details about the vandals, and no one seemed to know much about the attempted bombing. That morning, those incidents had instantly been transformed from the theoretical trouble of someone else, to the very real trouble staring him in the face.

When he reached the grave, Edelman discovered that his grandfather's headstone had been painted black. Over it was smeared the shape of a cross painted white. As Edelman stared at it, Jacob Cohen appeared at his side. "Who would do such a thing?"

Edelman shook his head. "I don't know."

"This is the third cemetery that has been attacked. They struck Beth Israel last month."

"You think it was an attack?"

"They struck Beth Israel last month."

"I heard about that."

"And they hit Home of Peace before that."

Edelman nodded. "I remember them now." He knew about those incidents and about several others Cohen had failed to mention. But right then he didn't care about those other incidents. The angst of seeing his grandfather's resting-place defaced pushed all other concerns aside and focused his thoughts solely on the moment at hand. "We must do something."

"But what?" Cohen lamented. "Apparently, no one saw anything."

Edelman's eyes still were focused on the defaced headstone. "Has anyone reported this to the police?"

"Hayyim Nieto is head of the burial society. Everyone seems to be waiting for him to act."

Nieto was almost ninety years old and no longer drove his

own car. His grandson cared for him and was the only person Nieto trusted to take him anywhere. The grandson, however, was in Chicago and would not return for three more days. Edelman gestured to the headstone. "This was my grandfather's grave. I am under no constraint to wait for Nieto."

"What are you going to do?"

Edelman turned away and started toward the car. "I am going to the police. You should, too." He gestured to no one in particular. "And so should everyone else."

✦ ✦ ✦

Thirty minutes later, Edelman arrived in downtown Los Angeles. Instead of going to his office, he went to the police station and filed a complaint about the vandalism of his grandfather's grave. The sergeant on duty glanced over his paperwork and gave it a cursory review, then looked up and told him, "We'll check into it, but we've had a lot of this sort of thing happening lately and we have other cases of higher priority."

Not satisfied with that response, Edelman went down the hall to the detective's section and found Ken Ryker, a friend he'd known for many years. Ryker was a supervising detective and someone who cared about doing a good job. Edelman told Ryker what happened, then said, "Can you look into it?"

"You filed a report?"

"Yes, but we both know that unless someone takes the initiative, all that will happen is a patrolman will go out there in a few days and have a look around and that will be it."

Ryker checked his watch. "Okay, I have three hours until I have to be somewhere. Ride with me out to the cemetery and I'll have a look."

Edelman had a thousand other things to do and his own schedule was getting tighter by the minute, but the opportunity to have Ryker personally involved seemed too important to worry about anything else. So he stood and straightened his jacket. "I'm ready. Let's go."

They rode to the cemetery in Ryker's car and as they turned from Downey Road and idled past the first rows of graves, Ryker's eyes opened wide with amazement. "You weren't kidding."

"They hit almost every grave out here."

"I can see that."

"That is my grandfather's grave over there." Edelman pointed.

Ryker brought the car to a stop and they got out. Edelman led him to Salman's headstone. Ryker stared down at it a moment, his hands clasped reverently. "Has anyone found anything other than the damaged headstones? Anything that might be evidence? Anything suspicious? Anything out of place?"

"Like what?"

"Well, it looks like they used paint." Ryker gestured toward the headstone. "Has anyone found a paint can?"

"I don't know. I was angry. I didn't really talk to anyone when I was out here before. I just came to the police station and reported it."

"Maybe we should talk to those who are still here."

From Salman's grave, Ryker and Edelman wandered through the cemetery. A woman three graves down was trying to right a headstone that had been toppled over. Ryker and Edelman helped her and they set it upright. As they did, others came forward, and when they learned that Ryker was a Los Angeles police detective, they complained about what had happened. Ryker took a small pad from the pocket of his jacket and dutifully took notes.

As each one told their story, Ryker and Edelman slowly worked their way across the cemetery. Near the backside of the property, they came to a grave where the headstone had been smashed. It was large, heavy, and had broken into sizeable chunks.

"This was the grave of Rabbi Dovber Karelitz," Edelman

explained. "He was a teacher and a scholar of great renown. He once gave a lecture at the University of Berlin that was attended by over a hundred rabbis and professors."

Ryker nudged one aside with the toe of his shoe to reveal a paintbrush that lay beneath it. The brush had black paint on it. Ryker squatted beside it. "Looks like they might have used this," he said, pointing to the brush.

Edelman leaned over his shoulder to see. "Think you can get a fingerprint from it?" He spoke with an expectant tone, and when Ryker glanced up at him, he smiled. "I hear the department is using them to identify all sorts of people now."

"Yeah, they can be helpful, but it's a cumbersome process."

"What do you mean?"

"The known prints are kept on file cards at the courthouse. Clerks have to go through them and compare new ones to the ones we have. It's rather tedious."

"But they're getting better, right? I mean, if the same people do the same task over and over, they get better at it. Right?"

Ryker nodded. "They're getting better at comparing the ones we have to the ones we lift in the field. But it's still more of a way to connect someone to a crime *after* they've been located—we figure out who did it, take their prints, compare it to a weapon or something from the scene—rather than getting prints from the scene and comparing them to ones we already have on file."

"But it's a start," Edelman noted.

"It's a start, but it's a long shot."

Using his handkerchief, Ryker picked up the brush by the bristles and walked with it back to the car. A small case in the trunk held a fingerprint kit and he used it to locate three prints from the brush handle. Edelman and half a dozen others looked on while he transferred the prints to a card, placed the card inside a flap on the lid of the case, then put the brush in a paper bag.

✦ ✦ ✦

Two weeks later, Edelman received a phone call from Ryker. "We found three prints in the file that might be a match for the ones from the paintbrush."

"Only three?"

"Like I told you, it's an imperfect process right now."

"Well, at least we have something."

"Not really."

"Why not?"

"I checked them out from the information we have available to us. Two of them are elderly. Confined to their house. Not really capable of doing something like what happened at the cemetery."

"And the other one?"

"His name is Allen Waller. A much younger guy. Joined the army as a teenager. Spent time in Europe during the Great War. Recently discharged. No indication of any criminal charges against him in our files. That would be a place to start, but I have another case that I have to work on right now and I can't get out to talk to him until maybe next week."

"Give me his address. I'll go talk to him."

Ryker hesitated. "I don't know . . ."

"Come on," Edelman urged. "I just want to talk to him. That's what I do all day. I talk to people. Find out what they know."

"Okay," Ryker said finally. "But just talk to him. And just you. Nobody else with you."

"Sure."

"And don't tell anyone how you found out about him. Not even him."

"Okay. I won't say a word about that. Give me the address." Ryker called out the address, and Edelman jotted it down on a notepad. As soon as the call ended, Edelman grabbed his jacket and the notepad, then left the office.

Forty-five minutes later, Edelman located the house that matched the address he received from Ryker. He parked the car out front and knocked on the door. An older woman wearing a housecoat answered. She had thin gray hair and pale skin with dark circles around her eyes. When Edelman asked for Waller, she answered, "I'm his mother."

"I'm an attorney," Edelman told her. "I think your son might have been a witness in a case." It wasn't quite true but not really a lie, either. "I was wondering if I could talk to him about it."

"He's not here."

"When do you expect him to return?"

"I don't know," the woman explained. "He hasn't been here much lately. Took some of his things and left."

"Do you have any idea where he's gone?"

"He might be living at a place near the Palisades."

"What kind of place? Does it have a name?"

"I don't know the name. Someone said they thought it was a commune."

Edelman pressed the question. "And you don't know the name?"

She sighed. "I think I heard him call it Cleary Ranch."

"Cleary Ranch," Edelman repeated.

"Yes. I'm not sure what it is. All I know is it's somewhere up by the Palisades." She shrugged. "At least, that's what they say. I've never been there and I don't really care to go."

"Has Allen been in any trouble lately?"

"Trouble?" A deep scowl wrinkled her forehead. "No. He ain't been in no trouble. I thought you said he was just a witness."

"He is, "but you said he'd moved out and was living someplace you thought was a commune. If he's been in trouble, then I don't know if I could use him or not."

"He was in the war." She said it as if it explained everything. "That's all. It's just taking time for him to adjust. War changes a person, you know. All of them had to adjust when they came back. He's a good boy."

Edelman listened patiently while she went on to describe her son in glowing terms, and he asked a few more questions, which extended the conversation another fifteen minutes. Finally he was able to bring things to an end. He said good-bye and made his way back to the car.

From Waller's house, Edelman drove back toward the coast and up to the Palisades, an undeveloped tract that lay atop a bluff overlooking the coast, with Topanga Canyon to the north and Santa Monica to the south. Sunset Boulevard, the only paved road in the area, meandered from Los Angeles up the bluff and back down. Edelman traveled it from one end to the other, looking, hoping, searching. For what, he didn't quite know. But he searched, nonetheless.

After an hour of driving aimlessly up and down the paved road, he stopped at a garage near the Pacific Coast Highway and described the site to an attendant. "I think they might call the place Cleary Ranch."

"I know where it is," the attendant said. "But it'll be difficult for you to find it."

"Explain it the best you can.".

"Well, you go back up Sunset like you're going into town."

"Okay."

"Once you get past the first curve up here." The attendant pointed to indicate. "You'll cross two or three ravines. A little way past the last one, you'll come to a road that goes off to the left." He looked over at the car and grimaced. "It's not much of a road. Be better if you were in a truck."

Edelman shook his head. "I don't have a truck."

"Well, drive slow and you might be all right."

"Okay. So I turn onto a dirt road. Does the road have a name?"

"Yeah," the attendant clarified. "We call it Sullivan Road.

I'm not sure if there's a sign for it. But the place you're looking for is about a mile up that road."

"Okay," Edelman said as he returned to the car. "Thanks."

"Be careful," the attendant added. "Folks say they've heard a lot of gunfire from up there. Not sure what they're doing."

Edelman thanked the attendant once more, then turned the car around and started up Sunset Boulevard as it wound its way up from the coast toward the top of the bluff. A few minutes later, he crossed what appeared to be the first draw. A moment later, he crossed the second. Just beyond it, a dirt road led up a hill. He turned the car in that direction and noticed that the engine strained as the grade steepened.

About a mile up the dirt road, a narrower freshly traveled road led off to the left. The location fit the description he'd received from the garage attendant, so Edelman steered the car in that direction. A moment later, he rounded a curve to find a gate blocking the road. He jammed the brake pedal with both feet to keep from hitting it.

The gate was manned by two guards, both of them dressed in black pants, leather boots, blousy red shirts, and black berets. They were armed with rifles and both carried a handgun in a holster on their hip. One of them approached the car.

"This is private property," the guard advised. "You're trespassing."

Edelman smiled. "I must be lost. I was looking for Don Webster's place, but I think I made a wrong turn." Webster was a friend from Santa Monica and the first name that popped into his head. He really didn't like the looks of the two men.

The guard shook his head. "Never heard of him."

"I think I made a wrong turn," Edelman repeated.

"I think you did, too," the guard sneered. "You need to get out of here."

Edelman nodded. "I'll just turn around and get moving."

With both guards glaring at him, Edelman backed the car away from the gate, found a place wide enough to turn it around, then started back toward the bottom of the hill. When he reached Sullivan Road, he made a mental note of where the drive up the hill was located.

This is the place, he thought. *And they're up to no good. I don't know what, exactly. But I know it's not good.*

From the Palisades, Edelman drove downtown and found Ryker at his desk. Ryker saw him as he entered the office and tried to wave him off. "Whatever it is, I don't have time for it today."

"You have to make time for this." Edelman took a seat. "It's important."

"What happened?" Ryker asked. "You didn't get into it with Waller, did you? I told you just to talk."

"I did just talk. And he doesn't really live there now. At least not much. It's his mother's house. But she told me he's been staying at a place in the Palisades. Some kind of commune or something."

Ryker had a knowing look. "And you went out there?"

"Yes."

"And what did you find?"

"Armed guards."

"What are you talking about? Armed guards at what?"

"I don't know what it is."

"You're not making much sense. Why don't you tell me what happened."

"I went to Waller's house. His mother said he was staying at a place in the Palisades. Some kind of camp or something. Called it Cleary Ranch. So I rode out there to see what I could find. After wandering around awhile, I stopped at a garage and asked them about it. A guy who worked there told me how to find the place. So I followed his directions and came to a gate manned by men with rifles."

Ryker had a serious expression. "And you think that's where

Waller is living?"

"Yes. Whatever's happening up there, I think Waller is involved and I think whoever lives there had something to do with what happened at the cemetery."

"Okay," Ryker responded. "I'll check it out."

"Today?"

"No. I'm in the middle of something else."

"You'll always be in the middle of something else," Edelman then urged. "Let's go up there now. I can show you where it is," Edelman said.

Ryker stood. "You're a real piece of work, you know that?" He slipped on his jacket. "I'll go. But you gotta drive."

"Why me?"

"If the shooting starts, I don't want them shooting up my car. The department just got it a few months ago."

Twenty minutes later, they reached Sullivan Road. Edelman slowed the car as they wound their way up the canyon, and pointed out the window. "That's the drive."

"You're sure that's it?"

"Yes."

Ryker gestured toward the windshield. "Let's go a little farther. Maybe we can park out of sight."

A short way up from the turnoff, the road made a curve. Edelman found a place to park and brought the car to a stop. The canyon fell away to the right and a hill rose to the left. "Okay," he said. "The place should be over the crest of that ridge." He gestured to the left. "We'll have to hike from here."

With Ryker in the lead, they made their way to the top of the hill and crouched low as they reached the crest. Below them was a newly constructed building made of concrete block. To the right of it, workers prepared the foundation for another. And beyond those, a grader smoothed off a spot, apparently in preparation for construction of a third structure.

"They're definitely building *something*," Ryker speculated. "But it's hard to tell what."

Just then, the sound of gunfire came from somewhere in the distance. Ryker's eyes opened wide and he shifted positions trying to get a better view.

"That was gunfire," Edelman whispered.

"Yeah, sounded like high-caliber rifles."

"What do you think they're doing down there?"

"Looks like they're setting up a camp of some sort."

They watched a moment longer and then, just as they were starting to leave, a squad of men appeared, coming over a hill into the construction site. They marched in formation and each one carried a file on their shoulder.

"This isn't good."

"No," Edelman replied. "It isn't."

"Looks like they're conducting military training." Ryker glanced over at him. "And you think this is where Waller is living?"

"It fits the description I got from his mother and the man at the garage. But why would these people care about the cemetery?"

"That's a good question." Ryker backed away. "Come on. Let's get out of here before someone sees us."

When they reached the car, Edelman looked over at Ryker. "What are you going to do now?"

"I need to get back to the office and finish what I was doing when you arrived."

"I mean about what we saw."

"I'll look into it and see who owns the property. Maybe follow up to find out what they're doing with it. But I'm not sure I can do much more than that."

"Can't you get someone to watch the place?"

"We don't have the manpower for that kind of surveillance.

Especially when we don't even know if they've committed a crime."

"Waller has."

"Maybe."

"But you found his fingerprints."

"Prints on a brush are a good lead. But it doesn't make a case against him. Besides, we don't even know for sure if Waller is living at that place."

"What about the gunfire?"

"It's not illegal to fire a weapon. Certainly not out here."

✦ ✦ ✦

Edelman was dissatisfied with Ryker's response and decided to check out the Palisades property himself. To do that, he went to the Los Angeles County land records office and searched for any mention of a Cleary Ranch or something similar. After two hours, he located a deed from two years earlier conveying forty acres to John and Pamela Cleary. He checked the description from the deed against a land records map and found it was the site of the camp he and Ryker had visited in the Palisades.

A search of the telephone book gave Edelman an address for the Clearys in the newly developed area of Beverly Hills, a planned restricted community that forbade non-whites, including Jews, from living there. Rather than simply knocking on their door, as he might have done when he wanted to question someone who lived in other areas of the city, Edelman went to the library and checked the city registry. There he found that John Cleary was in the oil business. A review of recent newspapers showed the Clearys had made a fortune in drilling for oil along the coast and the family was among the first residents in Beverly Hills.

Development of Beverly Hills included the construction of a hotel—aptly named the Beverly Hills Hotel—which had recently opened for business. It was located only a few blocks from where the Clearys lived. *Perhaps,* Edelman thought, *they might dine there.* And if they did so frequently, the hotel staff might remember them.

Late that afternoon, Edelman drove to the hotel, parked in back, and began questioning the hotel staff. No one who worked at the front desk wanted to talk to him, but a waiter in the restaurant admitted knowing the Clearys. "They dine here often," he told Edelman, "and they've had several out-of-town guests who have stayed here at the hotel."

As Edelman was leaving, one of the bellmen approached him in the parking lot. "If you want to know what they're up to, check out this man." He handed Edelman a newspaper folded to show a picture of a middle-aged man identified in the caption as William Griffin. The bellman pointed to the photo. "The Clearys were in here with him a month or two ago."

From the newspaper article, Edelman learned that Griffin was the director of the Crimson Legion of America. He already knew about the Legion from friends and family who lived in New York. It didn't take long to figure out that the Legion was using the Clearys' property.

✦ ✦ ✦

A few days later, Edelman went to see Hayyim Nieto, the president of the burial society that was responsible for the care of his grandfather's grave. "Has the headstone been repaired?"

"We have crews working in the cemetery now," Nieto told him. "These things take time. I understand you went to the police."

"Yes."

"You should have waited for me."

"Did you file a report?"

"Yes." Nieto shrugged. "But it did no good. They only sent a patrolman, as we knew they would. He asked a few questions, but that is all."

"I found out more about what might have happened."

"We know what happened. The cemetery was vandalized."

"But I learned a few things about the people who might have done it."

Nieto nodded. "I heard you were looking into it."

"The police found a paintbrush that the attackers used. It was beneath the pieces of Rabbi Karelitz's monument."

"I heard that, too."

"Turns out, the police were able to get a fingerprint from the handle of the brush."

"The things they can do these days."

"The print matches one from a person who is associated with a group called the Crimson Legion of America."

"I have heard of them. My brother in Boston said they had trouble with the Crimson Legion. Our cousin in Springfield had trouble with them, too." Nieto raised an eyebrow. "They are here now?"

"Apparently so."

"Why are you telling me this?"

"The Crimson Legion is using a place near the Palisades. It looks like they are creating some kind of base there. They are constructing buildings. Patrolling the site with armed guards. That sort of thing."

"Armed guards?"

"Yes."

"What are they doing there?"

"I don't know. But that's why I came to see you. I want to use the society's members to conduct surveillance out there."

Nieto looked puzzled. "Surveillance?"

"To watch them," Edelman explained. "See what they're

doing."

Nieto sighed. "I don't know . . ."

"I don't need you to do it with us. I just need the list of members. I'll take care of organizing them and setting it up."

"I'm not sure they would want to do that."

"They don't have to if they don't want to," Edelman responded. "But we have to do *something*. Unless someone finds a way to put a stop to these people, we'll face even more trouble than desecrated graves."

"And you think the society can make them stop?"

"I just need the members to help me keep an eye on these people."

Nieto opened a desk draw, took out a file, and handed him a page from it. "This is the list. These people who do these things to us. They don't respect private property anymore."

"No, sir. They don't. But I think this goes much further than that."

Using Nieto's list, Edelman recruited enough men to fill four teams. He assigned the teams to six-hour shifts and showed each of them the location for the Cleary Ranch. In the weeks that followed, the teams watched the site day and night from carefully concealed positions along the ridges that ringed the location. Each shift carefully logged each vehicle coming and going from the property. It was tedious work at times, often under difficult conditions. But the men in Edelman's teams never wavered in their resolve to discover the precise nature of the Crimson Legion's operation at the site.

CHAPTER 40

As Edelman suspected, Allen Waller did, in fact, live at the Crimson Legion camp. Jesse Nettles lived there also. Both men were members of the California National Guard, and both had been successfully recruited by Fred Payne to procure military weapons for the Legion's use. The weapons—which they stole from the Guard armories where they were assigned—were dutifully delivered to Mullins.

Not long after Waller and Nettles began their weapons-theft activity, a routine audit was conducted at the Burbank Armory. Waller, who was at the armory only part time, was not present when the count was conducted. The audit revealed that a dozen rifles and several crates of ammunition were missing.

The missing items were too many to attribute to general attrition, and a report of the deficiency was filed with the office of the National Guard's commanding general in Sacramento. Guard staff members reviewed the report and recommended a statewide audit. That audit was ordered and revealed similar deficiencies at three armories in the Los Angeles area.

While the statewide audit of California Guard armories was being conducted, a report of the original findings was forwarded to US Army Headquarters in Washington, D.C. It was reviewed by staff from the army's general counsel office and sent to Fort Rosecrans in San Diego for further action. At Rosecrans, the matter was handed to Floyd Hughes and Irving O'Toole, investigators from the army's base security service, for follow-up.

Three weeks after receiving the California Guard's report, Hughes and O'Toole arrived in Los Angeles and discussed the armory audit with the commander of the Burbank facility. He gave them a list of everyone who had access to the armory's weapons cache. With that list in hand, Hughes and O'Toole began interviewing personnel. Near the bottom of the list they came to the name of Allen Waller and paid a visit to his address on record. They were met at the door by his mother.

"Like I told the other man," Mrs. Waller insisted. "Allen doesn't stay here much now."

"The other man?" O'Toole asked. "What other man?"

"The one who came around here asking about my son." She had a frustrated tone. "I told him Allen took most of his stuff and left."

"When was that?"

"I don't know exactly. It's been a month or two, I guess."

"Do you know who that person was that questioned you before?"

She shook her head. "No. I don't know his name. I think he said he was a lawyer. Working on a case. He thought my son might have seen something."

"And what did you tell him?" Hughes asked.

"I told him exactly what I'm telling you."

"Do you know where your son is now?"

"Like I told that other man, I think he's living someplace near the Palisades. I'm not sure. They say it might be a commune, but I don't know. I've never been up there."

"Does this place have a name?"

"I heard him call it Cleary Ranch, I think. I'm not sure if that's the official name. Or if it even has a name. But the place is up by the Palisades, so they say. I've never been out there."

O'Toole spoke up. "Before your son left, did you notice anything different about him?"

"You mean has my son been in any trouble lately?"

"That would be important. Has he?"

"The other man asked me that, too." A frown wrinkled her forehead. "What's this about?"

"We're not at liberty to disclose the nature of our investigation."

She had a startled look. "Investigation? You're investigating my son?"

"We just want to talk to him," Hughes said.

She shook her head. "Why do you people keep asking me if he's been in trouble?"

"The other man asked you that?"

"Allen was in the war, okay, that's all. It has taken time for him to adjust from what he saw and did over there. War changes people, you know. It's nothing no one else hasn't experienced, but he hasn't recovered as fast as some of them. All of them have had to adjust. It's just taken him a little longer, that's all."

✦ ✦ ✦

From Mrs. Waller's house, Hughes and O'Toole went in search of the location she described. They followed the same path Edelman took and eventually came to the garage on the Coast Highway. When they asked the attendant, he gave them a puzzled look. "This is the second time someone has asked about that place."

"Someone else has been here looking for it already?"

"Yeah. A guy come in here a few weeks ago asking about it."

"Do you know who he was?"

"No. He didn't mention his name."

"A policeman, maybe?" Hughes suggested.

"No, I don't think so," the attendant replied. "I'm not sure he ever said."

O'Toole spoke up. "Did you tell him how to find the place?"

"Yeah. And I can tell you where it is, too, but like I told him, it'll be a little difficult for you, not being from around here and all."

Using directions supplied by the garage attendant, Hughes and O'Toole arrived at the same gate that Edelman had reached.

As they approached, two guards stepped forward. Both wore black pants, leather boots, blousy red shirts, and black berets. Each carried a rifle, with a handgun tucked into a holster on their hip. They stood there glaring at them with a serious and foreboding look.

Hughes, who was driving, opened the car door and stepped out. As he did, the guards moved closer, rifles at the ready. O'Toole stepped out on the opposite side of the car and showed his government identification. "We're investigators from the US Army."

"This is private property," the first guard replied. "You're trespassing."

Hughes smirked. "We're with the federal government. And we don't really care about your private property."

The second guard pointed his rifle in Hughes's direction. "You might learn to care a little more if you don't leave right now."

O'Toole pointed to the rifle. "That looks like a Springfield 1903."

"What of it?"

"Unauthorized possession of government property is a felony. If that's a weapon stolen from the National Guard Armory, you could spend time in prison just for having it."

The first guard spoke up. "You two need to get back in your car and get out of here. Before there's any trouble."

"Yeah," the second one added. "Because it won't be any kind of trouble you've ever had before."

Hughes looked over at O'Toole and both men chuckled. "Okay, we'll leave. But you haven't heard the last of this."

✦ ✦ ✦

When Hughes and O'Toole were gone from the gate, one of the guards walked up to the construction site and reported the incident to Mullins.

"They said they were investigators from the army."

Mullins had a curious expression. "The US Army?"

"Yes."

"What did they want?"

"They didn't say," the guard responded. "We told them to leave and they left."

"Good."

"But before they left, one of them pointed to my rifle and said it looked like a Springfield. He said that just having it in my possession was enough to send me to prison."

"I wouldn't worry about it."

"He seemed to know what he was talking about."

"It's okay. We'll take care of it."

The guard returned to the gate and as he walked away, Mullins crossed the compound to a tent where the trainers kept their gear. Lynch was in there, lying on a cot, resting from the morning's training exercises.

"Army investigators were at the gate," Mullins told him.

Lynch sat up on the edge of the cot. "When?"

"Just now."

"What did they want?"

"I don't think they said. One of the boys reported it to me just now. I think they just left."

"And they didn't say what they wanted?"

"No. But they recognized the rifles the guys were carrying."

"That's not good. I'd better go see Payne."

"Yeah. And what about Waller and Nettles?"

"You think we should take them out of training?"

"I think they are a link back to us," Mullins commented.

"They'll be all right."

"They'll both be compromised if the government is trying to find those missing weapons."

"I'll talk to all of them," Lynch replied. "See what I can find out."

✦ ✦ ✦

Meanwhile, on the ridge between the camp and Sullivan Road, and along the crest of a hill to the west, Edelman's team observed all that occurred at the Cleary Ranch facility. Enthusiasm for the work had grown, and additional volunteers made it possible for them to follow every vehicle that left the premises. When Lynch drove down the hall on his way to find Payne, two of Edelman's men followed in a nondescript vehicle, always at a safe and undetectable distance.

✦ ✦ ✦

Late that evening, Lynch returned and came to Mullins's tent. "I talked to Payne, Waller, and Nettles. And to the guards again, just to make sure we didn't miss anything."

"What did you find out?"

"It's not good." Lynch grimaced. "Waller says that a recent audit of the armory in Burbank came up light. Weapons and ammunition were missing."

Mullins nodded his head. "That's why those investigators came out here."

"Probably so."

"Has anything come of it?"

"They changed their procedures at the armory. Waller says he no longer has access to the weapons and explosives."

"Why didn't he tell us this before now?"

"He said it just happened the last time he was out there, which was a few days ago."

Mullins wasn't satisfied with that answer but it seemed there was nothing he could do about it right then. "They think Waller took the missing rifles?"

"I don't know. They did the same thing to a couple of other people who were assigned there."

"So," Mullins surmised, "either they don't know who took them and they're just being cautious—"

"Or," Lynch finished the sentence, "they know and are trying not to be obvious."

"What about Nettles? Does he still have access to the weapons at his place?"

"Yeah. I told him to get what he could and bring it out here to us."

"We should find a new source for weapons."

"I agree. And we should think about whether to continue sending Waller and Nettles out with the others."

"Can you do without them?" Mullins asked.

"Not really," Lynch responded. "They're the most experienced men on the team."

"And even if the army suspects them," Mullins noted, "they're not doing anything illegal with us."

"All the same. The more they are with us, the more they know."

"You think they might talk?"

"I think we don't know whether they will or not."

"I'll keep an eye on them," Lynch assured. "Waller and Nettles are our two best guys. They've actually worked under combat conditions. No one else on the team has."

"Maybe we should think about adding a class on resisting interrogation."

"Good idea."

CHAPTER 41

As work continued at the Crimson Legion camp, so did the practice of sending teams to conduct clandestine operations that were increasingly risky. After vandalizing Jewish cemeteries, Mullins moved the men on to defacing synagogues and the homes of prominent Jewish leaders. All the while developing the ability to get in and get out without being detected or caught.

In the midst of that, and without prior notice, Bradley Edwards and Kenneth Frost—Crimson Legion staff members from the office in Charlotte—arrived at the camp, ostensibly to check on progress. "Mr. Griffin sent us to see how things are going," Edwards informed. Mullins was unaware that any such trip was planned and was suspicious from the moment they arrived.

Nevertheless, he gave them a tour of the camp and had Lynch put the men through exercises, much the same as he had when Griffin visited. Unlike the way they acted toward Mullins before, this time Edwards and Frost seemed friendly and encouraging. Perhaps too much so.

As the exercises came to a conclusion and they wandered back toward Mullins's tent, Edwards reported, "The office has kept tabs on your work here and we all are impressed by how fast you've brought the men along."

"That's good to hear." Mullins didn't believe a word either of them said but there was no point in arguing right then.

"In fact," Frost added, "after careful consideration, we've

reached the conclusion your men are ready for their first serious challenge."

Mullins frowned. "And what would that be?"

"As you're probably aware, Jews control the motion-picture business. You've said so yourself. And they are using their advantageous position to poison the minds of Americans with their pro-Jewish and pro-Communist newsreels and movies."

Frost picked up the theme. "We've talked about the problem among ourselves. We've discussed it with politicians. Yet nothing has been done about it. Even your friend Senator Fisher has proved inept at addressing the root problem facing us today."

"Which means," Edwards continued, "it's time for us to act."

Mullins was put off by the contrived nature of their presentation, as if they had rehearsed the whole thing ahead of time and were only giving a performance—a very *bad* performance. "And what do you want us to do?" he asked, hoping they would get to the point quickly.

They were inside the tent then, and Frost leaned close. "We want you to assemble a team to assassinate the Jewish heads of the motion-picture industry."

Mullins was taken aback. "Assassinate them?"

"Yes."

"All of them?"

Edwards nodded. "It will cripple their industry."

This was just the sort of disconnected kind of violence Mullins had tried to steer Griffin away from. They didn't need single, sporadic events. They needed a strategy for sustained, coordinated action that took advantage of their strengths and exploited society's weaknesses. Killing someone important as a single gesture—or even as multiple gestures—would only provoke an overwhelming response from the government. Still, he forced himself to remain calm. "I assume you have someone in mind."

"We have a list," Frost offered. "We want them all gone. But we think you should begin with Arthur Klein. He is the president of Asterion Motion Pictures, one of the largest movie companies in Hollywood."

"This guy is the key," Edwards added. "With him gone, the entire industry will fall into disarray. The others will be much easier to take out."

Mullins was astounded by the flippant way they talked of killing someone. As if it were an act as simple as shaking someone's hand. He understood the point of their suggestion—he'd made the argument many times before about how Jews used entertainment to shape public discussion and thought—and he had moved to California specifically for the purpose of taking direct action against the threat they posed. But the downside of mere violence remained apparent to him.

"Without immediate action to follow it up," Mullins told them, "any undertaking like this will merely provoke a response from the police. They will come after us with all their might."

"That's part of the risk."

"They won't just come for me, or the men we have here at the camp," Mullins pressed. "They will come looking for *all* of us. And not just to arrest us."

Edwards bristled. "Is that a threat?"

"No," Mullins responded. "It's a reality. I've tried to explain this before. We can't—"

Frost cut him off. "We know about your conversation with Mr. Griffin."

"Then you know I'm right," Mullins countered. "If we confront the government with force—or even cultural institutions like the entertainment business—and do it without a broader strategy that takes advantage of the single act, the government will crush us."

"We are aware of the risks," Edwards snarled. "Mr. Griffin is aware of the risks. The risks have been discussed. But there are other aspects to the Crimson Legion's work that you are not aware of. You are to proceed with the plot at once."

It was those *other aspects* that troubled Mullins, but he knew that arguing with Edwards and Frost would get him nowhere. Instead of tossing them off the property, he agreed, "Very well. We will proceed as you say."

Despite assurances from Edwards and Frost that the assassination plot had been authorized by Mr. Griffin, Mullins was worried. Killing anyone would be a major undertaking with the best operatives and under the best conditions. He had neither. Using the trainees to do it could easily turn into a catastrophe.

Yet, with no one to contact for verification, Mullins decided to proceed as planned, at least with the necessary training. Preparing the men would take a while and perhaps in the intervening time he could think of something else to do about the order.

✦ ✦ ✦

When Edwards and Frost were gone, Mullins found Lynch and took him for a walk. On the far side of the property, they sat beneath a pine tree and Mullins got to the point. "They want us to assassinate Arthur Klein."

"What for?"

"That was my question."

"And did they have an answer?"

"They said I should do as I'm told."

Lynch had a troubled look. "They told you that?"

"In so many words."

"Klein is the head of a major motion-picture studio. Killing him makes no sense."

"I told them that. In so many words."

"So," Lynch said, "what are we going to do?"

"Kill Arthur Klein, I guess."

Lynch looked over at him. "You would really do it?"

"I don't really have much choice. But if you want out, you should leave now. I won't say anything."

Lynch looked away. "No, I'll stay."

"What about Davis and Gropper?"

"I'll talk to them, but I don't think they'll leave, either."

✦ ✦ ✦

As Lynch expected, Davis and Gropper were undeterred in their resolve to remain at the camp and train the men. "This is the sort of thing I've wanted us to do all along," Gropper said. "It's the reason I joined the Legion."

"Me too," Davis added. "We have to do more than talk about the issues or conduct demonstrations."

With the training staff on board, Mullins met with them to discuss how to prepare for the operation. "We should do this in stages," Davis suggested. "Get them up to speed on each skill they will need, one at a time."

"And we can use that time to evaluate the men," Gropper said. "We only need five or six for an assassination team."

"And we should not tell them what they're going to be doing," Davis added. "Not yet."

"I agree," Gropper nodded. "This will take weeks to prepare. We don't want the men thinking about it all that time."

"Okay," Lynch said. "We'll do it incrementally. We'll break the operation down into groups of skills and train them on each set, then gradually combine those skills into a tactical plan. And while we do that, we'll decide which ones get the actual assignment."

Mullins nodded approvingly. "Sounds like a good plan."

Lynch looked over at him. "You realize doing this with these men under these conditions is going to be rough."

"Yeah, I know."

✦ ✦ ✦

In the weeks that followed, Lynch and the training staff devised a rigorous regimen to prepare the men with the heightened skills necessary for an effective assassination—observing a target without being noticed, long-distance marksmanship, and working with explosives. Marksmanship practice quickly showed that the team's firearm skills were their weakness.

Use of explosives, however, proved a surprising strength—even with multiple complex configurations. It also confirmed for them that Nettles and Waller were the best in the group for clandestine assignments. Their prior military experience gave them an obvious advantage that schedule constraints would not allow the others to obtain. Lynch brought this up with Mullins one evening as they reviewed the men and their progress. "We need to select the team we're going to use for this Klein matter so we can begin training them specifically for the operation."

"Who do you want?"

Lynch handed him a list. "These six guys."

Mullins glanced at it, then looked over at him. "You really want Nettles and Waller?"

"As we've said many times, they're the best. And the work we've done lately makes it obvious."

"But what about the investigators from the army?"

"Well," Lynch replied, "they haven't been back."

"True," Mullins acknowledged. "But I don't know . . ."

"I don't think we can do this operation without them."

Mullins raised an eyebrow. "They're that important?"

"With the people we have right now, yeah. They're that important."

"Okay." Mullins handed back the list. "If those are the men you want, then that's your team."

✦ ✦ ✦

The men Lynch wanted for the Klein assassination were in the group of recruits that trained in the morning. Rather than making a point of their special selection in front of the others, he simply divided the group into six-man units and conducted the morning session in units.

After the session ended, and the other men went to work in the afternoon on the camp's construction projects, Lynch took the chosen six-man team aside for additional training while Gropper and Davis trained the regular afternoon group. That arrangement continued for almost two months.

When the team's proficiency with training exercises at the camp peaked, Mullins, Lynch, and the staff decided to send the men into the field to test their skills in a real environment. "We have no choice," Lynch insisted. "We have to find out what they can do before we send them to conduct an actual operation."

"And sending them out to observe and gather information is in keeping with our incremental approach," Davis said.

"I agree," Mullins responded. "But I don't like it."

Lynch had a questioning expression. "You don't like what we've done, or you don't like the idea of assassinating Klein?"

"I don't like the assignment. And I don't like the lack of a larger strategy that this operation fits within."

Lynch looked over at him. "Do we have an option?"

"No." Mullins sighed. "Not really."

"Then we should assemble the men and get ready to put them in the field."

The following morning, Lynch gathered the team in his tent. Mullins was present but only as an observer. Lynch ran the meeting.

"Well," Lynch began, "we've been sharpening the skills that are necessary for committing an effective assassination. And, as we have also discussed, assassinations are a good way of changing a situation in an instant. Think of a political leader. If you take him out, the entire government is thrown into disarray. And that disarray happens in an instant."

"Are we going to do that?" Waller asked. "Are we going to assassinate a politician?"

Davis spoke up. "One step at a time."

"Okay." Waller grinned. "But I'm excited about it."

"Today," Lynch continued, "we're sending the six of you out on an exercise as if you were going to conduct an assassination. You are the assassination team. You will function as a team, just as we've practiced. Everyone knows their role?" Heads nodded in response. Lynch went on. "Your target is Arthur Klein." Several of the men murmured, as they apparently recognized the name. "He is the president of Asterion Motion Pictures."

"That's a big target," someone spoke up. "I mean, he's a . . ."

"High-value," Gropper added. "That's the phrase you're looking for. Klein is a *high-value* target."

Nettles raised his hand. "Doesn't that mean he'll have tighter security?"

Lynch answered, "Almost every important figure will have some form of security. That's why we've stressed the need for planning. Which is what this exercise is about. You will be gathering information about Klein through observation. Which means traveling to the studio, to his house, and anywhere else he frequents. You'll get to practice observing the subject in a manner that does not arouse suspicion or attract attention to yourself."

"You're going with us?"

"Davis and Gropper will be on site to observe your work."

✦ ✦ ✦

Reconnaissance for the Klein operation lasted a week. During that time, the team observed their target at work, at home, and during several social outings. As Lynch had indicated, Davis and Gropper monitored the team's progress and reported that the exercise went off without a problem.

Convinced the team could handle that part of the assassination effort, Lynch suggested they test the team's ability by having them use the information they'd gathered to plan a bombing at the movie studio. Mullins approved and the work went forward.

Turning the team's attention to the details necessary to actually take action revealed several pieces of information they had missed or overlooked in their earlier observations. Gathering that information required additional reconnaissance missions to the studio for mapping and photographing specific locations.

✦ ✦ ✦

Despite all they had done to prepare for the assassination assignment, Mullins remained deeply suspicious of the whole affair. He wondered if Griffin really had given the order, if Klein really was a target because he was part of a Jewish conspiracy, or if Edwards and Frost were doing this solely for their own purposes.

In an effort to satisfy his suspicions and relieve the angst he felt over those doubts, Mullins assigned three men—Lyndon Burke, Curtis Dixon, and Leonard Freeman—to research Arthur Klein. None of them were on the six-man assassination team and weren't even in the morning training session where the team had been preparing. He called them to his tent late one afternoon.

"As we have stressed these past few weeks, planning an assassination is a tedious task. One of the keys to a successful operation like that involves minimizing the threat to the shooters. For that, you need information. Not just the kind of information you've been learning to collect in your exercises, but deep research on the target's associations, his lifestyle, his vulnerabilities."

"How deep?" Burke asked.

"As deep as you can go. Business. Home. Relationships. Girlfriends. Boyfriends. Whatever you can find."

"Some of that would be difficult to obtain." Freeman ventured.

"You'll need to get creative. Facts. Gossip. Rumors. Habits, hobbies, vices. We need to know anything the target does that might expose him to risk. The best at this typically find the riskiest activity a person regularly undertakes, and they use that to cover for the actual kill."

"You mean like a race-car driver who has an accident during a race?" Dixon asked. "Only, the accident is planned and intentional."

"Exactly. The hunter who gets killed in a hunting accident. The hiker who dies from a fall in the mountains. You get the picture."

"Right."

"I want you three to perform that kind of research on this man." Mullins handed them a photograph of Arthur Klein. "He's the man some of you already have been using as the focus of your training exercises."

"He's one of those movie guys."

"Right. So that should make it easier for you to find out information about him."

"And you want us to research him?"

"Yes. I want you to find out everything there is to know about him."

Freeman spoke up. "Are we really going to hit him?"

"Do your work as if you were."

"How much time do we have for this?" Dixon asked.

"I need it as soon as possible." Mullins looked over at Burke. "You coordinate what you find and give me a report."

"Okay," Burke replied. "We'll get busy on it right away."

✦ ✦ ✦

A few weeks later, Burke reported to Mullins. "Klein runs a tight ship. We went through his financial reports. Talked to some of his suppliers. The studio is a moneymaking operation, but we didn't find any obvious issues that could be exploited."

"No girlfriends?" Mullins asked.

"He has a mistress," Burke replied. "But that's not unusual for studio executives."

"And there was nothing else?"

"The only issue he faces," Burke responded, "is with the unions."

Mention of the unions touched an old sore spot for Mullins. "What about them?" he asked with obvious interest.

"They're trying to organize his stagehands."

"And this is a problem for him?"

"The union is bankrolled by Johnny Geraci," Burke explained. "He's a Mafia boss from Las Vegas. His man in Los Angeles is a guy named Alberto Mineo. They're trying to muscle in on Klein as a way of gaining access to his money."

"Any success?"

"So far Klein has resisted."

"I'm not familiar with Geraci or Mineo."

Burke showed him pictures of both. "This is who we're talking about."

Mullins glanced at the pictures. "Okay. Good work. Mind if I keep the photos?"

"They're for you."

Nothing Burke told him meant much until the mention of Geraci and Mineo. He knew the Jews were in the entertainment business. Now they were being joined by the Italians. *Dagoes and*

Kikes in the motion-picture business. He shook his head in disgust.

Knowing that Jews and Italians were involved convinced Mullins that Edwards and Frost were on the level. It also gave him one more assurance that he was correct in his belief that Jews and Italians were America's biggest enemies.

✦ ✦ ✦

Training the team to complete an assassination took longer than even Mullins imagined. Apparently, it took longer than Edwards and Frost imagined, too. A few months into the project, cryptic telegrams began arriving from Edwards, asking Mullins things like, "Is the baby overdue?" or "Has the shipment been sent?" Mullins put him off with equally obscure responses like, "Baby developing on schedule," or "Shipment delayed due to weather."

Finally, however, Mullins felt he could no longer ignore the issue. He met with Lynch and told him, "Whatever we have—however ready they are—we have to do this. We can't wait any longer."

Lynch smiled. "I was thinking of telling you the same thing."

On the appointed night, Nettles, Waller, and the other members of the team piled into two cars and drove from the camp to the Asterion movie studio. Nettles snipped the wire on a fence guarding the back of the property and squeezed through the opening. The others followed closely behind.

With no trouble at all, they entered a building designated as Sound Stage Four and placed a bomb, made with three sticks of dynamite, beneath a storage box in the building's prop room. A pressure trigger attached to the explosives was designed to detonate when the box was moved as little as three inches in any direction. When all of the pieces were arranged and in place, the team hurried from the building and retreated to the fence, then slipped through and ran to the car.

The team returned to the camp feeling pleased to have completed the operation and to have gotten away without being discovered. They spent the remainder of the night celebrating. Lynch was pleased. Mullins was relieved.

However, when three days went by with no word of an explosion, the men began to wonder if they had done everything correctly. Mullins wondered, too. Lynch remained confident.

"These things have a way of developing on their own schedule. Be patient. Give it some time. The point of setting the bomb in the way we did was to allow everyone to get away and to put distance between our presence at the site and the explosion. We wanted it to take a while to unfold."

Four days after the team set the bomb, Lynch was proved right when a stagehand pushed the storage box aside to reach a broom that had been placed against the wall behind it. Seconds later, a violent explosion ripped through the building, sending body parts and debris in every direction.

Reports of the explosion reached radio broadcasts within the hour. Articles about it appeared in morning newspapers the following day. Three people died in the blast. One of them was Douglas Gish, an up-and-coming motion-picture star who'd come to the building in search of a script he'd left behind a few days earlier.

CHAPTER 42

When the explosion ripped through the building at Asterion's sound stage, one of the stagehands notified the guard at the front gate. The guard phoned the police immediately. When the call reached the detective section at police headquarters, Ryker was out of the office, working to solve a murder that occurred near Thomas Jefferson High School, a new school on the south side in an area known as Alameda. The case was assigned to Linc Autwell. Ryker didn't hear about the explosion until noon when he stopped for lunch at a diner.

The case at the studio was important. The deaths were tragic—and everyone was talking about the loss of Gish—but Ryker gave it only passing attention. He was focused instead on the Alameda murder to which he'd been assigned, and rightly so. The principal at the high school had become one of his prime suspects. Solving the case quickly was a departmental priority.

That evening, Ryker arrived home as usual. He greeted his wife and tossed the baseball with his son in the front yard until dark. After dinner, as he and his wife were doing the dishes in the kitchen, there was a knock at the back door. Ryker answered it to find David Edelman standing on the back steps.

"We need to talk," Edelman announced.

Ryker stepped outside and pulled the door closed behind him. "What's this about?"

"You know that place I showed you out at the Palisades?"

"Yeah."

"I've had some guys watching it ever since."

Ryker frowned. "Watching it?"

"Yeah. You know. Conducting surveillance."

"Did something happen?"

"No, no," Edelman answered quickly. "Nothing like that. But we've had teams up there. Guys on the ridge in front. Where you and I were. They've been there since about the time you and I were out there."

"Right."

"Men in the front and men on a hill in back. We have the whole place covered."

"Look," Ryker said impatiently, "I'm in the middle of a big case right now. And my wife—"

Edelman cut him off. "I'm sorry to bother you at home. But this is important."

"Then get to the point. I really need to go back inside."

"A few nights ago, my guys saw two cars leave the camp."

"The Cleary Ranch place?"

Edelman nodded. "They saw two cars leave. It was night. My guys were curious. We have plenty of people out there watching. So some of the guys from out there followed the cars into the city and all the way to the Asterion studio."

Ryker's eyes opened wide. "And you think they had something to do with the explosion?"

"We know they did."

"What makes you think that?"

"My guys followed them all the way up to the time they cut a hole in the studio fence and went inside."

Ryker was very interested now. "Your guys saw them doing that?"

"Yeah."

"When?"

"About four days ago."

Ryker relaxed. "The explosion was today. Not four days ago."

"A trigger could be rigged to go off at any time," Edelman countered. "It didn't have to happen the night my guys saw them. In fact, an explosion right away would have occurred in the middle of the night when no one was present."

"There's already a detective assigned to the case. Your guys need to talk to him."

"No!" Edelman waved both hands in protest. "Not if it means disclosing our operation."

"Why not? Isn't that the purpose for your operation?"

"The men at that camp are dangerous. This is the Crimson Legion we're talking about—the Red Shirts. They're worse than any gang you've ever heard about. These guys are bad, and they mean to visit their evil on my people."

"Your people?"

"Jews. Klein is Jewish. The Crimson Legion thinks we are the enemy and that Jews in the entertainment business are the worst of all."

"Why?"

"Don't you read the newspapers? They think we are part of some sinister plot to rule the world."

"I've got enough to do with my own cases. Talk to Linc Autwell. I think he's the guy handling the case at the studio."

Ryker turned to go back inside, but Edelman caught hold of his sleeve. "Look," he insisted, "whatever they did at that studio, it was just the beginning."

"Your men could get killed doing this."

"And if we do nothing. They'll kill us anyway."

"Linc Autwell is the lead investigator on the explosion. I can't get involved as long as he's on the case, but I'll have to tell him about you."

"Okay." Edelman nodded. "But if he wants to talk, tell him to come see me in person. Don't call on the telephone."

"Don't call?"

"I'm not talking about this on the telephone," Edelman stated emphatically. "The operators listen to everything that's said. I'll be glad to talk to him, but we have to do it in person."

✦ ✦ ✦

The next day, Ryker told Autwell about the information he had received from Edelman. Later that morning, Autwell visited Edelman at his office, and Edelman told him the same thing he'd told Ryker.

"It's interesting information," Autwell decided. "But if you can't give me names or descriptions, there isn't much I can do with it."

"You could go out there to the Crimson Legion camp and question them."

"Which ones?"

"Well, you could send some people out there to work with my people and see for yourselves what they are doing."

"I don't have time for it. Or the people for it." Autwell turned to leave. "If you have a serious lead, maybe we'll look into it. But for now it sounds like one Jew covering for another."

Edelman was incensed. "What does that mean?"

"Look, we all know the owner of the studio is Jewish. You're Jewish. Someone got killed there."

"Three people were murdered there."

"And we're investigating their deaths. But you want us to go out there and roust a group of people based solely on your suspicions? And from what you *have* told me about them, they all are white, non-Jewish people you think are a threat."

"What if I told you that the incident I described was not the first time men from that camp came to the studio."

Autwell gave a dismissive gesture. "Many people go to the studio."

"These men weren't there to watch the filming of their favorite movie stars. They were drawing sketches. Maps, probably. And taking pictures."

"Casing the joint."

"Yes."

"Can your men describe the people they saw doing that?"

Edelman sighed. "No."

"And they can't describe the men they saw cutting through the fence."

"It was dark. They couldn't get a good look."

Autwell opened the office door. "Call me when you have something solid I can use."

"I have talked to Ryker about this group before," Edelman persisted, still not giving up on the issue. "I even took him out there and showed him where they are living and training."

Autwell paused in the doorway and looked back at him. "You took Ryker to the camp?"

"Yes. Would you like to see the place? I can take you out there right now."

"No," Autwell scoffed. "I don't have time for this kind of thing. I have *real* police work to do."

✦ ✦ ✦

Ten days after the explosion, Mullins gathered the six-man assassination team in his tent. "Now, we will go after even bigger targets. We will methodically eliminate the heads of the motion-picture studios. All of them are Jews. All of them are poisoning the minds of Americans and lulling them into doing whatever the Jews tell them to do. We will end it."

A wooden table stood near the tent flap. He brought the men around it, laid a file on the tabletop, and opened it to a black-and-white photo. "This is Arthur Klein. You've heard of him. You've seen him. We've talked about him before. He's the head of the studio we hit the other night. Now *he* is the target."

Several of the men leafed through the pages of the file while Mullins continued. "Klein is the most important man in the entertainment business. Taking him out will have the greatest impact of any single person we could remove."

✦ ✦ ✦

Meanwhile, Edelman's team on the hills around the camp reported daily on the activity they observed, giving him precise notes as to the dates, times, and locations of all the Crimson Legion movements. After reviewing the information, Edelman took the information to Autwell.

"This is nothing," Autwell scoffed after glancing at the notes.

"What do you mean?"

"It's a record of the movements of people in and around someone else's home. There could be a dozen explanations for it."

"Shouldn't we at least tell Klein the Crimson Legion has him under surveillance?"

"You can tell him. He's one of your fellow Jews. Don't you guys have some kind of connection?"

"Look, you don't have to like me. You don't have to like any of us. But I'm telling you Klein is their next target. These people blew up one of the buildings at his studio. Doesn't it seem likely they plan to detonate something at his house?"

"And what would you want me to do about it?"

"Talk to Klein," Edelman insisted. "Suggest that he increase his security."

"If I do that, then whoever you say is watching him will know that we know they are out there."

"So you would rather use him as bait?"

"I don't have much option," Autwell replied. "Like I told you, if your guys can get me descriptions of specific people, I can go talk to them. Otherwise, I can't go around harassing people on *your* hunch."

"You mean you can't harass *white* people on the hunch of a Jew."

"Exactly. Not in this town."

When Autwell proved unworkable, Edelman approached Ryker and told him what his men had observed. Ryker refused to get involved. "It's Autwell's case, and right now I have my own I'm working."

"But this man could get killed in the process."

"You don't know that," Ryker argued. "No one knows it. Not for a fact. If Autwell says he needs specific information, then get him specific information."

With neither Autwell nor Ryker willing to help, Edelman decided to approach Klein himself. Of course, there was no secret connection between them, as Autwell had suggested, nor did Edelman know anyone who knew Klein, but he could not let the threat go unreported and so he did the only thing he could do. He drove to the studio, talked his way past the guard at the front gate, and went inside to Klein's office.

Klein, however, was not present, so Edelman left a note for him with his secretary that read, "I think there is a threat to you at your house. Ask Detective Autwell about it. He knows."

✦ ✦ ✦

At the Crimson Legion training facility, weeks of surveilling Klein produced four notebooks filled with detailed information about his comings and goings. After reviewing it for himself, Mullins gathered the men at his tent, along with Lynch, Davis, and

Gropper, to discuss what the team had observed and how they should move forward with the assignment.

"We have all of this information. "Nettles gestured to the notebooks. "But Klein's routine is always the same. A driver brings the car to the house each morning, picks him up at the door, and drives him to the studio."

Waller added, "Then he parks the car in the same spot, and sits inside the studio most of the day, waiting to take Klein home in the afternoon."

"Leaving the car outside and unattended," someone added.

"But it's still within the studio compound," Nettles noted. "Which means that, although it's unguarded, people can see it throughout the day."

"However," Waller said, "at night the driver brings Klein back to the house and parks the car in the garage, then goes home for the evening."

Davis smiled as if he understood Waller's train of thought. "And what does that tell you?"

"It tells me," Waller replied, "that the obvious weak spot in Klein's routine is the car. And the car is most vulnerable when it is right there at his house. That car sits in the garage all night, unattended. The estate has no guard. Once the driver leaves for the evening, there is no one to stop us from gaining access to the car while it's sitting there. We can get in, plant a bomb in the car, and get out. And no one will ever know we were there."

Lynch nodded. "And that is what we'll do."

"Good," Mullins agreed. "Get to it."

✦ ✦ ✦

The following day, the team began designing a bomb for Klein's car. Two days later, they tested their first design. Later that week, they tried another. Afterward, they discussed the results.

"We can fit the bomb in place under the hood and connect it to the engine's electrical current. But we don't want it to explode when the driver starts the engine. We need to delay the explosion until Klein is in the car."

"How long will that take?"

Waller checked a page in the notebook. "Looks like the average time from the moment he starts the car in the morning until he picks up Klein is about seven minutes."

"That's a long time."

"And," Waller added, "there's some variation on the time."

"We can address that," Nettles added.

"How so?"

"We can wire it to a clock, set the alarm to a particular time, and use that as the trigger. Alarm rings, the bomb explodes."

"Where will we get the electrical charge to ignite the detonator?"

"The car's engine will be running," Waller explained. "Put the clock between the car's system and the detonator. When the clock reaches the predetermined time, its alarm mechanism will act as a switch and complete the circuit. That'll send an electrical charge to the detonator."

"So, what time do we use for the alarm?"

Waller checked the notebooks. "They leave the house between seven and seven fifteen every morning. If we set the alarm at seven twenty-five, we should catch them somewhere en route."

The next morning, they prepared a bomb that included a clock for the detonator and tested it at the target range on the far side of the property. The bomb worked perfectly. They made another just to be sure, then created the components for a third and packed them in a case for easy transportation.

Shortly after midnight later that week, the team slipped onto the estate of Arthur Klein, made their way into the garage, and wired the bomb to Klein's automobile, just as Waller and Nettles had suggested. Once the work was completed and the alarm was set, they retreated from the estate and traveled back to the camp without incident.

✦ ✦ ✦

Edelman's men who were watching the camp observed Mullins's team as they left the training facility. And, as before, two men from the surveillance crew followed the team all the way to Klein's estate. They observed the men entering Klein's garage and saw them leave a short while later.

Rather than return to their observation point around the camp, the men who followed the team went to Edelman's house. One of them awakened him and told him that they had seen men from the Crimson Legion camp entering the garage on Klein's estate. Edelman didn't like what he heard and, despite the lateness of the hour, went to Ryker's house and banged on the back door.

Moments later, the door opened and a groggy Ryker appeared. "What are you doing, Edelman?"

"My guys followed the men from the Crimson Legion camp all the way to Arthur Klein's house. They entered the garage and were there for a while. Then left."

Ryker looked sleepy. "Why are you bothering me with this?"

"There's going to be trouble. My guys couldn't get a good look at the men but they think these are the same ones they saw at the studio. Before the bomb exploded. This isn't good."

"I admit it sounds suspicious," Ryker agreed. "But we can't go over there now and wake up Klein."

"Why not?"

"It's the middle of the night," Ryker protested.

"When you find a bomb in his garage, he won't mind the disturbance."

"I'll think about it." Ryker turned away to close the door, but

Edelman stuck his foot in the way. "You can't ignore this," he insisted. "You have to do something."

"I'll do what I think is appropriate," Ryker snarled. "*I* will." He gestured in his own direction to emphasize the point. "Not you. You've done too much with this already." He leaned against the door to push it closed, and Edelman was forced to move his foot out of the way. When he did, the door slammed shut.

As Ryker turned away and started toward the hall, his wife came from their bedroom. "What was that?"

"Edelman," Ryker replied.

"What did he want?"

"It's nothing. Go back to bed." Ryker's wife disappeared down the hall, but Ryker took a seat at the kitchen table.

The information Edelman brought posed a quandary. If he took the information to Autwell—the detective already assigned to the explosion at Klein's studio—no one would act on it, if at all, until the middle of the morning. By then, a bomb at Klein's house—if there was a bomb—likely would already have exploded.

If he went over there to Klein's house now, on his own, he risked the ire of his supervisor for stepping into someone else's case. And if the perpetrators were nearby, watching to see that the explosion actually occurred, he risked tipping them off. If they saw him at Klein's house at that hour, they would know that someone had seen them. But if he did nothing, and Klein was killed. . .well, that would be bad in many ways.

After reviewing the situation for a moment, Ryker realized he had to act on Edelman's tip. Reluctantly, he rose from his place at the table, walked down the hall to the bedroom, and dressed quickly. As he did, a sense of urgency came over him and he hurried out to the car.

Ryker drove to Arthur Klein's estate and parked near the front steps. It took several moments of pounding on the front door but in a little while the door opened and the housekeeper peeked out, her face just visible through a narrow opening between the door and the frame. "What is the meaning of this?" she demanded in a whisper.

Ryker showed her his badge. "I need to talk to Mr. Klein."

"Absolutely not! Why do you want to see him?"

"We've had reports of someone around your garage."

"Reports?" The housekeeper frowned. "What reports?"

"Someone saw some men come onto the property," Ryker explained. "They saw them go into the garage. Could I at least have a look inside it?"

The housekeeper sighed. "Wait here." She disappeared from view and closed the door. A few minutes later, she returned with a key and escorted Ryker across the driveway to the garage. Using the key, she unlocked a side door, and Ryker went inside.

A quick glance around showed no sign of forced entry and nothing appeared disturbed. The housekeeper seemed to realize this. "You found nothing?"

"I don't see anything out of place." Ryker looked over at her. "Do you?"

"I do not come out here often, but it looks fine to me." She gestured over her shoulder. "And the door was locked when we came in, right?"

"Yes."

After another look around, Ryker turned to leave. "You will tell Mr. Klein I was here, please?"

"I will tell him. But if you think it is important, you should take it up with him yourself. Tomorrow, though." She wagged her finger. "Not tonight. He is a busy man and he needs his rest." Ryker stepped outside, and she closed the garage door, and locked it. "He is usually at his office by eight." The housekeeper led the way back across the drive. "You can call him there on the telephone."

CHAPTER 43

The following morning, Klein's driver reached the bus stop near the estate at seven, arriving there on the earliest city bus to travel that route. As was his customary practice, he walked from the corner to the driveway and made his way toward the garage.

When he reached the building, he used his key to open the side door. The car was parked in a stall on the far side, and when he saw it he thought about lifting the hood to check the engine oil, but he had checked it the day before and it was fine, so he decided to let it go. Besides, touching any part of the engine left his hands dirty and he smelled like grease all day. Better not to do that if he could avoid it.

A few minutes later, he raised the main door and started the car's engine. When it was warm and ready for the road, he backed the car from the stall and, as he did every morning, drove it slowly around to the front of the house. Near the steps, he brought the car to a stop and left it running at an idle.

Five minutes later, when Mr. Klein still had not appeared, the driver came from the car, climbed the steps, and knocked on the door. A moment later, the door opened and the housekeeper greeted him with a smile. "Mr. Klein is not yet ready. I think this may take a while."

"Why so?"

"He has a visitor."

"Perhaps I should take the car back to the garage."

"Leave it," she directed. "But come around to the back and let's have some coffee."

The driver, being a gentleman and more than a little attracted to her, followed a path through the garden to a patio outside the kitchen door. She was waiting for him and they sat at a small table enjoying the cool morning air and the taste of her wonderful coffee.

Sometime later, the housekeeper and the driver were on their second cup when a horrible explosion erupted. So forceful was the blast that it rattled the cups on the table as they rested in their saucers. The housekeeper, her eyes wide in a look of fear, flew from her chair and rushed into the house. The driver also dashed toward the front drive, coming around the house by the same path he'd walked a few minutes earlier.

As the car came into sight, the driver saw the hood had been blown away. The doors were open on either side and flames engulfed it from front to back. The force of the explosion shattered windows along the front of the house. Nearby shrubbery was singed, and the steps were covered in black soot.

Klein's housekeeper telephoned the police, and officers responded at once. Within minutes, policemen and firemen swarmed the location. Linc Autwell, the Los Angeles detective working the studio explosion, was dispatched to the scene at the house, too, and arrived as the flames that burned the car were extinguished.

Autwell stood near the front of the car, staring past a fender to the engine compartment, trying to make sense of what had happened. An assistant took photos. After a moment, a patrolman pointed to the charred remains of the car. "Looks like the bomb was near the engine. See how the hood has been blown off and the top of the car has been separated from the windshield?"

"Yes," Autwell replied. "I think you may be right."

Of course Autwell knew the patrolman was right. Edelman had tried to warn him that a bombing might occur, but he had refused to listen. He hated those Jews with their snarky ways and their money and their clubby sense of superiority. And he hated them even more when they were right.

The metal of the car was too hot to touch, so he took a statement from the driver, then went inside and took one from the housekeeper. She told him about having coffee with the driver, hearing the explosion, and rushing inside to see about Mr. Klein. She failed to mention anything about a guest. But as Autwell was finishing with her, she said, "I feel so bad about this. A policeman tried to warn us last night." Tears filled her eyes. "But I made him leave."

"A policeman." Autwell frowned. "What policeman?"

"There was a detective here. He came after midnight. Said they had received a report of someone snooping around the garage. He wanted to talk to Mr. Klein, but I wouldn't let him. Mr. Klein needed to rest. But I took him out to the garage and he had a look around."

"He didn't find anything?"

"No."

"Do you remember his name?"

"No, but I have a card he gave me." She retrieved a business card from the kitchen counter and handed it to Autwell.

Klein was upstairs and while Autwell waited for him to come down, he walked outside to view the scene once more. By then the car had cooled, and he poked through the remains more closely. That's when he noticed that the top of the engine was missing. From the condition of what remained, it appeared the carburetor and intake manifold had been ripped off. "The bomb was right here," he said to himself.

As he glanced over the car again, he caught sight of a round metal object lodged in an opening behind the steering wheel. He pulled it free and held it between his fingers, turning it from side to side to examine it.

Just then, the patrolman who had been outside earlier pointed to it. "That's the face of an alarm clock."

"Yeah," Autwell replied. "I figured as much."

"That's what they used for a timer."

"You think?"

"Wired the clock to the car's engine, then another wire to the bomb. When the alarm mechanism clicked over to ring the bell, it acted like a switch and completed the circuit, sending current from the car to the bomb."

Autwell looked over at him. "You seem to know a lot about this."

"We did this in the army," the patrolman explained.

"The army?"

"Yeah."

Autwell looked at him askance. "You blew up cars when you were in the army?"

"During the war. They taught us this kind of thing."

"For what purpose?"

"Some of us were sent behind enemy lines. We did this to the Germans."

Autwell gestured to the car. "And this looks like an army job to you?"

"I'm not saying that. I'm just saying—"

Autwell took a stern tone. "Why don't you make sure this place is secure. See if they need some help inside. And leave the detective part to me." The patrolman appeared not to like the way Autwell spoke to him, but he forced himself to keep quiet and walked away, while Autwell located a paper bag for the piece of the alarm clock.

✦ ✦ ✦

Talking to Klein yielded nothing of interest. He was upstairs when the bomb exploded but had been on the backside of the house. He saw nothing and was unharmed. Once again, there was no mention of the guest the housekeeper had mentioned earlier to the driver.

After he finished at Klein's house, Autwell returned to police headquarters and found Ryker. They talked in an interview room. "I understand from the housekeeper that you were over at Klein's house last night."

"Yeah." Ryker glanced away. "I heard there was an explosion, but no one was hurt."

"Destroyed a perfectly good car. But, no. No one was injured."

"They told you I was there?"

"The housekeeper did. You said something about seeing someone near the garage?"

"I had a tip about suspicious activity."

"There's no record of anyone calling in a tip."

"I know."

"Someone came to you, personally? Tell me about it."

"A guy came to see me. Said he'd heard there were people snooping around Klein's garage. And thought I should have a look."

"Just snooping around." Autwell was skeptical. "And you went out in the middle of the night to a studio owner's estate at the suggestion of an informant?"

"Yeah."

"Come on, Ryker. Tell me what really happened." He could tell Ryker didn't like him.

"I'm not telling you all of it," Ryker replied. "You'll just have to trust me."

"I don't think the chief will like that when he hears about it."

Ryker glared at him. "You aren't telling the chief anything."

"Why won't I?"

Ryker looked him in the eye. "Because you're in this as deep as I am."

Autwell frowned. "What are you talking about?"

"You know David Edelman just as well as I do."

Autwell leaned away. "Ah, man," he scoffed. "Not that crazy Jew again."

Ryker leaned closer. "He came to see you the other day and tried to tell you that someone was casing Klein's estate. And you refused to even look into it."

"All he had were his suspicions," Autwell defended. "It sounded like just one Jew covering for another."

Ryker arched an eyebrow. "Is that what it sounds like now?"

Autwell deflected the question. "Why's Edelman so interested in this, anyway? Far as I can tell, he's not friends with Klein. And there's no money in it. Isn't that the thing with Jews? Either they're related to a guy or they think they can make a buck off him?"

"Someone desecrated his grandfather's grave. I went out there and had a look around. The headstone had been painted over. A bunch of them had. We found a brush they used and took a fingerprint off the handle. Got a match to a print belonging to a guy named Allen Waller. That guy is living with a group at Cleary Ranch."

"Edelman wanted me to go out there with him."

"And you didn't."

"I don't have time for riding around the county with a Jew."

"Wish you had gone now?"

"What happened with this Waller guy?"

"I never found enough to charge him or even bring him in for questioning, but Edelman wasn't satisfied. He organized a group of volunteers to put the site under surveillance. That's how he knew about someone watching Klein. And he's the one who contacted me with the tip last night."

"Some of Edelman's volunteers saw these men at the house?"

"Yes."

Autwell sighed and looked away. "Well, now we have several problems."

"What's that?"

"Finding out who blew up Klein's car and keeping both of us out of trouble for letting it happen."

"I didn't know what else to do. It was just a tip. Not enough for a warrant. I went to the house. The housekeeper refused to let me inside and wouldn't wake up Klein. I went to the garage and had a look around, but I didn't find anything."

"No sign of forced entry?"

"No."

"Well," Autwell sighed, "at least there's that much."

Ryker looked over at him. "What's your excuse?"

"My excuse?"

"For ignoring Edelman."

"Like you said, it was just a tip."

"And he's just a Jew."

"Come on, Ryker. You know how it is. Jews are always looking after each other."

"I think you're right."

Autwell glanced over at him. "I know I'm right."

"Not about the Jews."

"Then, about what?"

"We should keep this between you and me for now," Ryker cautioned. "And you should lay off with the Jewish comments."

"What's that got to do with it?"

"I think it may be the difference between keeping your job and losing it."

✦ ✦ ✦

As with the explosion at the studio, reports of the bomb blast at Klein's home were reported on radio broadcasts and in the region's evening newspapers. Mullins was pleased that the operation at Klein's house went off without anyone getting caught, but he was not pleased with the result—Klein was still alive. To address that concern, he gathered the team—along with Lynch and the trainers—at his tent and showed them the articles. Like him, the team's sense of satisfaction was muted. The bomb went off, but no one was in the car and Klein was unharmed.

"You did a great job planning the operation and planting the bomb," Mullins noted. "But the timing didn't work out."

"Something happened," Waller had decided. "Something that wasn't part of his regular routine."

"Regardless, I don't think a car bomb will work for him. We need a plan to assassinate him another way."

"Maybe we should move on to a different target," Nettles suggested. "The police will be guarding Klein closely now."

"But we've already invested a lot of time in Klein," someone added. "We've been tracking his movements and habits. We have notebooks worth of information on him. We can't just walk away from that."

"Yeah," another agreed. "We should follow through with him and finish the job."

"But even if we do it a different way," Nettles countered, "and even if that different way proves successful, the police will relate his death to *this* bombing. They will see the two as connected."

"And to the bomb at the studio," someone else chipped in.

Mullins spoke up. "But does any of that matter?"

Waller responded, "What they're saying is, the more times we try, the more information we give them."

Mullins frowned. "Information?"

"About us," Waller explained. "Every time we try, every move we make, everything we do reveals something about ourselves."

"If they know about it."

"Right." Mullins continued. "But they know about the bombing at the studio. And they know about this one at the house. Both sites were owned by Klein. Both devices were bombs. They'll eventually figure out the kind of explosive we used and how the bombs were detonated. That gives them a lot of information about us."

"And you think they'll eventually connect it all up?" Someone asked.

Waller nodded. "I think the more times we do this, the more we give them to make those connections."

Nettles spoke up. "It's also more times we are subjected to the risk of being caught. I mean, we've managed to avoid getting caught so far. But the more times we go out, the more risk we incur."

"Yeah," another opined. "The law of averages, you know. It eventually catches up with you."

Mullins intervened. "These are all good points. But I think we should make one more attempt on Klein."

Davis, who had remained silent thus far, agreed. "But I think we should consider a different method."

Lynch looked over at him. "You have something in mind?"

Davis nodded. "Yes, but I think we should talk about it among ourselves first. Before we tell the group."

When the meeting ended, Mullins called Lynch, Davis, and Gropper aside. "I think we should create a new team."

Davis nodded in agreement. "I was going to talk to you about that."

"That was part of your new method idea?" Lynch asked.

"Yes," Davis replied. "And I think we should switch to a sniper."

"Kill him with a rifle?"

"Yes."

"You can discuss the merits of the methods among yourselves," Mullins instructed. "I think you should continue with Klein using the men you have, except for Nettles."

Lynch looked puzzled. "Why not Nettles?"

"I want to move him to a different team."

"You think this failed because of him?"

"No, I think, as we have mentioned before, that he and Waller are the best we have. So I would like to continue using Waller with the Klein operation and move Nettles to a team with a new assignment."

Gropper spoke up. "What assignment is that?"

Mullins took a file from the table in his tent and slid a photograph from it and pointed. "This man. Jules Bernstein."

"He's the head of another one of those studios," Davis noted. "I've seen articles about him in the newspaper."

Mullins nodded. "He's the head of Leramax Pictures. Not as big as Klein's studio, but still a major player in the motion-picture business."

Gropper raised an eyebrow. "And you want us to hit him?"

"Do you have a problem with that?"

"No." Gropper shook his head. "Not at all."

CHAPTER 44

Autwell and Ryker went to see Mrs. Waller and interviewed her yet again. "Why do you people keep bothering me?" she complained.

"We just want to talk to your son," Ryker urged.

"I've told you people before," she railed, "I haven't seen my son in months." And with that, she slammed the door.

Ryker looked over at Autwell, and Autwell shrugged in reply. As they walked away from the house, Ryker suggested, "We should put this place under surveillance."

"I agree, but the chief isn't going to like the expense."

"We could always ask Edelman to do it."

"Edelman already knows too much about us," Autwell replied. "I would rather deal with the chief."

"I'll talk to him. I get along with him."

That afternoon, Ryker met with the supervisor for the detective division and arranged for surveillance of Mrs. Waller's house. He also passed around pictures of Waller to the sergeants and asked them to alert the patrolmen to be on the lookout for him.

✦ ✦ ✦

News of the explosion at Klein's house reached Floyd Hughes and Irving O'Toole at their office at Fort Rosecrans in San Diego. After reviewing reports of the incident, and of the earlier blast at the studio, they decided to go back to Los Angeles to see if the two incidents had any connection to the weapons and munitions missing from the National Guard Armory in Burbank. It was a long shot, but they'd made no further progress since their initial interviews. Anything they might find would be more than what they had.

The next day, Hughes and O'Toole arrived in Los Angeles shortly after noon and met with Autwell and Ryker in a conference room at police headquarters. Autwell showed them photographs from the scene and gave them copies of the incident reports.

As O'Toole scanned the documents, he noticed a comment from a patrolman about the nature of the blast. He pointed to it in the notes. "Tell me about this."

"As you can see from the photos," Autwell responded, "the blast was rather powerful and appears to have been set inside the engine compartment. The patrolman noticed that right away and said something about it."

"What did he notice?" O'Toole wondered. "What did he point out, other than telling you it might be an army-style operation?"

"He noticed that the hood was missing and there was damage to the top of the windshield." Autwell pointed to one of the photos. "You can see the damage right there."

"And you also found pieces of an alarm clock?"

"Yeah." Autwell pointed to a different photo. "This is a picture of it. We have the pieces in the evidence room."

"Pieces?"

"After we found the face, we also located a piece of the clock's alarm."

"This was the detonator," Hughes noted.

Autwell nodded. "That's what it looked like to us."

O'Toole gestured to another of the reports. "I see that the patrolman agreed with you."

"Yes."

"Anything else?"

Autwell and Ryker exchanged glances. "Well . . ." Ryker hesitated. "We had. . .a tip. . .the night before." He seemed uncomfortable talking about it.

"What sort of tip?" O'Toole asked.

"A report of someone snooping around the garage."

"Did you check it out?"

"I went out there," Ryker said.

"And what did you find?"

"Nothing out of the ordinary." Ryker leaned back in his chair. "The housekeeper refused to awaken Klein, but she finally agreed to let me into the garage. We went out there and I looked around, but I didn't see anything."

Hughes spoke up. "Did you check the car?"

"No."

Hughes had a disapproving expression. "Wouldn't that have been an obvious thing to check?"

"Yes, I suppose. Ryker admitted. "But it was late at night. The housekeeper was impatient. I was impatient. I just didn't think about it."

O'Toole spoke up. "Was this tip from a telephone call?"

"No." Ryker scooted his chair closer. "Are either of you familiar with a group called the Crimson Legion?"

Suddenly Hughes and O'Toole's exchanged glances. "We might have. . .heard of them," Hughes replied.

"No." Autwell wagged his finger accusingly. "You know something specific about them."

Reluctantly, Hughes and O'Toole told them about the arms and munitions missing from the armory, their investigation into it, and about their attempt to locate Allen Waller. Ryker smiled at the mention of Waller's name. Hughes looked in his direction. "You know something about him?"

For the next twenty minutes, the four discussed David

Edelman, the trouble at Mount Zion Cemetery, and how their respective investigations led them to Allen Waller and the Crimson Legion camp in the Palisades. In the course of that discussion, Ryker explained, "We don't have the manpower to place the camp under surveillance with policemen. But Edelman has a group of volunteers out there, which is how we know that guys from the camp were the ones behind the two bombings. But Edelman's men didn't see enough to be able to identify anyone."

O'Toole frowned. "And they don't know where the explosives came from?"

"No, but if Waller is out there with them, it's a pretty good bet that he got the explosives from the armory."

"Along with the rifles we saw," Hughes noted.

Autwell spoke up, "We need to tie all of this together. Think you can help us?"

O'Toole asked, "What did you have in mind?"

"Maybe you could get some men to help with the surveillance. A couple of extra cars to follow people as they come and go from out there."

"Yeah." O'Toole nodded. "We can help with that."

Hughes glanced over at O'Toole. "And the Crimson Legion's offices in Charlotte. We should get someone moving on them, too."

Ryker looked perplexed. "Charlotte?"

"North Carolina," Hughes explained. "That's where their headquarters is located."

"I know about some of the things the Crimson Legion has been doing," Ryker added. "But I didn't know about their headquarters."

"They've created an extensive organization," Hughes said. "Pretty much nationwide. But they run the whole thing from an office in Charlotte."

"The Justice Department began investigating them a few years ago," O'Toole commented. "We'll ask them for an update on what they've found so far."

"And you'll share that update with us?" Autwell asked.

"Of course."

✦ ✦ ✦

As promised, Hughes and O'Toole arranged for extra manpower to help with surveillance of the Crimson Legion camp in the Palisades. Two days later, agents on that detail observed a car leaving the grounds. Four people were seen inside.

As the car left the grounds, agents followed it to the west side of Los Angeles. There they watched from a safe distance as the car slowly made the block around Jules Bernstein's house, stopping occasionally.

When the car began a second circuit around the house a Los Angeles patrolman—on heightened alert after the bombing at Klein's house—noticed it and became suspicious. He approached the car as it sat at the curb on the north side of the property. The window on the driver's door was down and the patrolman leaned over to look inside. "Do you mind telling me what you men are up to?"

"Just enjoying the scenery," the driver replied.

Someone seated in back spoke up. "It ain't against the law to sit in a parked car."

"No," the patrolman answered. "But I've been watching you and you've gone all the way around the house, stopping on each side. Now you've started around it a second time." The patrolman glanced over at the front-seat passenger and noticed a notebook open on his lap. "What are you writing in that notebook?" He pointed.

The passenger slammed the notebook closed and with a sullen tone said, "Nothing."

"Look, flat-foot," one of them snarled, "we haven't broken any laws and you've got no reason to harass us. So just get along with your work and leave us alone."

The patrolman looked over at the driver. "Let me see your license and the registration for this car."

"I don't recognize your authority," the driver replied. "I'm not giving you anything."

The patrolman stood up straight and opened the driver's door. "Get out of the car." When the driver didn't comply, the patrolman grabbed him by the shoulder and pulled him from the seat, then threw him against the front fender of the car. As the patrolman patted him down, he discovered a revolver tucked in the waistband of the driver's pants. He removed the pistol and placed the driver in handcuffs.

Federal agents parked up the street saw the officer as he wrestled with the driver. "Think we ought to help him?"

The second agent shook his head. "We're not supposed to intervene out here."

"Yeah," the first replied. "But we can at least call it in." He radioed the Los Angeles Police Department dispatcher to report the incident, then continued to watch.

As the patrolman hustled the driver to his patrol car, the doors of the car he'd stopped flew open and the remaining occupants bolted. Within minutes, however, additional patrolmen arrived and began a neighborhood search. Within the hour, all four occupants from the car were detained for questioning.

In a subsequent search of the car, officers found two sketch pads that contained drawings of the streets around Bernstein's house, including estimates of various distances between key landmarks. They also found a logbook with entries noting the times Bernstein came and went from the house and from his studio downtown.

The occupants of the car were taken to the city jail where they were fingerprinted, identified, and booked into a holding cell. During that process, one of the men was identified as Allen Waller. Because of recent inquiries about him, the booking clerk recognized the name and notified Ryker and Autwell.

While the men were being booked into the jail, Hughes and O'Toole, having been tipped off by the agents parked outside Bernstein's house, arrived at police headquarters and met with Ryker and Autwell. Hughes asked, "You have men from the Crimson Legion in custody?"

"Yes," Autwell responded. "A couple of your guys spotted them and called it in. I assume they told you?"

"Any idea who they are?" Hughes asked.

Ryker nodded. "One of them is Allen Waller."

"Good," O'Toole smiled. "Who gets him first?"

Autwell spoke up. "We've been looking for him since before you knew about him."

"We need to talk to him quickly. To find out about those missing weapons."

"You can talk to him after we're done with him," Ryker replied. "But give us first crack at him and then you can have a go at him after that."

"Okay," O'Toole said. "But we think you should bring in his mother."

Ryker frowned. "His mother?"

"Waller has prior military experience," Hughes explained. "Some of it was rather sophisticated. And he's been in combat. I'm not sure he'll respond well to your interrogation methods. We might need his mother for. . .leverage."

Autwell's eyes opened wide at the suggestion. "Good idea!"

"We could get a search warrant, too," Ryker offered. "Search her house while she's being detained."

"I like that," Hughes noted.

CHAPTER 45

With the district attorney's help, Ryker and Autwell obtained a search warrant for Mrs. Waller's residence. As they came from the judge's chambers with the warrant, Ryker turned to Autwell. "Get some patrolmen and go to the house. Search the place and bring Mrs. Waller in for questioning. But bring her to the office first. Don't take her to the jail. And make sure she arrives in handcuffs. I'll get started with Waller."

Autwell had a mischievous smile. "You want Waller to see his mother in handcuffs?"

"Yes," Ryker replied.

Autwell grinned. "You're starting to think like me."

While Autwell went to Mrs. Waller's house, Ryker brought Waller from the jail to an interview room in the detective division of police headquarters. The room was painted a drab gray and was sparsely furnished with only a table and four chairs. A bare lightbulb was suspended by a cord from the ceiling and cast a glare across the center of the room. A single window afforded a view of the hallway outside.

Waller was seated on one side of the table, his wrists bound in handcuffs. Ryker took a seat across from him and began with questions about the bombing at the studio.

As O'Toole had predicted, Waller was uncooperative. "I got nothing to say to you," he replied in a surly tone.

"Three people died in that explosion," Ryker reminded him.

Waller shrugged. "Three Jews, and if they wasn't Jews, they thought like Jews. Don't mean nothin' to me."

"That's murder," Ryker noted.

Waller shrugged again. "So?"

"You're facing three counts of murder. Might even be capital murder."

Waller leaned forward and lowered his voice. "I'm not afraid of what you cops think you can do to me."

When Ryker asked about the explosion outside Klein's house, Waller grinned, "I'll say this for them. Jews got one thing on their side: luck."

"So you admit you knew about the bomb?"

"Like I said," Waller replied, "I got nothing to say to you. You're an agent of Jews and I don't recognize Jewish authority over anything."

"What about Jules Bernstein?"

"What about him?"

"You were picked up outside his house. What were you doing there?"

"This is still America. The Jews ain't started flying their flag over us yet. And that means I got a right to be anywhere I want to be."

Ryker, undeterred, opened a package that contained items seized from the car, but as he prepared to ask about them, Autwell arrived with Mrs. Waller. As Ryker suggested, he paraded her past the window of the interview room, making sure to create as much noise as possible and pausing in plain view to check her handcuffs.

When Waller caught sight of her, his eyes opened wide. "That's my mother," he blurted.

"Yes."

"What do you intend to do with her?"

"We're serious about this investigation," Ryker shot back.

"We intend to find out what she knows about what you and the Crimson Legion have been doing."

"She doesn't know anything."

Ryker sighed, "We'll find out if that's true, I'm sure." He took a notebook from the evidence package. "Let's talk about this book."

"Wait," Waller frowned. "I'll tell you what I know. Just leave my mother out of it. She don't know anything about anything. She ain't been out there or helped me. She ain't done nothin'."

"And you'll tell us everything?"

"Yes." Waller was insistent. "I'll tell you everything. Just keep her out of it."

Ryker brought Autwell, O'Toole, and Hughes into the room and for the next two hours Waller told them about the Crimson Legion's work in developing the camp at Cleary Ranch, how they planned the bomb at Asterion's studio, the one at Klein's house, and the places from which they obtained explosives. He gave them names of the other men in the crew, information about Mullins, and about Lynch, Nettles, and Gropper. And he confirmed that Bernstein was their next target. He gave them everything except the one critical piece of information they still lacked—the time of the attack on Bernstein.

"I know they're going to hit him," Waller stressed. "And I know they plan to do it at his house. But I don't know when."

✦ ✦ ✦

Based on information supplied by Waller, and on the pending threat of further action, O'Toole notified the Justice Department and brought them up-to-date on the Crimson Legion's activities in California. Additional agents were sent to the Cleary Ranch site, and surveillance increased. However, with the exact time of an attack on Bernstein still unknown, Ryker and Autwell decided to meet with Bernstein and apprise him of the situation.

"So," Bernstein reacted after hearing the threat against him, "they tried to kill Klein. And now they want to kill me?"

"Yes."

"I'm not going to let people like this rule my life."

"I understand," Ryker replied. "But you can't ignore the threat, either. When they attack you, anyone around you would be in danger."

"What do you want me to do?"

"We want to monitor your activities. And when the attack seems imminent, we want to take you away to a safe location."

Bernstein frowned. "Monitor? What does that mean?"

Autwell spoke up. "It means we'll have you under surveillance, but at a distance. We don't want to tip off anyone who might be watching. If they see us with you, they will know that we know about them. And that might alter what they do. So we'll keep our people out of sight as much as possible but close enough to intervene before anyone gets to you."

Bernstein had a knowing expression. "You want to use me as bait."

"After a fashion," Ryker admitted. "But if you would rather, we can simply protect you in a straightforward manner. Put on a heavy detail. Cordon you off from public access."

"In other words, take control of my life," Bernstein said.

"I'm sure it would feel that way," Autwell answered.

Bernstein shook his head. "Like I said before, gentlemen. Giving in to fear is like surrendering to it and to the people behind it. I don't want these anti-Semites running my life."

✦ ✦ ✦

In the weeks that followed, alternating teams of detectives and federal agents tailed Bernstein's movements. As Bernstein wished, they kept at a discreet distance that allowed them to observe but still gave them the potential to respond quickly if necessary.

For a while, nothing out of the ordinary happened, and Ryker began to wonder if Waller's information was correct, or merely a ruse to keep them occupied. Then late one night a car with three passengers drove out of the compound. Officers conducting surveillance notified the police dispatcher. The dispatcher notified the detail at Bernstein's house.

Within minutes, Bernstein was taken from his bedroom and whisked away to a secure location. Ryker, Autwell, and a dozen police officers remained behind, hiding in the house and on the grounds, hoping the attackers were on the way to that location and not somewhere else.

Thirty minutes later, the Crimson Legion team arrived in the neighborhood. They circled the house once, then parked their car on a side street. From the street, they made their way across the lawn and entered the house, armed with handguns and rifles.

With Nettles in the lead, they moved methodically through the first floor of the residence, going from room to room, then made their way upstairs. Moments later, they burst into Bernstein's bedroom and opened fire. Bullets ripped through the bedding and splintered the headboard.

When the shooting stopped, Ryker and Autwell appeared behind them. Ryker placed the muzzle of his pistol against the back of Nettles's head and, in a calm and even voice, threatened, "If you move a muscle, I'll make your head explode."

Nettles surrendered without resistance, as did the others with him.

✦ ✦ ✦

While Nettles and the assassination team were being detained at Bernstein's residence, federal agents prepared to raid the

Crimson Legion facility at Cleary Ranch. Additional agents were brought in to augment those already on site and extra equipment was put in place. O'Toole and Hughes coordinated the operation, sending the new men to the crest of the hills that ringed the site and making sure all of Edelman's volunteers were gone.

When the agents were in place and ready, they moved slowly down the slopes to the camp in a deliberate manner. At the bottom, they methodically worked their way across the grounds toward the buildings, some of which still were under construction, and the tents where all but a few of the men slept. Along the way, they captured five Crimson Legion members who were on patrol. As agents drew closer to the central compound, however, a watchman spotted them and shouted a warning, followed by a burst of gunfire.

For three hours, federal agents fought their way through the compound, moving from building to building, tent to tent, point to point. Casualties mounted but gradually pockets of men defending the camp ran out of ammunition and surrendered.

A few, however, fought to the very end. Lynch, Davis, Gropper, and Mullins were among those few. As the agents closed in, they retreated to the building that had been designated for use as an armory. It had the thickest walls and held the group's supply of arms and ammunition, which allowed them to hold out until morning. But as the sun came up, federal agents had the building surrounded.

Rather than continue the fight with the agents at hand, O'Toole requested a detachment of soldiers from Fort Rosecrans to finish the job. They arrived later that day with an M1917 light tank that they hauled to the site on a flatbed trailer. When the tank was armed and ready, the soldiers wheeled it into position and fired a single round at the front wall of the armory building. The projectile from the tank ripped a gaping hole in the concrete block wall and it began to crumble in a cloud of dust and debris.

As the wall collapsed, automatic gunfire came from inside. Agents returned fire for a while, but then a hand appeared above the pile of rubble, waving back and forth as if to get attention. The shooting stopped, and in the silence of the moment Davis slowly emerged with both hands raised in the air. Lynch followed close behind.

Once Davis and Lynch were in custody, agents entered the damaged building and found crates of ammunition still inside. Mullins and Gropper were discovered in the back corner, crouched behind a stack of empty ammo boxes. Both had been shot multiple times. Neither was alive.

✦ ✦ ✦

In Cleveland, Ohio, Griffin was at his hotel room, preparing for a rally that was scheduled to take place the following evening. Edwards and Frost were with him. Late in the afternoon, as they were wrapping up the day's meetings, the telephone rang. Edwards answered, then handed the phone to Griffin.

Fred Payne was calling from Venice, California, to tell them about the raid on the Cleary Ranch facility. "I haven't been out there but I heard from one of the guys who escaped," he reported.

"How bad was it?"

"Most of the facility is intact."

"That's good."

"No, sir. It's not. The men held out through the night, but this morning they brought up a tank from San Diego and—"

"A tank!" Griffin erupted.

"Yes, sir."

"They used a military tank against civilians?"

"Yes, sir."

"There's no end to what these people will do!" Griffin shouted. "Did they use it?"

"Yes, sir," Payne replied. "They blasted the front wall of the armory with it."

"Was anyone injured?"

"I don't think the blast hurt anyone. Mullins, Gropper, Lynch, and Davis were inside the building when it hit. They were the last holdouts. Lynch and Davis eventually surrendered."

"And Mullins?"

"Mullins and Gropper are dead, sir."

They talked awhile longer, but Griffin only listened as Payne gave further details. He was ashen as he hung up the phone. Edwards looked over at him. "What's the problem?"

Before Griffin could explain, the door to the room burst open and federal agents rushed inside. Griffin was seized immediately, but Edwards and Frost scurried into an adjoining room where they attempted to escape by climbing out a window to the fire escape. They made it from the room, but agents were waiting for them on the street below, and they were arrested on the spot.

✦ ✦ ✦

In Charlotte, North Carolina, Dorothy Miller was at home, just finishing dinner with Travis Fielding, when the front door was forced open. Agents grabbed them before they could leave the table.

At the same time, an additional team of agents seized the Crimson Legion headquarters office. No one was present and they took it without resistance.

CHAPTER 46

The following day, Grace left the boardinghouse, walked to the corner, and caught the streetcar for the ride to Senator Fisher's office on Capitol Hill. Since the party convention, she'd followed that routine every day.

Most of her time at the office was devoted to organizing events and rallies in an effort to keep Fisher's name always before the public. The work was consuming for her and required long hours, but she didn't mind. Every minute she spent working for Fisher put her another minute farther from her past—a past she hoped no one ever discovered.

At the office that morning, the past came crashing down on her as she read the headlines of the morning papers. "Police Raid Camp in California," was one. "Rebel Group Defeated," read another. "Griffin Arrested, Crimson Legion Comes to an End," proclaimed yet another. She scanned the articles quickly and saw that Griffin had been arrested in Ohio, and Dorothy had been arrested in Charlotte, but there was no mention of Mullins. Only that the camp in California had been seized by federal agents.

Grace was worried—about Mullins, but more about what it might mean for her—and she thought about making a few calls. By then, she knew people in places who could provide her with a report of precisely what occurred. One call was all it would take. One phone call with the senator's name and she would know what happened. But that would embroil him in what would appear to the public as a sordid affair. It would involve her in it, too. But wasn't that coming anyway? Mullins was out there. Once they looked into him, it wouldn't take long for them to connect him to Fisher.

This is going to be trouble for us, she thought. And instead of calling to find out about the raid, she began working on ideas to distance the senator from Mullins and the Crimson Legion. It wouldn't be easy, but she had to try. Both of their careers might be on the line—hers and Fisher's.

Grace worked late that evening, still without a clear story that would deflect attention from Fisher, should the press ask about his connections to Mullins. But no one had mentioned the raid in California, and she had no intention of bringing it up.

As she left the building to hail a taxi, a car came to a stop at the curb beside her. The front door opened, and Graham Hawthorne stepped out. Through the open door she saw Martin seated at the steering wheel.

Hawthorne and Martin—the federal agents who first approached her while she was living in Springfield. It had been a long time since she'd seen them and in the intervening period she'd almost forgotten them. Now here they were again. She knew what they wanted.

Without asking, Hawthorne opened the rear door of the car and gestured with a nod for her to get in. She slid onto the back seat, Hawthorne closed the door, and they continued on their way.

At the corner, they turned and traveled down Pennsylvania Avenue toward Georgetown. As they did, Hawthorne turned sideways in the seat and looked over at her. "You've heard about the raid in Los Angeles?"

"Yes," Grace replied. "I heard."

"And I assume you also heard about the recent explosions out there."

"Yes. What does this have to do with me?"

Martin, still at the wheel, turned his head to one side. "Bryce Mullins is dead."

The news hit Grace hard. She hadn't seen him in a long time and he hadn't written her, either. And she was sure he was romantically involved with Dorothy, but still . . . Tears filled her eyes at the thought of him dead.

"You didn't know that, did you?" Hawthorne said.

"No," she whispered.

"Federal agents raided the ranch. There was a shootout. Several Legion members were killed. Mullins was one of them."

"That figures." She forced a smile. "He always was loyal to the end."

"I know this is difficult for you," Hawthorne continued, "but we're all but certain Mullins was involved in those explosions I mentioned. And in a plot to kill Jules Bernstein."

Grace turned away. "That doesn't surprise me, either." As she stared out the window, she thought of the first time she saw Mullins. At a Crimson Legion rally in Springfield. He was so handsome. So vibrant. So full of energy. They were going to change the world. Just the two of them. Now it seemed the events and causes that had brought them so close before had driven them far apart.

"People died in those explosions," Hawthorne continued.

"I know."

Martin piped up. "We're talking murder now."

"We've seized the office in Charlotte and arrested Griffin," Hawthorne said. "Now we're making sure we have everyone and understand the full situation."

Grace glanced up and caught his eye in the rearview mirror. "Surely you don't think I had anything to do with any of it."

"We don't know what to think," Hawthorne answered. "But anything you can tell us about the Crimson Legion's recent activity would be very helpful."

"Bryce was in California. I haven't seen or heard from him

in months. And I don't have any idea what they were doing in Charlotte."

"But is there anything you've been holding back from us? Something you know but didn't think important before?"

With news of the raid on the ranch in California, Bryce's death, and the mention of murder, Grace was more worried than ever. Not about Mullins, but about herself. She wanted to stay in Washington and stay with Fisher. She'd carved out a good place for herself and she didn't want to give it up. And so she decided to tell them everything she could remember about all that had happened since she and Mullins became involved.

When she finished talking about Mullins, she moved on to tell them about Fielding, the church in Virginia, and how Fielding's ultimate loyalty was always to the Crimson Legion. "That's what got him fired from Fisher's office. His loyalty was to the Legion, not the senator, and he had been shaping the senator's views to suit Mr. Griffin."

None of what Grace said seemed to interest Hawthorne. "But what about Mullins and California? Is there anything more you can tell us about him and what he was doing out there?"

"He went out there to build a training camp for the Legion. They wanted to train people for military-style action."

"What were their likely targets?"

"I don't know. I do know that Bryce absolutely hated the Jews. I'm sure you already knew that. He blamed them for starting the Great War."

"And the death of his brother," Martin added.

"Yes, that's how he came to find the Legion. He was looking for answers to why his brother died, why there was a war, why things turned out the way they did. When we were in Springfield, he used to listen to Walter Jones on the radio. Jones said the Jews started the war to make money. Bryce believed him. Walter Jones's broadcasts led him to the Legion. And I think in some ways he saw Mr. Griffin as a substitute for his brother. He would have done just about anything Griffin told him to do."

"So if Griffin wanted him to plant those bombs, he would have done it?"

"Absolutely," Grace replied.

"Was there a concerted effort by Mullins or anyone associated with the Crimson Legion to acquire weapons or explosives?"

"Not that I am aware of. They could have," she added. "And I suppose they couldn't do what they were trying to do without them. But I didn't know anything about it. He was always talking about how we needed to actually confront the people who were a threat to the country, but he never said, 'We should kill this one,' or anything like that."

"And by threat to the country, he meant the Jews."

"Yes, Jews, Negroes, Communists—those were the biggest enemies he saw."

Hawthorne looked her in the eye. "And you're sure you haven't seen him since he moved to California?"

Grace glared at him. "You've been watching me the whole time. You know I haven't been anywhere except wherever Senator Fisher has sent me."

"You weren't continuing to see Mullins romantically after he went to California?"

She looked away. "I haven't seen him in any manner—romantically or otherwise—since he left to go back to Charlotte."

"So, you two weren't. . .together?"

"There was a woman at the headquarters in Charlotte. Dorothy Miller. She seemed to like him. If he was romantically involved with anyone, it would have been her."

"Do you think Dorothy knows what he was doing?"

"From my work with her, I would say nothing happened with the Crimson Legion that Dorothy Miller didn't know about. She knew it all. She might not have been in charge of everything they did, but she knew about everything."

"And she would know what Mullins was doing?"

"Yes. If you seized the office, then you already know all of this. Didn't you arrest her?"

"Yes, we have her in custody. We're just tying up loose ends. What do you know about Travis Fielding?"

"Not much. He used to work for the senator but, like I said, his loyalty was to the Crimson Legion. Once the senator realized that, he fired him."

"Any chance he spent time in California, too?"

"Perhaps, but I haven't seen him since Senator Fisher fired him. He didn't go to Charlotte with Bryce. I know that much. But I don't know where he is."

They talked awhile longer, but Grace knew little else to tell them. By then they were near the boardinghouse, and Martin brought the car to a stop at the corner.

"You should get out here," Hawthorne said. "The less others see of us, the better."

"Does this finish it with us?" Grace asked.

"Yes," Hawthorne replied. "We might need your help as we dig deeper into the Crimson Legion, but for now I think we're done."

"And what about the thing in Virginia?"

"You won't have to worry about that. We took care of that before you came to work for Fisher." He smiled at her. "We couldn't have something like that blowing your cover."

✦ ✦ ✦

A few days later, Patrick McNair, the Springfield police officer who responded to Rabbi Tabick's complaint about the pigs, came to Temple Beth El. Edward Talmy was there with Tabick when McNair arrived.

"You've seen the reports from California about the federal agents who raided the facility operated by the Crimson Legion?" McNair asked.

"Yes," Tabick replied. "Very tragic."

"The men who desecrated your building with pigs were members of the Crimson Legion."

"Yes. I remember."

"While federal agents raided the location in California, a second team seized the Crimson Legion headquarters in North Carolina."

Talmy spoke up. "What does that mean?"

"It means," McNair explained, "that the Crimson Legion no longer exists."

"That is a good thing, right?"

"Yes. It is a great thing," McNair responded. "And I wanted you to know that reporting the trouble the way you did set in motion the series of events that led to that organization's demise."

"We put an end to them?"

"Yes," McNair replied.

"How is that so?" Talmy asked. "How could such a big thing come from the simple act of reporting trouble to the police?"

"Reporting trouble is like standing up to the people who did it. From the simple act of standing up and speaking out, you set in motion a chain of events. You reported it to us. We investigated and reported it to the Justice Department. They assigned agents to investigate. The federal investigation led to the raids that happened this week. And to the end of the organization."

"There must have been many people along the way."

"Yes. Many others. But it all started right here. Literally right here. At this building."

After McNair left, Rabbi Tabick looked over at Talmy. "That was a good thing you did. Reporting it to the police."

"I did not want to, but Levine insisted. Reporting it was

actually his idea. I went to the police station with him, not him with me."

"Then, come," Tabick beckoned. "We should tell Levine what McNair said to us."

Tabick and Talmy left the synagogue and started down the street toward Levine's house. On the way Talmy related, "Back in Belarus, where I come from, nothing like this would have ever happened."

Tabick frowned. "The desecration of a synagogue would not happen there? They burned synagogues to the ground in Belarus."

"No, in Belarus, a policeman would never have come to say that he followed up on our complaint and arrested the people who were responsible. They did nothing like this for us."

"Ah," Tabick said. "But the difference is, in Belarus, no one would have bothered to speak out against such atrocities. Here, you and Levine spoke out."

A few minutes later they reached Levine's house and went inside to tell him the news.

ACKNOWLEDGMENTS

My deepest gratitude and sincere thanks to my writing partner, Joe Hilley, and to my executive assistant, Lanelle Shaw-Young, both of whom work diligently to turn my story ideas into great books. And to Arlen Young, Peter Glöege, and Janna Nysewander for making the finished product look and read its best. And always, to my wife, Carolyn, whose presence makes everything better.

BOOKS BY: MIKE EVANS

Israel: America's Key to Survival

Save Jerusalem

The Return

Jerusalem D.C.

Purity and Peace of Mind

Who Cries for the Hurting?

Living Fear Free

I Shall Not Want

Let My People Go

Jerusalem Betrayed

Seven Years of Shaking: A Vision

The Nuclear Bomb of Islam

Jerusalem Prophecies

Pray For Peace of Jerusalem

America's War:The Beginning of the
    End

The Jerusalem Scroll

The Prayer of David

The Unanswered Prayers of Jesus

God Wrestling

The American Prophecies

Beyond Iraq: The Next Move

The Final Move beyond Iraq

Showdown with Nuclear Iran

Jimmy Carter: The Liberal Leftand
    World Chaos

Atomic Iran

Cursed

Betrayed

The Light

Corrie's Reflections & Meditations

The Revolution

The Final Generation

Seven Days

The Locket

Persia: The Final Jihad

GAMECHANGER SERIES:

GameChanger

Samson Option

The Four Horsemen

THE PROTOCOLS SERIES:

The Protocols

The Candidate

Jerusalem

The History of Christian Zionism

Countdown

Ten Boom: Betsie, Promise of God

Commanded Blessing

BORN AGAIN SERIES:

Born Again: 1948

Born Again: 1967

TO PURCHASE, CONTACT: orders@TimeWorthyBooks.
comP. O. BOX 30000, PHOENIX, AZ 85046

MICHAEL DAVID EVANS, the #1 *New York Times* bestselling author, is an award-winning journalist/Middle East analyst. Dr. Evans has appeared on hundreds of network television and radio shows including *Good Morning America, Crossfire* and *Nightline,* and *The Rush Limbaugh Show,* and on Fox Network, *CNN World News,* NBC, ABC, and CBS. His articles have been published in the *Wall Street Journal, USA Today, Washington Times, Jerusalem Post* and newspapers worldwide. More than twenty-five million copies of his books are in print, and he is the award-winning producer of nine documentaries based on his books.

Dr. Evans is considered one of the world's leading experts on Israel and the Middle East, and is one of the most sought-after speakers on that subject. He is the chairman of the board of the ten Boom Holocaust Museum in Haarlem, Holland, and is the founder of Israel's first Christian museum located in the Friends of Zion Heritage Center in Jerusalem.

Dr. Evans has authored 93 books including: *History of Christian Zionism, Showdown with Nuclear Iran, Atomic Iran, The Next Move Beyond Iraq, The Final Move Beyond Iraq,* and *Countdown.* His body of work also includes the novels *Seven Days, GameChanger, The Samson Option, The Four Horsemen, The Locket, Born Again: 1967,* and *The Columbus Code.*

✦ ✦ ✦

Michael David Evans is available to speak or for interviews. Contact: EVENTS@drmichaeldevans.com.